I0670496

Deacon

The A**hole Club Series

Tiya Rayne

Perceptive Illusions Publishing
Bayshore, New York

Tiya Rayne/Perceptive Illusions Publishing, Inc.
PO BOX 5253
Bayshore, NY 11706
www.TiyaRayne.com

Publisher's Note: This is a work of fiction. Names, characters, places, and incidents are a product of the author's imagination. Locales and public names are sometimes used for atmospheric purposes. Any resemblance to actual people, living or dead, or to businesses, companies, events, institutions, or locales is completely coincidental.

Cover Designed by Covers by Combs
Ordering Information:
Quantity sales. Special discounts are available on quantity purchases by corporations, associations, and others. For details, contact the "Special Sales Department" at the address above.

Deacon: The A**hole Club Series/ Tiya Rayne. -- 1st ed.
ISBN 978-1-941924-09-9

The greatest gift you can give yourself is love. Love yourself first and everyone else will follow your guidelines.

–Tiya Rayne

PROLOGUE

The Race

Deacon

I rake my fingers through my hair and chuckle at this group around me. It's hilarious to me how serious they take this race shit. All these rich assholes with fucked-up daddy issues, trying to find a way to piss off their parents. These guys don't know shit about struggle or fighting to survive.

Shit, they don't even need the money up for grabs if they win. I guess it's the only thing that makes us alike. I don't need the money either.

Hell, I'm not even here to win the race. I have an ulterior motive to be here. A very lucrative motive.

While the rich douchebags chase a twenty-thousand-dollar bag, I'm taking notice of cars. On this track alone is about half a million in parts. All I need to do is point out the easiest target and the most valuable car.

I give a signal to my guy in the crowd, and he takes photos of the car and driver. Next thing they know, they're without a car. I've been running this scam since I was fifteen.

That's how old I was when Griff took me under his wing. Now I'm in a fucking race every few months. You would think these dudes would put the shit together, but it goes to show you being rich doesn't always mean being smart.

I quickly send a text to my guy, Q, in the crowd. Q is the computer whiz and my tail for tonight. I work with a team of four, Griff being the leader.

We all play a part, if you see me, know Q is close by. I give Q the signal, letting him know I've spotted our first victim. I then slide the phone in my back pocket once it's done.

Q's job is to give us all the information about the car, the cost of the parts, and what buyers are looking to pay for it. Leaning my back against the car I'm driving; I take another look around the strip we've met on for tonight's race.

The usual suspects are all here. Pretty boy, Kelex is leaning against his Mustang. Like most rich fucks, he don't know shit about cars, they think putting the money into a sports car is enough to win these races. It isn't.

You need a lot more than a fast car for this shit. You need to have the guts and eye for this. It takes talent.

On the other side of Kelex is Luke Reynolds and his weird ass friend. I swear, those dudes are fucking.

The only real talent on the track is probably Will Pitman. The punk actually has a gift for this shit. It also helps that his car is souped up as well. I watch as the brunette with him nails him in the arm.

She must have caught him gawking at the new black chick. I scoped her out too. The chocolate beauty is new to the race world.

I've been to a ton of these motherfuckers and I've never seen her before. Judging by the ride she's in, she knows what the fuck she's doing. She's also my second victim.

Raised voices catch my attention.

"She's not racing with us. She has no business out here."

I roll my eyes at the sound of bitch ass Jeremy's voice. I've been dying to whoop his punk ass. He's a sneaky little prick. You have to watch him.

I've already noticed how those shady eyes have been tracking all of us. Just a few months ago, he was in a race where a young kid died. I only heard about the shit.

Supposedly, the eighteen-year-old driver got clipped, his car flipping a few times. Most said it was an accident, but I know a few people who said otherwise. So, I don't trust the fucker.

My phone rings, taking me out of the conversation between the rich boys.

"Titus," Griff says through my phone. He never waits for me to say hello.

"What's up, Griff?"

"How's it looking?"

"We got a Mustang and Martin. If we keep them in tack, we can get a little under two hundred thousand."

Griff grunts. It's more lucrative to sell the cars whole on the black market once we change the VIN number, but it's also a lot riskier. I know Griff is thinking through the risk and analyzing in his head. You don't run one of the best chop shops in the city without knowing what the fuck you're doing.

"Nah," he eventually says. "I want pieces."

I smile because I knew he would say that.

"All right, I'll see you back at the shop."

"Hey." He stops me before I hang up. "Be safe," he says, as if I had no choice.

I wouldn't say Griff and I have a father and son relationship, but we're as close as two criminals can be.

"Always."

Hanging up my phone, I catch the tail end of Reynolds telling the others to shut the fuck up and drive.

I couldn't help but agree. I wanted to get this shit over with so I can get some rest, maybe even take the chocolate beauty home.

I've never fucked a black chick, but she's got me reconsidering my taste in women.

Climbing into my car and shutting the door, I start the engine, revving it. Despite not giving a shit about winning, I do love the adrenaline rush I get while behind the wheel of a car.

I roll up beside Pitman, he's watching me with an over fucking confident look in his eyes. I flip him off and speed off to cut in front of him. I enjoy the scowl that crosses his face.

I'm lined up in the middle, Pitman on my left, Kelex on my right, and beside him is chocolate beauty. It's official, I'm definitely fucking her tonight.

Seth announces the race is about to start right before two skinny chicks take a slow walk across the starting line, trying to be sexy. They fail.

The flag drops, and my foot is on the gas pedal. The race is in full speed. It's neck and neck at first.

Pitman, Kelex, Jeremy, and CB are in the lead. Reynolds looks pissed beside me. He must have got caught sleeping.

Pitman starts to pull away from the race, but I have to keep my eyes on Chocolate Beauty and Kelex's ride. Those are the two I plan on taking with me tonight.

I notice Jeremy's car starts to swerve. What the fuck is he doing? I realize his intention at the same time Kelex must have.

Jeremy jerks his car to the left, on track to ram his car into Beauty's. I try to pull up to intersect it, but Kelex rams the front of his car into the back-right side of the Beauty's, taking on the full force of Jeremy's hit. Kelex's car takes fucking flight in the air, flipping like an acrobat before crashing onto the side of the road upside down. Beauty spins around in a circle for a second before coming to a stop.

Jeremy wasn't expecting Kelex's approach. He tries to gain control of the car, spins a few times and then stops facing away from the starting line. His shit immediately catches on fire. I'm out of my car instantly.

My phone goes off in my pocket.

"What the fuck is going on?" Griff barks. I'm sure Q informed him the moment the first car was hit.

"Fuck, it's bad, man."

"Look, Titus, get the fuck out of there. Leave now, no bullshitting." The phone goes dead after his command.

I should get the fuck back in my car, but I don't. I'm the last person who needs to be here when the police show up. However, instead of following the smart plan, I rush toward the wrecked cars.

"Help! Please, help me."

Jeremy's cries cause me to stop. Looking around me, I notice everyone helping beauty and Kelex. There's no one here to help me with this fucker.

The fire at his engine hasn't made it to Jeremy yet. In fact, all I have to do is reach in and grab him out of the car. I smile as I watch him.

"Deacon, please," he pleads again.

I take a step toward the car and squat down so he can better see me.

"Fuck you. You deserve this." Jeremy's eyes widen as I wink and rush away from his car.

I get to Kelex's car just in time to hear Pittman asking for help to pull him out. I grab one arm and shoulder and heft Kelex out of the car. Shit, he's on fire, I wasn't expecting that. Reynolds quickly throws a blanket on him, putting out the flames.

Just as we get the fire on Kelex out, an explosion sounds. Without looking, I know it's Jeremy's car.

"Oh God, he was still in there," Beauty cries out.

Some stoned-looking motherfucker is swaying beside her.

"Fuck him," I snarl. "He caused this shit."

Besides, it's what the fuck I wanted to happen. After seeing this shit tonight, I know what they said about the young kid in the other race was true.

"Let's get him in my car. We all need to get out of here," Pitman says as he picks up Kelex.

"We have to take him to a hospital," Beauty announces like we don't already know this shit.

"You need to get the fuck out of here. Anyone connected to this shit is going to jail. Go," Pitman roars at her.

"You're bleeding," Luke points out.

"Damn," I say under my breath. Her head is bleeding badly. I wouldn't be surprised if she has a fucking concussion.

I help Pitman get a passed-out Kelex into the back of his car.

Once he's situated, Pitman turns to the girl. "Can you still drive your car away from here?"

"Yeah, that guy only clipped me after. He took the impact for me."

She has no idea Kelex was the one that tapped her bumper, but he did it to save her life. If Jeremy would have had his way, she'd either be dead or severely fucked up.

"One of you follow her to somewhere safe," Pitman orders and I'm trying to figure out who the hell made his ass the team leader.

"You on the call list?" he aims his question at Beauty.

Seth keeps a list of all his drivers. We're all saved by nicknames. For a fair price, he lets me see who's on the list before I enter into a race.

In the distance, I hear sirens. Fuck, I need to get out of here.

"Yeah, I'm Skittles," she answers, drawing my attention back to her.

I bet her ass is as sweet as Skittles. I'd taste her fucking rainbow. I shake my head. Damn, even in this fucked-up situation, all I can think about is fucking her.

Pitman continues to bark out orders, but I'm too focused on getting the hell out of here. I'm not exactly on the good side of the law. My juvie record alone is enough for them to want to toss me in jail and hide the key.

Whereas these rich kids can have daddy bailing them out by the morning, my pasty ass will be fucked. I tune back into the conversation just in time to hear Pittman say, "I'm going to be the lowlife my father says I am. None of you were here. None of you know what the fuck happened. I'll get him to the hospital. This is all on me, I'll take this one."

I'm not going to argue with his ass. I clap him on the back, my sign of thanks for taking this rap. Then I turn to race back to my car. The moment I get in, my fucking phone goes off again.

"Yeah," I say this time before Griff speaks.

"Why the fuck aren't you back at the shop?"

I glance behind me at the cops I just passed heading to the wreck site. Damn, that was close.

"I'm on my way."

"I don't have time for you to be playing superhero. Get your ass here, now."

The phone goes dead, and I drop it on the seat. My heart's still pounding after that shit. I run a shaky hand through my long hair.

I've been doing this shit since I was fifteen, it's getting old. Hell, I'm getting old. I think it's about time I start my retirement plan. I think it's time I get serious about opening up my tattoo shop.

CHAPTER ONE

Friends

Deacon
Three months later...

I don't know why I let that short-ass girl talk me into this shit. When I first saw Skittles on that race strip, I visualized all the ways I would fuck her brains out. After spending time with her these last three months, I can't make up my mind if I want to kill her or pat the top of her head.

I guess this is what having an annoying ass little sibling feels like. I can't be too mad at her. She has been a lot of help with me getting my tattoo shop off the ground. She's even gone to different locations with me to help me find a building.

I park my brand-new custom black-on-black Harley Fat Boy near the curb of the bar Skittles told me to meet her at. Taking off my helmet, I then store it in my leather saddle bag. I spot Skittles waiting for me and I go straight to her, a frown already plastered on my face.

"What the fuck are you wearing?" I say in reference to the tiny scrap of material she's sporting as a dress.

"My father is at home, thanks though."

Her snarky comment only pisses me off further. I glare at her. Once thinking her curves were enticing, now I see them for what they are.

"Don't get some guy in here fucked up," I warn, accepting the hug she offers me.

"Ugh, I'm so glad I don't have brothers."

"Are we going in?" I ask when she turns back to the parking lot.

"Not yet, we're waiting on someone."

I grumble under my breath. "Come on, not this bonding shit again."

I don't know why this woman is so hell-bent on getting all of us together. This ain't a damn after-school special. We're not going to magically realize we have a lot in common and start holding hands and shit.

The rumble of a car cuts off anything I was going to say. Skittles face lights up and her shoulders lift, pushing her chest slightly forward. I roll my eyes, already knowing who's joining us.

Will Pitman climbs out of a Viper. His big ass unfolds out of the compact car like a giant. Beside me, Skittles is practically drooling.

"You all right? Do you want me to hold him down while you ride his face?"

"Shut the fuck up, Deacon," she hisses, never dropping her smile.

Pit eats up the space between us with his long strides, his hands in his front pockets. He stops in front of us.

"What's up? You asked me to meet you here." I bet his ass grabbed a box of condoms before he got here. I can tell by the disappointed look on his face, he thought he was getting some pussy tonight.

"I thought we could all hang out," Skittles says, shrugging. "It will just be the three of us. Tak's too young to get in, Luke is out in California, and Kelex..."

"Is too busy running through children's nightmares with knife hands," I joke.

Skittles frowns at me, but Pit snorts.

"Just come on," Skittles says, turning to head into the bar.

I nod my head for Pit to go in front of me. I chuckle when his attention goes straight to her ass. These two are funny.

The bar isn't too packed tonight. The music is pumping a pretty good mix of top 20 hits and hip-hop. It's low enough that I don't have to shout to be heard.

The place is broken up in three sections. Near the back are the pool tables. The dance floor is in the middle and the bar is near the front of the building.

Right now, Pit and I are leaning against the bar. He has a glass of whiskey and I'm babysitting a beer. Both of us have our eyes on the dance floor where Skittles and her friends are dancing.

Even though we are both watching, I'm pretty sure it's for two different reasons. I'm only making sure none of these wasted fucktards get too handsy with her. Pit's tensed jaw and stalker-like gaze is for another reason I imagine.

"You finished eye fucking her yet, or are you still doing foreplay?"

He turns to me, narrowing his eyes. For a moment, I think he's going to swing on me, but he seems too laid back for that. He takes a sip of his whiskey, emptying the glass. Turning to place it on the bar, he then turns back to the dance floor.

"You still stealing cars for your designated daddy?"

On the inside, I'm taken off guard and a little shocked he knows that much about me. On the outside, I casually lift a shoulder as if I don't give a fuck.

"Worried about me stealing daddy's birthday gift to you outside?" His gaze lands on me, piercing and direct.

"You don't know shit about me," he says in a low tone I assume is supposed to scare me.

"I can say the same to you. Don't make assumptions about me like you know me."

We stare at each other for a long moment, neither of us willing to back down. The truth is, I don't dislike Pit. I just don't give a fuck about him. He was the least annoying of the others Skittles was so determined to make me bond with.

"Hey, you guys all right?" Skittles says in a cheery voice when she approaches.

Only she is capable of breaking the standoff between Pit and me. We both turn our attention to her.

"We're great," he grumbles.

"Just peachy," I add, taking a sip from my beer.

"I bet you are," she says, rolling her eyes. "Why don't you guys come dance?"

"Hell, no," I quickly add.

"Come on, Deacon. You're the biggest manwhore I know. There has to be at least one soon-to-be-disappointed woman you want to take home tonight."

Pit snorts. I stick my middle finger up at Skittles. She laughs away my action.

"What about that one?" she asks, pointing to the blonde in the middle of the floor.

"The one that's having a seizure?"

Skittles laughs out loud. "She's dancing, at least I think that's what that is."

"Someone needs to stick a spoon in her mouth to make sure she's not swallowing her tongue."

"What about that one?" This time she points to a redhead.

"I've watched her dance for two hours and her ass hasn't caught the beat yet," Pit answers for me. I thought I was the only one that picked up on that.

"She almost had it on that last song," I joke. Pit grunts a short laugh.

"Fine," Skittles says. "What about those two?" This time she directs our attention to the two chicks in the middle of the floor dry humping each other.

Both Pit and I tilt our heads as we admire the two women.

"Now that might be fun," I admit.

"You are so disgusting," Skittles halfheartedly reprimands. "What about the girl at the end of the bar? She's pretty."

I turn to check out who she's talking about. "The cockeyed one? She's looking at me and the door at the same time."

Pit laughs out loud.

Skittles punches me in the arm. "God, you're so picky. Just come dance with me."

I didn't have to turn to look at him to know Pit tensed beside me. I bet if I looked over at him his brows would be creased and that vein in his neck would be throbbing. Part of me wants to fuck with him and agree to dance with her, the other part knows better.

"Naw, I'm good."

Skittles' brow lifts to her hairline. "Wait, why won't you dance with me?"

I take a sip from my longneck. "Because your ass is fat, and my dick might get hard. And we ain't trying to have that type of relationship."

She scoffs. "You know what, forget it. You two stay over here and be miserable. I'm going to have fun and put my fat ass all on some guy's dick."

"Don't forget my warning from outside." I remind her.

I had no problem kicking somebody's ass for her. She shoots me the bird over her head and storms back off to her friends.

"Don't you think you missed your opportunity?" I say, glancing over at Pit.

"She's not for me."

"Half of the men in here are probably glad you feel that way."

He turns to me, once again eyeing me up and down. "You looking for a shot?"

I almost laugh at how quickly he flipped. For someone not interested in her, he sure the fuck is worried about me.

"You can relax, I'm not your competition." I laugh. "We don't have that kind of relationship."

"What kind of relationship do you two have?" This time he doesn't ask as if he's concerned. I think he genuinely wants to know.

"Mayven is like my little sister. What she lacks in height, she makes up for in hostility."

This brings a smile to his face. "It's always the short ones. Their like fucking pit bulls in a toy poodle's body."

I laugh out at his accurate analogy.

"Hello." We both turn to the sound of the female in front of us. She's a tall leggy blonde. Nice rack, but her face is plain.

"I was checking you guys out from the pool table." She flips her hair over her shoulder. "So, which one of you is with that Black chick." My hackles go up at the way she mentions Skittles.

I look to Pit, and I think he got the same vibe. I plant a smile on my lips, one I've been told is charming.

"Actually, we both are. We share her."

She grimaces, trying to pretend she's disgusted, even though her nipples are nearly poking out of her tight shirt.

"And you're okay with that type of thing?" She directs her question to Pit.

"She's talented, she can handle us." He shrugs, probably only playing along for my benefit.

Blondie licks her lips. "Well, if you guys are looking for an upgrade..." She leaves the end of her sentence open for us to interpret.

"You're supposed to be the upgrade?" I asked, stunned by the audacity. "You come over here with those rolled over cheap ass heels and you have the audacity to act like you're the upgrade."

"How dare you talk to me like that?" she screeches like I give a fuck she's drawing attention.

"Take your desperate ass back to your pool table and get the fuck out of our face," Pit says, not even looking at her.

Blondie huffs and stomps off. Her ankle gives in her haste and she takes three steps, wobbling like a newborn fawn before she can correct herself. Pit and I look to each other before laughing.

"What was that about?" Skittles ask as she approaches.

"Nothing," Pit answers her. "Go back to your dancing."

Skittles narrows her eyes at him. She looks as if she was about to say something else, but her words are cut off by loud voices.

"Who the fuck disrespected my sister?" Some big ass dude with fucked-up neck tattoos says. Blondie is beside him, pointing in our direction.

"Welp, tonight is about to be fun." I place my beer down on the bar behind me.

As soon as the big guy and his equally thick-necked friend approach us, Pit grabs Skittles' arm and moves her to the other side of him. After, he leans back against the bar, folding his arms over his chest.

"Did you assholes touch my sister?"

I look to the chick in question. She looks boldly back at me as if she didn't tell a lie.

"Nobody touched her. I did toss her lying ass out of my face though," Pit says in his laid-back tone.

"You calling my sister a liar?"

"Yeah, he called her a liar, but before that I called her a broke down desperate slut."

"With cheap shoes," Pit reminds me.

"Damn, those shoes are cheap looking," Skittles joins in. "And they're leaning."

"Same thing I said," I tell her.

"Shut up," the brother barks. "Either you apologize to my sister, or you get this beatdown."

"Are those my only two options?" I ask, smirking.

"Fucking right they are," the thick-necked friend says, coming up on the other side of the girl, standing right in front of me.

I look to Pit, and he glances at me. In this moment, we have an understanding. We were by no means besties or some shit like that, but we do have a mutual agreement.

"I guess we'll see what's behind door number two." I shrug. Flying my fist into the friend's face just as Pit lands a blow to the mouthy brother. The lying blonde tried to jump in, but Skittles nails her ass in the face, and blondie lands in a heap on the ground. In the end, both guys go down without much work.

As Pit and I get kicked out of the bar, we share a laugh and fist-bump.

"What you got planned for next weekend?" I ask after we both see Skittles off.

He shakes his head. "Hopefully, not that shit again."

I smile. "We got about twenty or so bars around here, maybe we can get kicked out of another one next weekend."

Pit eyes me, not saying much. Finally, he nods. "Sounds like a plan."

We parted ways, but something about it seems like a pivotal moment in our friendship.

CHAPTER TWO

Happened in Vegas

Deacon
Fourteen years later...

"Daddy. Daddy. Look, I can read this."

I roll my eyes at the asshat on his phone as I stand in line at this fucking store. As big as this place is, you'd think they'd have more than one damn register open. I'm the fifth person in line and I'm tempted to put this shit back and say forget it. However, the message two nights ago has me clutching the box of condoms in my hand like it's my lifeline.

"Look, Daddy, I can read it," the little boy calls out proudly to his father, and like before, the man on the phone doesn't acknowledge his kid's excited words.

The little boy's shoulders slump as he places the magazine back on the rack. I swear some people shouldn't procreate. I should fucking know.

My parents were two of those people. I have a soft spot for kids. I don't have any of my own and I don't want any, but I still have a soft spot for them.

Kids are innocent. They should be protected and cared for at all times. And if you're going to have them, pay the fuck attention to them when they're trying to show you they can read.

"Hey, kid," I say to the little boy standing in front of me.

He turns his wide blue eyes to me and unbelievably, they seem to widen even more. I don't blame him, I'm a bit scary. I'm six-three, two-hundred-fifteen pounds, and I'm covered in tattoos. My presence makes grown men shit themselves. I have no doubt this kid thinks I'm the fucking bogeyman.

"You want to show me what you can read?"

At this, the boy forgets about his fear as he smiles at me. He reaches for the magazine, but I stop him.

"Read this," I advise instead.

"Ccc... con... dddd.... doms. Condoms," the little guy says proudly.

"Good job, kid. Now, when you go home to your mom, tell her you learned the word condom at the store with your dad."

The kid nods, whispering the word over and over again as he moves up in the line. I pull out my phone and check the time. I still have fifteen minutes before I have to meet her at the diner.

Talk about a ghost from my past. I thought after Vegas I would never see her again. Damn, just thinking about her and our time together gets my dick hard.

I've fucked plenty of females. I'm not running up any astronomical numbers, but I've had my fair share. Yet, there was something about her.

She wasn't the most experienced lay. I've fucked females that could do shit I'd never dreamed of. I knew a chick who had no gag reflex, and she could choke down my cock like a fucking circus freak.

However, none of them compared to this girl. I still don't know what it was about her that's made her so unforgettable. I'm hoping this out of the blue message on Facebook means she's ready to go at it again.

Maybe after this second time. I'll realize the sex wasn't all I thought it was. Maybe I'll realize I was drunk and making it out to be something it wasn't.

I can't say. All I know is I'm ready for this fucking meeting.

I finally get to the front of the line and toss my box of condoms on the register. The cashier looks me over like I might be a pack of meat she wants to buy. Apparently, she approves of what she sees.

A brown-toothed smile slides over her jaundiced, pockmarked face. She slips her stringy hair off her shoulder. The nerve of this chick.

Some women think just because they have a pussy, they can get any man they want. This meth-head-looking broad is out of her damn mind.

"The extra-large size," she says, reading the label on my condoms.

"Yeah," I reply, only half paying attention as I pull some cash out of my pocket.

"I read somewhere most men can actually fit the regular size and they are only showing off when they buy extra large, but I find it hard to believe with you."

"First of all, you know your ass hasn't read a damn thing since first grade so you can stop lying. And if you're so fucking concerned about the size of my dick, I can pull it out and lay it on your wide ass forehead for measurement."

Her eyes bulge and her meth-toothed smile falls for only a second before returning. She bites into her bottom lip and runs her gaze back over my body. I'm guessing she likes being talked to like shit.

"What do you plan on doing with these extra-large condoms?"

I check my watch one last time before looking back up at the cashier. "I'm going to make fucking balloon animals. What the hell you think I'm going to do with them? Will you ring my shit up so I can go? Damn."

Her stunned face turns bright red as she quickly rings me up. I toss my money on the counter and grab my condoms before heading out the door. I'm on my bike, rushing to the diner as fast as I can go.

***

The place isn't too crowded for a Tuesday afternoon. The parking lot is rather small though. I stop behind a pickup truck that's holding up traffic. The truck is waiting for a Cadillac to get out of their parking spot so he can park.

I hate shit like this. I pull my bike around the truck and as soon as the Cadillac pulls out of the way I park my bike in its spot. The truck driver blares on its horn while I turn off my bike.

"You fucking asshole," the man yells out of the window.

I take off my helmet, tuck it under my arm, and turn to face the truck driver. He quickly drives away. I head inside.

I was hoping I would get here early enough to see her when she walked in, but it looks like she had the same idea. Like a moth to a flame, I spot her easily, even though her hair is different this time. In Vegas she had long wavy hair that fell to her hips.

Today, her hair is in a short chin-length cut. I know it's her because her shoulders are out and that dark chocolate skin is glistening from the sunlight. I head straight to the table.

My focus only on her. She's not facing me, so she hasn't spotted me yet. The flowery scent I remember so well from Vegas has me hard as fuck already.

That's one thing I thought I had made up in my head, but it's real. She smells like heaven. I come around to stand in front of her and I pause.

I wasn't expecting it. Damn, she's beautiful. Her hair is pushed behind her ears, showcasing her diamond shape face. Her upturned brown eyes and long lashes giving her a sweet innocent look. She has a button nose and plump lips I want wrapped around my cock so bad I can almost feel it.

"How ya doing, Noni?"

A smile slips over her face, the one that drew me to her in Vegas. Noni is a beautiful woman. She's built like a model, only not as tall.

She's about five six or five seven, with curves in all the right places. Any man can see her beauty with one look at her, but there is something about her. The same thing I noticed the night I met her, something draws your eye to her no matter where you are or who you're with.

"Hello, Deacon."

I lick my lips at something else I thought I'd made up about her. She has a raspy sultry voice like Demi Moore. I remember after hearing her speak the first time, I wondered what her voice would sound like screaming my name. I can testify, it's sexy as hell.

I take a seat in the booth across from her, placing my helmet down beside me. She picked a table in the back, close to the bathrooms. I assume it's for privacy. If I remember correctly, she's a bit shy at times.

Watching her for a minute, I allow that one crazy night to play back in my mind like a porno. She must read where my thoughts are from my face, because she blushes, ducking her head.

The waitress comes to the table, ready to take our order. I wait for Noni to place hers first. I'm not hungry for anything on this menu. I want to skip this whole lunch and get straight to what we both want.

"Deacon, are you getting anything?" Her voice brings me back to the present.

"Just a cup of coffee. Black," I say with a wink over to my dark beauty.

I get another grin from her and a blush. The waitress walks off and I go in for the kill.

"Let me guess, you called me up because you couldn't stop thinking about the best sex you've ever had."

She tosses her head back and laughs. I never thought the column of someone's neck could be so fucking sexy. Her eyes sparkle and I can tell she has a retort on the tip of her tongue, but she shakes her head and sits up straight.

"Actually, I wanted to talk about something else."

"Why'd you stop?"

She tilts her head slightly to the left and quizzically lifts a perfectly arched brow. "What?"

"You were about to say something."

She shakes her head, ready to lie, but I won't accept it. "Say it," I demand.

She did this a lot in Vegas too. It's like she's always second-guessing her response. Again, she ducks her head before looking up at me.

Closely watching her face, I can almost see the war her mind must be churning over in her head. She watches me for a moment, not saying anything. Then, she shakes her head and squares her shoulders as if she's come to a decision.

"I think it's funny you assume you were the best sex I'd ever had."

A pleased smile spreads over my face. "Baby, your pussy was so tight and underused, I thought you were a virgin. I had to check the sheets for blood after you left."

She scoffs and rolls her eyes. "God, I thought I imagined how much of an asshole you were." Her eyes widen as if the reply slipped out on its own. She drops her eyes to the table. "Sorry."

"Don't apologize. Say what you feel."

Those cat-like brown eyes lift even more when a small smile touches her face, making her even more gorgeous.

"So much of our night together felt like a dream. It was hard to remember what was real and what wasn't," she admits softly.

My smile turns into a prideful smirk. "You've been thinking about me?"

She quickly sits up straight, placing her hands on the table to play with the straw paper, twirling it around her finger. "No, I haven't thought about you."

It's nice to know I can still read her. I thought it was the tequila shots that made her so expressive, but no, it's just Noni. She's lying.

The way her gaze has been running away from mine this entire encounter and the way she's so interested in twirling the straw paper around her finger like a ribbon, lets me know she's still been thinking about me. The waitress walks up, placing my cup of coffee in front of me and refills Noni's iced tea.

"What's the deal, beautiful? You contact me out of the blue after nearly three months. I know it's not for another round." I nod to the large rock on her left hand. I spotted it the moment she moved her hand to the table, which I'm disappointed about. "Why the impromptu meeting?"

She looks nervous for a minute. Another thing I remember from Vegas, she was all flirty when we were in the club, but the moment I got her back to the room, she sobered up a little and turned nervous and shy.

"Do you remember the incident?" she asks, lowering her voice.

I frown. "You mean the broken condom?"

Hell yeah, I remember. That shit sobered both of us up completely. We had been fucking nonstop and I was down to my last damn condom, trying to make the shit stretch.

I fucked straight out of the damn thing. Even had to do a mission impossible search to find it inside her. It was about eight in the morning. After that was when she crawled out of bed, talking about never seeing each other again.

"Yeah, and…"

She twists her hands. "I was supposed to go and grab the morning-after pill, but I ended up having to talk my friend down after she caught her husband in the bed with her sister and well."

I watch her cautiously, already knowing where this is going. I still needed to hear her say it though.

"I'm pregnant."

"You're pregnant?" My question comes out much louder than I had expected. The people three tables over turn to look at us.

"Yes," she answers a lot quieter than me.

A lot of things go through my head. First off, I never wanted to be a father. I didn't have one growing up and I know I'm not in the right mindset to be one.

Secondly, I always knew if a mistake like this was made—and it has never been made in my entire thirty-five years—I vowed I wouldn't be like the low-life motherfuckers who spawned me. I sink back into the bench cushions behind me, locking my gaze with hers.

"You keeping it?"

Her eyes flare with anger and fuck me, the shit excites me.

"Absolutely," she says confidently as if she's daring me to say something against it.

I nod, feeling a little proud. "And you're sure it's mine?"

This question knocks the wind out of her sails. I knew at the first glance of Noni, no matter how tight and tiny her little gold dress was, she wasn't wild. She had goody-two-shoes written all over her.

I was shooting my shot when I asked her to go back to my room with me. It shocked the hell out of me when she agreed. I imagine Vegas was a new experience for her, and me having to question her gets under her skin.

"I've only been with one other man. Jason and I had been broken up for three months before I went to Vegas. Besides, we've never had sex without protection. We were going to wait until after the wedding to..." She trails off. "Look, if you don't believe me, I can get a test."

I already had questions about this boyfriend, but if he's got a girl like Noni and he's waiting until after marriage to sleep with her, he's fucking crazy. Her pussy is top notch. Hell, I want it now and she's wearing his ring.

"No need for all that, I believe you." And I did. "Sorry, I had to ask."

She nods. "I understand."

I exhale, sitting up a little straighter. News like this has a way of making you sit up and get your shit together.

"Well, how do you want to do this? You're up in Bridge Lake, right? You're about twenty minutes away, I can come up for the weekends until he gets old enough to come stay with me.

"I want some holidays though. I guess I can let you decide which ones you want first. And I want to be there when he's born."

"Deacon," she calls my name, cutting into my list of demands. "That's what I wanted to talk to you about. You see, Jason and I are getting married at the end of the year. He wants to adopt the baby and raise it as his own. I'm here to ask you if you will sign over your rights?"

It takes about two seconds for what she's asking to register. I don't think she could have cut me more if she actually took the dirty butter knife off the table and stabbed me in the chest with it. The scars of my childhood rush back to me and I have to momentarily close my eyes on the barrage of thoughts and feelings trying to consume me. My hands are lying flat on top of the table and I have to try not to use them to flip this fucking thing over.

"Are you out of your fucking mind?"

This time when I shout, I mean to. Everyone in the entire diner turns toward our little booth. Noni looks around nervously.

"Keep your voice down," she whisper-yells.

"Let me get this right. You want me to sign over my rights to my child so you and your little dick fiancé can raise him as your own."

"Okay, there is no need for name calling. Be reasonable, Deacon."

"Fuck reasonable. I'm not giving up my kid." I don't give a shit what people think about me. I'm not going to be a deadbeat dad in my own kid's life.

"Do you even want kids?"

"Hell no, but that's beside the damn point. I have one now."

She shuts her eyes, taking a deep breath before she opens them and looks at me again.

"Jason and I just think—"

"I swear if you mention his bitch ass to me one more time, I'm going to go the fuck off. He wasn't there the night I had you coming so hard on my cock you were screaming like a dying cat. He doesn't have a say in this."

"My god, you're such an asshole," she says, rolling her eyes. "We had one night of sex. I was in a bad place and I wasn't thinking rationally."

"Is that the bullshit excuse you told him?" I mock, leaning forward in my seat, bringing my face closer to hers. "You can tell that shit to him, but I was there."

I run my tongue over my bottom lip. I want her to remember how hard she came with just my fucking tongue running over her little unused clit. She wanted me like a drowning man wants air.

Her breath comes out staggered as her chest rises suddenly. Yeah, she remembers.

"Not the point," she says, forcing her eyes closed briefly. "What we had is over. I just want what's best for my child."

Those words hit me in the gut like a sucker punch. I sit back in my seat.

"I'm not what's best? I was good enough for you to fuck, but not good enough to share custody of a kid?"

She looks hurt by my words, but I don't care. She's not the only one hurt here.

"If you want custody of my kid, you will have to take me to court to get it."

I throw some cash on the table to cover the coffee I never drank. I'm done with this conversation. I slide out of the booth, taking my helmet with me.

"Deacon, wait," she pleads for me to come back, but I don't.

I honestly don't know if a judge will rule me as the best fit for a child. I mean, my past isn't squeaky clean, but I'll be damned if I let them take this kid from me without a fight. Shit, I don't even want to be a dad, but the fact I have a child on the way changes all that. My pop didn't stick around long enough for the nut to dry on my mom, but I won't do that to my kid.

My phone is at my ear the moment I step outside.

"Hey, Pit, call me back when you get this message. I need you to pull some strings. I need a lawyer."

I put the phone away, place my helmet on my head, and hop on my bike. I make it back to the shop in less time than I should.

CHAPTER THREE

Good Girl

Noni

I smack my hands against the steering wheel of my car as I stop at a red light. I won't wipe at my eyes because it would be useless. How did I find myself in this predicament?

I've lived my entire life on the straight and narrow. I got good grades all throughout school. I had no behavioral issues.

Hell, I barely even spoke. I graduated at the top of my class in high school and college. I even kept my virginity until I was an adult, and then one stupid bachelorette party in Vegas and now I'm the trollop with a baby on the way that isn't my fiancé's.

I have fallen so far from the perfect fiancée I've been trying to be. The memory of Deacon's expression when he asked me if he wasn't good enough crosses my mind. And once again, I feel as low as a snake's belly.

This is a truly shitty situation. On one side, I'm hurting the man who I vowed to love, and on the other side, I'm hurting a man who for eight hours, one night, made me feel more alive than I've felt in all my thirty-one years on this earth. For some reason, the latter seems to bother me the most.

No one would ever accuse Deacon Clarke of being a sweet man. He's too vulgar and rough around the edges. Yet, when he was with me, we had a connection.

A connection so strong, I swear, I've been off since I came back from that trip. I've had this lingering feeling like I'm trapped in a small prison and I can't fully stretch out or breathe. Until today.

Being with him today felt like the first day since Vegas I could move. I could fully take a deep breath. The more I try to explain the situation to myself, the more stupid I feel. How can I have a connection like that with a man I hardly know?

The speaker in my car starts ringing, bringing my mind away from the thoughts it had been heading toward. I tap the hands-free option on my steering wheel just as the light turns green and I start moving again.

"Hello."

"Best friend." The high-pitched squeal brings a needed smile to my face.

"Porsha," I cheer, so glad to be hearing from one of my two best friends.

I met Porsha my freshmen year in college. We were both in line waiting to buy books and she sparked up a conversation with me. We've been close ever since. It was Porsha's bachelorette party I attended in Vegas where I met Deacon.

"You finally leave the beautiful island of Jamaica to come back with us peasants?"

She snorts. "Girl, if I didn't have to work, I'd still be there. Marcus and I loved it."

A proud smile spreads over my face. "How is married life treating you two?"

Porsha and Marcus have a beautiful love story. They met on a business trip. Their flight got canceled and they were stuck in the airport for six hours getting to know each other.

They realized they were only three hours away from each other and when they left the airport, they kept in touch. After only eight months of dating, Marcus popped the question and eight months later, they got married. Their love is so remarkable to be around, it made you envious.

"Perfect," she says in answer to my question. "Marcus showed me the finished house."

I gasp, removing my hand off the steering wheel to clutch my chest. "Did it turn out exactly like you dreamed?"

Her voice drops and becomes breathless. "Even more beautiful."

I'm so happy for my friend. I don't think there is a person I know who deserves good fortune as much as Porsha. She had a rough few years.

First, the bad breakup with Chance. Then, the death of her father and the murder of her brother. She needed to find her happiness.

"Well, enough about me. What's going on with you? Has Stick Up The Ass, aka Jason set a date yet?"

I roll my eyes and laugh at her nickname for Jason. Those two have never gotten along.

"Well, there is something I need to tell you."

Before *I'm pregnant* can fall from my lips, my phone goes off again. The cheerful mood I was just in immediately gets sucked out of me.

"Porsh, let me call you back. This is Jason."

She sucks her teeth on the other end. "Fine, but let's schedule to go out to lunch this weekend. We need to catch up."

I agree and quickly press the button on my steering wheel to click over.

"I was just about to call you," I lie easily.

"How did it go? Did he agree to sign over his rights?" Jason asks.

I can tell by his tone he's distracted. Probably working on something for work. I usually only get half his attention nowadays.

"Not really."

There's a pause on the line. I don't speak. I know he has more to say, he likes to make me wait.

"You told him I'm willing to raise the kid?"

"Yes, Jason. He's not going for it. He wants to share custody with me."

There is another pause from him, followed by a long sigh. "That can't happen, Noni. I'm not sharing my family with some asshole you drunkenly slept with."

He releases another breath. "This isn't what I had planned for my life. I was supposed to marry a woman who only knew me. Then we were going to be married for a few years before starting a family. Now here I am, trying to raise a child who isn't mine because my fiancée can't keep her fucking legs closed."

My mood from my previous conversation is completely gone. I remain silent on the phone, there's nothing I can say. Don't get me wrong, I have a lot to say.

For instance, if he'd never cheated on me, then I would have never been in Vegas, single and feeling lonely enough to sleep with anyone else. I might have even said I didn't give a shit about what he had planned for himself, because I, too, had plans he never asked me about. However, I don't say any of that even though it's on the tip of my tongue and clawing at me to open my mouth so it can come out.

No, I keep my mouth shut and count to three. I'm the perfect girl, perfect daughter, and perfect fiancée. I don't say mean and cruel things to my future husband.

He wouldn't like it. *Deacon wouldn't mind.* The thought comes through so loud and prominent, it's almost like the words were spoken outside my body.

The light feeling accompanies a smile when I think about Deacon telling me to say what's on my mind. He didn't seem to have a problem with me speaking my truth, even if I was calling him an asshole.

"I'm sorry I ruined your plans," I say into the empty car. "I'm trying to make this better."

That's the truth. I'm trying my hardest to give this baby the best chance at life I can. I was already eight weeks when I found out I was pregnant, but from the moment those two lines showed up on the test, I wanted this kid to have all the things I didn't have growing up.

That meant a mother and a father who lived together and who loved them. I never want my children to feel the way I felt as a child. If that means getting Deacon to sign over his rights so Jason can raise this baby with me, then so be it.

Jason releases another one of those condescending sighs. "I know, baby. I know you're trying to do the best you can with the situation. Maybe we need to give it a few days. Let him come to terms with it all. I have a feeling he will take our offer after he thinks about it. No man wants to raise a child with some easy one-night stand."

I ignore the barbed words. Instead, I force my irritation down as I pull my car to a stop in front of my mother's house.

"You're right."

If my life were ever turned into a book or a movie that would be the title of it. You're right. Someone else is always right.

"Are you at your mother's?"

"Yes."

"Good. I'm working late tonight, but I want you to go straight home after you leave there. I love you, Noni."

"I love you too."

The line goes dead before my reply is out of my mouth and I'm met with the silence of my car. I exhale, taking a moment before pushing my door open and climbing out. The two Cadillacs in the yard let me know my aunts are here, so hopefully, I can make this trip quick.

The walk up the short steps of my mom's bungalow-style home gives me time to prepare. A lot of my childhood friends talked about their loving relationships with their mothers. Porsha and her mother are like best friends.

Even my other best friend Amira and her mother, who argue like an old married couple, are like two peas in a pod. I can't say the same for me and my mother. Every day after I get off work— as the perfect daughter—I come by to see my mother and help with any chores she may need done. It doesn't matter how tired I am or how shitty my day is.

It's expected of me to do what my mother needs from me. It's what the perfect daughter does. I knock before opening the screen door and walking in.

"You're late today?" my aunt Mildred says as soon as I walk in. Her glass of wine already in her hand. She's still in her postal uniform. A job she's held for as long as I've been alive.

"Leave her alone, Mildred, she might have been helping that fine fiancé of hers," Aunt Judy says, winking suggestively.

I swear, I have to be careful with my fiancé around my aunt. From the moment I brought him home, she's been after him.

My mother comes around the corner with a pitcher of tea and a glass in her hand. She sets both down in the middle of the dining room table. Right beside the deck of cards. I don't think a day has gone by without my mother and her sisters getting together right after work to gossip and play cards, more specifically gin rummy.

"Don't be talking nasty around my daughter," my mom says, looking down her nose at her youngest sister. "Noni is waiting until after marriage to lie with her husband."

A perfected smile graces my face. One I can do in my sleep. I've mastered it over the years. It's the *I can't tell you the truth so I will stay silent* smile.

Mildred scoffs before taking another sip from her wine glass. "You might as well give that up, Shondra. After the mess she's made, ain't no reason for her trying to act like a virtuous Mary now."

"I know that's right," Aunt Judy agrees, and she and Mildred laugh.

Mom frowns and then cuts her eyes to me. Embarrassment and shame look back at me before she turns away and storms back into the kitchen.

"Face it, sis, your perfect little girl ain't so perfect anymore." Mildred downs the rest of her drink.

Aunt Mildred is the middle child out of the three sisters and she and my mother seem to always have some battle going on between them. I never witnessed the original fallout, but I'm always a victim to the war. Aunt Mildred watches me with a jutted chin and a sneer as I pass their card game and follow my mom into the kitchen.

"Mom, I'm sorry," I say right away.

I've said those three words more to my mother than I think I've told her I love her. It doesn't matter how insignificant her conceived injustice is, I'm always apologizing. Like in fourth grade, when I—among only one other student in the entire district—was asked to write a speech for our state board meeting about the love for our schools.

It was a huge honor. My speech was even placed in the newspaper for how well written it was. However, I found myself apologizing to my mother because the other kid mentioned his mother in his speech, and I didn't. That night I was ungrateful and unappreciative.

"Did you get the lowlife to give up his rights?"

I flinch when she calls Deacon a lowlife. I never talked about him. All I told Jason was I'm pregnant and it was by the guy I met in Vegas.

He doesn't know anything more than that. Whatever idea he or my mother have of Deacon is solely what they have cooked up in their heads.

"It's not going to be that easy. He wants to be in his child's life."

She scoffs, her nose scrunching up as if she smells something awful. She closes the fridge door with a little more force than is needed. The bottles in the door rattle with the force.

"I can't believe you, Noni," she hisses toward me. "I know I raised you better than this."

Raised? Is that what you call shutting me out and blaming me for everything that went wrong in your life? The reply flutters against my lips like butterfly wings, but I keep it caged in.

My lips seal tight. The perfect daughter wouldn't dare say anything like that.

"You're right, mother. You didn't raise me this way."

I drop my chin to my chest, averting my eyes away from hers so she doesn't catch my eye roll.

"Foolish," she mutters, never fully understanding when she's won an argument there's no need to continue to argue her point. "I should have never let you go to Vegas."

Let me? She says this as if I'm not a grown ass woman.

"I knew those worthless girls were no good for you. They were always jealous."

This is my mother's delusional side. She hates Porsha and Amira—not because they are jealous—but because they like me. She never could understand why.

"Porsha and Amira aren't worthless. Porsha is one of the youngest principals in the state and Amira is a successful realtor."

She waves her hand, dismissing my claims. "That's always been your problem. You don't know nothing about the world. Those women are jealous because you were able to find a good man like Jason."

I trap the laugh behind my clenched lips. If Porsha was here, she'd throw up even thinking about her wanting Jason.

"Not many men would take you back after the foolishness you pulled."

The comment steals the laugh from my lips. Not many women would have taken his ass back after catching him with his pants down and his paralegal with her lips wrapped around his dick. Granted, he had already called it off when I walked into his office, but I had only gotten the text message that we "needed a break" twenty minutes before his dick was down her throat. And yet, no one's telling me how great and forgiving I am.

She glares at me then shakes her head. "You're selfish, just like your father." I flinch at the words.

The gaping wound from my childhood opens up like a fresh cut. Anything I do that's not up to standard for my mother that she finds unappealing, I get from my father. My tight curls, I get them from my father.

Needing braces in fifth grade, that was from my father. My inability to carry a tune, yup, I get that from my father too. All the things she hates about me comes from him.

"Do you need my help today?" My voice breaks and comes out high pitched, something my usual raspy tone doesn't do.

She kisses her teeth. "I need you to take those towels over to the church and then run some money to the bank."

She walks past me and into her living room. I take a moment to gather myself in the kitchen that's cut off from everyone else.

This pregnancy so far has been relatively easy. Only occasional sickness and tender breasts, but I've been extremely tired. Many days I've wanted to do nothing more than come home from work and nap.

Yet, I don't get that chance. I place a hand over my still flat stomach and smile. This isn't how I would've wanted this little life inside me to start, but it's here now.

"Mommy will get some rest soon," I whisper to the fetus inside me. I steel my nerves and square my shoulders before joining my mother and aunts back in the living room.

***

By the time I get home I'm so hungry and exhausted, I can't think straight. I shower and warm up some leftovers, then plant myself at the kitchen table to eat and look over a few of my design ideas for a new dentist's office downtown. Five years ago, I opened up my own interior design business.

Three years later, my best friend, who is a realtor, joined me in the building. We united forces and now we work side by side. Often times, I'm hired to stage homes for her and recently we've started to buy and flip houses together.

I'm lost in my work when my phone goes off on the table. I pick it up and look down at the screen. It's my Messenger app.

The name DC Ink appears and my heart stops. My hands shake slightly as I slide my finger across the screen to see the message. It's a single word.

DC INK: Hey

When I found out I was pregnant, I immediately looked Deacon up. I only knew his name, that we didn't live far from each other, and he owned DC Ink, a tattoo shop. We didn't talk too much in Vegas.

The only reason I knew about DC Ink is because he had it tattooed on his chest and after licking across it, I asked him what it was. My face warms at the memory.

I took to the internet to track him down, found his page on Facebook and then sent him a message. Now, when I see the little Messenger icon on my screen with a conversation bubble, my heart starts to race. I don't exactly know if it's a good racing or a nervous one.

Part of me wants him to sign over his rights. That would be the easiest thing for me and Jason. However, part of me hopes he won't give in so easily. I wanted him to put up some kind of fight over this child.

I'm pretty sure this message is going to be him saying he will sign the papers. I mean, everyone is right. Why the hell would he want to raise a kid with someone he had a one-night stand with?

DC INK: I'm still pissed the fuck off you came at me like that, but it isn't okay for me not to at least ask you, are you okay? How's the baby treating you? Any cravings or anything yet? I don't know how this shit works, but do you know what you're having?

I cup my hand to my mouth and my eyes blur. He has been the first one to ask me this since I found out I was pregnant. Not what I am having, but the general question of am I okay? Not my mother nor my fiancé ever thought to ask me those three words.

My fingers fly over the screen in reply.

Noni Kaye: Thank you for asking. I'm fine. Tired mostly. I'm only ten weeks, so no, I don't know what I'm having yet.

I hit send and watch as his picture moves down to read the message. I chew on my bottom lip, waiting for his reply. When I see the little dots appear on the screen, I get even more nervous.

DC INK: Glad everything is okay. You should get some rest, I'm pretty sure you need it.

At the exact same time I read that message, another one appears.

DC INK: Thanks for telling me about the baby.

I smile at that last one. Not telling him did cross my mind. The day I took the test and found out for sure, I honestly did think about it. I mean, he couldn't truly miss something he didn't know about, but deep down I knew that wasn't the right thing to do.

Noni Kaye: No problem. Good night, Deacon.

DC INK: Good night.

I place the phone face down on the table. The moment the conversation ends that confined feeling comes back and the odd stomach fluttering stops. It's the same feeling I felt in Vegas when he first approached me. The moment those hazel eyes connected to mine at the club, the ripples in my stomach went off.

I'd never seen a man as gorgeous as him. Jason is easy on the eyes and turns women's heads everywhere we go, yet he is no match for Deacon. His tanned skin looks even more golden in contrast to the artwork that graces his arms, fingers, chest, back, and thighs.

His tattoos are like a suit of armor on him. His body was trim and long sinewy muscles had stretched out the fabric of his gray shirt. That dark hair was long up top and shorter on the sides and had been pushed back out of his face with the exception of a piece in the front that fell just on his forehead.

His eyebrows sat like dark slashes over his stunning eyes. Then there's his full thick beard. I was never a beard girl until I met him. Until I felt how amazing the silky hairs could feel brushing against my skin.

The alcohol in my system gave me all the courage to catch and hold his eye across the bar. Well, the alcohol and realizing I'd wasted nearly six years with a man who would break up with me in a text and not even an hour later have his dick down another woman's throat.

In the few hours I spent with Deacon, wrapped up in his arms on that dance floor and lying beneath him in bed was incredible. And because of that magnificent night, I'm now having his baby.

My phone goes off again and exhilaration fills my veins as I quickly pick it up. The feeling dies down when I see the text from Jason.

Jason: Change of plans. I'm coming over, wait up for me.

Well, there goes my plans of getting any rest. I place the phone back on the table and finish going over my work.

CHAPTER FOUR

The Old Man

Deacon

The chime on the front door of my shop dings and I look up from the paperwork on my desk to catch sight of my old boss. I smile, welcoming the distraction. It's not like I was getting any work done anyway.

I need to be looking at the books for my three tattoo shops, but all I can think about is her. My mind can't figure out what it wants to focus on. It switches back and forth between reliving that night in Vegas and yesterday in the diner.

What the fuck did she mean by asking me some shit like that? I don't have much. I'll never be a billionaire or own my own yacht or anything, but I have enough in the bank to live comfortably and take care of a kid. And yeah, my past is pretty fucked up, but since that race, I've gotten my shit together. Haven't done anything outside of the law since.

"Hey, Griff," my tattoo crew calls out.

Standing, I forget the paperwork and walk out of my office. As soon as I hit the main area, the smell hits me.

"Who the fuck got my shop smelling like wild onions?"

I turn to my crew. They are all here today. They shake their heads. Turning back to my receptionist, Karly, she points to the kid standing at the front counter with baller shorts on.

I storm over to him.

"Let him be," Griff says with a chuckle, but I ignore him.

I approach the guy filling out the paperwork and almost get knocked out by his funk.

"I know damn well you didn't bring your ass up in my place smelling like hot ass on a cold day."

The punk looks at me nervously. "I… um, came over right after I left the gym."

"How old are you?"

"Eighteen, sir," he says, looking at my receptionist for help.

"Does he check out?" I look to Karly. The guy looks like he's sixteen instead of eighteen.

"Yeah, he's eighteen."

I snatch the clipboard out of his hands and toss it back on the counter.

"If you're not responsible enough to wash your funky nuts before coming into my shop and think one of my artists are going to sit close to you and tat you, then you're not responsible enough to get a damn tattoo. Take your ass home and shower, got my shit smelling like old hotdog water. Get the fuck out of here."

The guy quickly turns on his heels and hightails it out of the shop. My crew and the other patrons burst out in laughter.

"I knew you were going to say something," Money Mike, one of my tattoo artists says.

"I thought that was you, Money. Thought you got kicked out again," Maverick, another artist, says jokingly.

"Fuck you, Mav. That was one time. I sprayed with body spray." The crew laughs again, and I join them briefly before turning back to Griff.

"What's up, old man?"

Griff and I give each other a quick one-armed hug. "Titus, my boy, I see you haven't changed a bit."

The years have been good to my mentor and friend. He's on the far side of fifty but is still in great shape. He may even give me a run for my money in the physical fitness department. His short salt and pepper hair is trimmed almost identical to mine.

"I'm good," I say, embracing him in a quick one-arm hug. "What brings you by? Going to let me start that sleeve?" I joke.

Griff laughs, the lines around his eyes growing more prominent. "Hell no. I don't have the time for that shit. I was wondering if I could take you out for lunch?"

I stand there for a moment watching him. This isn't the first time Griff has come to my shop, or we have gone out for lunch, but I've known this man long enough to know something is off.

"You all right?"

His gaze flashes to the front door before looking back at me. "I'm good. Just haven't seen you in a while." He claps me on the back. "Are you free for lunch or not?"

I shake my head. "Yeah, I can have lunch. Let me put some stuff up." I grab my bike keys off my desk before closing and locking my office door.

We go to one of our favorite spots and grab one of the tables outside. A repeat of last night's basketball game plays on the TV over our heads as a waitress in tiny orange shorts places our wings on the table. Griff winks at the young girl and her face turns as red as her hair before she walks away.

"Keep it up, one of these young girls is going to give your old ass a heart attack."

He laughs. "Don't worry about me. I've been ruining women's lives longer than you've known how to get your dick hard."

This time I laugh. His phone goes off on the table for the fourth time since we sat down. He looks down at it and grimaces before silencing the device.

"You owe somebody? That damn phone hasn't stopped ringing." Griff's face pales before he looks away.

"Naw, just an old friend."

A beat of silence drips between us. The kind that lets me know he's lying about something. I've never been one to get in anyone else's business. If he wanted me to know he would tell me, so I don't push him.

Griff watches me with a smile on his face then shakes his head.

"What the hell is wrong with you?" I chuckle.

His smile grows as he laughs lightheartedly. "Just thinking about all the shit you used to pull. Remember that damn Shelby?"

A booming laugh erupts from me, causing the people at the next table to glance over at us.

"It was my first job," I say in my defense.

Griff narrows his eyes in mock anger. "I was so damn mad at you. I couldn't use shit off that car after all the damage you caused."

We take a second to laugh about the memory.

"I kind of miss those days," I admit.

I don't miss the danger or living life looking over my shoulder bullshit, but I do miss all the time I spent hanging with the crew.

He lifts a hand as if he's holding up traffic. "Not me. I'm glad you pulled me out of it."

"Me?" I rear my head back.

"Yeah you. You were the best. No one could lift a car faster than you or know the value of the parts like you. Once you left, it wasn't the same anymore and I realized I just didn't have the passion for it."

This is all news to me. I had no idea Griff came out of the game because of me. I always thought he just got tired of it.

After the night of that race that killed Jeremy and almost killed Kelex and Tak, I left the car heisting business. I told Griff that night I was taking my money and going legit. He never argued. In fact, he told me upfront the day I started, if I ever didn't want to do it anymore, I was free to walk away.

"And you've been enjoying retirement ever sense?"

A broad smile lifts his lips and brightens his eyes. "Retirement is the way to go, kid. Now, I'm just waiting until the day you make me a grandpa."

I damn near choke on the sip of beer that just went down my throat. Griff laughs out loud. I place the bottle back down on the table and tug at the collar of my shirt.

I don't want to tell him in just under six months he will get his wish. At this point, it's still up in the air if I'll be able to see my own damn kid.

"I don't know about that," I say, voicing my true concerns. "I may not be the best role model for a kid. Hell, I wouldn't know the first thing about being a dad."

He leans onto the table on his elbows, his eyes narrowing. "You know how to be loyal don't you?"

I nod.

"You know how to put a bullet in a motherfucker's head if they fuck with your loved ones?"

"Definitely."

"Then you know how to be a father." He shrugs then leans back in his seat.

I chuckle. "I'm sure it requires more than that."

"Titus, look, kids don't require much. I mean, yeah you have all the basic shit like diapers and milk, but the important thing is they need to know you love them and you'd do anything for them. To know you'll always have their back no matter what."

I stop and think about that for a minute. If that is all that's needed, then hell, I could do that. No man would love my kid more than I would. Growing up, I didn't have much.

My mother couldn't stay off the pipe long enough to make sure we had food or a roof over our heads, but I would have dealt with an empty stomach and staying in shelters if she would have cared about me just a little. If I'd known even deep down beneath that hard exterior, she loved me, I would have gone through hell with her. But she didn't.

So maybe Griff is right. Maybe I did have everything I needed to be the father my kid deserved.

"How do you know all this shit about fatherhood?" I tease him, steering the conversation to a less depressing topic.

"I figured it out after I became a dad to a skinny ass homeless kid trying to break into my car."

I snort at the memory. "I still to this day don't know why you didn't call the cops on me."

He shrugs, lifting his longneck to his lips before placing it back on the table. "I felt sorry for you. Plus, I knew sending you to juvie wasn't what you needed."

"And how'd you know what I needed?"

"Because I knew what I needed when I was your age trying to survive on the streets."

"Thanks for that," I say, sobering up.

In all honesty, Griff saved me. I was tumbling headfirst down a dark path. I made worse and worse decisions by the day.

I was done with the bullshit situations in foster care and had refused to go back. However, the streets were no place for a kid and I was on the verge of saying fuck it and ending it all. When Griff pulled me out of his car and dragged me into his chop shop, it was the best thing for me.

On the outside, living with a criminal who taught me how to steal and break down cars was probably not the ideal situation, but Griff loved me like a son and made sure I was taken care of. No one fucked with me, not on his watch. I owe this man my life. We spend the rest of lunch reminiscing on the old days and shooting the shit.

***

I'm back in my office going over those papers when my phone goes off in my pocket. I pull it out and look down at the screen before answering it.

"About fucking time you called me back. I could have been dead," I say the moment I answer.

William Knight formally known as William Pitman snorts on the other side of the phone. "Your ass is too stubborn to fucking die."

I laugh at that. He might be right.

Will 'Pit' Knight is the owner of Fuck Off bar and one of my closest friends. He is also part of the Asshole Club, the name given to us by the honorary member Mayven *Skittles* Knight.

"What's such a big emergency I had to call you back immediately?"

I take a deep breath, lean back in my chair and fill him in on the Noni situation. Pit listens intently without interrupting until I'm finished.

"Let me get this straight, the chick you had a one-night stand with in Vegas is pregnant?"

"Basically."

"Damn, your pull out game is weak as fuck."

"Fuck you, Pit We had a prophylactic mishap. Besides, condoms are only ninety-eight percent effective."

Loud laughter comes through the phone, causing me to pull it away from my ear for a moment. "You know a motherfucker is scared when he starts reading the fucking stats."

I allow Pit his moment to laugh and get the shit out of his system. I don't blame him. If the shoe was on the other foot, I'd find this situation funny as hell too.

"Are you done?" I ask when his laughter starts to die down.

"For now, but give me some time," he says, getting that last little bit out. "A kid, huh?"

He snorts. "Well, I guess someone's got to carry on the asshole legacy. Congrats, man. Leo is too young for that shit and Scarlett better keep her shit covered in cement, so I guess that makes your kid my first niece or nephew.

"And just so you know, I'm going to be the favorite uncle. Don't tell Kelex though, his ass will try to outdo me."

I don't say anything because we both know Tak's childish ass will probably be the favorite uncle.

"I can't get too excited, remember? She still wants me to sign over my rights."

He grows silent on the other end. "What do you think about that?"

Despite how rocky our relationship started, the guys and I have all grown close over the years. Just like I know all their issues, they all know my issues with my mom and my fears of that shit rubbing off on me as well.

"Fuck that," I say adamantly. "That's my kid. I may not be perfect, but the kid deserves to know me. I don't care what her and her limp dick fiancé wants."

"Wait, she's engaged?"

"Yeah, apparently they got back together sometime after Vegas." I run my hands through my hair, pushing it off my forehead.

"And you're sure the kid is yours?"

I have no right to be mad about that question. Hell, I even asked it myself, but I didn't like him assuming anything about Noni. I have no fucking clue why I care.

"Yeah, I know it's mine. Look, I just need some legal advice. I'm hoping your ass has some of that law shit in your head on this. I need to find out if I have a chance against her in court if I want joint custody of my kid."

"All right, calm down," Pit says, seeming to pick up on my irritation. "I see how you could be concerned, but I think you have a good shot. Most of your shit is juvenile stuff. A judge won't even look at that in court. You also have a few legit businesses that show consistency in employment. All you have to do is prove to the judge you're just as involved and responsible as the mother."

"How do I do that?"

"Easy, you need to make sure you make every doctor's appointment. Any classes she takes and anything she does, you need to make sure you're there too. And keep documentation of it.

"Take pictures with the date showing, get doctor's notes. You need anything you can get that verifies you were there. Don't stop there though, while you're there ask questions. Let the doctors and nurses see you as a concerned father. You can call them in as character witnesses later."

"I doubt she will let me attend all that. She doesn't want me in the kid's life, she's probably not even going to tell me when she has the appointments."

"She will if she thinks you'll do what she wants."

His plan starts to sink in. If I make Noni think I will sign over my rights or at least I'm thinking about it, she will probably allow me to be as involved as I want to be.

"Thanks, Pit."

"Hey, no problem. You know we got your back. Assholes for life, and all that bullshit?" he says tauntingly.

"For life," I agree before hanging up the phone.

I quickly go to my Messenger app and send Noni a message.

DC INK: Ok, I've had time to think about it. I'll consider giving you what you want under one condition.

I place the phone down, waiting to get her attention. I want to give her time to get the wrong idea. It only takes a few minutes for her picture to appear beside my message and then the dots to alert me she's messaging me back.

Noni Kaye: I'm listening.

A smile spreads over my face.

DC INK: Give me the remainder of the pregnancy. Allow me to be involved as much as I possibly can, and I'll consider signing over my rights.

That shit was hard to even type, but I wait for her response. The three dots appear and then disappear as if she was about to write something and then decided against it. Finally, her message appears on my phone.

Noni Kaye: Okay.

DC INK: Okay? You're cool with that?

Noni Kaye: I have no problem with it. So how involved are you trying to be?

My fingers fly over my phone to explain to her what all I want, but then a thought crosses my mind and I erase all the other stuff I had typed.

DC INK: Have coffee with me tomorrow? I can tell you everything then.

I sit back at my desk, fixated on my phone. For a few minutes, she doesn't respond. Yeah, I could have told her what I wanted in a text, but I'd rather do it face to face.

I know things can't happen between me and Noni anymore. I usually don't put much thought into fucking a chick. I don't care if she's got a boyfriend or not, but with Noni, if she's happy with this dude, I don't want to ruin it.

I do, however, want to spend more time with her. I mean, we're about to have a kid together, we should at least be able to be friends. My phone chirps letting me know a message has come through. I swipe the screen to read the message.

Noni Kaye: Okay. When? Where?

A wide grin spreads over my face as I lean up in my chair.

DC INK: Same time and place as last time. Is that okay?

Noni Kaye: Yes. See you then.

So far this plan is working out well. Excitement thrums through my veins like the buzz of my machine in the middle of a tattoo.

However, I know enough about life to know shit can go south real quick. What will happen if the judge does rule me unfit or I fuck up and can't make all the appointments?

The thought sobers me. This is nowhere near over. I'm just as helpless in my own kid's life as I was in mine.

CHAPTER FIVE

Memories

Noni

"He wants to meet up with me tomorrow," I say, reading the message back to Jason.

We're sitting on the couch when the first message comes through. Me trying to order fabric and Jason watching the basketball game at a volume loud enough to burst my eardrums.

"Good," Jason says. "Tell him you will meet him."

I send the message and ask him where. He replies back instantly. I place the phone down on the coffee table in front of me.

When I first read Deacon's message my heart sunk. I've been on pins and needles the last two days. I knew the text was going to be him telling me he would sign over his rights.

However, I was shocked when he said he had stipulations and wanted to be there for the pregnancy. I'm happy that he wants to be involved in that part. I wasn't expecting it at all.

Although I have to admit, I'm not as sure as Jason is about this plan. Deacon said he would consider signing over the rights after I have the baby, but I don't think he will. I won't lie and act like I know this man so well. Hell, I can't even tell you his middle name, but I get this feeling he isn't going to be able to let go.

"This is perfect," Jason says muting the TV, giving me the quiet I've been wishing for since he came over.

"I don't know. I don't think he's going to give up that easily," I say, voicing my opinion.

Jason scoffs. "You have no idea what you're talking about, babe. I'm a man and I know how other men think." He shakes his head like what I said was stupid.

"This guy is trying to play hard ball, probably hanging around to see if he can get something out of the deal. Trust me, after he sees how much work it is, after going to all the dumb appointments and classes, he's going to realize how much time a kid requires. And I don't care how good his intentions are, no one is going to stick around after that."

He lifts his chin. "This works perfect. See how I have to fix your mess? You're lucky I love you. Most men wouldn't deal with this type of shit."

He turns back to the TV and unmutes the noise. The slew of curse words that run through my head would make a sailor blush. The nerve of him. He didn't fix shit.

All he did was demand I apologize and make it right. I'm the one who came up with the signing over the rights idea. I thought it would be the best way to go.

It would assure Jason he could be the only father this child would know and I could at least rest knowing I'd told Deacon about the baby.

"You need to make sure you let him know about all the appointments. The more the better. And remind him how much the stuff cost too. By the time this baby comes, he'll be begging to sign those papers. I know I would," he says the last part to himself. "Hey, go get me a drink."

I look at him dumbfounded. I've told him three times how tired I am and how much my feet are bothering me. I'm on them all day viewing homes for remodels and pinning designs to whiteboards.

"Jason my feet hurt and I'm trying to make sure I order the right chevron fabric for Amira's remodel that starts next week."

"Are you serious?" He turns to me and narrows his eyes.

"Yes, I'm tired."

He stares at me aghast for a second.

"Wow. Just wow, Noni. You know, after all the crap I've had to put up with lately, you would think me making a simple request wouldn't be so awful for you. Way to make me feel welcome."

He moves to get up. I let out a breath before stopping him.

"I'm sorry. I'll get it."

"No, don't worry about it."

"I said I got it."

I lift the stack of fabric folders along with my laptop off my lap and place it down beside me. Getting to my achy feet, I go to get his drink. He did come over here to spend time with me, I could try to make him feel more welcome.

Even though I didn't ask him to come in the first place. However, that isn't what perfect fiancées say. I place the drink down on the coffee table in front of him and turn to go back to my seat, but he tugs my arm, dragging me into his lap and places a kiss on my lips with a bright smile.

"I shouldn't have raised my voice. I love you so much, Noni."

I return his smile.

"I love you too."

He kisses my lips briefly before pulling away. For a moment, I get excited. Maybe this is the moment he will break my dry spell.

My hormones have been on a thousand during this pregnancy. I've been so horny, I'd probably dry hump his leg among other things. Yet whenever I even try to hint like I want sex, Jason immediately shuts me down. He's still so stuck on us waiting until marriage.

I go to kiss him again and he leans away from me.

"What are you doing?"

Isn't it obvious? "I thought you were in the mood to fool around."

He scoffs. "Are you kidding? The game is on."

When he first suggested we wait to have sex again until our wedding night, I thought it was romantic. Sex was always nice with Jason, nothing like when I was with—I cut that thought off. I wouldn't give it life, not even in my thoughts.

I figured waiting a few months until the wedding would be easy. I didn't plan for the way my body would crave intimacy during this pregnancy. All of my nerves are like live wires and the slightest touch seems to set them off.

I am in need of some attention. I poke my bottom lip out. Usually, just a little manipulation has been able to win Jason over in the past.

I run my hand down his chest and toward his joggers where I know his manhood lies. He grabs my wrist and pushes it away.

"I said no," he says, nudging me up out of his lap. Standing, I feel a little embarrassed by his blatant rejection. "It's unattractive for a woman to be desperate. Did Porsha teach you that?"

He looks at me like a misbehaving child before turning back to the television. Feeling even more embarrassed and now angry, I snatch up my things off the couch and head to my room. The moment I get inside, the sound of him cheering at something on the television reaches me.

I shut my door and drop my work on my bed before climbing on. How dare that man? He acts as if I can't do anything on my own. As if I can't have one original thought in my head. And who the fuck says a woman wanting to touch her man's dick is desperate?

The more I think about it, the angrier I get. Deacon sure had no problem with me touching his dick. In fact, he grabbed my hand at one point during our night and wrapped it around him. I close my eyes as the memory starts to play out.

I'd never seen one so big, veiny, and long. Even my muddled brain knew I was looking at something unique. It felt so strong under my grasp.

He had commanded me with his deep voice. "Touch that shit, beautiful."

I pop my eyes open when a moan comes from out of nowhere. I look around to the corners of my room, trying to figure out who moaned out so loudly. Then it dawns on me, I'm the only one in the room and that sound of wanton bliss came from me.

My face flushes at the realization, but instead of feeling ashamed or disgusted by the act, I feel bold and empowered. I slide my bottom lip between my teeth and throw my body back onto my pillow. My thoughts go to that night again.

Deacon's tattooed hand wrapped around mine as he showed me how to stroke him. I was mesmerized by the way the precum had glimmered off the tip. He had hissed when he cupped my mound with his palm, telling me how hot it felt.

I close my eyes as I remember his thick fingers finding the trimmed kinky coils between my legs. I'd never been touched that way before. And even though back in Vegas it was thick roughened hands that had slid over my flat stomach to my slick nub—in my bedroom right now—the fingers that find themselves coated in my essence are a lot slimmer.

I buck off the bed when I slip my fingers into my core the same way his had in Vegas. The word fuck coming out of his mouth once he felt my tight fit.

"Damn, this pussy is small," he'd fumed as if he was angry about it.

I thrust my hips up off my mattress here at home as I use the same circular motions he had used. He was so enraptured while he played with my sensitive pearl. His eyes stayed glued to it the entire time.

His lip between his teeth and that one piece of hair on his forehead. He took his time going back and forth between his fingers slowly moving in and out of me to smearing my wetness over my hardened nub. He did it until my breathing grew labored and my hips wouldn't stay still, like now.

My hands don't have the same feel or expertise Deacon's had, but when I close my eyes, I can't tell the difference. I can tell it's my other hand and not his that tugs at my sensitive nipple. The one he spent forever lavishing and running his tongue over.

He didn't have a problem with me being too forward when his face was buried between my legs and he demanded I play with my own breasts. That slow burn starts to rise up in my body. The one I felt for the first time with him.

I know I'm getting close to my orgasm. This time when I focus on Vegas, I remember what his face had looked like as he moved inside me. He surrounded me.

His heavy body on top of me, his hands were all over me, his taste in my mouth, and his dick so thick inside me, I felt every ridge and vein. Then, I remember those gruff words whispered in my ear.

"Come all over this cock, beautiful. Give me what I want."

And just like then, I follow his command. I bite down on my lip, trapping in the moan that wants to escape. I slam my thighs shut, closing around my hand even while my finger still dances over my clit.

When the orgasm fades along with Deacon's face and the memories of that night, guilt hits me like a ton of bricks. My fiancé is in the other room on the couch, and here I am in the bedroom, getting off to another man. I feel utterly disgusted with myself.

No matter how annoyed I get with Jason, I know how much he loves me and how much he will love this child. I would never want to lose that. So why the hell am I thinking about Deacon?

Despite knowing how wrong I am, I still can't help the flutters in my belly when I think of him. I get up and head into the bathroom to wash away my sins. I try to avoid all the mirrors.

I'm determined to wash my body and any and all thoughts of Deacon out of my mind. I have Jason and we're getting married.

CHAPTER SIX

The New Plan

Noni

Even though I had that pep talk with myself about getting Deacon out of my mind all night and this morning, I still took a little extra time today picking out my outfit and doing my hair. My black wide-leg jumpsuit fits my body well, showing the swell of my hips. I paired it with a yellow cardigan.

Bright colors always accent my deep brown skin tone. My hair is down today. The lace front is parted on the side with big waves that fall to my mid back.

I look like a woman who's meeting her one-night stand to talk about the child they're about to share. I shake my head at the thought. Climbing out of my car, the roaring of a motorcycle causes me to turn my head toward the noise.

The sleek black machine pulls up right beside me. I've always loved motorcycles. Even dreamed of riding one, but good daughters didn't ride motorcycles.

The rumbling stops and the man lifts his leg up and climbs off the bike. Even with the shiny black helmet on, I know it's Deacon. He pulls the helmet off and rakes his fingers through his hair, pushing it off his forehead.

The way his black shirt fits snug to his chest has my stomach and my limbs flooding with warmth and a shiver runs up my spine. My cheeks heat as I remember what I did to memories last night.

"Hey."

I have to clear my throat first. "Hi."

He tucks his helmet under his arm and takes a step toward me. His scent sends those flutters in my belly on a faster flight. Sandalwood and spice.

I'll never forget his smell for as long as I live. It fits Deacon so well. It reminds of faraway lands and forbidden meetings.

"What kind of bike is that?" I ask the question to distract from the way my nipples seem to tighten from his closeness.

He smiles and glances down at the bike before turning back to me. "It's called a Fat Bob Harley. Its custom made."

"Is it safe?" I ask, running my hand over the matte black paint, not truly interested in the beautiful machine.

"As safe as your car, but don't worry, I won't put the kid on the bike." I look up from the bike to him. "I do have a car to take the kid around. I just rarely drive it."

I watch him, it's the glint in his eyes. Again, I get the feeling he isn't going to comply with our request so quickly.

"Thought you were thinking about signing over your rights?"

A wide grin spreads over his face. "Yeah, of course."

Deacon may be fooling himself and Jason, but not me. I know he has no plans of signing over his rights to this baby, but I'm not going to argue with him. I'm going to see how far he's going to take this.

"You ever rode on a bike?"

I recite the reminder I give myself. "Good girls don't ride on the back of bikes."

"And you're trying to be a good girl?"

"I am a good girl," I retort.

He slips his bottom lip between his teeth as his eyes roam over my body. I push my shoulders forward, hoping to make my still pebbled nipples not so obvious.

"Stop thinking whatever you're thinking," I fuss.

"I'm not thinking about anything."

"You're thinking about Vegas."

I didn't even need him to admit it. I know what's on his mind the moment that lip goes between his teeth and his eyes glaze over. I know the look.

I've caught the same look in the mirror many times as I thought back over the one night we shared. Hell, I looked that same way last night.

Deacon shrugs. "I'm just saying, I can think of a couple non-good girl things you did that night."

My face heats. "It was a momentary lack of judgment."

He moves closer to me, eating up the little space between us in two steps. His towering height has the ability to make me feel small and protected all at the same time.

"Something tells me you need more days like that."

No truer words have ever been spoken. Vegas was freeing. First time in my life I felt like I was in control, like I was living and not just surviving.

"Come on, you need to eat," he says, placing a hand at my lower back and ushering me into the diner. The moment his hand touches me, those live wires erupt, and I become so aroused I nearly stumble.

"You okay?" he asks, grabbing my arm to keep me on my feet.

The genuine concern on his face causes those flutters to go haywire. I can only nod my head out of fear I may say something stupid if I open my mouth. I take a step away from him, placing distance between our bodies.

I hope he doesn't notice, but from the way his brow dips, I know he does. Thankfully he doesn't comment. Instead, he allows me to lead the rest of the way to a table.

We find a seat and the waitress comes to take our drink orders. The waitress comes back quickly and hands us our drinks before asking us what we want to eat.

"Grilled chicken salad for me," I say.

"Are you sure that's all you want? You're eating for two now." His concern is adorable.

I smile. "Yes, it's fine. Besides, all the books say eating for two doesn't mean I need to eat more. It means I have to make healthier and smarter food decisions."

"What books are you reading?"

I tilt my head to the side and stare at him. "Why?"

"Because I want to know what you're reading, so I can read them too. I told you, I want to be involved in all of this."

Watching him closely, I take in the determination set in his brow. He's serious. He actually does want to know.

I nod my head. "Okay, I'll send you the list of books."

His smile grows before he takes a sip of his drink. I go to place my straw in my cup and realize the waitress forgot to give me one. I turn in my booth, getting ready to stand and go get my straw. Deacon's hand falls on top of mine, halting me in my movement. I turn to him.

"Where're you going?"

"To get a straw."

He frowns. "Stay here, I'll get it."

He unfolds his long lean body off of the bench and walks over to the counter. He grabs one of the straws out of the holder before heading back my way. Watching him walk is like watching the moon control the waves.

Deacon has a swagger about him. He commands your attention the moment he walks into a room. He even catches the eye of some of the other people in the restaurant. He joins me back at the table, handing me the straw.

"Thank you."

"No problem."

I take off the paper and place the straw in my cup. "So," I say. "What are these requirements?"

He doesn't reply right away. Instead, he leans back in his chair. He raps his long fingers against the table as he watches me.

He shrugs. "Nothing major. I want to experience the pregnancy with you. I want to go to all doctors' appointments and the classes.

"Basically, I want to be involved with anything you do that involves the baby. I also need my name on your call list. If anything happens to the baby, I don't want to be the last to know."

"Very specific requirements for someone who wants to sign over their rights." I place my elbows on the table, leaning forward.

"I said I would consider it. I never said I would do it."

I don't comment on that last statement. "You just want doctor visits and classes?"

"No, I want to know everything. From the moment your stomach flutters with the first kick to what you crave and what you feel. I want to be involved in all of it."

"And then what happens when the baby is born?"

After being involved like that, how is he supposed to just walk away? That is my real question. The one thing Jason hadn't considered.

Yes, being so heavily involved in this pregnancy could deter Deacon, but what if it doesn't? What if he makes it the entire remainder of this pregnancy—going to the appointments and being involved in all the small things, like cravings and picking out baby furniture? How does he walk away then, and can he?

"Well, hopefully, I'll see what I'm looking for."

"And what's that?"

"That you and your man can take care of my kid better than I can. That you can love him more than I will."

I have a feeling this part isn't a lie. This isn't part of his well thought out plan. The other things he said lacked the conviction these words have.

"And if we prove it?" I ask the question hesitantly. Not sure I want the answer.

He drops his shoulders and his eyes cast down. "Then I'll step out of the way and sign the papers."

Him signing over his rights is my plan. The one chance to save the relationship I have with my fiancé, but hearing Deacon now, it doesn't sit right with me. My stomach tightens at the thought.

"What do you think?" he asks.

A lot is going through my head, none of it I want to process at the moment.

"I think I need more time."

"How much time?"

"I don't know, Deacon," I say testily. Taking a breath, I sit back in my seat. "This isn't ideal for me either. Not exactly how I planned to bring a child into this world."

He tilts his head to the side and raises his eyebrows. "What was your plan?"

I smile and briefly lift one shoulder to my ear. "I would be married," I start, and he rolls his eyes. I laugh. "What do you have against marriage?"

He gives a shrug from those broad muscled shoulders. "Nothing. It's just not my thing."

"Not your thing? You have something against being in a committed relationship with someone?"

"No, I don't, but being married has shit to do with commitment."

I wouldn't necessarily call the sinking feeling in the pit of my stomach disappointment. What would I have to be disappointed about? I mean, I understand what he's saying.

People who are married cheat, but ever since I was a little girl, I've wanted that happy complete family. Husband and wife, with three kids and a dog. I explain this to Deacon, and he chuckles.

The sound both familiar and foreign. Familiar with the fact I remember it from our night in Vegas, foreign because I don't recall the sound having this same odd effect on me.

"Three kids and a dog? Will little dick Jason be up for the role or will I have to step in to give my son some siblings?"

I roll my eyes and blow out a breath. "Every time I try to have a decent conversation with you, you remind me how much of an asshole you are." I sink back into the vinyl cushions of the bench seat and fold my arms over my chest.

Deacon sits up and reaches across the table to grab my arm and pulls it away from my chest. He clasps my hand in his on the table and doesn't let go.

"I'm sorry," he says and even pokes out his lip to show his remorse.

"No, you're not," I argue only halfheartedly.

"You're right, not sorry for what I said, but I didn't mean to upset you."

He smiles at me and for a moment I get lost to that wicked grin. I'm reminded again of the pull I feel to him, so strong the hairs on my arms stand up. Whenever we are in the same room, it's like a strong magnetic force draws me to him.

I wonder if he feels the same thing. Maybe that's why in Vegas whenever I looked up, his eyes were on me. It takes the waitress dropping our food off to get me to realize he's still holding my hand and that isn't a good look for an engaged woman.

After the waitress leaves, Deacon and I spend the remainder of the meal discussing my plans for the pregnancy. I tell him I want to have a natural birth. Preferably a water birth, but I opted out of that route for my first child.

We discuss if I want a boy or a girl. He obviously wants and truly believes I'll be having a boy. I tell him I don't care, and my only preference is to find out when the baby is born. He likes that idea.

By the time my phone starts vibrating on the table, we have sat and talked for three hours.

"I should be heading out," I say, digging into my purse for some cash to pay my bill.

I don't even get my wallet out before the money is placed on the table and Deacon stands over me with his hand out to me.

"Come on, I'll walk you to your car."

I oblige, placing my hand in his and allow him to help me from my seat even if I don't need it. The live wires are back, but instead of trying to avoid them, I embrace the feeling. We make it out to my SUV parked beside his bike.

Three men are on the other side of my KIA, leaning against a large black truck. They seem to take us in briefly before losing interest. We stop at my driver's door and I turn to face him.

"Thanks for the meal," I say.

He lifts one of those dark brows at me and takes a step forward. Not exactly crowding my space, just enough to send those flutters in a frenzy again.

"You still haven't given me an answer on my request," he says.

"I still need to think about it."

"What is there to think about?"

"You're asking for a lot, Deacon."

"No more than any other father would want."

It's those words that slap me in the face and settle heavily on my heart. He's right and I can't refute that. So, I won't.

"I'll get back in touch with you."

I turn to leave, but he grabs my elbow, stopping me and causing me to turn back to face him. He looks down into my eyes and again I get a glimpse of his truths. Not the arrogant asshole who came up with this plan, but the man underneath. The man I assume only wants to be a part of his child's life.

"You promise?" he says.

I run my tongue over my bottom lip. "I promise." And I do.

Deacon lets me go and I climb into my SUV and head out. I glance back in my rearview. He's watching me, his hands tucked into his pockets.

As reasonable as his request is, I fight against it. I don't know why, but somewhere deep down—you can call it women's intuition—I know this is a bad idea.

CHAPTER SEVEN

Russians

Deacon

She's going to say yes. No matter how bad she doesn't want to, Noni is going to say yes. That's just the person she is.

I smile to myself at that fact. Spending this time with her—sober and without my dick in her tight pussy—I'm learning more about her. That crazy pull is definitely still there and my desire to be balls deep in her isn't going anywhere either.

When those nipples—I know to be like little black berries poked out at me—I almost said fuck my morals and pinned her up against my bike. Thankfully, I got a hold of myself because I was able to get to know her more.

"Damn," one of the three guys parked beside me says, drawing my attention. "I've never had black pussy before, but if it has my guy gazing off in space like that, then maybe I need to give it a try. Or maybe it's just that chocolate pussy? That bitch was fine."

69

"What the fuck did you just say?" I take a step toward the young punk.

I noticed these three when I walked out of the diner with Noni. They were trying their best to seem uninterested in us, but I knew that was a lie. I wasn't going to alert her of their presence.

The skinny kid with the piercing in his lip and the sunken-in heroin cheeks is the one with the mouth. The big dark-skinned guy with dreads steps in front of his mouthy friend. I don't give a shit.

I've never backed down from a fight, I don't care how the odds were stacked against me.

"My apologies," the big black guy says, holding his hands out in the universal sign of calm down. "Mad Dog didn't mean you any harm, he's just fucking around."

Some of my anger abates. It's hard to take a motherfucker serious when his name is Mad Dog.

"Tell your pup he doesn't know me well enough to play with me." I spin around to leave, done with these punks.

"We know you well enough, Titus."

I freeze. No one calls me that name except for Griff and people I no longer associate with. The big guy nods his head, he knows he has my attention now.

"You might want to check in on Griff."

This has me walking back over to the three. If they thought I was pissed off when he mentioned Noni, they are about to see the real fucking Titus. All three stand shoulder to shoulder.

The angry puppy isn't going to be a problem, he's the smallest of the three. A strong wind could knock his ass over. The big black guy who has done all the talking looks like he may be able to handle his own.

However, I can tell the bald silent guy with the thick neck the size of my fucking thigh believes himself to be my match. He isn't.

"What did you say about Griff?"

"He could really use your help."

"Griff has my number, if he needs me, he can call me. So, what the fuck are you doing here passing on messages like a fucking pigeon?"

Lil pup takes a step forward, but the big guy holds up a hand to stop him. I laugh, this shit is hilarious.

"Just get in touch with Griff," big guy says, then turns around, taking his band of merry men with him.

I watch them climb back into their big ass truck and speed out of the parking lot. They don't have to worry about me calling Griff, I'm going to pay his ass a visit.

***

Griff's Auto and Restoration Shop was home to me. From the day he found me trying to steal his car, this has been my sanctuary. From the sound of motors and drills going to the smell of the oil and gas, this is my familiar place.

"Hey, Titus. How's it going?" Mr. Johnny, an elderly man with skin the color of coffee without cream and the resemblance of worn leather says. He's knocking on sixty's door, but Griff can't keep the man away from this shop. There's no one who knows their way around an engine like Mr. Johnny.

"Good, Mr. Johnny. How about you? Griff ain't working you too hard, is he?"

A wide toothy smile spreads across his face. He throws his hands out like he's shooing away my comment.

"Naw, he needs me around here. Wouldn't be able to do shit without me."

Now that I'm pretty damn sure of.

"Where is he?"

"Back in that office. He's been back there all damn day."

I nod my head as I make my way back to Griff's private office. The auto shop is where Griff runs his legal business. A few years back he almost lost the shop to some gambling debts and back taxes. I came in and bailed him out, buying the place from him.

His name is still on the building and he handles all the day to day shit, but technically the shop is mine. It's not something we talk about and no one really knows it.

I greet a few other employees who've gotten to know me over the years before I stop at the glass door of Griff's office. His head is down as he looks over the papers on his desk. I tap my knuckles against the glass before I walk in. He looks up and smiles.

"Hey, what're you doing here?" he greets me genuinely.

I take a seat on the couch pressed against the wall. I slept here more often than not when I was a kid.

"You need to talk to me about something?"

He frowns. "No. Why would you ask that?"

"I met three little fuckers today who felt like I needed to check in on you."

He releases a breath, his shoulders slumping before he sits back in his chair. "Those assholes. I swear, it's like wrangling fucking toddlers." He runs a hand over his head before looking back to me. "Look, whatever they told you, don't worry about it, I can take care of it."

Now I was worried. "They didn't tell me anything, but now you've sparked my interest. What's going on?"

Just then his phone lights up. He looks down at it and pulls a face, the same way he did when we went out for lunch.

"It's nothing," he says, canceling the phone call.

"Who keeps calling you? And before you say it's nothing again, know I have other ways of finding shit out."

If all else fails, I can always go to Pit. Nothing happens in this city, on the legal or illegal side, without Pit eventually knowing about it.

Griff eyes me, giving me that same stare down he did when I was a kid being a dick. It didn't work then, and it won't work now. He relents, his chin dropping to his chest.

"I may have gotten into a small bind."

"What kind of a bind?"

"You know how I am when I get drunk and run my mouth. Met up with LeCosta about a month ago, you remember him?"

"He used to be one of the guys you collected parts for? Big deal out in Miami, right?" I ask.

"Yeah, well, we were shooting the shit and I was talking up the old crew and he said he had another crew who was bringing in ten times the parts we were."

I scoff and Griff smiles. "Same thing I said. Anyway, there was a new guy there, big Russian dude. He offered me a job, told me he thought I was just the guy to do it." Griff runs a hand down his face. "I'd been talking shit all night, taking down bourbon like a fucking fish with water. I wasn't thinking straight. So, I agreed."

"What's the job for?"

"Six by six."

"Six hundred thousand in parts? That's not too bad. You can have that in six months."

He shakes his head. "Six hundred cars?"

I suck in a breath through clenched teeth. "What the fuck, Griff? Were you tossing back crack with those drinks? You know how hard it is to move that many cars?"

"Yeah, I know, and it isn't just any cars, he has specifics. Like really specific."

I shake my head at the shitstorm Griff has gotten himself into. Moving that amount of cars is dangerous. The heat from the cops would be all around the city.

And to pull off something like that would require nonstop moving. It can't be done. Well, it could, but not by just anyone.

"No." Griff's voice pulls me out of my thoughts. "I know that look. You're not helping. When you got out, I wanted you to stay out. I told you, your job now is to make me a grandfather," he says it as a joke, but the look on my face wipes the smile off his. "You got a kid on the way?"

I rub the back of my neck and spend the next seven minutes running down my dilemma to Griff. He listens, quietly nodding his head throughout.

"First of all," he says when I finish my story. "Did they stop selling condoms in Vegas? What the fuck have I told you since you were fifteen?"

"Wrap it up," we both say at the same time.

"But seriously, congratulations, Titus. I'm fucking proud of you."

"Did you miss the part where she and her fiancé want to raise the kid without me?"

He waves away the comment as if it's an annoying gnat.

"Fuck that. No motherfucker is raising my grandson but us." On this he and I agree. "This is even more reason for you to stay far away from my shitstorm. Look, I can handle this. I've been in this game long enough to know how to take care of my shit."

"Yeah, but how well do you know this Russian guy? And is he the one who keeps calling you?"

A smile spreads over his face. "You sound like you're the old man and I'm the kid. This ain't my first rodeo. This guy is no worse than any other motherfucker I've come across. I got this," he says, sounding a lot more assured than I am.

I stay for another thirty minutes, shooting the shit with Griff and the rest of his employees, but I leave there with a heavy heart. This doesn't sit right with me and for some reason I believe this time Griff has, in fact, bit off more than he can chew.

***

Later that night I got a text from Pit asking me to swing by the bar. It's been a minute since I last saw the crew, so I don't put up much of a fight. The first thing I notice is the bar looks packed, but that's like any time you come to this place. Fuck Off is one of the hottest spots in the city.

I park my bike in one of the employee spots, despite not being an employee. Walking into the bar, I see a few of the regular patrons. I wave to a few who call out my name.

I spot Terry walking through the tables heading in my direction. I go to meet her when a cloud of perfume hits me.

"Hey, handsome. You looking for me?"

Looking down at the skinny chick with the smeared lipstick and war paint makeup. "Does my shirt say wildlife reservationist? Why the fuck would I be looking for you?"

It takes a second for her drunk mind to catch the insult, when it does her face crumples. I walk past her, leaving her thirsty ass behind.

I get to Terry, stopping her before she can walk by. The leggy brunette has gotten my attention a few times. I would've had her by now, but Pit forbids us from fucking his waitresses.

"Hey, Terry."

She pushes her shoulders back a little more and her breasts nearly spill out of her little black tank top when she notices it's me.

"Hey, Deacon," she purrs. "You looking for Pit?"

"Yeah, you know where he is?"

She tilts her head back in the opposite direction. "He's in the back. They're waiting on you."

They? What the fuck is going on? I leave Terry and head back to Pit's meeting room. The place is closed off and used for Pit's shady shit. I have to pass through the game room first to get to his private room.

I push the lever on the door and open it before walking in. The second I do, the word *congratulations* is shouted at me and I'm hit with a ton of condoms.

I start to laugh, shaking my head.

"You know what, fuck y'all," I say, walking into the room. "Pit, I should have known your gossiping ass wouldn't be able to keep a secret."

My words are lighthearted. Even if Pit hadn't told them I was going to tell them myself. The entire crew is here.

There's Pit and his beautiful way out of his league wife, Skittles. She's the first to approach me and offer a hug.

"I'm so happy for you. Maybe it will be a girl and I'll finally get some estrogen in this group."

"No fucking way will fate give us a niece," Pit says, pulling Skittles away from me and back to his side as if I'm going to sneak her away from him.

"Same thing I thought," I agree, taking his hand and giving him a quick hug. "I'd kill any motherfucker that even thought of touching her."

Pit laughs and Skittles punches him in the belly.

"Oh, what, you're scared she'll run into assholes like you six?"

"There are no assholes like us," Reynolds says, stepping forward to shake my hand.

"What the fuck are you doing here? Shouldn't you be training one of your new fighters," I ask the MMA champion.

"You know I wasn't going to miss out on an opportunity like this. Apparently, you need a lesson on putting on condoms."

I shove him playfully and step around him to greet Tak. The youngest of the group. I give him a stern look before I pull him into me.

I used to have to ride his case before Jazz came along. The kid has a shit ton of talent, but I've had to threaten every dealer in the city about selling to his dumb ass.

"How you been, kid?"

He lifts his shoulders to his ears briefly. "Living my best life, but I can't shake being a condescending asshole. Jazz told me I should work on it. Yeah, right."

"So, nothing's changed," I quip.

The next face that greets me makes me take a step back. "Now I know this is a special occasion. Who the fuck got pretty boy here?"

It's been forever since I saw Kelex. Lately his ass is never around. As the only blond in the entire group, we fuck with him constantly about being the good-looking one, even with the burns hidden beneath his clothes.

"First, I had my balls threatened. Then I was told you're going to be a daddy. There was no way I was getting on a plane and missing this."

He gives a pointed look at Skittles and a lopsided smile tugs at the corners of his lips as he turns his gaze to me. "I was hoping to meet the poor woman who let you close enough to fuck her."

"It was your mom. She told me to tell you, hey."

This time his smile lifts higher as he shakes my hand and embraces me in a hug. When I look past his shoulder and spot Jeff Harrington, I have to question my own vision.

"Now, I know someone had to drag this rich bitch out of the house kicking and screaming," I say, folding my arms across my chest.

Jeff gives me a smug smile while shrugging. "You know I love charity work. Giving my time to the poor is what makes me a good businessman."

"Calling yourself a businessman is like calling Al Capone a community activist."

Jeff shoots me the middle finger. "Like calling yourself a tattoo artist when your work looks like something written on the bathroom walls in this place."

"Fuck you," I say before giving him a one-arm hug and hitting him on the back.

He whispers in my ear before I let him go. "I already put together his trust fund for college. That shit is paid for."

I nod, feeling a bit speechless. Of all the assholes, Jeff and I argue the most. Well, he's an unofficial asshole, but I'd still go to war for the stuck-up bastard. I glance at the round table in the middle of the room and a proud big smile lifts my lips.

"Let me guess, you pussies came to give me all your money?" I say, pointing a thumb over my shoulder to the poker setup.

"You fucking wish," Skittles says with a laugh. "You know you play poker like you fuck." She winks and blows me a kiss as she walks past me.

Kelex snorts. "Yeah, he never knows when to pull out."

The room goes up in laughter. I flip all the assholes off.

We all sit at the table and another one of Pit's waitresses comes from behind the private bar with beers and shots for all of us. We take the shots in my honor and immediately start dealing out cards and catching up.

"Hold up," Jeff says, leaning up in his seat he places three hundred-dollar chips down on the table. "She wants you to sign over your rights so her and her short cock lover can play house with my nephew?"

I take a sip of my beer and nod. That about sums it up.

"Wait, you're not going to let that happen, right?" Skittles asks, rubbing her hands up and down Pit's back as she tries to get a good look at his hand. He catches her in the act and moves his hands.

"They can get the fuck out of here with that," Pit answers for me, adding two more chips to his pile. "He's fighting that shit."

I nod again and add my own two chips to the pile. "That's the plan. I'm just waiting for her to tell me yes."

A calculating smile lights up my face. I still had no doubt Noni would cave. I didn't care how much time she thought she needed.

"What plan?" Kelex asks this time, his attention momentarily moving from the cards in his hands.

I quickly run over the plan Pit and I concocted.

"And you think it'll work?"

I turn toward Jeff to answer his question. "Hell yeah. I'm already waiting for her to call and tell me yes. I know this girl; she wants me in that kid's life just as bad as I want to be there."

After saying those words out loud, they feel real. I don't know what's giving me that vibe, but there's something about the way she watches me. The way her breath catches in her throat every time she sees me.

Even the light in her eyes tells me Noni doesn't want me to give up my rights. I don't know who came up with the fucked-up plan and I don't care. I just know Noni's heart isn't all the way in it.

"But why go through all the trouble? You don't even know this girl. If some prick wants to raise the baby, why not let him?"

Everyone at the table collectively rolls their eyes at Tak. We love the kid to death, but he has the most jaded fucking view of the world.

"Shut your young ass up, Tak. No one is looking to you for responsible advice. Your ass better be glad you can write a damn song," Skittles says.

Reynolds snorts, nearly choking on his beer. And I can't help but shake my head.

"Why, grandmother, you wound me with your inconsequential opinion of me," Tak delivers in his sarcastic tone that oftentimes makes us want to kill him.

"Call me grandma one more time, little boy and I'm going to beat your ass like a grandma should've."

Tak winks and blows Skittles a kiss.

"Keep that shit up, Tak. I'm going to let her kick your ass one day," Pit adds before turning to me. "Say the word, what do you need from us?"

This is what makes our bond so strong. We fuck around and get on each other's nerves, but we have each other's backs.

"Just hold me accountable," I say honestly. "My childhood shit can't keep me from this kid, but you know my life. Trouble lands in my lap. I just need you guys to make sure I don't do anything dumb to fuck this up. And then maybe I won't fuck this kid up."

"You're not going to fuck the kid up." Skittles places a hand on my arm briefly.

"Of course, you won't," Reynolds says. "We got your back with that too. I'm just not changing diapers, but I will take him to his first titty bar at twelve."

"You can't take him to a strip club at twelve, you moron," Skittles says, placing her cards down and calling out of the game. Pit, Reynolds, and I all add more chips to the pile while Kelex, Jeff, and Tak pull out.

"I went at twelve," I say, shrugging.

"You don't count. You practically raised yourself." She waves me off. "Besides, it's going to be a girl. I'm calling that shit now."

"Fuck no," I argue.

"Hell no," Pit agrees.

"I hope the fuck not," Reynolds says, putting his cards down and letting us know he's done. "Can you imagine a female Deacon?" He shudders like he's envisioned a monster.

"Fuck you, she'll look like her mother."

Reynolds laughs before taking back the rest of his beer.

"What you got, Deacon?" Pit asks, placing his cards down on the table.

"Son of a…" I mumble as I throw out my hand. Pit slides the chips in the pile on the table toward him.

"Damn, Deacon," Kelex starts. "You still haven't learned how to pull the fuck out."

The entire group erupts in laughter and I have to remind them to go fuck themselves.

I laugh and hang with the crew until the sun is nearly up in the sky. Before they leave, they all make sure to tell me they have my back. Even Tak tells me he's with me.

CHAPTER EIGHT

Best Friend

Noni

"Well, hello, Mrs. Porter," I say in greeting to my best friend.

Porsha jumps up when she sees me. Today is an easy day for me. I stopped by a new client's house to check out the space and start on a design plan, but I didn't have anything on the schedule for the rest of the day.

That means it's the perfect time for me and Porsha to hang out and catch up. As always, she's well dressed. Her plaid linen pants are paired with a turtle neck and black ankle boots. Her low-cut fade is stunning, and it plays up her gorgeous feline features.

"Look at you, you're glowing," she says, pulling me into a quick hug.

I don't feel like I'm glowing. I barely got any sleep last night, not after I left Deacon at that diner. His last words to me keep playing back in my head. He wasn't asking for anything more than a real father would. Yet my brain still yelled to proceed with caution.

"No, you're the one that's glowing," I say, directing the conversation back on her.

We take our seats on the veranda of the restaurant. The waitress takes our drink and appetizer orders before walking off.

"Okay, so what's been going on?"

"Nothing."

The word comes out high-pitched. It isn't even believable to my own ears. She raises one of her perfectly threaded eyebrows.

"Okay, what's going on? Is this about Stick Up The Ass or does this have something to do with why I can't get in touch with Amira?"

Amira is the other part of our friendship trio. It was because of her misfortune I forgot to get the morning-after pill.

"No, Mira is fine. Well." I rethink that response, because my sweet and bubbly best friend who would give you the shirt off her back is definitely not fine. "She's doing better."

Kind of. She's been back at work for a while and she seems to be functioning, but she's not the same. I imagine it may take some time.

Carlos was the love of her life. None of us would have expected to find him sleeping with her half sister.

"Well, that's good. I've tried to call her a few times."

I don't want to tell her Amira isn't ready to hear from her yet. Porsha is unapologetically honest and raw. We love her for it, but when we're going through stuff, her honesty isn't always desired. I know Mira just needs time and eventually she'll heal from her hurt.

"Then is this about Jason?" Just then the waitress brings our drinks and I have a small reprieve before I'm forced to answer her.

"Kind of," I start, taking a sip of iced tea. I decide to give her the good news first. "I'm pregnant."

She spits her coke out and nearly gets it all over my face. "Oh my God. Are you serious?"

I laugh and nod my head. She jumps out of her seat, wraps her arms around my neck and gives me a hug while I remain seated. She lets me go and turns to the table behind us and announces, "I'm going to be an auntie."

The older couple smiles back at us and even offers me congratulations. Porsha returns to her seat across from me.

"I can't wait to meet my niece or nephew, we have so much to buy—wait." I was waiting for realization to come to her. "Didn't you say you and Jason were waiting until marriage? Did he realize how dumb that is?"

I take another sip of my drink, cutting my eyes down to the table. "Not exactly. I'm three months pregnant."

Her brows meet in the center of her head and her nose crinkles as if she's trying to decipher the math problem.

"But that would mean—"

Her words cut off and she gasps, covering her mouth. Her eyes open so wide they look as if they will pop out of her head.

"Sexy white boy from Vegas," she whispers as if someone around us is going to hear her.

I nod my head and hide my face. The peal of her laughter causes me to look back up. Her head is back and she's laughing so hard people are watching her.

"Porsha, what's so funny?"

"Are you kidding? Have you told Stick Up The Ass yet? Please tell me you haven't and that I can be there when you knock that smug ass look off his face."

I shake my head and bite into my bottom lip to try to hide my smile. "I've already told him."

"Dang it." She pouts. "What did he say?" she asks, leaning forward for the tea.

For the next twelve minutes, I give her all the details as we enjoy our chorizo con queso.

"Wait, you seriously asked that man to sign over his rights?"

"Well, yeah. I didn't think he would care."

She grimaces. "Girl, one look at that man and I can tell he wasn't going for that. Honey, white chocolate was a real man. And real men don't play shit like that with their kids."

"Well, he agreed to it."

Her eyes widen momentarily.

"He says he will think about signing over his rights, only if I agree to allow him to be involved in the pregnancy and I mean, fully involved."

Her wide-eyed expression turns into a smirk. She leans back, taking a sip from her cup. "And you believe that?"

I think about lying. To tell Porsha I was absolutely sure Deacon was going to do just what he said. However, I know she will be able to read that lie miles away.

"No."

She starts to laugh. "That man is not letting that kid go. And honestly, I don't blame him. What are you going to do? Are you going to give him access during the pregnancy?"

This time I blow out a breath and slump down. "That would be the right thing to do, right?"

"Oh no, ma'am, I'm not giving you any advice. I'm just going to sit back and let fate happen."

"What's that supposed to mean?"

For a beat of silence, she doesn't answer me. She just stares into my eyes. Her lighter brown bearing down into my dark brown. She straightens.

"Noni, I've known you for twelve years. Yet that night in Vegas, when you were with him, I saw something I'd never seen in you. It's like life had come back into your body."

I blush at just the memory. He definitely made me feel alive.

"Look at your face," she says, pointing to my obvious smile. "When we left Vegas, all the light went out of you. You looked like you were going home to serve a life sentence. And that light hasn't been back, well until now." She picks up her glass and winks at me. "Girl, this is fate."

I take a moment to absorb all she just revealed. None of it's new to me. I know I wasn't the same after that trip.

"Okay, I'll admit it. Deacon brought out a spark in me, but it was a onetime thing. I want my life with Jason. I want my perfect family."

She opens her mouth as if she's going to say something else. My phone goes off on the table. I pick it up and answer.

"Hello?"

"Hey, babe. I left my lunch at home and I'm swamped at the office. Can you bring me something to eat?"

"Sure, what time? I can bring you something from here when I leave."

"Actually, I'm pretty hungry now. Can you bring it now?"

"Oh, I thought I told you I was out with Porsha for lunch today." I told him this three times and each time I brought it up, he never commented.

"So, I'm supposed to starve while you yak it up with your friend? You know what, don't worry about it. I'll ask someone from the office to go."

"Jason, relax I'll bring it."

There is a short pause on the other end of the phone.

"Thanks, baby. I want Thai though, not Mexican." The line goes dead, and I place the phone back down on the table.

"Let me guess, man-child all of a sudden needs you?" she says, then takes an exaggerated long sip of her drink.

"I know what you're thinking, but he left his lunch at home."

She rolls her eyes but doesn't reply. I quickly gather my belongings and take out enough cash to cover my drink and appetizer. As I stand, Porsha grabs my hand.

"I know you, and I know how your mind works. You want what you think is the ideal perfect family, but don't keep this man away from his child. Things happen for a reason."

"You told Mira that too, remember?" Right after Mira had cried her eyes out over losing the man she thought she would grow old with to her half sister.

Porsha removes her hand from mine and smiles shyly into her glass. "Someone gave me that advice and it worked out pretty well for me." She shrugs. "I figured I'd pass it on."

"I'll keep it in mind. See you later, Porsha."

I leave my best friend behind. Unfortunately, I don't get to spend as much time with my bestie as I had planned, but anytime I see her or Amira is always good.

***

Peterson, Gibson, and Peterson is one of the top estate law firms in the city. Jason was so proud when he was hired on here. Even though Mr. Peterson is his uncle, he wasn't going to give the job to Jason.

He made him apply and work for it. Jason thought once he got the job, he would make partner just like his cousin. Hasn't happened yet.

I make it to the fourth floor of the building where Jason's office is located. Mrs. Peggy, the sweet older lady who runs the front desk greets me with a smile. I step through the doors to the offices of the lawyers and the cubicles of the paralegals.

I spot a few familiar faces. I've been to enough office parties to be well known around here. Off to my right, I catch sight of the paralegal I caught with Jason.

Her skin is a light creamy brown, like Amira's. The kind that makes you think she might be biracial. Her hair is wavy and reaches almost to her ass.

She cuts her eyes at me and quickly turns to mumble something to the woman beside her. They both look at me and start to laugh. I ignore their taunts.

I would never sink so low as to beef with a woman over a man that's mine. I head toward Jason's office only to get cut off by Mr. Gage Peterson.

"Noni, how's it going?"

I greet Mr. Peterson with a genuine smile. "Hi, Gage," I say even though I would like to call him Mr. Peterson because he's old enough to be my granddad. He, however, refuses to let me call him that.

"Congratulations again on the engagement. I told Jason he'd better hurry up and put a ring on it. I'm glad he decided to listen. My nephew has a hard head." He leans into me and whispers. "And congratulations on the you-know-what."

He looks toward my belly and winks. His dark brown skin hiding his age well until he smiles and the lines around his eyes and mouth tell his secret.

I fight the instinctual urge to place a hand over my belly. Thankfully, I have the bag filled with Jason's lunch in it. Jason and I agreed we would wait to tell everyone other than certain family and friends. Especially with the whole situation with Deacon.

Why would he tell his uncle?

"I was telling the team the other day we needed more family men in this office. We haven't had a new baby in the family since Parker and Renee had Cody."

Parker is Gage's son and a partner at the law firm.

"Oh wow, how old is Cody now?"

"Six," he says with a proud smile. "Has Patricia called you yet?"

"No," I reply, a little confused about why his wife would call me. I liked the Petersons. They accepted me right away when they first met me.

"Well, she's having that annual banquet and they like to award up-and-coming new businesses in the area. And she nominated you."

"Me?" I wasn't expecting that.

I'm proud of my little company. It was a huge risk, but it was one of the first things I'd felt so strongly about that I didn't let anyone deter me from it. Even before Amira partnered with me, Royal Designs was flourishing.

"Of course. What you've done with that company in just five years, not to mention all the ways you've given back to the community with the design of the Boys and Girls home and the free DIY classes at the community center. You're the perfect nominee.

"Although we will understand if you have to miss it because of the pregnancy, I realize you'll be quite far along by then. However, if you can make it, we would appreciate it."

"I'll see what I can do."

He gives me a quick pat on the arm before wishing me well and heading in the opposite direction. I head to Jason's office to find him on the phone with his feet propped on the desk.

Spotting me when I walk in, he nods for me to come to him. I walk into the room, closing the door behind me. I place the food on the desk and spot a white take-out tray. I wait for him to get off the phone.

"You had food?" I ask, pointing to the Styrofoam plate with the remnants of a chicken salad sandwich and fries.

"Oh, yeah." He grins and shakes his head. "When I got off the phone with you, Troy said he was going and could grab me something." He shrugs that news off like it's nothing.

"And you didn't think to call me and tell me this? I was having lunch with Porsha. I haven't even eaten yet."

He rears his head back. "I'm sorry, did my wanting to see my fiancée inconvenience you and your friend's gossiping? I'm sorry I'm not a priority to you like you are to me."

Jason knows the right words to make me feel like crap. And even though I know he's doing it; I always feel guilty.

"That's not what I was saying."

"Seriously, you're treating me like the one who's bringing another man's baby into this marriage. The other day I come over to hang with you and watch basketball, but you wouldn't even put your work away to enjoy it with me and then you left me. It's like I can't do anything right with you anymore."

I walk around his desk to cup his face between my hands. "I'm sorry."

Could I have told him I never asked him to come over? Yes. I could have pointed out the fact I told him when he called I had a lot of work to catch up on.

Yet he insisted. I even could have brought up how I tried to spend some time with him, but he turned me away. I could tell him all these things.

I could even explain I still would've come over to see him today, but a quick courtesy call would have kept me from rushing, and I would've been able to grab some lunch myself. However, I don't say those things. Those aren't things the perfect fiancée says.

He removes my hands from his face and grabs my chin, pulling it down to get my lips closer to his for a kiss. I've been so deprived of intimacy. I moan at just the idea of a kiss.

However, the quick touch of lips does nothing to feed my appetite. He pulls away too soon and goes back to his computer.

"Have you been by to see your mom today?"

"No, I'll go at the regular time." I take a seat in the chair across from him.

"You should go see her earlier than that. I called her this morning on my way to work."

This catches me off guard. "Why would you do that?"

He looks up from his computer to stare at me like I've asked him why he's breathing. "She's my future mother-in-law, Noni. I would think you would be a little more appreciative that I'm bonding with her."

He huffs and shakes his head. "You remember Jeff Rodgers? He was telling me the other day he hated his mother-in-law, and it was a huge issue for him and his wife. And you're complaining about me calling your mom."

"I'm not complaining, I'm just wondering what you needed to talk to her about."

Silence surrounds us as he watches me closely. His gaze neither friendly nor angry.

"Well, someone needs to check on her," he replies, going back to his computer.

I'm glad he looks away because if he didn't, he would have seen the glare I just gave him. I guess going to her house every damn day after work and on the weekends isn't enough? I don't argue, it's not worth it. Instead, I change the subject.

"I ran into Gage in the hallway."

He lifts his head and wide interested eyes meet mine. "You did? What did he say? Did he mention me?"

"He congratulated me on the engagement and the baby. Told me how excited he was to have a baby in the family again."

A proud smile sets on his face. "That's my little junior. Already networking."

Is it normal that I cringe inwardly when he mentions the baby? I want to raise this child with him. I've loved this man for six years. Hell, I'm going through all this trouble with Deacon so Jason can be a father to this child, but every time he mentions the baby, I can't help but cringe.

"Speaking of networking," I say to segue into another topic. "Has Gage mentioned anything to you about that banquet?"

"No, what about it?"

"Patricia nominated me for the small business award."

His eyes sparkle and gleam and a wide grin spreads over his face. "Are you kidding, that's fantastic. Gage hardly ever invites anyone to those events."

"Yeah, I told him I'd think about it."

And just like that, the gleam and the smile are gone. "Think about it?" He shakes his head. "There is nothing to think about, you're going."

"Jason, the event is in a few months. Who knows what I will feel like by then. Even Gage understands this."

He pinches his brow as if he has the beginning of a migraine. "I can't with you. Look, your job might not mean much, but mine does. And if my uncle invites you to hold his balls while he takes a piss, you say, yes sir. Understood?" His gaze narrows on me and I have to wonder, has he lost his mind?

He can kiss ass all he wants to, but I don't have to ride anyone's coattails to get ahead. I'm actually just that good at what I do. And I also love it. Besides, I'm the one being honored and not him.

"Sure," I reply through clenched teeth.

The perfect fiancée doesn't tell her future husband she could drop on her knees to suck Gage Patterson's dick, and it still wouldn't lead to Jason getting that partner promotion.

"Perfect, I'll let my uncle know you will definitely be there. In the meantime, you need to persuade that guy to sign over his rights. The sooner we can get that behind us, the better."

I guess it was time I made a decision about Deacon. He has waited long enough.

CHAPTER NINE

Bad Luck

Deacon

How hard is it to get a decent blow job these days?

I flinch as the chick on her knees scrapes her teeth on my dick for the tenth fucking time. I don't mind some teeth action, but damn, I don't know if she's sucking dick or eating a pickle.

"You like this, sir?" she moans, and it sounds like the fake shit in bad pornos. If my dick is in her mouth, why the fuck does she think I want her talking?

I blame this on Noni. I've been thinking about her and that bullshit request all day, so I figured I'd pick up a chick and take my mind off of things. However, this one and these Mr. Ed ass teeth are about to make me lose my mind.

"Sweetheart, I'm going to need you to do less talking and more sucking."

She frowns and goes back to her mediocre blow job. My cock is big, so I know she can't get all of it in her mouth, but this is starting to feel less like head and more like a sad hand job. When her teeth nip at my sensitive crown, I'm fucking done. I shove her ass away from me and she falls onto her back.

"Fuck this, you got to go." I put my shit away and stand.

"Wait, what? You don't want me to finish?"

"I'd rather stick it in a garbage disposal. I picked your ass up at a bar. I'd think you'd be a lot better at sucking dick."

"You know what?" she says before snatching her purse off my couch. "Fuck you."

"Trust me, I'll pass. If you can't suck dick, I can only imagine how lazy that pussy is."

She scoffs as if I've said something to hurt her feelings. "Forget you ever met me you asshole."

"That'll be easy, I don't even remember your name."

She flips me off before she storms out my door and slams it. I flop down on my couch, listening to her car back out of my driveway. I hate that my thoughts immediately turn back to Noni.

Why the hell hasn't she called me yet? My phone rings and I pull it out of my pocket. The name on the screen brings a smile to my face.

"I hope this call brings me good news." I say into the phone the moment I answer.

Her chuckle chimes through the line. "Hello to you too, Deacon." Hearing her voice puts me in a much better mood than my earlier company.

"What's the verdict?" I lean forward on the couch, propping my elbows on my knees.

She exhales. I already know it's a sigh of acceptance. "You have a deal." The smile widens on my face.

"Seriously?"

"Yes, look, Deacon, I only want what's best for this baby. I know it isn't starting out on a very promising note, but I just want to do what's best."

I bite back my retort, I'm what's best for my kid. I don't say it because I know this is hard for her. And I don't blame her questioning me.

What do I know about being a father? The only one I knew was a thief. And though I know what that sounds like, Griff was still a better fucking father than any I ever knew.

"I understand. Believe it or not, I want what's best for him too."

And I honestly say this with the mindset that if I'm not what's best for this kid, I will step down. I don't want to have a hand in ruining a child's life. Not like my parents did me. I will break that fucking curse with my child.

"So," I say in no rush to get off the phone. "What are you doing?"

She laughs. "Well, I'm sitting in the middle of my bed eating a banana because apparently this kid likes cold fruit. I'm finalizing some orders for a house renovation and compiling some paint swatches for a client."

"That's right, you're an interior decorator," I say as I make a mental note of her love for cold fruit. I'll stop by the grocery store tomorrow and pick up some fruit for her. "You own your own business, right?"

"Yeah, I own Royal Designs. And you're a tattoo artist?"

"Yeah, I am. Have you made your mind up about what tattoo you want yet?" I ask the question, bringing up the conversation we had in Vegas. I kissed every inch of that unmarked body. I know she has no tattoos.

She laughs again. "Still can't think of anything important enough to put it on my body permanently."

"You'll think of it soon."

"You're so sure."

"You just haven't found that thing you love enough, that thing that represents who you are as a whole. The thing you want the world to know about you even without you telling them."

"Do all your tattoos have a meaning?"

This time I laugh. "Not all. I can admit I got some just for the hell of it, but most have a significance to me. Like the number 126 on my ribcage. That's the number of days I lived on the streets before my adoptive father found me."

Griff never legally adopted me. He just gave me a safe place to stay and rest my head, provided me with food and money. All the things a parent is supposed to do for their kid.

"I didn't know you were homeless once." The laughter is far from her voice when she speaks.

"There's a lot we don't know about each other, Noni. But we'll learn before this kid comes, I want to know all about you."

"Let's see." She giggles. "I'm five foot seven. I enjoy late-night binge-watching TV and looking through fabric magazines. I don't like the taste of coconut unless it's in Rum and I'll try almost anything once."

I don't tell her how well I know that last part. She was so eager to do whatever I asked her. I inwardly groan when I get hard thinking about her slow tentative licks when she was learning how to suck me off. I'll take that over piranha teeth any day.

"What else is there to know?" Her soft voice pulls my thoughts out of the gutter.

"Trust me, I have a lot more I want to know about you, but I'm not your man, so I can't ask those questions."

The sexy sudden intake of her breath is going to help me rub one out later. I know that comment probably crossed a line, but I can't help it. A beat of silence follows my statement and I imagine she's blushing and probably scolding herself for it.

"I should be going, Deacon. I'll text you the next appointment information." I'm not surprised by her response. Noni will always make the decision to do the right thing. "Goodbye, Deacon."

"Goodbye." The phone disconnects and for a moment I stare at it, feeling excited. Everything is going to plan. I vow in that moment not to allow anything to fuck this up for me.

***

My phone going off on the nightstand has me reaching out for the annoying contraption. I try to look at the screen, but the brightness of it has me squinting at the sight. I slide my thumb across the front, answering the call.

"Hello?"

"Is this Titus?" The voice of a male has my attention. I pull the phone from my ear to glare down at it. The number says Griff, but it isn't Griff's voice on the other end of the phone. He also wouldn't be calling me at four in the fucking morning.

"Who the fuck is this?" I say, sitting up in my bed.

"A friend of Griff's. He told me to call you if anything ever happened to him." Those words have ice running through my veins and the last bit of sleep slips away. "They messed him up real bad. He's in the hospital."

"Which one?" I had a lot more questions than that, but that was the first one to come out.

I'm already on my feet, throwing on my clothes before the man on the other end can answer. After I find out which hospital, I hang up and finish dressing. If I wanted more information, I'd get it from Griff.

I don't remember anything about the trip to the hospital. I vaguely remember stopping at red lights. I rush to the reception desk as soon as I arrive.

"James Griffin's room," I say hurriedly.

"Are you a relative?"

I have to bite the inside of my jaw so I don't curse her ass out. "Yeah, I'm his son."

She looks up the information on the computer. "He's in room 242. Visiting hours…"

"Fuck your visiting hours." I walk away and head to the elevators.

I get off on the second floor and head directly for his room. I find Griff lying motionless in his bed. In all honesty, this man is my father.

His face is swollen, his eyes are closed, and his lip is split. He looks like he took a serious beating. I pull one of the chairs in the corner of the room up to his hospital bed.

The beeping of the machine is the only noise in the room for a while. A nurse walks in and smiles sadly at me as she checks his vitals.

"Now I know I've died and gone to heaven. Are all the angels this beautiful?" Griff's voice is raspy and weak, but it's still good to hear from him. Even if it's a god-awful pickup line.

"How're you feeling, Mr. Griffin?" the nurse says.

"Much better now that you're here." The nurse shakes her head with a smile.

"It's good to see even in this state, you can still manage those weak ass pickup lines," I say.

Griff turns to me and blinks a few times. "What're you doing here?"

The nurse looks at me and smiles, but it doesn't reach her eyes. "Why wouldn't I be here?" I say, trying to ease the woman's apprehension.

"You should be home resting. When that baby comes you won't get any." Griff turns to the nurse. "My son's going to be a father."

The nurse only smiles and gives me a quick "congratulations". I shake my head and smile, leaning forward in the chair.

"I'll be back to check on you later, Mr. Griffin," she announces before walking out of the room. I wait until I'm sure she's gone and not coming back in.

"What happened?"

He turns away from me, his eyes fixed on the ceiling. "The Russian didn't appreciate me avoiding his calls. Sent his little punks by to remind me of my deal."

I tamp down on my anger. This isn't the time for hothead Titus, I need to stay calm.

"This is when I need you to be honest with me. I need to know if you can make good on this deal."

For a long moment, he doesn't react or speak, just continues to stare at the ceiling. When he turns to me, his one good eye is red with unshed tears.

"I'm in over my head." His voice breaks. "I thought I could do this, but the team is…" He pauses and sighs. "They aren't you."

I sink back in my chair, my mind racing. I left this shit behind after that wreck that nearly killed Kelex and Tak. Seeing them and Skittles nearly lose their lives sobered me up quick. It made me realize just how dangerous of a life I led.

Griff is right, without me he will never fulfill that order, but it comes with a lot of risk. With the heat that will come from this size of a job, there is a huge possibility I may get pinched before my fucking kid gets here.

That thought more than anything else gives me reservations. All my dreams and plans of not being my fucking parents are withering away right before my eyes, but I guess the best thing about that is if I fuck up at least my son will have Noni.

"All right," I say, swiping a hand down the back of my neck. "I'm in, but we have to do this shit my way. I got a lot at stake."

"I know. I know, Titus, and I wish like hell I didn't have to bring you into this."

I wave my hand to cut him off. "You're my old man. I got your back. You just worry about getting out of here and getting better."

I clutch his hand in a tight fist and he brings our combined hands to his chest. That's how he falls back to sleep, my hand clutched in his. My mind continues to race. I didn't want to let my kid down, but part of me doesn't want to let Noni down more.

CHAPTER TEN

Heartbeat

Noni

"I thought you told this guy the appointment is at ten?"

Jason glances down at his watch. It's only seven minutes before ten and we just got here about three minutes ago. It's not like we've been waiting long.

It's been two weeks since I called and told Deacon I would allow him to be involved. This is the first appointment I'm having with the OB-GYN. My regular doctor is the one who confirmed my pregnancy.

"I did, but he has to come from farther away, remember?"

Jason scoffs. I thought it funny he had no intentions of coming to this doctor's appointment until he found out Deacon would be here. Suddenly his calendar became much more open, whereas before he couldn't fit this in.

We climb out of his Jaguar and off in the distance the rumbling of a motorcycle has a smile stretching across my face.

The matte black bike turns into the parking lot, stopping right beside us.

"Please tell me this is not the father of the child," Jason groans near me.

I ignore him, I'm too busy trying to slow my heart rate down. Deacon cuts off the bike, then rips his helmet off. His smile is wide on his face as he uses his free hand to push his hair off his forehead.

"Hey, Noni."

Before I can speak Jason cuts into anything I'm going to say. "He's white? You didn't tell me he's white?"

I turn to face my fiancé, a little put off by his tone. "I didn't think it mattered."

"Didn't think it mattered? We're both black," he says the last part as if it explains everything. When I don't immediately catch onto why Deacon's race should matter, Jason goes on to explain. "What am I supposed to tell my family or my colleagues?"

"You said you could handle this. You said as long as the baby was half mine, we could make it work."

"Come on, Noni, you can't be that damn dumb. I only said that when I thought the other half was black."

"If it makes any difference," Deacon cuts in, reminding Jason and me we aren't alone. "I might have some Cherokee somewhere down the line."

I rub the stiffness out of my neck before turning to him. "Shut up, Deacon."

"You were so much nicer in Vegas. I'm starting to think you're lacking a sufficient amount of white boy dick."

"Hey, look asshole, don't make this anymore uncomfortable than it has to be."

"Who's uncomfortable? I'm not. You're the one talking about my kid matching up to you like a fucking pair of socks. If taking care of a kid who isn't yours is too much, maybe you should leave now." Jason takes a step toward Deacon who tilts his head slightly.

"Oh, you would like that, wouldn't you? You want me out of the way so you can diddle in my fiancée again."

I cringe at the reminder of Vegas and partially at his use of the word diddle.

"You might as well forget it. Noni is mine. I was her first and I'll be her last. And this little stunt you're trying to pull won't last long. Eventually, you'll lose interest and go running back to the streets you came from leaving me to raise the kid you created."

"Jason, that's enough." I step forward, placing a hand on his chest to calm him down.

I don't like the implication that Deacon wouldn't stick around or that he would lose interest in his child. My childhood fears came rushing back to me. Not only that, but I also didn't like the way Jason's words seem to cause physical harm to Deacon. He flinched as if he was struck by the comment.

"Can we get along long enough to get through this appointment?"

Both men take a step back, letting the tension die down. I turn away from them both and head into the office building. The sound of their distinct footsteps, Jason's hurried pace, and Deacon's slow, assured walk, follow behind.

I walk into the brightly lit room filled with comfortable looking cushy seating and pictures of happy women caressing their protruding bellies. There's a couple sitting together with their heads lowered, looking in a magazine. A woman with a small toddler playing at her feet and a rounded belly, plays on her phone.

Another woman in her pantsuit and stilettos looks down at her tablet. They all look up briefly when I enter. I head toward the reception desk.

"Noni Scott here to check in." The older brown-haired woman looks up over her glasses and gives me a warm, inviting smile.

"And who is here today with mommy?"

She looks over my shoulder at the two men behind me. A grimace hits her face as her eyes go back and forth between the two. As I open my mouth to make the situation a little less awkward, Deacon takes it up to a whole new awkward level.

"The dick that got her pregnant and the dick she wants to raise the baby with."

I close my eyes, praying and hoping for once my prayers will be heard and I can truly wake up and this unbelievable moment will be over.

"This is ridiculous," Jason scoffs before turning and walking away.

"Um, I have you checked in," the receptionist says, trying her best to stay neutral. I imagine this may not be the craziest situation she has ever seen, but still, it's embarrassing.

I follow Jason back out of the building to the parking lot.

"Jason, where are you going?" He turns to glare at me.

"I can't do this. You slept with that prick?"

"Obviously. Why the fuck else would we be here?"

I had no idea Deacon followed us out, but his reply makes me aware of him.

"Deacon," I warn. He holds his hands up in surrender.

"Noni, I love you, but I can't understand how you could betray me in this way. And you walk around without an ounce of remorse for how this is making me feel."

His words are like a slap across the face. I've done nothing but apologize from the moment I told him about Vegas, that was even before I found out I was pregnant. I've bent over backward trying to acknowledge his feelings and figure out how to make this easier for him. Everything I have done has been in my attempt to still be the perfect fiancée for him.

"I've apologized countless times. What else do you want me to do?"

"I don't know," he huffs. "Maybe not walk around acting as if you did nothing wrong."

"Hold the fuck up," Deacon says, getting our attention again.

"This part doesn't concern you." Jason tries to cut off whatever Deacon is going to say, but just like the man that he is, Deacon just barrels through anyway.

"If I'm remembering our very drunk conversation right, didn't you tell me you two were broken up during that time because he had his dick in some other chick's mouth?"

I completely forgot I told him that and can't believe he remembers.

"You told him that?" Jason's narrowed gaze zeroes in on me.

"I was drunk and hurt."

"Don't get mad at her. Look, it looks to me like you're doing a lot of finger-pointing. You fucked up first and she had fun in Vegas.

"Shit happens, but no one is at fault. I'm pretty sure if you weren't getting your dick wet down another chick's throat she wouldn't have been going so hard on tequila shots in Vegas and my ass could be at my shop right now instead of talking to you. So, get the fuck over yourself and stop whining like a pussy and pushing your shit off on her. We need to get back in there so I can see how my kid is doing."

Though it was so brutally and honestly said, Deacon is right. It's about time that Jason understood we both hold a bit of responsibility in this situation and the only innocent bystander is this baby. Also, hearing Deacon stand up for me did crazy things to my belly.

"Jason, you know how much a family for this child means to me," I say, taking a step toward him. "I don't want this child to grow up the way I did, but if this is too much for you, I understand if you walk away. I won't hold it against you."

I hold my breath because I don't know what the hell I will do if Jason walks. Yes, single parenting has been done before. I know there are women and men out there doing it every day, but since I was a little girl, watching family's play together at parks, I've wanted that for my child. Hell, I wanted it for myself.

Jason cuts his eyes over to Deacon and I don't know what he sees there, but something changes in him. A smile spreads over his face and he holds out his hands for me.

"Come here, baby." I go to him and he wraps me in a tight hug. "We can get through everything as long as we are together."

I hear the words, but for some reason they don't sound as reassuring as they should. In fact, they fall kind of flat in my ears. I don't let on to it.

Instead, I let him lead me into the doctor's office with one hand placed at my lower back. We sit in the waiting room. Deacon is on one side of me and Jason on the other.

I haven't been able to get Jason's attention since we sat down. He's been glued to his phone. Deacon rests his head against the wall behind him.

I can't stop bouncing my leg. I know it's probably all in my head, but I feel like everyone is looking at me and judging me. I'm not stupid. I know what I must look like walking up in here with two men.

However, it isn't as uncommon as they're making it seem. Deacon's hand lands on my knee, stopping my movements. I look over at him and he's watching me.

"You okay?"

I lean toward him, keeping my voice down. "Is it just me or is everyone looking at us?"

Deacon lifts his head to look around the room. The mother with her toddler isn't the least bit focused on us. The toddler is staring, but he's a baby, that's what they do.

The woman in the pantsuit seems interested, but more so in the two handsome men beside me. The couple, however, glares at me with their noses up.

"Don't I know you from somewhere?" Deacon says to the woman. She looks completely shocked before shaking her head.

"I don't think so."

"Yeah, I do. I'm viewing from the wrong angle, last time you were on your knees sucking me off."

The guy beside her gasps, turning to the woman quickly.

"Laura, what is he talking about?"

"Laura, that's right. Me and the guys called you nasty Laura. You still got that weird birthmark?"

The man leaps up from his chair and glares down at the woman. "He knows about your third nipple birthmark."

"Sam, I don't know this man," the woman pleads.

Sam doesn't want to hear it. He storms out of the doctor's office. Laura follows behind him swearing that she doesn't know Deacon. The waiting room grows quiet again.

"Do you really know her?" I ask Deacon.

He looks at me and flashes a grin. "Hell no, never met her a day in my life, but they're not looking at you and judging you anymore."

He's right. No one else is paying me any attention. I look at him and shake my head, trying to trap a laugh behind my smile.

"You're so bad."

"And you know it." He winks and I have to squeeze my thighs together.

We don't sit there much longer after that before my name is called. All three of us get up and head to the back. I go alone into a small room with a nurse as she takes my vitals and weighs me.

Everything checks out well. The moment I come out of the room, Deacon asks, "how'd it go?" The nurse smiles and explains I'm doing well.

After peeing in a little cup, I'm ushered into a small room with a little bed and a chair in the corner. The nurse brings in an extra chair for Deacon. He places it up by the top of the bed.

"Ms. Scott, you can take off everything below the waist and put this on." She hands me a gown. "Do you want your guests to wait outside?"

"No, thank you, darling. We've both seen the goods," Deacon answers for me. The nurses face flushes before she slips out of the room.

"You should step out while she gets undressed." Jason takes the lead on this.

"Why? I'm the one that saw her naked last, maybe you should leave," Deacon says, shrugging.

I shake my head and roll my eyes at him. I can't believe the things that come out of his mouth. He was never supposed to know that Jason and I haven't had sex again. I catch the accusation in my fiancé's glare before turning back to Deacon.

"Could you at least cover your eyes?"

He places his hands over his eyes, but keeps a huge gap between his fingers. His hazel eyes peeking through.

"Real immature," Jason scolds him, but I have to trap my laugh behind my lips.

I quickly slip out of my pants and underwear and fold them up in a chair then climb on top of the table, placing the paper thin cover up over me. Lying back, I stare up at the flower mural on the ceiling. I'm guessing it's supposed to make this situation less awkward.

The room is quiet, the only sound is the clicking of the keys on Jason's cell phone and the heavy swooshing of my heart in my ears. A lot of my fears are coming through. What if something is wrong? What if the doctor tells me I'm not capable of carrying this baby? What if...

My thoughts are cut off when a heavy hand wraps around mine.

"You all right?" Deacon's warm breath brushes against my ear.

I nod my head.

"I guess it's just me that's nervous as hell?"

I turn to him, the paper beneath me crinkling with the movement. "Okay, so maybe I'm a little nervous," I whisper back.

He smiles and it's the first time I pay attention to how beautiful his smile is. The one dimple and the pearly white teeth that are just straight enough adds charm to his bad boy flair.

I'm once again reminded of the first night I met him and how gorgeous he was. Those damn flutters let loose in my stomach.

"What if it's twins?" He flinches at his own question.

My breath catches. "Do you have multiples in your family?" This is the type of stuff you find out before you get pregnant by a guy.

He shrugs. "I don't know. Don't know much about my mom's side and I never met my pops."

That kind of makes me sad. Something else you should know about your partner before you get pregnant.

"Well, I'm an only child from my parents. My dad's kids aren't twins and neither of my parents have multiples in their family. So, we might be all right."

He gives me another one-dimpled smile.

The door opens, and the doctor walks in. She's a tall, middle-aged black woman with a warm, friendly smile.

"Hello, Noni. I'm Dr. Shay."

I go to sit up but can't manage it. Before the doctor can hold out a hand, Deacon has me sitting up and is standing right beside me. All of this is done while Jason has yet to look up from his phone.

The doctor sits down on the little rolling stool and pulls it up to the foot of the bed. She asks a lot of personal questions about pets and advises me to stay away from cat litter. We talk about fish and raw meats with a bunch of other questions and warnings. When she's done, she gets up and goes to the sink to wash her hands.

"Do you have any questions?"

I open my mouth to say no but get cut off.

"I have a few."

Deacon pulls out a piece of paper and unfolds it. He has about five sentences written out on it and the thought of him having his own questions warm my heart. He's so prepared for this.

"What do you consider an emergency and when should Noni contact you?" The doctor smiles at the question and so do I. I didn't even think of that one.

All of Deacon's questions are good and well thought out. The only question I had to ask was if it was safe to have sex. Hopefully, the answer will convince Jason to sleep with me. Lately, he's been using the health of the baby as an excuse.

I have a lot of pent-up sexual needs. I need some release. Touching myself two weeks ago was fine, but it didn't satisfy me.

"I have a question." We all turn to Jason, who hasn't seemed interested in any of this. "How much weight is she supposed to gain?"

"As much as she wants," Deacon says before the doctor can reply.

"Look, it may not concern you, but I'm the one going to be married to that body when this is over with."

I flinch at his words. I haven't thought about my weight gain or if I'm gaining too much.

"And this is who you want to raise my kid with?" Deacon has a pretty fair question.

Dr. Shay answers Jason's question as politely as possible, but I can tell she doesn't like it either.

"All right," Dr. Shay says when the nurse enters the room. "We're going to do a pelvic exam and then we will get to hear the heartbeat."

The pelvic exam is less awkward because Deacon stayed up by my head and holds my hand during most of it. The room grows silent when Dr. Shay pulls out the little microphone-looking device to hear the heartbeat. I hold my breath during this time.

All the books I read said the moment the machine touched their stomach they heard the heartbeat. As another second passes and then another with nothing, the swishing of my heart starts to pick up.

"What's wrong? Can't you find the heartbeat?" Jason asks the question I'm too nervous to voice. "Is something wrong with the baby?"

"Will you shut the hell up," Deacon scolds him.

"Something is wrong, can't you see? Noni, have you been taking those vitamins?"

I have to hold tight to Deacon's hand so he doesn't walk over to Jason like he starts to do.

"Yes, I take them," I say defensively. His ass has never asked about me taking vitamins before today.

"Well, you must've done something."

His words are forgotten when I hear the sweetest sound I've ever heard. Tears spill from my eyes and a collective breath follows it.

"There it goes," Dr. Shay says and I can tell for a moment she got a little nervous, too. "It's strong."

I can't see anything because the tears have blurred my vision. Suddenly, a Kleenex appears in my face, I take it and mumble thank you to Deacon.

Dr. Shay and the nurse both leave to allow me to get dressed. Jason slips out too, to make a phone call. I'm left alone with Deacon, who helps me off the bed.

"Seems we have a little prankster. That heart stunt had you going for a minute?" He laughs.

I slip my panties back on while his back is turned to me.

"She almost gave mama a heart attack with that prank."

"She?" he says, glancing over his shoulder to look at me.

"Yes, it could be a girl, Deacon." I slip my pants on and button them up.

He scoffs and shakes his head. "The world isn't ready for me to be the father of a daughter."

His statement brings a smile to my face.

"Are you telling me you'll be an overprotective dad?"

He turns to look at me and hands me my purse off the counter.

"Hell yeah. She's not dating until she's forty and I'm going to teach her everything I know about everything. None of that bullshit about a girl can only do girl things. I want her able to change the motor out of her own car and rebuild a deck if she has to. She's going to be fiercely independent and a princess."

Watching him talk so proudly about our imaginary daughter brings a smile to my face. This is how a man should feel about his child. Watching the excitement dance in his eyes as he talks about raising his kid is refreshing. It again reminds me this plan we agreed on won't work.

"That's if you don't decide to give up your rights, right?" I ask with a teasing smile.

Deacon blinks as if he's brought back to reality.

"Yeah. Of course," he says, even less believable than the first time he said it.

The door opens and Jason pokes his head in.

"Hey, come on. I have to get back to work."

I walk out of the room and head to the receptionist to schedule my next appointment. She makes two reminder cards, one for me and one for Deacon.

We part ways outside, but the visit stays with me. More so the things Deacon spoke of. Every little girl deserves a father like that.

CHAPTER ELEVEN

Shit Show

Deacon

Nine hours after the doctor's appointment, I look down at my phone and check the time as I stand outside of Griff's chop shop. I still can't get over hearing my son's heartbeat. It was a surreal moment for me. It's been real for me since the moment Noni told me she was pregnant, but being there, waiting to hear that sound while holding my breath.

At first, when it didn't pick up, I started to panic, but when I looked down and saw the fear on her face, I knew I had to be strong for her. I couldn't fall apart because she needed my strength. I also had another idea, one I'm a little ashamed to admit.

I told myself if this heartbeat didn't pick up, we would try again. The thought came so fast and without delay, I had to remind myself Noni isn't my girl. Then dip shit started tripping like he couldn't pick up on the fear coming off of her in waves.

And what was that shit he asked her? If she's taking her vitamins. Like it was her fault if something happened.

I also didn't miss that second of hopefulness in his tone. Fuck him.

"Hello?" Her voice is soft and pleasant when she picks up the phone. "Deacon, is everything okay?"

I smile. I don't fucking know why. "Yeah, I was just checking in on you."

I have no idea why I'm calling, but I've wanted to since we went our separate ways today.

She laughs. "I'm good. Just lying here in bed. Jason is here," she says it as an afterthought.

"Cool," I say because telling her I don't give a fuck seems rude. "Do you need anything?"

"What does he want? Does he know what time it is?" jackass says in the background.

She ignores him. "No. I'm fine. Getting ready for bed."

"Good. You need to get some rest. Did you eat today?"

"Sure did. Just had a cold banana."

After she told me about her love for cold fruit, I picked some up for her the next day and met her with it. She was so happy she wrapped her hands around my neck and gave me a hug. At the time, I couldn't help but think how something as basic as fruit brought her so much joy.

It made me question if tiny dick Tim was taking care of her. After meeting him today, I know the answer to that. I laugh and then catch Griff waving to get my attention.

"That's great. I just wanted to check in. Hey," I say as the thought comes to me. "Can you do me a favor, put the phone to your stomach so I can tell him good night?"

Silence. Maybe that was a bit much. A bit too personal.

"Okay, hold on." The sound of rustling noises through the phone alerts me she's doing what I asked.

"What the fuck are you doing?" Jason's muffled voice comes through the speaker.

"He wants to say good night."

"Are you fucking serious?" he roars, and I smile.

"It's not that big of a deal," Noni's reply is preceded by her calling out. "Go ahead, Deacon."

"Hey, little Ace." I don't know exactly what to say. I hadn't planned this, but I don't want my son to only know Noni's voice. Or that prick's. "I just wanted you to hear my voice. I'm going to warn you, you're going to hear another man's voice too, but don't get it confused. He's not your daddy. In fact, your first job when you're born is to piss in his face. We'll keep that between us though, okay? Night, Ace."

The phone rustles again. "Are you done?"

"Yeah. Thanks again, Noni."

"No problem. Good night, Deacon."

The phone goes dead, and I place it in my pocket before walking into the old workshop. I haven't been in here in years.

The place still looks the same. Enough equipment to strip a car down to nothing but the frame in less than ten minutes. A sitting area with enough seating for twelve and storage space to hold at least five cars at once.

Griff is already setting up the whiteboard when I walk in. The three stooges from the day at the diner are also here. I look around for the rest of my crew.

"Guys," Griff gathers everyone's attention when I walk up. "This here is Titus. The best to do this shit since myself."

"He doesn't look like much," the one they called Mad dog sneers. He's sitting backward in a chair like a fucking clown.

I ignore him. "Where's the crew?" I direct my question to Griff.

I hear the sniggers from the boy band behind me.

"Well, this is your crew." I turn back to the fuck boys. "Steel is your command center."

The quiet, bald guy waves a hand. I can't see him sitting behind a laptop unless it's to look up porn. He looks more like a meathead who tries to fight his way through his problems.

"Mad Dog's your trail and Chris is the jacker. This is your crew." Griff waves his hands out like he's presenting me with a shitty prize at a game show.

"Are you fucking serious? Where are my guys? Where's Tony, Shank, and Q?"

"Well, Tony got clamped about a year ago. He's serving five years for possession of stolen goods. Shank went legit. Took that girl he was crazy about and moved back east with his family. And Q, well after you left, he started feeling betrayed. Ran off to work tech for LeStova."

Damn, he must have really felt betrayed. We didn't actually have rivals because we weren't a gang, but I guess, LeStova's crew would be the closest we had to enemies. If Q went to work for that motherfucker, he's dead to us.

I look back at the team I have now and shake my head. This just made this job ten times harder.

"I know they don't look like much, but they're good." Griff must read my mind.

"Look, old man." The one called Mad dog pushes up from his seat. He saunters over to me with more bravado than he should have. "We're the new and improved crew. I know that may be scary, old timer, but we will try to slow down for you to keep up."

He chokes out the last part of that sentence while curled in the fetal position on the floor after I throat punch his ass. His friends jump up and I lift my chin, questioning if they really want this fight. I will put all three of them on their asses tonight.

"Can we please chill the fuck out?" Griff shouts. "The kid had it coming, and I assure you, Titus may not look like much, but he ain't the one to try."

The other two are much smarter than their Mad counterpart. They back up. Chris helps his friend off the floor.

"Show me what we're up against." I direct my command to Griff, and he escorts me to the whiteboard.

"The Russian has specific cars he wants. If we break them up to about twenty-five a week, we can knock them out of the park and not draw too much police attention. That will be our biggest issue with a job like this. If we can keep the police off our backs, we will be okay."

"Where are we holding these cars that we take?"

I look around at the area we have here. There is definitely not enough room for that many cars, that also becomes risky. We can't store that many stolen cars in one place.

That's why parts are easier. You bring the car in and within ten minutes the car is broken down in hundreds of small parts that can be hidden well.

"Storage facility over by the harbor. We take the cars there and they will ship them off. All we have to do is get the cars there."

I nod in approval. That makes it a little easier.

"What's first?" I ask, ready to get this shit show over with.

Griff turns to the whiteboard. "These will be the easiest." The first car I spot is a 1969 Chevrolet Camaro Z28 convertible, yellow with black stripes. Damn, this guy is specific as shit.

"Steel has been able to track all these cars down locally. The first one only a few blocks away from here. We scouted it out a few weeks ago and tonight is a good night to take it."

"It's an old guy, and he has an early bedtime," Mad Pup says with a sneer. "You can probably relate."

"How's your throat?" I reply, and he narrows his eyes at me.

"All right, y'all get the fuck out of here before you get into it again. The guys have all the places we're hitting tonight. And remember, Titus runs this show. What he says goes out there," Griff says before turning back to the board.

I hate that I'm back into this shit, especially with that heartbeat still on my mind, but I would do anything for the man who raised me. Even risk my own freedom, it seems.

I head outside toward the white work van. Mad Dog goes for the front seat. I grab him by the back of the neck and shove his ass toward the back.

"I called shotgun," he argues.

"Get your ass in the back," I say, climbing into the passenger seat of the van beside the one they call Steel, who has yet to talk.

Chris laughs as the pup curses me out under his breath. This is going to be a long six months.

We pull up to a subdivision not far from the warehouse. Steel slows the van down.

"The third house is your spot. The car is in his garage."

That makes the job slightly harder. I have to get the car out of the garage before I crank it. Not difficult, just annoying.

"You might want to leave this one for Chris," Mad Dog says arrogantly.

I climb out of the van, ignoring his attempt to make me beat his ass. "Go to the drop-off. I'll meet you there."

"You don't need us to stay around for backup?" Chris asks.

I look at him pointedly before shutting the door. I can do this shit with my eyes closed.

I creep up to the house, making sure to look as inconspicuous as possible. Keeping my eye out for motion detectors, I find the side entrance to the garage. Most of suburbia live on a false sense of safety, meaning they don't worry about things like locking doors.

As suspected, the side door isn't locked. I slip inside of the junky garage. Shit is stacked in corners like statues.

The car is in the middle of the space with a sheet placed over it. Another car is here as well. A Thunderbird. If I had the choice, I'd take that one, but it isn't about me.

My phone goes off in my pocket and I curse as I fumble with it. Who the fuck would be calling me?

"Hello?" I snarl into the phone without looking at the caller ID.

"I'm sorry, is it a bad time?" Even though I know the voice, I still pull the phone from my ear to look down at the screen to make sure I'm not crazy.

"Noni, is everything okay?"

"Yeah. If it's a bad time, I can call someone else."

"No. No, it's not a bad time." I'm just in the middle of trying to steal a car, but even though that's true I wouldn't dream of rushing her off the phone.

"Is Ace okay?"

Her chuckle comes through the line. "You've already named the baby Ace?"

"Yes," I say leaning up against a work bench as if I have all the time in the world.

"I'll take that name into consideration when the time comes."

"No, you won't," I chuckle. She laughs. "So, what's wrong?"

She sighs. "I can't sleep. I'm tired, but I can't fall asleep."

"Isn't Limp Dick there with you? Wake him up to keep you comfortable."

Another laugh from her comes through the phone. "We kind of got into another argument after your call and he left. He says he needs time."

I hate that this information seems to bother her. She doesn't need to be worried about his ass. She needs to be getting her rest so she can be healthy for our kid.

"Well, what can I do to help you fall asleep? Besides the obvious."

"What's the obvious?"

I shake my head at how adorable her inexperience is. "Dick, Noni. I can come and fuck you to sleep."

A startled gasp and a beat of silence proceeds her next words. "Maybe." She stops and clears her throat. "We should stay away from the obvious."

I laugh only because I know she wants the obvious. I can tell by that breathy reply. Also, the question she asked the doctor let me know she's in need as well.

Dumbass didn't even look up from his phone when the doctor said she was okay to have sex. I would have sent everyone out of the room that minute to part her thighs and bury myself in that warmth. I readjust my dick in my pants as I remember her snug fit.

She's not yours, Deacon.

She exhales. "Can you tell me what you saw in me that night? What made you approach me?"

Okay. I wasn't expecting that. "Is this truly what you want to hear?"

"Yes." She yawns.

I run a hand over my head, then push my hair off my forehead. I look out the glass on the side door. Everything still looks clear.

"Your eyes," I admit honestly. There were a few more things that factored in, like the way that gold dress stood out against her beautiful dark skin. "You looked happy, very sexy, and drunk, but your eyes told a different story."

"What story?" Her sleepy voice is barely over a whisper.

"They said you were sad. Possibly hurting, and you had a good heart."

"You could tell all that from my eyes?" I think her words were meant to be teasing, but she's too sleepy to pull it off.

"Yep. I can tell a lot about people's eyes."

"Well, I can tell a lot about people's eyes too."

I laugh. "Oh really? What do my eyes tell you, sleepy Noni?"

She yawns again. "They tell me you aren't giving this baby up."

Silence greets us. I can't argue with that, because she's right. Not even if I'm not worthy. I don't think I can walk away from this kid.

I look around at my surroundings. I say those words, yet here I am, in this cold, filthy garage, putting my life and my kid's happiness at risk. Even when I think of that, I think of seeing Griff in that hospital and not having him in my life.

"I think you're right," I say the words, but I don't fear her hearing the truth. The soft snores coming from the other end of the phone tell me she was much more tired than she let on. "Good night, Noni and Ace."

I slide my phone off and place it back in my pocket. I pop the lock to the car, using the tool kit in my back pocket. I quickly lift the garage door, leaving no fingerprints with my gloves.

I put the car in neutral and roll it out of the driveway before hot-wiring it and pulling out of the subdivision. I want to make quick work of this night. The faster I can get this shit done, the better.

CHAPTER TWELVE

Getting Away

Noni

For three weeks straight, Deacon has called me every night to talk to Ace before I go to bed. It's to the point I not only expect his call, but I plan ahead for it. Jason still isn't a fan of it and I understand.

This situation isn't the best, but I have to point out, I tried to tell Jason this in the beginning. It wasn't a good idea, but he wouldn't listen.

Porsha says that I shouldn't feel guilty for enjoying his calls. This is the father of my child and we should get along. However, she doesn't know that after the calls I fall asleep and dream about our night in Vegas.

"That boy still calling you at night?" My mother's voice cuts through my thoughts like ice water.

"Who told you that?" I look up from the flower garden she has me digging weeds out of today.

She and the aunts are sitting on the porch enjoying tea while I tend to her prize rose garden—or maybe I should say my prize rose garden since I'm the one always doing the work.

She shrugs and turns her nose up. "My future son-in-law and I have a very good relationship."

"It ain't natural," Aunt Judy mumbles under her breath before shooting my mom a pointed look.

"Hush, Judy. You just mad because your son-in-law hardly comes around you."

"For good reason. He's always working, taking care of my daughter and their real kids." Judy looks to me pointedly. I roll my eyes and go back to my work.

"I can't keep him from talking to his kid," I argue as politely as the perfect daughter can.

My mother sucks her teeth. "That white boy ain't caring about that baby. He just trying to see if he can get some money out of Jason." Again, I never told her Deacon was white, but I imagine I know who did.

"Wait, he's white?" Aunt Judy asks the question with glee in her eyes.

I imagine she can't wait to spread this juicy tidbit to the rest of the family. My mother shakes her head in disgust.

"Deacon doesn't need money," I say, bringing the conversation away from his race.

At least I don't think he needs money. The only time he's mentioned money is if he's offering it to me. He's determined to purchase anything I can even think of wanting.

He hates that I want to wait until further in the pregnancy to start purchasing things for the baby, but he understands my superstition. He's always willing to spend his money on my needs.

"You don't even know that boy," she snarls down at me from her seat on the porch. "Trying to tell me what he wants. I know men, Noni."

If you knew men maybe you would have known enough not to get involved with a man who didn't want you or your kid.

Those thunderous words appear in my head without my permission. They want to be set free so bad, but I don't say it. My phone vibrates, distracting me from those words. I glance down at the screen once I take it out of my pocket and frown.

It's a text from Jason saying he won't be stopping by again tonight. That's the fourth night this week. He's spending less and less time with me.

There's always an excuse. An important case that just has to be solved in one night, he needs a bigger bed to relax, or he's too tired to drive to my house. At this point, I saw him more during our breakup than now that we've gotten back together.

"Is that my son-in-law?"

I look up at my mother, slipping my phone back in my pocket. "Yeah."

"Tell him I'm going to make him a pound cake." She turns to my aunts with a proud smile. "He loves my pound cakes."

"I just bet he does," Aunt Mildred goads, taking a sip of her tea.

"He's not coming over tonight," I say low with the hope she won't hear me, but I already know she will.

"Uh oh. How many times has it been this week, Shondra? Three or four?" Aunt Mildred says over the brim of her cup of ice tea. Mama cuts her eyes to her sister, then back down at me.

"You're not going to be happy until you run that man off, just like you did your father. I can't have any happiness with you. And I don't even blame him, I wouldn't want to pay for your mistakes either."

She slams her cup down on her small end table then rapidly gets up before storming into the house and letting the screen door bang shut.

"Don't make no sense. You should be ashamed of yourself, upsetting your mother like that," Aunt Mildred remarks, before following my mother inside.

The words, *bitch, you're the one that started with her*, are left dead on my tongue.

"Don't let it get you down, Noni," Aunt Judy says, placing her cup down to go after them.

I finish my weeding outside alone, the way I prefer. When I'm done, I leave. I don't even say goodbye. I just climb in my car and go.

It's a Saturday and I have nothing else to do. Even though Porsha and Amira would both be free and willing to hang out, I drive by both their homes. I drive until I get to where I'm going even though that destination isn't made clear to me until I pull up into the parking lot out front.

The words DC INK are scrolled across the building in black swirls. The brick building is plain, with large, tinted windows facing the front. A neon open sign hangs in the doorway, beckoning in new customers.

I don't even know if he's here today. It's a Saturday and he could be off work for all I know. I have no idea where he lives.

I pull out my phone and call him. This probably wasn't part of his idea when he said anything that involves the baby, but for some reason my subconscious brought me thirty minutes out of the way.

"Hey, everything all right?" I smile at how concerned he is for Ace. He always asks me that, even though people close to me have yet to ask.

"Um, so I was driving by your shop and I thought I'd stop by and see you." That hopefully sounds a lot more casual than it sounds in my head.

The line is silent and for a moment I think he might have hung up the phone. That is until I see him standing at the front of his shop, the phone at his ear. A smile spreads across his face when he sees me.

"Get out of the car, Noni," he says then hangs up the phone.

I drop mine back into my purse and climb out of the car in my gardening overalls. I'm without my makeup or my signature lace front today. My thick course hair is in two low ponytails that look like fluffy clouds sitting at the back of my head.

I tug at the little curly pieces I have down by my ears as I climb out of my car. I look a hot mess and really should have rethought stopping by to see him. Deacon scans his gaze up and down my body, taking in my dirty-kneed overalls, my hair and my cloth Chuck Taylors and then smiles.

He grabs my hand, not commenting on the fact that I look so far from the woman he met in Vegas. We walk into his shop and I'm a little caught off guard by how nice it is. The space is wide and open, with only a few closed-off doors that signify privacy.

There's plenty of sunlight and recessed lighting to give it a bright feel. The walls are a soft matte gray. Black picture frames hang on the walls with sketches of some of the most unique and beautiful artwork.

Chrome and black is the color scheme for the furniture and the fixtures. The floors are a light hardwood and emblazoned in the center of the floor is the logo DC INK.

"Your place is beautiful," I say.

He turns back to me and smiles. "What did you think it would look like?"

"I don't know what I thought. I've never been in one before."

When I'm no longer caught up in the decoration of the place, I notice we have gathered a bit of attention. I feel exposed. All these eyes on me.

It's an eclectic bunch. A tall guy with a shaved head and neck tattoos stands behind a black chair wiping it down. A blue-eyed girl with pink hair and black-framed glasses is behind a desk that looks like the receptionist section.

A tall black guy with a low fade and gorgeous full lips wipes his hands on a white towel near the back, and another woman with jet black hair who reminds me of the late Amy Winehouse is hovering over a boy with a humming tattoo gun in her gloved hand.

"Everybody, this is Noni Scott."

A chorus of *hi Noni* goes around the room. Even the kid that's getting a tattoo greets me. I lift my hand and wave.

"Right there's Karly," Deacon says, starting with the pink-haired girl at the front desk. "Up front is Pat." He points to the young, tall guy with all the neck tattoos.

"Money Mike in the back." The black guy winks at me and smiles. "And the queen of black work back there is Chloe. Her line work is the best in the city." I love how proudly he speaks of his employees.

"Maverick is the only one who isn't here. He's out running errands for me, but this is DC Ink main. I have two other locations, but this is the main spot and the one I work solely in."

"Look at that gorgeous brown skin," the one named Chloe says with a smile. "You're going to have us fighting over who gets to mark it up."

The crew laughs and I step closer to Deacon. He chuckles beside me, still holding my hand.

"Hey, no one touches her skin until she drops my kid." He beams, looking down at me. "But even so, I get first dibs marking this skin."

I know he's talking about a tattoo, but I feel that comment in my core.

"Hold up, you got a kid on the way?" Pat says, taking a step forward.

Deacon turns back to the crowd. "Yeah, but we're not making a big deal about it yet."

Before he can finish his sentence, his crew is surrounding him, giving him claps on the back and handshakes. Once they've all congratulated us, they step back.

"It's going to be fun having a baby around the shop. I can babysit. I have five younger siblings," the one name Karly says as she skips back to her desk.

Deacon laughs but doesn't answer. We wave to the crew before slipping into a back room. He opens the door and I notice it's an office.

It keeps up with the clean lines and chrome and black of the front room. He shuts the door behind us, still without letting go of my hand. He walks me to the leather couch and sits me down.

"All right, you going to tell me why you drove all the way here to see me or do you want me to pretend like I don't know something is wrong?"

I stare at him with an open mouth. I don't know why I'm so shocked, he has had a way of reading me sense we first met. I exhale and fall back into the couch cushions.

He watches me with a smile.

"I just wanted to not think for a while, and it seems I get to do that when I'm with you. I get to turn off and not try so hard." I shrug. "I guess I'm not making sense."

"No, I get it," he says, rubbing his knuckles over his bottom lip. "It's that perfect thing, right?"

I open my mouth again, but nothing comes out.

"What do you know about that?" I ask.

He lifts one shoulder briefly before lowering it. "I told you, I'm good at reading people. And, you might have mentioned something about being the perfect daughter in Vegas. It was right before you let me put my dick in your mouth."

My entire face and body heat up at the memory. I'd never given head before and I didn't know if I was any good at it. Jason had said oral is for whores and gay people and we wouldn't be sharing it in our marriage bed. Yet, of course, his dick was in that lady's mouth.

"You're so crass," I say, covering my face.

He pulls my hands away. When I look up at him, he's grinning. "I'm just fucking with you. I wanted you to loosen up."

"That's just it, I'm always loose around you." He lifts a brow. I realize what I said and how it could be misinterpreted. "Maybe I should stop talking."

He laughs, and it causes that fluttery thing in my belly. "I like when you say inappropriate things. You look cute when you blush." I roll my eyes at his teasing. "Why are you out on a Saturday dressed like a sexy farmer?"

Yes, my face does heat at him calling me sexy. I look down at my grassy knees. "I was weeding my mom's rose garden."

"You like gardening?"

"No." I snort. "But she loves those roses, and her knees are too bad to be on them so long."

I shrug as if it's no big deal. I'm not actually sure if that's the reason my mom doesn't tend her own garden, but that's the reason I tell myself. Deacon doesn't comment.

Instead, he watches me, but I don't get uncomfortable like I would if someone else stared at me like that. I watch him too. I watch the way his hazel eyes lazily stare back at me.

I watch the way his narrow nose seems to flare under my scrutiny. I even follow the slow rise of his pink lips as they lift up into a smile.

"Let's go for a ride," he says, pulling his bottom lip between his teeth.

I lift a shoulder. "Okay."

I didn't care what we did, I just want to get away. He stands and helps me up off the couch. Not that I needed it, I'm not even showing yet.

"You do know I'm not that big yet? I can get up off the couch without help."

"Not when I'm around." He winks at me as he leads us out of his office. "Hey, Karly, tell Maverick to lock up for me, please. I'll be out for the rest of the day."

The blue eyed girl with the lip piercing and warm smile nods at Deacon. She waves at me and I wave back.

"It was nice meeting you all," I say to the group and they all tell me bye.

When we get outside, I go for my car, but Deacon tugs at my hand clutched in his. I turn to look at him, a little confused.

"We're not taking your car."

"Then what are we taking?"

He pulls me to him, his mischievous eyes gleaming down at me. "I'm going to turn you into a bad girl."

He nods his head to the left. I follow the direction until my gaze lands on his matte black bike I'm just now seeing.

"Oh no. I can't get on that."

"Yes, you can. And you will. Remember, you're here because you don't want to think. Let me do it for you. Come on."

He leads me toward the bike. I go, but I still have no intention of getting on that thing.

"Deacon, I don't think this is safe. What about the baby?"

Yes, I'm not too good to use my unborn child as a reason to not do something. He stops and turns to look at me, his brows bunched together.

"First, I would never do anything to hurt you or Ace. Second, I've been riding bikes since I was fifteen. I need you to trust me."

Such a huge request. It takes years to earn trust and only seconds to break it. Yet, the moment he asks me to trust him, I do.

"Okay," I reply.

He takes me to the bike and hands me the helmet then helps me put it on and fasten it down. I have to tug on my ponytails to make it fit.

"I like your hair like this," he says, tugging at one of the large afro puffs. Something I wouldn't let him do with the two-hundred-dollar lace front in Vegas.

"This is actually mine," I reply for no other reason than I have nothing else to say to fill the silence. He winks and then helps me onto his bike before climbing on in front of me.

"Wrap your hands around my waist and hold on." He gives the direction before the engine roars to life.

I wrap my hands around him so tight, I wonder for only a moment if I'm hurting him. However, that concern goes flying out the window when he rips out of the parking lot like a bullet. We don't talk and after a while I loosen my grip and place my chin on his shoulder and allow the world to zip by me in a blur.

I don't know how far we ride. I just know not too long ago we turned off the main roads and we've been on a scenic route ever since.

Finally, Deacon pulls his bike to an open field of wildflowers. He parks and quickly hops off the bike before helping me off and taking off the helmet.

"How was your first ride?" he asks with a knowing smile.

"Worth every horrifying second of it."

He takes my hand again and walks me over to the field before taking a seat on the ground. I plop down beside him, tucking my feet under my butt. Deacon has one knee folded and the other leg extended out in front of him. He picks up a blade of grass and breaks it into smaller pieces before tossing them back to the earth.

"This is the place I come to when I need to clear my head," he says.

"I can see why. It's perfect."

And it is, a breathtaking view of nothing but nature. The silence is therapeutic along with the smell of fresh grass and uninterrupted nature. This place is peaceful.

"I spent so much time out here when I was a kid. I used to skip school and take the bus up this way. I would dream about running away and living off the land." He chuckles at his words as if the thought is absurd.

"I had visions of building a cool house up in the trees with ropes and pulleys and a slide that would get me down to the forest floor. I would hunt for my food and dig wells for my water."

"That's a pretty well-developed plan for a kid," I say. "I just had dreams of marrying Nelly. I didn't even put any thought into how we would meet."

Deacon's shoulders shake as he laughs out loud. "You were a Nelly fan."

"No, I was his future wife, thank you very much," I say, rolling my neck.

He gives another deep laugh. "My apologies," he says, holding up a hand in surrender. "I never meant to downplay your relationship."

We both chuckle before letting the silence surround us again. I stare off in the distance. Taking in the serenity of this place.

I'm not exactly an outdoor person. I go outside because I have to, but I don't take leisurely hikes through the forest or anything. However, being out here is tranquil. Or maybe it has nothing to do with the location.

"Why is it so easy with you?" My question cuts through the silence.

"What do you mean?"

I shake my head and turn to look at him. He's studying me, those dark eyebrows bunched in thought.

"When I'm with everyone else, it feels like I'm putting on a show. Even with my friends who love and support me, it feels like I'm always so worried about saying the wrong thing. I have to second-guess everything I want to say and hold myself back, but when I'm around you, I feel like the mask is off and I can be real."

He watches me for a while, I like the fact that he listens and takes into consideration what I say before responding.

"I think Noni just needs to be Noni. Stop looking at yourself as a participant of life. Claim your space in this world."

I blow out a breath. "It's not that easy."

"Yes, it is. And the moment you realize that is the moment you will realize how perfect the real Noni is."

Perfect. A title I've been striving for since I was five years old. If only it were that easy. If only I were truly enough.

We spend the remainder of the day talking. I learned a little about his childhood. He doesn't go too much into detail, just that it was rough.

He learns I was raised by a single mother and I have no real siblings. We talk until the sun goes down and the stars spot the sky like confetti.

***

"Okay, Deacon, I'm home now," I say into the speaker of my car as I pull into my driveway. He made me promise to call and talk to him the entire thirty-minute ride. I yawned one time, and he was terrified I would fall asleep at the wheel.

"All right. Get some rest. You too, Ace."

I smile when he mentions his nickname for the baby. I'm so focused on Deacon on the phone, I'm not paying attention to Jason's car parked on the curb near my townhome. He rips my door open, causing me to startle and gasp.

"Where in the hell have you been?" he yells down at me.

"Noni, who is that?" Deacon calls through the car speaker. I quickly push the button on the steering wheel to disconnect the call.

"Who was that?" Jason steps back to allow me space to climb out of the car.

"I thought you weren't coming over tonight?"

"Are you serious? Is that all you have to say?" he screeches.

"You told me you weren't coming by, so I was in no rush to come home."

He narrows his eyes at me with so much accusation. "Were you with him?"

I have never lied to Jason and I didn't see why I should start now.

"I was on his side of town, so we hung out for a while talking about the baby." Which is true, technically.

Jason shakes his head. He looks at me as if I'm a stranger.

"Look, obviously nothing happened."

"Oh, is it obvious? You opened your legs up to him once, what's to stop you from doing it again."

His biting words leave me with no retort. Never have I cheated on Jason or gave him a reason to doubt me. However, he on the other hand, is quite known for breaking up with me only days before getting into a relationship with someone else.

This last instance wasn't the first time. Though I'd never walked in on him in the act with someone else so soon after a breakup. So how is it he gets to treat me like the bad guy?

He went back to work with his lover, and I never questioned him or asked him about her. I've given him the benefit of the doubt and trusted him. He could at least show me the same damn courtesy.

"I think you should go back to your place tonight."

I turn and walk away. Hopefully, done with this conversation. It's best we call it a night before things get said or should I say more things get said.

"What's gotten into you?" he asks, following behind me.

I turn to yell at him to just go home but pull up short when I see the hurt in his eyes.

"I'm trying to love you, Noni, but you're making it hard. You're turning into someone I don't know. You're not the woman I fell in love with.

"Where is the sweet, considerate, thoughtful woman I met in the library? The woman who actually cared how she treated others and made them feel."

Have I really turned into that bad of a person? I mean, I was gone all day spending time with another man and instead of apologizing or explaining it, I got angry with him. I would have never acted this way before.

Claim your space in this world.

Deacon's words come back to me, but instead of empowering me as they were meant to, I remind myself of the day I was five years old and my father left, without even turning to acknowledge me.

I have to be perfect in order to be loved. My shoulders sag and I let out a breath.

"I'm sorry," I say. "You're right, I'm being selfish. I was having a bad day and I just needed to let off some steam. Deacon helped me take my mind off things."

"Aww, baby." He opens his arms and I walk into his embrace. I stay there, but it does lack the comfort I wish to find there. It doesn't even have the same effect as being on the back of Deacon's bike. "You should've come to me."

"I know."

"I could have helped you see that compared to other people; you don't have problems."

His words settle over me like a two-ton block. I pull away from him, too dumbstruck to even reply to that asinine comment.

"Come on. I haven't eaten and I could sure go for one of your omelets right now."

He walks up to my door, using his key to go inside. My phone vibrates in my hand, and I look down at it. The smile is instant and so is the feeling I was searching for minutes earlier.

Deacon: Please answer or text back to let me know you two are okay. I'm two seconds away from jumping on my bike and heading to you.

I hadn't even realized I'd missed any calls.

Me: We're good. No need to come.

It takes a few seconds before his text appears.

Deacon: Get some rest. Let me know if you need anything.

Me: I will and thank you for today.

"Noni, what are you doing? I'm starving in here," Jason calls from inside the house. I stuff my phone back down in my purse and head in.

CHAPTER THIRTEEN

Just A Kiss

Noni

A month later, my loud laughter can be heard throughout the restaurant.

"I'm just saying, Carlos fucked like he was scooting in a chair to the dinner table."

I erupt into laughter. It feels good to have the old Amira back. It took us a while to pull my best friend out of the state she was in, but we eventually got her. I don't blame her for taking her time.

She and Carlos were childhood friends and had been together longer than me and Jason. They married not too long after Amira graduated college. They'd been through a lot together.

I thought when she found him in the bed with her newly reconnected half sister, she was going to lose her mind. For a while, I think she did, but she's recovered.

"See, I would've been kicked him to the curb. Y'all know how I am about dick. That shit has to be good."

"Oh please, Porsha," I say, holding in my laugh. "You remember that Darius boy, junior year?"

"She was crazy about him." Amira laughs. "And if I'm not mistaken, didn't you say the first time you had sex with him you counted the tiles on the ceiling?"

This time I snort, laughing, thinking about Porsha and all her stories.

"That's right, he had the curve," I say jokingly.

Porsha glares at us. "A waste of a damn curve. That shit was bent like a cashew."

I nearly choke and Amira laughs so hard she has tears in her eyes.

"And to think, you cried for two days over him."

"Shut up, Amira. I was young and dumb. And Noni, you're going to piss your pants. You know how weak pregnant women's bladders are," Porsha playfully sneers, sticking her tongue out at me.

"Don't get mad at my bladder because you got sprung over some baby dick."

This time Mira clutches her chest and laughs so loud the woman beside us gives us the evil eye. Porsha stares at me with her mouth wide open.

"Wait a minute. Look at my little Noni. Where did you get a mouth like that from?" she says.

I look down at my virgin margarita and shrug.

"Oh no, don't get all bashful on us now. I like this Noni," Amira says with a smile.

I shrug. "I guess I've been hanging with a bad influence."

"Bad, my ass." Porsha chuckles, taking a sip of her margarita. "Seems to me like baby daddy is just what you needed."

"Don't start."

"What? Telling the truth?" She leans up in her seat, placing her glass down on the table. "I told you, you're glowing, and it isn't because of my niece or nephew."

"She's right, No'," Amira says without the laughter. "We've even noticed it around the office. Especially on Thursday when a certain someone makes the fruit delivery. Although, it's still funny knowing you're having a baby by that fine ass white boy I sold a cabin to a few years ago."

I try so hard to keep the blush from my face. I press my lips so tightly together they ache, but nothing keeps the smile from my face. I dress much better on Thursdays, even go as far as reapplying my makeup by noon because I know he's coming.

"He brings fruit to her job?" Porsha directs her question to Amira.

"Mmhmm. Every Thursday."

Porsha turns back to me with a raised brow.

"He knows that I crave cold fruit. He's just doing it for the baby."

Both women turn to look at each other.

"What?" I say, rubbing my four months pregnant belly.

"Girl, no man drives twenty-five minutes every week just to bring you fruit unless he wants another type of fruit."

She glances down to my lap. I gasp.

"It's not like that. Deacon is just nice."

"I just bet he is," Porsha says and they both laugh. "Tell me this, how is Stick Up The Ass taking this situation? We all know Jason isn't exactly a team player."

Amira takes a suspicious sip of her drink, making sure to drown out her mumbled words.

"He's doing fine."

I shift in my seat. Porsha raises an arched brow.

"This is the same man who calls you a hundred times a day just to keep track of you. You want me to believe he's all right with Deacon coming to your job and being in the picture?"

I shrug. "Yes."

"Bullshit," Amira blurts out.

I gasp. "I've done nothing wrong. He has no reason not to trust me."

"Jason's issue has nothing to do with trust. He knows you're not going to leave his ass. His issue is control."

"Bingo." Once again, Amira puts in her two cents.

"That man is a control freak. The first thing he did when you two started talking was to try to break in between us. Remember, he said I was checking him out." Porsha scoffs at the memory. "You had to convince that man he wasn't my type. And when that didn't work, he got in good with your mama so he could further take control."

"She has a point there, Noni," Amira says, shaking her head. "His relationship with Ms. Shondra is weird."

"You know how I am about Paulette," Porsha says in reference to her mother. "Any man in my life has to get along with my mama, but Jason and Shondra are weird, even to me."

It's not like I haven't thought the same thing. I even called attention to this with Jason, but he's right, it could be worse. I never said Jason was perfect, but at the end of the day, he loves me, and we've been together six years. Obviously, we are doing something right.

"Jason isn't a control freak. He's just attentive."

"If you say so." Porsha shrugs. "But enough about the man-child. Tell me more about Mr. Deacon."

The smile I try so hard to fight against spreads across my face the millionth time.

"Noni, girl, you got it bad."

Porsha and Amira both burst out laughing. I can't help it, every time that man's name is mentioned these damn flutters in my belly go off.

***

"I agree you should totally do the Parisian theme," Amira says, two hours later as we head to my car in the dark parking lot.

After lunch, the girls and I went for a pamper day and a little shopping. Porsha left about twenty minutes ago. She was ready to get back to her hubby. That left me and Amira to hang out and catch up.

"You don't think the Parisian would be too much if it's a boy?"

"Not at all. We could add a few subtle touches to bring it down a little. Maybe a cute accent color."

I don't get a chance to reply because I notice right away that my tire is flat.

"Oh, shit." I rush to the back driver's side tire. "What happened?"

"It looks like you might have hit a nail or something," Amira chimes in, standing beside me.

That's just great. It's almost seven at night and the parking lot is nearly empty.

"Do you have roadside assistance?"

"Yeah, I do," I say, still looking at my flattened tire.

I dig through my purse to pull out my phone and the second it's in my hand, it starts ringing. A wide smile spreads over my face from the name on the caller ID.

"Hey, Deacon."

"*Oohhh*, Deacon," Amira sings beside me before giggling. I shh her before tuning back into Deacon.

I hear his laughter on the other end. He must have heard Amira. "Are you with friends? I don't want to bother you."

I shake my head as if he can see me. "No, you're not bothering me. Amira and I were out, but I got a flat tire so I'm going to call for a tow."

"Flat tire?" he repeats, I'm guessing to verify what I said "Where are you? Are there any other people around?"

His concern-laced words make me smile. "We're at Oakdale shopping plaza. The parking lot is kind of empty, but I have roadside assistance."

"Get in the car and wait for me, I'm on my way."

"Deacon, you don't have to do that. Don't come out of your way for me."

"Noni, put my son and your friend in that car and wait for me."

Well, I can't argue with that. His tone isn't demeaning or rude, it's the tone of a man who isn't going to argue about the safety of his child. Besides, every time he mentions this baby, my knees get weak.

"Okay," I say before he tells me goodbye. I click off the phone and turn to Amira.

"He wants us to wait in the car for him."

A wide smile spreads over her face. "I'm going to claim it now, I want to be the maid of honor at your wedding."

She grins as she heads to the passenger side with her bags. I unlock the car door and toss my things in the back seat before climbing into the front.

"What are you talking about, you're already the maid of honor."

Amira shuts her door and turns to me. "Okay, Noni, I'm going to say something to you I wouldn't have said a while ago." That makes me a little nervous. She takes a deep breath before blowing it out. "I don't like Jason. There, I said it, it's out."

I know Porsha isn't a fan of Jason. I also know that stemmed from him trying to accuse her of wanting him when we first started dating. However, Amira has always encouraged our relationship. Even when we broke up, she would say, don't worry it will all work out.

I had no idea she didn't like him. I mean, I kind of got that idea today, but she was also tipsy. I don't even know how to respond to that.

"I didn't know."

She looks away before turning back to me. "He isn't a bad person. I just don't like him for you. And I know I'm the last person who should be giving advice on men."

"Don't say that, you never thought Carlos would do that to you."

She shakes her head before looking down at her hands. "I had an idea."

"What?"

This is news to me. Carlos and Amira were like the perfect couple. He doted on her, he was so loving and always bought her flowers, just because. I think Porsha and I were just as shocked and betrayed by his betrayal as Mira.

"Sometimes people show you signs, but you're so caught up in your own version of your life, you miss them. Carlos and I have known each other since we were babies. Our families are close. We fell right into a relationship because it was easy. And expected."

Her shoulders drop as she turns her gaze outside the car. "We were never perfect, but for the last two years things had changed drastically between us. He even mentioned he was unhappy. I thought it meant he wanted me to do something more, you know. So, I started trying to change up our sex life, I tried to do more adventurous things."

"You cut your hair," I say, pointing to the layered short cut.

Porsha and I were shocked when Amira cut her bra-length hair up to her ears. However, the pixie cut with long bangs complemented her diamond-shaped face.

"Yes, cutting my hair was another thing." She laughs before growing serious again. "Instead of listening to him, I kept trying to fix us."

She heaves a breath. "We talked after everything happened, you know. He apologized to me about what he did and who he chose to do it with, but he wasn't in love with me any longer."

This is hard to hear. Before Vegas, Amira was talking about having babies with this man. She was so excited about the idea of kids. I know what she felt for him was real, it's hard to hear he didn't return the feelings.

"I'm sorry you had to find out that way. And I know how much you loved him."

She waves her hand to dismiss my words. "I never got the butterflies."

Her words catch me off guard. It's like she took them out of my deepest thoughts and said them out loud.

"What do you mean?"

She chuckles. "It's stupid," she says, downplaying her thoughts.

"No, seriously, what do you mean?" I turn to her, placing my back to the door.

She combs her hands through her bangs, pushing them away from her forehead. "Remember when Porsha was telling us about when she first met Marcus?"

Of course, I remember, it was like hearing someone tell you the beginning of a romance novel. It was complete with chills, long gazes in crowded rooms, and even the occasional dry mouth when the other was near. Watching their love unfold was epic.

"She said he gave her chills whenever he was in the room with her," I recite the memory back to Mira.

"Exactly, and I remember trying to think if I'd ever experienced that with Carlos, but I hadn't. Not even those flutters in my stomach."

The mention of the flutters causes me to look away from her.

"I was upset at first when all this happened, but after a while I realized I wanted those flutters and those chills. I told myself I would not waste another second of the day on a man who didn't bring those things to me."

She turns to me again, giving me all her attention. "I want you happy, Noni. Not that fake happiness that I had. If Jason truly makes you happy, then I wish you all the success, but if I can give you any other advice, I would say follow the butterflies."

Easier said than done. Butterflies are fine, but they're fickle. Here today, gone tomorrow.

My mother preached that my father was the love of her life. She swore their passion was like fire. Yet, he still walked out of that door and left.

I can't depend on butterflies, I need security. I need to know my partner will stay with me until the end. That he won't walk out on me and our child because he no longer desired the commitment.

I don't say this to Amira. She can afford butterflies, I can't. I clutch my hand to my belly, finding comfort in the child who needs me to be smart.

Not too much later, the sound of a motorcycle has my blood rushing in my veins. Deacon pulls up beside us and on the other side of him is a black Charger. I slip out of my car to meet him as he gets off the bike and takes off his helmet. I ignore the flutters and the way my heart seems to pound when those hazel eyes turn to me with a smile.

"Hey, you all right?"

I take a step toward him before I catch myself. Fighting my desire to hug him, I look down bashfully. "Yeah, I'm good."

"Noni, this is Maverick," he says, introducing me to the tall Asian guy who steps out of the charger.

Wow, he's attractive, but he has a cold glare in his eyes. I wouldn't say it's frightening, but it is a bit disturbing.

"Nice to meet you," Maverick says with a slight dip of his head.

His bone structure is amazing, those dark downturned eyes nearly hidden by thick dark eyebrows. The slight five o'clock shadow adds a sexier appeal. Even his ears that slightly sit out from his head added to his beauty.

"Nice to meet you too," I say and then realize I'm staring openmouthed. This guy has to be six-seven if not nine. He completely dwarfs my five-seven.

"Hey," Amira says, gaining my attention. "Nice to see you again, Deacon."

"You too, baby girl," Deacon says, nodding his head.

She giggles and clutches her invisible pearls. When she turns to look at me, I glare down at her. She sobers and shrugs.

I don't blame her for her actions, Deacon is sexy as hell. Even as attractive and mysterious as his friend is, Deacon still stands out as the gorgeous one.

"I'm Mira," she says toward Deacon's friend.

Maverick steps toward Mira and grabs her hand, that cold look deepens as he brings her hand up to his lips to kiss. If I weren't there to experience it, I would never have believed it. It feels like electricity is crackling between them.

Maverick stops with her hand halfway to his lips as he gazes into her eyes. Amira's mouth hangs open and her whole face is a deep plum color. Deacon clears his throat and it helps to snap the two out of their trance.

Maverick releases Amira's hand and takes a step back. "Nice to meet you."

"You, too." Both sentences are said in a mumble and barely coherent.

"So," Deacons says, cutting the awkwardness. "I brought Mav to help me. You got a spare?"

He takes my keys out of my hand and heads around to the trunk of my car. We all follow behind him like little ducklings. He pops the trunk and looks under the floor mat. However, there's no spare tire.

"Oh yeah," I say, remembering at the same time it isn't there. "Jason used my car a few months ago, and he took the tire out for something. I guess he forgot to put it back."

"He took out your spare and didn't put it back?" Deacon turns to me, the glare in his eyes tells me he isn't so much asking the question, but more likely trying to understand the reasoning.

"Yeah."

He shakes his head and shuts my trunk.

"Nothing I can do without a spare. I'll have to have it towed to the shop."

He looks down at my tire and then walks around the entire car, kicking and checking all the tires. When he comes back to stand in front of me, he wipes his hands down the sides of his jeans.

"All your tires could be replaced, actually."

I sigh. "I'll call it in to get towed in the morning."

"No, you won't. I'll have my pops come get it and get new tires put on."

What? Is he serious? He opens my door and grabs my purse out like he didn't just offer to put hundreds of dollars on my car.

"That's entirely too much money," I argue. "You can have your father get the car, but I can get used tires."

The way he looks at me after I tell him I'll get used tires is like I might have suggested I'd put bike tires on it.

"Maverick, do you mind taking Amira home? I'd do it, but I don't think I can get both ladies on my bike."

"Not a problem." Maverick holds up his hands to show his ease.

"Do you mind?" Deacon turns his question to Amira. Her café au lait skin tints with a rose-colored hue.

"Sure, no problem."

"I'll help you get your bags," Maverick says and even though that cold look in his eyes remains, it eases slightly with the smile on his dimpled face.

With my back to Deacon, I watch my friend grab her things out of my car and give me a halfhearted wave before climbing in Maverick's Charger. I will definitely have to question her tomorrow.

"Ready?" Deacon asks, grabbing my attention.

He hands me my purse and keys. "Anything else you need out of the car before tomorrow?"

"No, we can just move my bags to the trunk," I say, following him back to the car. "You know you don't have to do this. I can get a tow truck…" He turns around, his brow lifted toward his hairline.

"It's done. You're carrying the most precious cargo anyone can have. I won't trust that with used fucking tires. Not happening. This should have been checked sooner. When's the last time your oil was changed?" He quickly moves my bags from the back seat to the trunk of my car.

"I don't know, I took it awhile back."

Deacon shakes his head. "Tell Limp Dick to keep up with that shit or I will."

I don't argue. In fact, I do the very opposite of that. I agree.

When we get to his bike, Deacon adjusts the helmet on my head. This time it goes on a lot smoother with my shoulder-length body wave wig. Once I'm situated on the back of the bike, he climbs on and revs the engine before taking off.

Deacon

Who the fuck let's their girl ride around without making sure her tires are up to standard? Or at the least making sure he puts the damn spare back in the trunk. I almost lost my shit when I realized the spare wasn't there. And what would she have done if I hadn't been there?

This is the shit I won't fucking tolerate with my girl. My train of thought comes to a screeching halt. What the hell am I saying, Noni isn't my girl.

My only concern is my kid. She didn't need to be stranded on the side of the road with my son in her belly. Or God forbid, what if this shit happened and she had to deal with a baby carrier?

She taps my arm, getting my attention, reminding me I'm near her house. I pull up to her town home. It's an architectural craftsman double unit.

It has a very modern style. Each home has its own garage. Turning off the bike, I hop off first and then help Noni.

She takes off the helmet and hands it to me. I place it on the seat of the bike. She stands in front of me, not saying anything, but the way she's working that bottom lip between her teeth, I know her mind is racing.

I think she wants to invite me in. I'm hoping like hell she does, but I'm pretty damn sure she won't.

"Your home is nice."

"Thank you."

Silence surrounds us again. Her eyes dash from me to the door. She's contemplating hard about inviting me in.

I take a step toward her, bringing us so close the tip of my sneaks touch the toe of her flats. I place my thumb on her chin and pull her lip from between her teeth.

"Relax," I tell her.

She exhales and a smile breaks across her face.

"Better?"

"Yeah."

"Do you want me to come in?" I put the ball in her court.

Look, I never said I was a fucking saint. Hell, yeah, I want to fuck. I haven't stopped thinking of that shit since I had it in Vegas.

And I can tell by the way her breathing is labored and the fact that her tits are damn near poking through her top she wants this dick too.

If I step foot in that house, I will be between her legs before the night is even over. I know this, and from the way she's working that lip again, she does too. She closes her eyes and exhales.

"I don't think that's a good idea."

I smile and lean in, bringing her so close if I exhale deep enough, my chest will brush her nipples.

"And why is that?"

I know why, I just want to hear her admit it. I want to hear her say out loud, I'm not the only fucking one feeling this way. She tries to turn away, but my finger under her chin turns her gaze back to me.

"Answer me, Noni. Why isn't it a good idea?"

Her tongue peeks out to dab her bottom lip before disappearing again.

"Because I don't think I would make a wise decision tonight."

"Do you have to?"

"Deacon," she says in warning. "I'm engaged."

I laugh and take a step back. I'm an asshole, but I'm not a dick. I would never try to persuade Noni to do something I know she would regret. When she comes to my bed again, I'm going to keep her there.

I quickly pump the brakes on my thoughts. What the hell? That shit's been happening more times than not lately.

I keep forgetting Noni and Ace aren't a package deal. My concerns start and stop with my son. His mother isn't mine and never will be.

"Go inside. I'll call you tomorrow with the details on your car. Will you be all right tomorrow without it?"

"Yes."

She starts toward the house but stops in her tracks. She comes back toward me. I lift my brow when she stands in front of me.

For a second, I think she's changed her mind. I won't lie, my dick jumped in my jeans. Her sweet scent surrounds me when she places a hand on my chest and raises up on her tiptoes to place a kiss on my cheek. She lingers longer than a friendly kiss, but not too long for me to misconstrue the kind gesture.

When she leans back, she smiles and says, "Thank you, for everything."

I only nod. If I open my mouth, I'm afraid I'll tell her to forget about her fiancé, and let me remind her how my dick tastes. With the willpower of a fucking god, I stay in my spot as she turns and heads to the house.

I watch her ass dance in her jeans as she walks. When she gets to the door, she turns one more time to wave at me before disappearing inside. I pull out my phone and call Griff.

"Are you on your way?" he asks as soon as he answers the phone.

"Yeah, but I have a favor I need to ask." I grab my helmet off the seat and place it in my satchel before climbing on the bike.

"Anything," Griff says with no hesitation.

I tell him about Noni's car before ending the call and starting my bike. The entire time to the shop, all I can think about is the kiss she gave me and the look in her eyes that told me she wants me too.

CHAPTER FOURTEEN

The Picture

Deacon

"Everything looks good, Noni," Dr. Shay says as she moves the wand around on Noni's stomach.

I love the small swell to her belly. She's midway into her second trimester. Today she turned twenty-one weeks which is five months and we're getting our first ultrasound.

"There's the head." Dr. Shay points to the grainy black-and-white screen. The white outline shows the rounded shape of a head.

"Are those the lips?" Noni points to the little white lines on what looks like a face.

Dr. Shay laughs. "Yep, and there's a thumb in its mouth."

"We're going to have to break that habit. Thumb-sucking can lead to problems," Tiny Penis says from his position above Noni's head.

I think it's fucked up he hasn't been to any more doctor appointments since that first one. Yet the day we are to have an ultrasound he brings his ass with us. He has sat on his phone through most of the visit, but now he wants to put in his two cents.

"My kid can suck his thumb all he wants."

"Good thing you'll be signing over your rights and it won't matter what you want."

I take a step away from Noni's side. I'm not in the mood to deal with this fucker. I've been getting little sleep lately, dealing with Griff's situation.

When I'm not working at the shop, I'm checking on Noni and Ace, which is the best part of my day. We always find time at least once a week to have lunch or dinner. Despite the shit that happened at her place three weeks ago, we've continued to stay in touch.

Doesn't matter that whenever I'm close to her, my dick gets hard, and her nipples always seem to greet me through her shirt. We talk on the phone most nights until she falls asleep. She hasn't had many problems during the pregnancy, but she does struggle with sleeping.

Then I turn right back around and steal cars for Griff. I'm working my ass off, but it feels like we aren't getting far with this shit. Working with the three fucking stooges is like trying to teach kindergartners how to color in the damn lines.

I should be bringing in way more cars than I am. The goal was twenty-five a week, we're only bringing in about twenty. When I say I don't have the fucking patience to deal with Tiny Dick Tim, I mean that shit.

Noni wraps her small hand around my wrist, stopping me from whooping her man's ass.

"Look at that, she's moving."

"You mean he's moving," I joke. Noni looks up at me and shakes her head.

"Does mommy want to know what she's having?" Dr. Shay asks with a kind smile.

"No," Noni says.

"Yes," Dumbass says over her.

Noni and I both turn to Jason.

"Noni, the whole point of me coming to this appointment was to find out what we're having."

"I told you, I want it to be a surprise," she replies.

She's only mentioned it seven hundred times. How the fuck does he not know this? I have no problem with waiting to see what we were having.

It's what she wants and since it's her body carrying this child, she gets to make the decisions. Especially the ones that are as basic as waiting until the baby comes to see what she's having.

"Well, you can wait, but I want to know," Jason says, stepping closer to the screen like he's going to be able to make out the grainy picture.

"She said she doesn't want to know," I restate for him.

"Well, I won't tell her."

"Jason, you're horrible at secrets. I know it will slip out and I don't want to risk that."

I hate to hear her pleading with this asshat about something that shouldn't even be an issue.

"This is stupid, what's the point of having the technology if we're not using it." He tosses his hands in the air like a child that doesn't get his way.

"It's her decision. We need to respect that," I say, heat pulsing through my body.

I try to remind myself if I lose my shit in this doctor's office it may mess up my plans to be involved in Ace's life. And not even beating the fuck out of Noodle Dick is worth that. The narrowing of his eyes lets me know he's about to say something that will eventually make me toss that caution to the wind.

"Look, she doesn't get to decide what she wants. She owes me that much."

Her long exhale draws my attention to her. "You know what," Noni starts, and I can tell by the defeat in her voice she's about to give this fucker what he wants.

I'm not having that. This is her fucking decision, and he doesn't get to guilt her into changing her mind. What kind of narcissistic shit is that?

"No," I say, crossing my arms over my chest. "She doesn't owe you a damn thing. If you don't like it, there's the door. You will wait like the rest of us to find out the sex of the baby. Those are her wishes, and they are final. Now if you have a problem with it, you're welcome to talk to me outside about it."

I'm not much of a praying man, but I pray like hell he will take me up on that offer. I still have an ass whooping waiting on him for not putting the fucking spare back in the trunk, and for the night I overheard him yelling at her through the phone. I had to calm myself down to keep from driving all the way out to her house and kicking his ass.

I don't give a fuck if my kid isn't here yet, no one gets to disrespect my son's mother. The room goes silent as I stare down at Jason, waiting to see where he wants to go with this. He lifts his hand up in the air as if he's surrendering before stepping back.

"You know what, I'll just leave. I see I'm not wanted here." He cuts his eyes to Noni before grabbing his jacket off the chair.

"Jason," she calls out to him, but he continues out of the room.

It grates my nerves the way he plays with her emotions like that. He says shit just to make her feel guilty.

"Sorry about that," I say over my shoulder to her. I'm not sorry for telling her fuck boy fiancé off, but I am sorry for upsetting her.

"It's okay and thank you for standing up for me." I turn this time to see her fully, and she has one of those bashful smiles on her face.

"No problem." I shrug.

"To be clear, you don't want to know the sex, right?" Dr. Shay asks.

Noni chuckles. "No, I don't. She will be a surprise for us."

"She means he," I correct.

Dr. Shay smiles before hitting a few buttons on the machine. She puts away her ultrasound probe and hands Noni napkins to wipe the jelly from her belly. I take the napkins from her and help her sit up while she tugs down her top.

"Well, everything looks on track for your due date." Dr. Shay hands Noni a few printed pictures of the ultrasound.

"I'll see you back here in a month." With those words, the doctor and the nurse slip from the room. I watch as Noni stares down at the little black-and-white pictures of Ace.

"Is it crazy to love something that you haven't even seen yet? She's so beautiful." She traces the outline of the white lines that make up our child's face with her fingers.

"Noni, babe, you have an incredible imagination because I can't make out any features."

She snorts in laughter and shakes her head. "Well, I already know she's going to be beautiful."

"If she looks anything like her mom, then yeah, she will be."

The words are out of my mouth before I realize what I've said. It isn't a lie and I have no problem admitting that to her. She's fucking gorgeous. She ducks her head to hide her smile.

"Thank you."

"It's the truth, no need to thank me for that."

She blushes, giving me a shy smile. I hand over her purse off the chair.

"Which picture do you want?" She hands the ultrasound pictures to me and takes her purse. I'm about to tell her it doesn't matter until I see one that makes the sentence die on my tongue. It's the picture of Ace sucking his thumb.

"I want this one."

She smiles and nods. "Good choice."

***

"These next few cars will be tricky," I say as Griff and I stand in front of the whiteboard going over the list of cars for tonight.

These aren't privately owned. They're showroom cars, which means I'll have to break into a few dealerships and a car museum to steal them. It adds a little more risk to the situation. It also means if I get caught, it will add another ten years to my sentence because now we're moving away from grand larceny to a first-degree felony.

"That Porsche will be a tough one. It's going to have a showroom tracker and the tracking system built in."

"Don't worry, my jammers are foolproof," Steel brags. "But you're going to have to pull that showroom tracker off yourself. How long do you think that will take?"

He and Chris are both here on time. Other than being young and dumb, these two aren't too bad. It's the dumbass that's late who I could get rid of.

I look down at my watch again. "Probably a good five minutes, depending on where it's located. The biggest issue is not triggering it. Which is why I'm ready to get this night started." I fold my arms over my chest. "So where is your boy?"

Steel sighs and Chris shakes his head.

"Not sure, he should be here by now," Chris states.

Just then, loud rap music blasting from a radio comes from outside.

"What the fuck is all that commotion?"

I'm wondering the same thing Griff is. All four of us head to the door to see what's going on. The sight that greets me pisses me off further.

"Hey, you fuckers." Mad Pup is leaning against the Porsche Cayenne we had on the list for tonight. The one from the museum. Chris and Steel walk up to the car admiring the beauty.

"Man, this is a beautiful ride," Chris says, stroking the car.

"See, you old guys like to sit around and talk about what needs to be done, I get shit done." He tosses a small device to Steel who catches it, I'm assuming it's a jammer.

I storm up to the kid, fed up with his bullshit. I send my fist across his face, knocking his ass in the dirt. Griff grabs me and keeps me from pounding the boy even more.

"Calm down, Titus," Griff pleads, he then turns to the kid.

"What the fuck, Griff? You need to control your guy," the kid cries as he gets up.

His lip is split and bleeding. I didn't even hit him as hard as I could have. "You snuck that one. Y'all saw it. He snuck me."

I push around Griff. I didn't sneak shit, but since he has so much mouth, I want him to see this ass whooping coming. Griff grabs me again, keeping me from laying this little punk out. Chris stands in front of the mutt, trying to get him to calm down.

"No, let me go, Chris. He's just mad I was able to get the car he was too fucking scared to get. We don't need him and all his planning bullshit. I got the car he couldn't."

"Shut the fuck up, boy," Griff roars at the kid. "There's a reason we were taking our time with that car. Tell me you took the showroom tracker off?"

The kid's brow's bunch up. "The what?"

That's it for me. I push Griff aside and when Chris steps up to block me, I knock his ass in the dirt too. I grab the kid by the collar of his shirt and lift him off the ground before slamming him on top of the hood of the car.

"You fucking idiot. The car has a tracker on it and you just brought that motherfucker to our spot. I would blow your damn brains out if I thought you had any." I lift him just to slam him back against the car again. I could kill this kid and I'm sure society would thank me. "Get this car out of here and ditch it."

"Can't we just take off the tracker here?" Steel asks, stepping forward.

"No, the tracker has to be taken off at the museum. Think of it like a dye pack from a bank heist. The moment you take the car from the showroom floor the tracker sets off small microchip currents into the motherboard. The entire car is the fucking tracker now," Griff snarls, tossing his hands into the air.

"Fuck," Steel growls appropriately. He glares down at the kid with the same anger and annoyance I have.

Griff exhales a calming breath before speaking again. "Chris, take the car, and your boy. Go wipe it down and dump it somewhere."

I release the kid and step away from him. This dumb fuck just jeopardized everything I've got going on because he's careless and trying to prove some kind of point. Who the hell is he trying to impress?

Chris walks over and helps the kid stand. He and the pup climb back in the car and speed out of the driveway.

I turn to Griff. "I'm done," I say, heading into the old warehouse for my jacket and helmet.

Griff and Steel follow me. "Titus, it's just a minor setback. We have to strip this shop tonight and move on to another one. I'll deal with the police. In the meantime, Steel will locate another Porsche to fit the request."

I spin around to face him. "No, you don't get it. I'm risking my fucking kid for this shit and that fuckup just jeopardized me."

"I know." Griff holds up his hands in surrender.

"No, you don't fucking know." I run my hands over my hair, feeling like I'm losing my damn mind.

What the hell am I doing here? I'm making leeway with Noni. We're getting to know each other and she even trusts me. If I continue to build our relationship, who knows what will happen. Hell, she may toss that fucking idea of me signing over my rights out the window.

"What's going on?" Griff asks.

I shake my head and drop my shoulders. I pull the little picture out of my wallet where I put it this morning when Noni gave it to me. I hand the black-and-white grainy picture to Griff. He looks down at it, his brows bunch in confusion before a wide smile spreads across his face.

"Is this what I think it is? Is this my grandson?"

"Yeah, that's my Ace."

Griff runs a finger over the picture.

"I want to help you, but this kid is..." I stop to gather my thoughts. "The kid is my everything. I'm already treading over thin ice trying to stay in his life, I can't risk fucking that up."

Still looking down at the picture, he nods before handing it back to me. I take it from him before glancing down at the thumb in Ace's mouth. I tuck the picture in my wallet and place it back in my pocket.

"I understand, but I need you, Son. I'll manage the boys better. I promise, but if you walk away now this job won't get done."

My jaw aches from clenching it too tight. He's right, if I back down, this shit isn't going to work, but the picture in my wallet feels heavy. It feels like I now have something in my life truly worth fighting for.

"How about you take a few days? I'll clean this shit up and get rid of the heat. When you come back, we can start again."

I don't want to. I want to walk out that door and leave this shit for good. That picture in my wallet is telling me that's exactly what I should do. However, I owe this man, because without him there would be no Ace.

Hell, there wouldn't even be a Deacon. Without Griff coming into my life, I would have been dead or doing some hard time. That's how far gone I was before we met. And if I pull out of this deal and something were to happen to him, I would never forgive myself.

"Okay," I say, relenting. Griff claps me on the back.

"Get out of here. We can meet back in a week at the Riverside location."

I don't argue, I get my shit and hop on my bike, speeding out of the gravel parking lot. My mind is crowded with thoughts. My past is chasing me like hellhounds.

I'm feeling more and more like a fuckup. Everyone told me I was worthless as a kid. They said I was destined to be a piece of shit.

For a while, I lived up to it. Making one bad decision after another. Then it felt like I had finally got my shit together.

Even though I didn't start this bullshit with Griff, I again feel like I'm self-sabotaging. Like I'm making all the wrong decisions.

After getting home and settled, I pull out my phone and call the one person I probably shouldn't be calling, but as I've pointed out, I make bad decisions.

"Hey, Deacon, is everything okay?"

I smile at the concern in her voice. I've already made my nightly call to talk to Ace, so I guess this does seem odd to her.

"Yeah, I'm good, just wanted to check on you and Ace again."

She laughs on the other side of the phone. "We're fine. Ace decided that instead of sleeping he would rather have a bowl of cereal.

"Oh, Ace decided that huh?" I tease.

"Of course, it was him. I would never be eating a bowl of Cinnamon Toast Crunch with freshly sliced bananas at midnight." She giggles.

I lay my head against the back of the couch, enjoying the sound of her voice. I never thought I'd be someone who wanted to sit around and listen to a woman talk about my kid, but here I am. Listening to Noni talk about Ace is like a soothing balm. No matter what mood I'm in, it calms me.

"Well, whatever Ace wants, he gets."

She laughs and when it trails off, the phone goes silent. "Are you okay?"

I let out a long breath. "Not really," I admit. "Can I be honest with you?"

"Always."

"I don't know shit about being a parent." I scrub a hand down my face. "My dad left before he even caught my mom's name. And my mother didn't have a parental bone in her body. I just have this fear that I'm going to fuck up Ace's life."

"You're not."

"How can you be so sure?"

"Because you care," she replies so assuredly, as if she's stating a fact. "You care enough about your child to be concerned about being a good dad. Look, no one is ever prepared to be a parent, not even if you think you are."

She pauses. "Honestly, I'm scared too. The only thing I know for a fact is that I love Ace. I will do whatever I can for him or her.

"And that's all I need to know. I'm pretty sure I will mess up along the way. I will probably do something that will embarrass her or make him scream he hates me, but I know she or he will never have to question if I love them."

I take a moment to soak in her words. To fully allow them to penetrate. Basically, she said the same thing Griff did.

And I don't care where I am or what's going on, my kid will know that I love him. I'll make sure of it every chance I get.

"Has anyone ever told you you're perfect?"

"I'm not perfect."

"You're close enough," I say.

She snorts. "Depends on who you talk to. If it's my fiancé, he will definitely not agree."

I sit up in my seat. I'm glad she brought him up. I want to know what she sees in the guy.

I picked up on some instability in the relationship. Not just his current lack of concern for her welfare and the baby's, but even as far back as Vegas. I mean, I know alcohol was involved, but it was obvious Noni was sexually frustrated.

I had her little kitten purring for me with only the slightest of touches, and then there were the things we did. I literally had to teach her how to suck cock, thankfully she's a fast and enthusiastic learner. Still, what motherfucker doesn't have his girlfriend giving him head?

What's the use of a long-term girlfriend if she doesn't come with automatic blow jobs? That should be a fucking requirement for the position.

"Why is that?"

"I don't know. I guess I can't blame him. I did put him in an unfavorable situation."

Her comment brings to mind something else I noticed. "Why do you do that?"

"What?"

"Make excuses for him. Look, you told him what happened, he had the chance to walk away. He said he wanted to stay, right?"

"Yes."

"Well then you don't owe him anything. Stop apologizing."

"You just don't understand," she huffs.

"Then help me understand."

She's quiet for a moment. "You know how you said you never met your father?" She continues before I reply. "Well, I know my father. I spent the first five years of my life with him. And then one day, he came home and told my mother he didn't want to be with us anymore."

"He just left without an explanation?" That's fucked up.

"Basically. He said he never wanted the responsibility of being in a committed relationship or to be a father."

Damn, that had to sting. My mother showed me with her actions she didn't want me. She never told me to my face. She said other degrading shit, but not that.

"We pleaded with him to stay," she goes on to say. "The both of us, but he walked out the door and never looked back. For years, I felt like if I could just be the best daughter ever, he would come back. If I was perfect enough, he would see I wasn't a big responsibility."

"Let me guess, it didn't work?"

"Nope. He never even tried to contact me. Then right before I graduated high school, I ran into him at the mall. He was happily married with daughters. When I tried to speak to him, he walked right past me like he didn't see me."

So much about Noni starts to make sense to me. I now understand her need to be perfect. Even why she so desperately clings to her fuck boy fiancé. He gives her hope of having the perfect family she always wanted.

"I'm sorry, Noni."

"It's okay. I'm over it." She isn't, but I don't point that out to her. "I just don't want that for Ace, you know?"

I get it now. It didn't matter that I'd be there and never let her or Ace go without. It's the image of the perfect family Noni is after.

The loving husband and happy children are what she craves. And let's face it, even if we were together, I would never want to get married.

"So," I start to change the subject to a less upsetting topic. "How many times have you looked at that picture the doctor gave us?"

Her light laughter floods my ears. Again, I find myself smiling at the sound. I like it when she laughs.

"About a thousand times," she admits. "What about you?"

I gaze down at the black-and-white picture I just took out of my wallet and smile. "About the same," I mutter.

It's after two when Noni and I say good night. I lie in my bed for an hour longer wide awake, thinking about things that will never be.

CHAPTER FIFTEEN

Enough

Noni

"It's just a stupid idea, Noni. Who doesn't want to find out the sex of the baby?" Jason's angry voice carries through the phone, making my head throb even more. It's been two weeks since that ultrasound and he hasn't let me forget it. "And you run around with that man like I'm nothing to you."

"I haven't been anywhere with Deacon."

I honestly haven't. Since the night we talked until two in the morning, I've tried to keep my distance from him. It's not that we've done something wrong or that I'm feeling guilty.

Other than the one night with the flat tire when I had to make myself walk away, he and I have never crossed the line. No, I'm keeping my distance because of this bullshit.

"No, but you have no problem taking his side over the man that loves you. The man who cares about you."

162

"It's not like that." Despite how many times I have said this, he still won't believe me.

"I don't know what to do here. Are you just not happy with me?"

I pinch the bridge of my nose and close my eyes to tamp down the pain in my head.

"Are you even listening to me?"

Yes, how can I not? You've been bitching about this for weeks. Instead of saying that, I reply, "Yes. You know I still love you."

The words taste funny coming off my lips. They have an acidic after taste. I do love Jason. We have years behind us. How could I not love him?

"Well, you don't act like it."

I huff, leaning my head back in my chair. "How about you come over tonight? I'll cook a nice dinner and we can just hang out. You can leave work at home and I can—"

"So now it's my fault we don't hang out? Because I'm trying to make a living to take care of my family, it's my fault?"

"I didn't say that. I just suggested for tonight we could leave the work out of it."

A knock at my door causes me to look up. I forgot it's Thursday and today is my fruit delivery day. I wave Deacon in, and he places the bag of fruit on my desk. Before he turns to leave, I hold up a finger to stop him.

I had a late start this morning, so I didn't eat much, and I've been on the phone with Jason all morning. I haven't been able to stop for lunch. It's at this moment Ace decides to notify his father of my neglect. I clutch a hand over my loud, grumbling stomach.

Deacon smirks at me before pulling a banana out of the bag and peeling it back before handing it to me. I take a bite and smile. It's cold, just the way I like it.

Jason's voice over my speaker phone causes me to turn my attention back to him.

"I work because someone has to pay for this baby, Noni. That little business you run may not be around forever."

I stare down at the phone and can't believe his nerve. I've been up and running for five years now and haven't slowed down once in all that time. I have projects booked a year out in advance. I'm so good at what I do even his boss recognizes it. However, as always, I bite back my retort.

"Of course, Jason. I have to go. I need to eat. Can you come over tonight?"

He sighs. "I guess everyone comes before me nowadays. Goodbye, Noni." The phone goes dead and the throbbing in my head increases, causing me to rub at my temples.

"Everything okay?" Deacon's voice, as always, is filled with authentic concern.

"Yeah. Everything is fine."

Thankfully, Deacon doesn't call me out. I'm pretty sure he heard enough of that conversation to know that's a lie.

"I didn't think you were coming today," I say, finishing up my banana and tossing the peel in the trash under my desk. "You usually call me when you're coming."

He smirks. "Would you have taken the phone call?"

Shame coats me. I forgot that quick I'm distancing myself from Deacon. Other than his nighttime calls to Ace, and the Thursday fruit drops, I don't talk to him.

I have the feeling Deacon noticed the sudden change. As I sit across from him, my attention locked on his hazel eyes, I get that sinking feeling in the pit of my stomach again. It comes every time I avoid his calls or remind myself I can't have lunch with him. It's even worse now that I have to face him.

I feel horrible because it's not his fault his presence in my life irritates my fiancé. Nor is it his fault that when I think of him, my body gets hot flashes from memories of Vegas.

The desire and the fluttery feeling in my stomach let me know I need the distance.

"I'm sorry. I'm just—" He holds up a hand to stop me.

"No need to apologize to me. You know I'm not trying to make it hard for you, right?"

I do know that. Despite his initial reaction, he's actually been the least stressful person during this situation.

"Yeah, I know."

"Good. And you should also know, no one else needs to make it hard for you either." He gives me a pointed look.

I could argue, maybe tell him Jason isn't making it hard for me and he should stay out of my business. However, he has a right to be concerned.

He stands. "What do you want for lunch?"

"You're bringing me lunch?"

"I'd rather take you out to get something, but I'm assuming you wouldn't want that since you've been blowing me off lately."

Not for the first time, the cold touch of shame slithers down my spine. He knows exactly what I've been doing.

I feel so bad about how I've been treating Deacon lately. I don't want him to go out of his way to get me lunch. However, Ace doesn't share my feelings. My stomach grumbles again, louder this time.

We both chuckle.

"I guess I could do a chicken salad sandwich from that café up the street. Make sure they give you an extra pickle."

"And the kale and apple salad instead of the chips, right?"

I blush at how accurately he knows my food choices. "Yes."

"All right, I'll be back." He bumps into Amira on his way out.

"Hey, Deacon," she says cheerfully.

"Amira." He nods to her but keeps going.

She walks into my office with today's mail in her hands and a smile plastered on her face. There's been something different about her, but I'm not sure what it is. I've been trying to put my finger on it for a while.

"Where is he in a rush to?" Stepping further into my office, she takes a seat before putting the mail down on my desk.

"Getting me lunch. I've been occupied with Jason all day, I forgot to eat."

"That man still giving you a hard time?"

I roll my eyes. That's an understatement.

"Lately, I can't do anything right with him. Two weeks ago, I bought some sexy lingerie. He wouldn't even look up from the case he was working on to look at it. If I suggest we hang out, he's too tired. If he is over, he complains the entire time or he's too busy working. I don't know what to do."

A sad smile touches her lips, but not her eyes. "Have you tried talking to him about it?"

"Yes." My voice wavers, and the urge to cry burns my eyes. This pregnancy has me crying about everything. Yesterday I cried because I couldn't find the right houndstooth fabric. "Talking leads to arguing."

"Have you ever considered maybe you aren't the problem?"

"What?"

"I'm just saying. You seem to be jumping through a lot of hoops to make him happy and he won't even meet you halfway. I think it's time you sit back and evaluate this relationship. I know you want stability, but what about peace of mind?"

Her words start to register. I've been so concerned about being perfect in order to have a happy family, but I think I'm missing the happy part. What does it matter that I have a husband if both of us are miserable?

In the past two weeks, I've been attentive and supportive, cooking meals, giving back massages, damn near running myself ragged just for Jason. Yet, he still complains. Maybe Amira is right. Maybe it's time I start thinking about this relationship.

My phone lights up on my desk, alerting me of a phone call.

"It's my mother. I need to take this," I say to Amira as I pick up the phone.

"Okay, but think about what I said," she says, getting up. She doesn't know I'm already thinking about it.

"Hey Mom, is everything all right?"

"No, it isn't. I need to see you immediately after work." As if she doesn't every day, anyway.

"Okay, is something wrong?"

"No. I'm just going to finally put a stop to something."

My heart stutters before it picks up a normal beat. What could she put a stop to? It's pretty common knowledge my mother blamed me for my father walking out on her all those years ago.

She's often told me I was the reason, even though I distinctly remember him saying he didn't want to be a father nor a husband. All my life my mother has treated me as if I was the sole cause of his betrayal. Despite all I do to try to appease her, she is never happy.

My only wish has been that one day, she will open her eyes and see she wasn't the only one hurt by my dad's actions. Maybe she will even realize I lost a father and mother that day. Could this be what she's trying to make right?

"Okay, I'll be there," I say before hanging up.

The knock on my door causes me to look up again to find Deacon with a bag in his hand. I smile and wave him in. My mood is a lot better than when he left. He sits down and dishes out my food.

"Eat," he demands. "I'm not leaving until I know Ace is satisfied."

I laugh. "When it comes to eating, your son is never satisfied."

I have lunch in good company. Deacon keeps his word. He stays until I have eaten all my food and half of his sandwich.

I spend the rest of my day anxious to get it over with. For the first time in years, I can't wait to get to my mom's house.

***

I'm shocked to see my aunts' Cadillacs aren't in the yard today. It takes me by surprise to see Jason's car, though. A slight bit of trepidation runs through my mind.

I shake my head. Of course, it's not anything bad. Jason and I are having a few issues, but we're trying to work them out. He must be here for moral support, or maybe he's the one who got my mom to see how she's been treating me lately.

I power forward because I need this apology and this conversation. I know she isn't all that happy about the baby and I'm hoping things will change before the baby comes. I climb out of the car.

Before I get to the porch, the front door opens. My mother is there with a glare on her face and a hand on those wide hips that I inherited.

"What took you so long?"

I actually work and I can't just drop everything to run to you just because you have come to your senses about your attitude toward the only fucking child you have.

"Sorry," I reply instead.

She turns around and heads back into the house, leaving me to follow her inside. I spot Jason sitting on the couch, looking more comfortable in my mother's house than I ever have. I smile down at him and he winks at me.

I take a seat on the loveseat beside him and my mother sits on the couch across from us. I look back and forth between the both of them, waiting for her to start. Jason gives my mother a subtle nod and she speaks.

"Noni," she starts. "Jason and I have been talking and I honestly don't like the things he has been telling me."

I turn to a straight-faced Jason. "What has he been telling you?"

Hopefully, he's telling her how hard I've been trying to make things right between us? That no matter how tired I am, I still make time to cook and give him attention? From the look on his face, I don't think he's told her any of that. I also don't think I will be receiving that much-needed apology from her

My mother continues. "You're allowing that scumbag to talk to Jason any kind of way, and what's this thing about you not allowing him to find out the sex of the baby? I mean, such a simple thing. A real wife would give a husband like Jason anything he wants."

Are you fucking kidding me?

Apparently, those words were not said in my head like they usually are. Both my mother and Jason turn to look at me with shocked expressions.

"See what I mean, Mama?" Jason says, turning to my mother.

"Disgraceful," she mutters. "You haven't been the same since that sinful trip to Vegas. I knew I shouldn't have let you go. You have your father's unfaithful spirit."

Okay, fuck this. I shoot to my feet.

Claim your space in this world.

Deacon's words come back to me and I let them sink in. I don't owe either of these people anything.

"I have been busting my behind trying to please your ungrateful ass." I direct my anger to Jason.

"That is your job."

"I'm not talking to you." I don't even turn to my mother when I speak to her, but I hear her gasp.

"Noni, that is no way to talk to your mother."

"For the love of God, shut the hell up." I roll my eyes and bring my hands up to cover my ears briefly. "I am sick and tired of you trying to play the victim here. We hurt each other. Neither of us are blameless in this."

"Yeah, but my screwup didn't result in me having a baby." Jason glares up at me.

I scoff. "That's the thing you think redeems you? Because your nut went down her throat instead of in her coochie?"

"Noni Kaye Scott, who taught you to talk like that?"

I turn to my mother and reply proudly, "An asshole that has respected me more than either of you two ever have."

Jason shoots up and points a finger in my face. "That's what this is about? You're acting like a disrespectful brat because of him." He turns to my mother. "I told you he was no good, white trash."

"You know nothing about him."

"I know enough to know he doesn't care about you. You were probably just some token black girl fuck he wanted to scratch off his to-do list. After he gets what he wants from you, he's going to leave you and that bastard in your belly."

So now the truth is out. How can you call a child you swore to treat as your own a bastard? Maybe I'm naïve for believing he could or for expecting him to be able to do so.

I wanted so badly for Ace to have what I didn't have growing up. I wanted that perfect family for my child, but I'm starting to see perfection is unattainable. Amira was right. I was striving for stability, but losing my peace.

The best thing I can give my child is a mother who will love it unconditionally, and not raise it with a man who could call it a bastard. I wipe away the tear that wobbles at the rim of my eye before it can fall. I slide the diamond engagement ring off my finger and place it down on the coffee table in front of me.

"What are you doing?" my mom cries out in a panic.

"Pick that ring back up and put it back on," Jason says in a harsh tone.

I don't. My eyes are open, and I now see the manipulative man who stands before me. I was so desperate to be a wife and mother, I was willing to commit myself to a man who didn't know how to love me without overshadowing and controlling me.

I head to the door, giving them my back. They don't deserve to see my tears.

"Noni, if you walk out that door, I won't take you back."

"Do you hear that?" my mom shrieks. "You're about to ruin the best thing that could ever happen to you."

I spin on my heels as I swing the door open and say, "Then you marry him." Slamming the door shut on my way out, I then rush to my car and climb in.

My eyes blur the entire ride home. I'm surprised I'm able to make it safely. At a quarter after six, I climb in my bed, bury my head under the covers, and cry. My tears are a mixture of pain for losing the man I thought I loved for six years and the relief of not making the mistake of marrying him.

CHAPTER SIXTEEN

Close Call

Deacon

It crosses my mind to call Noni again. That shit I walked in on today wasn't good. I thought she was pulling away from me because she and Dipshit were working things out.

I had no problem with stepping back if that were the case. However, hearing the shit he said to her and watching the pain etched in her face as she rubbed at her temples had me pissed. She wasn't avoiding me because they were working it out, she was avoiding me because he's being a little bitch.

I couldn't help but worry that Little Dick would convince her to push me out of the picture altogether. I still get my phone calls and I'm included in the doctor visits, but what if he talks her into keeping me from those things too?

I can't even fathom not being there for Ace now. Not after experiencing the first few months of this pregnancy. That shit has me distracted tonight, because when I called her for my nightly conversation with Ace, she didn't answer.

She's never done that. I send her a text telling her to please call me before slipping my phone back in my pocket.

Tonight, I'm breaking into a car dealership to take a 2019 red Ferrari Portofino, along with a Ferrari 488 Spider and the Stradale. These cars are fucking beauties.

"Everything is clear on this end," Steel's voice comes through my wireless earbuds.

Tonight's job is slightly complicated. Unfortunately, I couldn't pull off this one on my own. I'm good, but not that damn good. I'm stuck with taking Chris and the little pup with me.

I turn to both men standing behind me. "No shit in here," I say, pulling my black leather gloves on.

I'm wearing a plain black hoodie and black pants along with plain black tennis shoes. My hair is tucked underneath a black face mask. None of my body can be seen through my clothes.

I'm purposefully wearing basic clothing. I don't need anything to make me stand out on the security footage. Steel tried to hack the camera system but found it too difficult. It's times like this I miss the old crew.

"We have a total of fifteen minutes from the time we get in and that alarm goes off. Everyone know what they need to do?"

Chris nods his head. "I let the back gate up so we can drive the cars out," he reiterates the plan.

"This ain't our first rodeo," the kid argues. I have to count to five in my head to calm down before I fuck him up again.

"Just do your fucking job," I say, pulling the ski mask down over my face. The other two follow suit.

"You ready, Steel?" I ask through the earpiece.

"Setting the timer now."

I look down at my watch, taking in the time. "Let's go," I say before moving out.

We stay close together and low. When I get to the door, I'm mindful not to look up at the camera. I keep my face down as I pick the lock to the glass doors. The moment I swing the door open, the alarm starts blaring.

I glance at my wrist and hit the stopwatch, then rush inside. Chris heads to the back door and starts to roll the large garage-style door up in the showroom. Pup goes straight to the Stradale.

"Damn, this thing is nice," he says as if he's planning on fucking it. I rush to the Spider first, holding the jammer up to the door, waiting for the light to turn green. As soon as it does, I turn to Pup.

"The Spider is ready."

"You guys got seven minutes," Steel says through my earpiece. Pup tosses the key to Chris and he catches it out of the air. Steel made us a dummy key. Pup's job was to keep up with the key.

"The Stradale is ready," Pup lets us know, putting away his jammer.

I'm taking the Portofino tonight. Once the jammer turns green, I call out to Pup to toss me the dummy key. He cocks his hand back and tosses the fucking thing as if he's in the Super Bowl trying to make a fifty-yard pass. The key flies over my head and lands somewhere behind the counter.

"Shit, sorry, Titus," he says.

"You guys need to hurry up." Steel's panicked voice comes through the earpiece. "They just called it in. There's a car in route."

Fuck. I want to yell to the rooftops. This day just couldn't get any worse.

"C," I say careful not to use names. "You two take off, I'll get the last car."

"Just leave it, we can get another one."

No, we can't. I don't need another fucking delay. I needed to get these cars and be done with it.

"Get in the car and get out of here," I say, not staying to make sure they listen.

I run to the circular service desk, leaping over the top. I slide across the slick surface and land on the other side. The other two cars crank and shortly after speed away.

It's dark as fuck and I can hardly see. I pull out my phone and turn on the flashlight to search in the area where I think the key dropped.

"Get out of there now," Steel insists.

"Not without this car," I tell him.

I spot the key under the desk and quickly grab it up. Leaping back across the counter, I speed to the Portofino. I can hear the police siren in the distance. Thankfully the Portofino is still in show form, which means the top is still down.

I hop in the car and immediately push the button on the steering wheel. I studied all the cars before tonight, so I know how to work this one. The car roars to life.

I put the car in gear and then step on the gas, causing the wheels to spin out before jerking me forward. As soon as I come out onto the parking lot, two police cruisers turn in. They quickly make a U-turn and pursue me. I press the button to roll the top back up on the car.

Griff's voice cuts through my earpiece. "What the fuck, Titus?"

"Mishap with the keys. Can't explain it right now, got heat on my ass."

I turn left at the last minute, cutting off traffic. The sound of blaring horns greets me. Glancing in my rearview, I notice I lost the cruisers, but damn near run head on to another cop car.

I make a sudden right. The Ferrari rakes the tight turn like a dream. The new cruiser is hot on my tail.

Fuck. How did I get here? Even as I keep my eyes on the road and maneuver around cars zipping in and out of traffic as safely as I can, all I can think about is my Ace. And I won't lie, I think about Noni too and how her silence tonight has been fucking with me.

"All right," Griff says reminding me he's still here. "I got you pulled up on my screen, at the next light take a left on Taggert and then the immediate right."

I follow his directions, narrowly missing an oncoming car when I turn left. I take the right like he said, the road is clear. I push the gas pedal down, flooring it. Glancing in the rearview mirror, the cops on my tail are nowhere in sight.

"Lost the cruisers," I say to Griff. Not even two seconds later a spotlight overhead has me peering up through the windshield. "Fuck," I yell.

"Damn it," Griff follows up. "They got a chopper on you."

"No shit."

I run the red light and blaring horns sound behind me. Looking through my rearview, I spot three new police cruisers turning at the light to follow me. This night is absolutely going to hell fast.

"Okay, take the next left on Westview."

"A left on Westview?" I ask, questioning his sanity. "That road is always congested."

"Just trust me. Turn now."

I whip the car at the last minute. Again, thankful I'm doing this in a Ferrari.

"At the stop sign coming up, I need you to turn left."

I do as he says.

"I need you to push that car, Titus. You've got five minutes to get to the railroad tracks or you're shit out of luck. Drive that damn car," Griff shouts in my ear.

I push the gas all the way to the floor. Tonight, I'm going to make physics my bitch. I dust the police, leaving them in the distance. They can't match my speed, but the helicopter is a different story.

My heart is pounding, and adrenaline has me gripping the wheel in a death crush. I hear the train in the distance. The trains on this road are known to take forever. If I can get past that train, I can lose the cops. If I don't, I'll be a sitting duck until they come.

At this moment, my life is flashing before my eyes. Not exactly my life, more like my future. With the train up ahead and the helicopter over me, all I can think about is my future and my Ace.

If I make it out of here, I've got my son. The only thing in this world I want. Behind me, well, I don't even want to fucking think of what is behind me. Something else is made clear now too. It isn't just Ace on the other side of that track; Noni is there too.

I have no right to want her, but I do. That's why when she started distancing from me, it bothered me so much. I don't just want my son, I want his mother too.

I say a prayer to whoever is listening as the sound of the train whistle blows, letting me know its nearing the intersection. At the rate we are going, we're going to hit the track at the same time. I near the tracks and shut my eyes, envisioning her smile.

If I go out, it will be to her beautiful face. The sound of the train is thunderous in my ears. I hit the track, and the car lifts as if I went over a ramp. I open my eyes right as the car comes down on the other side. Ahead of me is freedom and behind me is the train completely cutting off the police.

"Fuck yeah," I cheer into the empty car.

"Damn, you nearly gave me a heart attack," Griff exhales into my earpiece. "We still got the chopper on us. Turn off on Pleasantburg, head downtown. We're going to cut off their view with the buildings."

Following Griff's directions, I head into the business district, zooming through the streets. I spot a parking garage and head there. Once I'm safely hidden from the helicopter, I catch my fucking breath. My heart is beating so hard it feels like it may come out of my chest.

"Quick thinking," Griff says, exhaling. "The chopper is pulling back. They lost you. Get that fucking car to the waterfront and get home. I think we've had enough excitement for the night."

The earpiece goes silent, but my heart is still in my throat and my adrenaline is still pumping. It's going to take me awhile to come down off this high.

I make record time getting the car to the checkpoint. I pull into the carry crate and turn it off before climbing out. As soon as I step out Chris and Pup are there to greet me.

"That was some crazy shit. I thought you were down for real," Pup says excitedly.

I grab him by the throat and slam him up against the side of the holding crate.

"You got one more time to fuck up, and I'm kicking your ass out. Do you understand?" I yell down in his face so loud I can feel the vein in my forehead throbbing.

Pup turns his terrified gaze to Chris, who for once doesn't come to his rescue.

"Do you fucking understand me?"

I apply a little more pressure to his throat, and he chokes out a yes. I push his ass away from me and he falls to the ground. I don't look back at him as I exit the crate.

I climb into the white van beside Steel. When Chris and Pup join us, we speed away and head back to Griff's.

***

The time on my phone reads after 4:00 am. However, after what I went through tonight, I need to call her. I figure the phone will go to voicemail and I can tell her everything I need to say.

I want to tell her I'm not going to let her cut me off and treat me like a stranger in my own kid's life. I'm going to fight her to stay in Ace's life even if it takes every dime of my money.

I'm ready to let her know the real deal through her voicemail, so it takes me completely by surprise when her croaking voice comes through on the other end of the phone.

I pull the phone from my ear to make sure I called the right person.

"Noni, are you okay?"

The sound of her sniffling has me alarmed.

"Is it Ace? Are you two all right?" I don't give her time to answer. I spent most of the night thinking she was avoiding me, and something was actually wrong.

"I called it off," she says, barely above a whisper.

"Called what off?"

"I couldn't do it anymore. He couldn't love the baby. He couldn't love me enough to love the baby."

Her sobs come again, and it feels like a sucker punch to the gut to hear how torn up she is. I let out a long breath and drop my head, running my fingers through my hair.

"I'm coming over."

"What? No, don't come all the way over here just for me."

"I'm coming. I'll be there in fifteen minutes."

She only holds out for a second before saying okay. I haven't been back to her place since I dropped her off the night with the flat tire, but I kept her address programmed in my phone in case of an emergency.

"See you soon."

"Thank you, Deacon."

I slide my phone into my pocket and climb on my bike, speeding out of the parking lot. I drive as fast as I legally can to get to my family. Yeah, my family. It's time I claim that shit.

CHAPTER SEVENTEEN

Where I should Be

Deacon

I pull my bike up beside Noni's black KIA and cut it off. She's standing inside the garage at the entryway to her home and hits the button to close the garage door down as soon as I enter. I head toward her and the moment I'm within reach, she wraps her arms around my neck and buries her tear-streaked face into my chest.

I wrap a hand around her and take in her scent as I place my nose at the top of her head. I allow her to take from me whatever she needs. When she pulls back, she looks up at me with puffy eyes and a weak smile.

"I'm sorry."

"Don't apologize." I grab her hand and give it a comforting squeeze.

"Come in," she says, stepping back for me to enter her domain. There is no hesitation this time.

We walk into the kitchen from the garage. The room is light and airy. The floors are a light wood and pale seafoam green paint coats the wall.

The cabinets are white, and the marble countertops are also white. She ushers me past the kitchen into the living room. This area is the same as the kitchen, with clean lines and white accents.

I start to laugh. She turns to me before sitting with one leg under her on the gray sectional. I take a seat down beside her.

"What's so funny?"

"I'm trying to figure out what you're going to do with all these white surfaces when Ace gets here."

Her face lights up as she gazes around her living room at the light-colored furniture, with pearly white accent vases in groups of three scattered around the room. Even the accent pillows are white.

She smiles widely before she turns back to me. "I guess I never thought about that."

"Your home is nice, but when he gets in those terrible two's he's going to wreak havoc on this couch."

"That's when he will have to go live with his dad," she jokes.

Those words coming off her lips give me pause. She's never once called me his dad. I know I am, and she's told me I'm the father, but she's never called me his dad. It sounds fucking amazing coming from her.

The room grows silent again. When I look over at her, I can tell her mind has drifted back to her problems. I don't like it.

I reach out and grab her small hand in mine. She lifts her sad eyes to my face and a weak smile greets me.

"Talk to me. What's going through your head?"

Her gaze drops down to her lap and a single tear falls to her cheek. "Why am I so unlovable?" Her brown eyes turn up to me only briefly to show me the depth of the hurt this realization has caused her. "Everyone who's supposed to love me or claims to love me always lets me down. One way or another, they prove to me I'm not good enough. No matter how perfect I try to be."

"Look at me." She lifts her gaze to find mine. "That shit ain't your problem. That's their problem."

I point to the door, indicating those people who hurt her. "You are enough. You don't have to do shit to prove that to anyone. And if they find you lacking, then that's their issue and they should move the fuck on," I say vehemently.

I've only spent a little time around Noni, but I know enough to know she has a good heart. She's caring, thoughtful, and loving. I want my words to uplift her, to cheer her up. I wasn't expecting the results I got.

One moment she's looking at me with sad eyes and the next she's on her knees on the couch and her lips are sealed to mine. The kiss is unexpected and catches me off guard, but it doesn't stop me from answering the demand she's making. I have my hand at the back of her neck, tugging her toward me.

She moans into my mouth when my teeth sink lightly into her bottom lip before sucking it into my mouth. At the back of my mind, I know this isn't the right move. I know she's just feeling vulnerable, the same way she was in Vegas.

However, my cock is not getting the memo. All it can think about is that tight fucking warmth it remembers from that night. She moans into my mouth. I tug her into my lap.

She comes immediately, her hot center cradling my cock. I can't get as close as I want to her because her little baby pudge is keeping me at a distance.

She tugs at the hem of my shirt and pulls it up just to run her hands over my chest. I deepen the kiss. I want her so damn bad I can't think straight.

The soft nudge against my stomach makes us both pause. She pulls back and I look down at her tank top-covered belly. Another bump against my stomach, and this time, I can see the little movement underneath her shirt.

"Did you feel that?" She smiles up at me.

"Is that Ace?" I place my hand flat against her stomach. This time the kick is a little stronger.

"This is the first time I've felt him move." She covers my hands with hers and again the little thump comes. "He must know you're here."

Or more like he knows I'm about to fuck things up. I want Noni, real bad. My dick feels like granite, but I think I want this shit more. Once it seems like Ace has settled down and is no longer trying to entertain us, I still don't remove my hand.

"I think we need to slow down."

Damn I sound like a bitch, but I'll be one in order to get the outcome I want. And that outcome is her and my son. She goes to climb out of my lap, but I tighten the hand I have on her hip, making her stay put.

"I don't want you to do something that you will regret."

She cups my face with her hands. "Do you know why I tried so hard with Jason after finding out I was pregnant?"

I shake my head no, even though I don't think she's asking a real question.

"I tried to make it right because I haven't been the same since I got back from Vegas."

This is news to me. It seems like she has been going through the same shit I was. I haven't been the same either, constantly thinking about her and what we did.

"I didn't know what it was at first. I felt like I was in the wrong body, like I was shoved into a tight box and I couldn't stretch out," she admits.

"What are you saying?"

She sighs, her warm breath brushing across my face. "I'm saying, I felt wrong, but when I'm around you, just like back in Vegas, I feel right. Like I'm where I'm supposed to be."

I don't think this time. I don't allow my doubt to deter me. I lean up in my seat, placing one hand at her back and the other at her throat as I position her beneath me on the couch. I plunder her mouth. I feel like I'm where I should be. Right here with my little family.

CHAPTER EIGHTEEN

First Date

Noni

I wake from the best sleep ever. This was the first time I've slept so long and so hard. The first thing I notice as I come awake, even before I open my eyes, is that I'm wrapped in strong arms. A familiar scent cradles me, and I take a deep breath in.

"You all right?" his deep voice causes flutters in my belly and this time it isn't Ace.

I open my eyes and look up at him. Those hazel eyes shining down on me. I chastise myself for not taking what I wanted last night, but he has a point.

We should take it slow. I did just end a six-year relationship. Funny, thinking about my relationship with Jason doesn't hurt anything like it probably should.

"How did you sleep?" he asks.

"Great."

"Do you have any plans for today?"

The entire time he's asking me this question, his hand rubs circles over my belly.

"I usually go to my mom's on Saturdays and help dig in her garden."

He smiles down at me. "Not today. Today, you're going to the shop with me. I have two appointments and then you and I are going on our first date." He plants a kiss on my lips, then climbs over me off the couch to stand and stretch.

"A date?"

"Yes, a date. Things normal couples do?"

Those familiar flutters hit my stomach and again, they aren't due to the baby.

"Oh, we're a couple now?" my words are said teasingly. I sit up, placing my feet on the cold floor.

He tilts his head slightly, gazing down at me. "I've always been a go-getter, Noni. When I want something, I go after that shit. It got me in trouble a few times when I was a kid, but I'm a grown fucking man now."

"Well, what do you want?" My heart is racing despite how calmly I ask the question.

He furrows his brow and his alert gaze fixes on me with so much unwavering determination. "You," he says without pause. "I want you and I want my kid. I was okay with not having you when I met you in Vegas.

"I let you walk out that hotel door. Then when you came back engaged, I agreed to step off. If you were happy, I could live with that, but last night made me realize something. I want us. I want my family."

If my jaw could be on the floor, I think it would be. Never has a man said something like that to me. Deacon claims me like I'm his to own. I have no problem taking things slow and getting to know him.

I want a family for Ace, but after all the crying I did yesterday, I've come to the realization that if I have to do this on my own, I will. And I'm okay with that.

Families come in all different shapes and sizes. I don't have to have a piece of paper to make a happy family. I could give my son the perfect family with just me. What I won't do is allow a man to come in and out of his life or to abandon him.

"All right," I say, hopping up. "We can give this a chance, but Deacon, when it comes to this kid, I won't take any risks." I hope he can understand what I mean.

He nods his head. "Go get dressed. We'll grab some lunch before we head to the shop."

"I have a spare toothbrush if you need it and you can shower here," I offer.

A smile cracks across his face. "I'm already getting my own toothbrush."

I laugh as I lead him to the guest bathroom and hand him the toothbrush. I leave him and head into my bathroom but stop and grab my phone off my nightstand where I left it to charge last night. Thirty missed calls and text messages from my mother, but nothing from Jason.

I'm not entirely shocked. He's probably still waiting for me to call him. He's going to be highly disappointed.

I place my phone back down on the nightstand and head for the shower.

***

"You're so talented," I say, watching Deacon wipe down the large tattoo he just did on a guy's ribcage.

I've been sitting here for four hours watching him outline a huge snarling dragon with large wings on top of a castle. I thought I would grow bored with watching him work, but I was so caught up in the work, I hate he's calling it for the day.

"Are you going to leave it like that?"

He places the clean bandages over the guy's tattoo.

"No, he'll come back in three weeks for me to fill in the color."

I shake my head, trying to imagine how much more gorgeous it will be once he adds the color.

"Deacon is the best in the state. Nobody has line work or detail as good as him," the man that so nicely allowed me to watch his tattoo says.

Deacon stands and removes his gloves before dropping them in the trash can, he and the guy shake hands.

"Make your next appointment with Karly."

"All right. See you later, Deacon and congratulations on the kid."

I smile and duck my head. Deacon has been proudly making that known to everyone who has come into the shop. Once we're alone again, Deacon turns to me with a smile.

My phone goes off for the hundredth time today. It seems my mother didn't get the notice last night when I ignored her. Not only has she been calling and texting, but she has started to recruit others into the game.

I pull out my phone to look down at the message. This one is short, only the words, *you are a horrible daughter.* And to think, this one was probably the nicest one I have gotten.

"What's that one say?"

I place the phone back down in my purse, too embarrassed to show him. Unfortunately, he saw one of the other messages that popped up. He didn't say anything, but that vein in his neck started to throb when he read it. He has glanced over at me every time my phone chimes.

"Doesn't matter," I say, shrugging my shoulders. "So, tattoos don't look too painful after watching you do one."

Yes, I changed the subject. I don't want to ruin the day we're having with my mom issues. I'm genuinely having a great time. Although he doesn't let on, I'm pretty sure Deacon doesn't like it.

"No, they aren't that bad. If you like, I can give you a nice little tear drop right here," he says reaching out to touch my cheek right under my eye.

I laugh and smack his hand away. "Don't even think about it."

He laughs before he continues to clean his workstation and put away his tools.

"But," I start softly. "If you were to give me a tattoo, where would you put it?"

I trail my finger along the arm of the chair. I don't look up, though I know he's looking at me because I don't hear him rummaging around anymore.

"You sure you want me to answer that?"

I force myself to look up at him. He's watching me with a smug look on his face.

I cut my eyes away again, then back to him. He folds his arms over his chest.

"Okay," he starts, taking a seat on his little black rolling stool. "I have a few ideas. The first, probably your shoulder or collarbone. Some place you can show off if you want and cover if you desire. Your legs work well for that too."

I like that idea. I would want to show it off when I could, but I definitely would need to be able to hide it. I don't want to scare off a potential client with tattoos. I have no problem with them, but some people would find it hard to take me seriously.

"Now the second place," he says, and a smirk tugs his lips up on one side. "Would be something just for your man to see." He slides his chair closer to me, leaning into my space for a moment. The smell of his fresh and woodsy cologne invades my senses the same way it does every time I'm around him. "I would put it only in a place where your clothes would always cover it and the only time it's revealed is when your body is on display."

With one of his long thick fingers, he makes a trail from my inner thigh to my knee, and I have to clench my vaginal walls to contain the ache. It's been so long since she's been touched or given any type of attention by someone other than me. Deacon isn't making it easy.

"What would you put there, in the secret place?" my words are breathlessly spoken.

His tongue runs over his bottom lip. And I watch the entire process before it slips back into his mouth. That kiss from last night is still humming through my body.

It was supposed to be a quick kiss. A thank you for saying such nice things, but the moment my lips touched his, heat soared between us and that feeling—the one I'd been craving since I left him in Vegas—came back.

"Climb on the table." He gets up and immediately goes to a small desk that houses his supplies.

"What are you talking about? I can't get a tattoo now."

He turns back to me and lifts a brow. "I know that. Now get your ass on the table and take off your shirt. You don't want me to say it again."

I should be put off by the way he's speaking to me. Jason was manipulative and selfish. I refuse to put myself through that again.

However, the way my nipples are so hard and nearly cutting through my bra, I'm not close to angry. It also helps that Deacon's words don't have the same bite or demeaning tone that Jason's used to. Instead of overthinking it, I pull my shirt up over my head, leaving me in my bra and leggings, and climb my ass onto the table. Thank God for the privacy curtains.

Deacon sits back down on the rolling stool and rolls over to me, placing a handful of permanent markers down on his tray.

I burst into laughter.

"I'm going to give you the best two-day tattoo you've ever seen." He winks before taking the top off the black marker.

I love watching him work. His tongue hangs out slightly, his brows pinch in concentration, and his hair hangs over his forehead. He's so gorgeous.

Is that a thing? Can you say a man is gorgeous? My fingers twitch to push his hair back off his forehead.

"If you keep looking at me like that, I'm not going to finish this tattoo."

I gasp. How does he know?

"I can't help it. You look cute when you're concentrating so hard."

He looks up at me briefly before looking back down at his work. "You're just trying to get fucked."

I nearly choke on my laugh. He's so vulgar.

"What if I am?"

Okay, that came out without me thinking. The old me would have never said anything like that. Jason hated when I was too forward about sex.

However, the way Deacon eyes me, I don't think he has a problem with it.

After holding my gaze for what seems like an eternity, he shakes his head and gets back to work. He won't let me see the full tattoo and makes me promise not to look down at it. Not that I can make much out at this angle.

"Done," Deacon says.

It took a total of an hour to create the design that covers most of my left side. The tattoo starts right at the base of my left breast and moves all the way down to my hip.

Deacon holds out his hand to help me stand up. He takes me over to the body-length mirror and stands behind me. When I catch sight of the tattoo, my breath catches in my throat.

It is phenomenal. The roses, done in black and shaded to look real, look absolutely stunning. So detailed I can even see the drops of dew on the large petals and in bold calligraphy letters is the name Ace.

"What do you think?" he asks the question as his finger runs over the tail of the E on my hip.

I spin around and wrap my arms around his neck. "I love it."

He smiles, then drops a peck on my lips before pulling away.

"Get dressed, I need to feed you two."

"Good," I say, tugging my leggings back up. "I'm starving." Immediately my stomach grumbles, expressing just how hungry I am.

He smiles down at my belly and drops a hand over the swell. "Relax, Ace. Your dad's going to make sure Mommy feeds you."

He winks at me before stepping away, then grabs my shirt and hands it to me. I pull it over my head. He quickly takes my hand before heading out of the shop.

CHAPTER NINETEEN

James

Noni

My laughter rings out around our little booth. The couple at the table next to us again looks over at me and frowns. They aren't that much older than us.

The guy is very clean-cut with his square glasses and neatly trimmed beard. The female with him has those overly drawn eyebrows and a long face that reminds me of something I just can't put my finger on. I'm not saying I'm not too loud, but I can't help it.

My belly is fed and I'm here with good company. Deacon has had me dying laughing with some of his funny stories about him and his friends he has dubbed the Asshole Club. He even showed me the tattoo on his stomach they all supposedly have alike.

"Did he do it?"

"Fuck yeah, he did it." He laughs. "Next thing we know Pit's naked ass is running through the hotel lobby singing at the top of his lungs."

I laugh so hard I have to hold my belly. Scoffing comes from my right and the couple frowns at me again.

"We got kicked out of the lodge and told to never come back."

"Oh, my goodness, I bet that was hilarious."

He shakes his head. "It's always some shit when me and the gang get together."

"I would love to meet them. They sound so fun."

He smiles over at me but doesn't reply. I realize I just made a very personal request. Most people only take girls they're serious about around their friends and family and here I am, just getting to know him and already I'm requesting to meet his friends.

Before I can correct myself, he shrugs and says, "You will."

I try to fight the blush that covers my face, but it's no use. I've enjoyed everything about today, from watching him work to talking over Mexican food. All of it has been the best first date I've ever had.

"But I'm warning you, if you think the guys are bad, you haven't seen anything yet. Skittles is a fucking terrorist. She got mad at me once and superglued my balls to my thigh while I was asleep. I had to go to the ER to get them unstuck."

I throw my head back and laugh.

"Hey, enough," the dark-haired man at the other table says, slamming his hand down. "Do you mind keeping it down, my wife and I are trying to have a peaceful lunch."

I hold up my hand, ready to apologize.

"What the fuck did you just say to her?"

Turning to Deacon, I try to calm him down. "It's okay. I'll be a little quieter."

He cuts his eyes to me in warning before turning back to the couple.

"She's being unnecessarily loud, disrupting the peace," the guy says boldly.

I wouldn't say I've been that loud. No one else seems the slightest bit disturbed.

"So is your wife's long-ass horse face, but I didn't call her out on it."

I will hate myself for it later, but I can't help it, I burst out laughing. That's exactly what she looks like.

"How dare you," the woman says.

"Buddy, you are way out of line."

At this, Deacon laughs. "Out of line would have been if I threw carrots at her ass like I started to do when I walked in."

I cover my mouth, fighting off my laughter.

"You know what. We don't have to take this. Let's go, darling." The man tosses his napkin on the table and shoots up from his seat. He grabs the lady's hand and pulls her up.

"That's right. Gallop her ass on out of here."

"Deacon," I half scold as we watch the couple leave.

He looks at me and shrugs. "What? You know I was right. I should have asked her how much it cost for a ride."

I shake my head, still laughing. "You're so mean."

He grabs my hand on top of the table and squeezes. "He better be glad all I did was call his girl ugly. I wanted to fuck him up for talking to you that way, but I refrained."

I duck my head, hiding my blush. Jason has never stood up for me like that. He probably would have agreed with the guy. It feels good to have a guy in my life that has my back.

"Well, thank you for protecting me, kind sir."

Heat blazes in his eyes that cause the smile to fall from my face and my thighs to tighten. When his tongue rolls over his bottom lip, my body feels like it's about to melt into the chair.

"Sir? I think I like that coming from your pretty lips."

There goes my blush, heating my face again. This time when I duck my head, I'm forced to lift it again when a man calls out the name Titus. I wouldn't have thought anything of it, but the way Deacon stiffens at either the name or the voice is alarming.

I look up into the face of an older guy, maybe in his late fifties. However, if there was ever a poster model for a sugar daddy, this guy would be it. A headful of thick salt and pepper hair that is shaved low on the sides.

I think they call the look a fauxhawk. Thick black eyebrows sit low over blue eyes and a nose that's only slightly too big make up his handsome features. A full, well-trimmed beard and mustache add to his appeal.

He's built like a man who spends plenty of time working out, but he has that rugged swag like his muscles were obtained from lifting heavy logs or something. His black T-shirt is molded to his body, showing off his muscles. He's a very attractive man, and the genuine smile on his face makes him even more appealing.

"You going to introduce us?" the man says without taking his eyes off me.

"Noni, this is my… adoptive father."

"How's it going?" he says, reaching out a hand toward me. "I'm James, James Griffin."

I shake the hand he holds out to me. "Noni Scott."

He drops his eyes to my belly and then back to my face, and the smile spreads wider. "You're the one carrying my grandson?"

I place my hand on my belly and smile. "Yes, but just like I've told your son, it could be a girl," I say, giving Deacon a pointed look.

"Damn, I didn't even consider that," James says, rubbing his chin. He turns to Deacon. "Are we ready for that?"

Deacon snorts. "Are they ready for it?" I have no idea what they're talking about.

James laughs and pats Deacon on the back.

"What are you doing here, Griff… uh, James?"

Despite the cover-up, I don't miss the fact that Deacon was about to call him another name.

James nonchalantly lifts a shoulder. "Same as you, I'm on a date."

Deacon's mouth drops open. "A date? With who?"

"Mind your business, kid." He retorts and I chuckle.

"Well, Noni, it was nice meeting you and finally laying eyes on the beauty that's giving me my first grandchild." He lifts my hand and places it to his lips for a quick kiss before releasing it.

"It was nice meeting you too." I smile.

James nods before turning to Deacon. "I'll see you tonight?" The clenching of Deacon's jaw leads me to believe whatever they're supposed to be meeting for, he isn't a fan of it.

Deacon nods and that seems to be enough for James. He tells me goodbye once more and then walks away. I wait until he's completely out the door before I turn back to Deacon.

"He's nice."

"Yeah, he is. He took a poor homeless kid in and gave him a family when no one else would." His face softens as he rubs his arm.

"That's amazing. Sounds like he means a lot to you."

I watch a smile break across his face, softening his features even more. "He's the only father I've ever known. I'd do anything for him."

I envy their relationship. I wish I had that growing up. "I bet he was fun to grow up with too."

"You have no idea." He shakes his head and laughs. "Let's head out. We need to stop and get you a few things before we head back to my place."

Deacon stands and holds out a hand for me. We had already paid and tipped our waitress, so we were free to go.

"What few things?" I ask as I climb out of the booth.

He rocks back on his heels and lifts his lips in a smug smile.

"Things you will need to spend the night. Remember what you said during your tattoo?"

My mouth drops open and I nod.

"Yeah, well your ass is about to get fucked tonight."

The elation that runs through my body and heats my blood makes me smile hard like an idiot. It's been so long. The many nights of trying to please myself has only slightly sated my desire. I need this just as much as I need my prenatal vitamins.

I don't argue when he tugs my hand and heads back out to my car. My excitement is building, the butterflies in my stomach are swarming. Finally, I'll get what I've been craving since that one night in Vegas.

CHAPTER TWENTY

Home

Deacon

I tried it. I gave it a good run, but I can't go another fucking second without being buried inside her. Noni is beautiful.

That dark rich skin that looks like there's sunshine beneath it, those full pouty lips, and button nose.

However, looking at her all day, her stomach round with my kid is a fucking turn-on. How the hell do men get anything done when their girlfriends or wives are pregnant? My cock goes hard the moment she does anything.

He was about to pull a Hulk through my jeans while I was drawing her tattoo. Just pretending to mark her skin with my design had me hard as granite. My plan tonight is to put us both out of our misery.

I pull my bike up to my cabin. I wish I could be in the car with her when she sees my home. The three thousand square foot home is settled on ten acres of secluded land. It's the closest I could get to my tree house in the woods.

The entire front of the house is made up of triangular-shaped thick glass. It's three stories, four bedrooms, a fully done basement with a bonus bedroom, and five baths. I designed the entire build from the stone and wood for the foundation to the placements of the furniture. Even the circular flagstone driveway with a fire pit and gazebo out front were all my ideas.

I left the chop shop business with a pretty sizable bank account. I tripled it with my tattoo shops. Like I said, I ain't a billionaire, but I do damn good.

I pull my bike into my garage, and she pulls her KIA up beside me. By the time I climb off my bike, she's out of her car.

"Oh, my goodness, Deacon, your home is gorgeous. Did you design this?"

Damn if her admiration doesn't have me feeling as tall as this house.

"Yeah, I had a hand in it," I say as humbly as I can.

"Is this the tree house you dreamed of when you were a kid?"

My cheeks hurt from the wide smile on my face. She remembers. "Not even close. I made some big boy improvements to it."

She tosses her head back and laughs. My sights are trained on the column of her neck. I have a lot of dirty plans for that damn neck.

"Come on, let me give you a tour. I'll come back and get your bags."

I reach for her hand and she places hers in mine. We head into the house. I kick off my boots in the mudroom and she takes off her tennis shoes. I give her a quick tour before showing her the master bathroom.

"If you want to shower and freshen up, the towels are in the linen closet and I'll head out now to get the things we picked up."

Her gaze bounces around the large bathroom, taking in the travertine tile I used for the floors and walls. Once we start toward the bedroom, I notice she hasn't been able to make eye contact with me. Just like now.

I take a step closer to her and wait for her to turn to me. When I get tired of waiting, I lift her chin and turn her head to me.

"What's wrong?"

"Nothing," she answers quickly, a little too quickly.

I arch one eyebrow in disbelief. She shuts her eyes on an exhale.

"I'm nervous."

"About?"

She opens her eyes and slumps. Yes, I'm going to make her say it out loud. My dick is too hard, taking all the blood from my brain at the moment, so I can't try to decipher her feelings. She wants something, she's going to have to say it.

"If you don't want to do this," I say, taking a step back. "Just say it. We can go as slow as you want." I would need a cold-ass shower, but I had no problems lying down with her and just holding her like I did last night.

"It's not that I don't want to do it. It's just that things have changed."

"What things?" We were in agreement about things when we left the store. What has changed since then?

"Remember that slim and trim body I had in Vegas?" She doesn't give me time to respond. "Well, Ace has taken certain liberties and spread things around. I'm not—"

I cut off her bullshit rant with a kiss that has my hand on that luscious ass of hers, squeezing it. Noni moans in my mouth. She brings her fingers up to grip my hair. I don't even remember moving, but eventually, her back is pressed to the shower door and the hand I had been using to grab her ass now has one of her legs pressed against my hip.

The ringing of my phone is the only thing that pulls me out of the lustful haze that almost has me fucking her up against my shower door. I let go of her leg and her foot drops back to the floor. With panting breaths, I step away from her. We both watch the other. I wait for any sign that I should ignore this phone call and get back to what we were doing.

"Get in the shower. When you come out, I want you naked. I want to admire your body all night."

Without listening for her rebuttal, I turn around, putting distance between us before I forget my plans and bend her over my sink. As soon as I'm far enough away, I pull out my phone and return Griff's call.

"Hey, what time are you getting here tonight?" he says the moment he answers the phone, in normal Griff fashion.

"I'm not coming tonight," I reply quickly as I slip back out of the house into the garage.

"What do you mean, you aren't coming tonight, Titus? We have a tight schedule and we're already behind."

"Yeah, I fucking know that. And don't come at me like that, if it wasn't for me, you would be a lot further behind than you are now."

"All right, you're right," he concedes. "But still, we can't take nights off anymore."

"Look, after that shit last night I need a break."

There's a pause on the other end of the phone.

"You sure this is about last night, or is it a certain chocolate beauty?" I run my hands through my hair, pushing the piece that falls over my forehead back.

"It's one and the same. I have a real shot here."

"A real shot at what? Is this about the kid or her?"

"Both, damn it." My voice raises, and I exhale before starting the conversation back. "It's about my new plan."

"In this new plan," he starts. "Did you factor in her fiancé? Last time I checked she was engaged."

"Not since yesterday."

He pauses for a long time. "Titus, I need you to be careful with this. It's one thing to stay friends with this chick so you can stay in your kid's life, but this is dangerous."

"I'm not a fucking teenager, Griff."

"Then stop acting like one and start thinking with something other than your dick. You're nothing more than a temporary fantasy for this girl. Her one walk on the wild side before she tosses you to the side for her suit and tie fiancé."

I don't let on how those words dig into me like talons. Noni isn't my first good girl. I've had quite a few of those.

The girls who only want to sample the wild bad boy side just to say they've had it. In the past, I had no issues with it because I wasn't trying to play anyone's boyfriend, but it's different now. She makes me want different.

"You don't fucking know her."

"I'm an old man, kid and I've been around the block a time or two. I don't have to know her. I know her type."

"And what's her type?"

"Not men like us," he replies. "I know you, because I raised you. We aren't the types to take home to meet the parents. Hell, we aren't even the marriage and family type. Trust me on this. Whatever you think is about to happen isn't. This isn't a fucking fairy tale."

"I know that," I nearly yell into the phone.

"Then wake the fuck up."

That silence finds itself in our conversation again.

"Look," he speaks. "I have to go. The crew is here, and we have shit to do. You can stay home and play temporary husband until she kicks your ass to the curb."

The line goes dead, and I place the phone in my back pocket. I lean against the door of Noni's car. My thoughts are racing and I'm not in a good headspace.

By the time I walk back into the house, an hour has passed. I don't imagine Noni is still in the shower waiting for her soaps and things. I place the bag down on my sofa before heading into the bedroom.

The house is dark and quiet. For a moment, I think maybe she has fallen asleep. I'm not that fucking lucky.

She's sitting on the side of the bed, wearing one of my old T-shirts. Her hair is in a large puff at the top of her head like a crown. Her hands are under her thighs and her toes barely touch the floor.

When she looks up at me, her big brown eyes flare with anger and hurt.

"Where've you been?"

"Took a walk to clear my head."

"Just a walk?"

She leans back, narrowing her eyes. I don't answer. It's obvious she's already sent me to trial and found me guilty of something. My silence draws her ire even more.

"Who were you talking to?"

So that's what this is about. Damn, how much did she hear?

"You eavesdropping on me?"

She looks over at me for a moment, neither of us speak. She then gets up and reaches for her leggings that I notice are on the side of the bed.

"I'm sorry I interrupted your night. By all means go to whoever the hell you had planned to be with tonight."

The curse sounds funny coming from her mouth, but I don't point that out because now isn't the time. I walk further into the room and reach out to halt her hasty dressing. She snatches her arm away from me.

"Who were you talking to? And don't lie to me, I saw you on the phone. I couldn't get the water to turn on, so I went looking for you and saw you."

"All right," I say, holding my hands up in surrender. "I was on the phone with my pops."

The truth knocks some of the wind out of her sails. She softens only slightly. The tightness in her expression is still there though.

"Well, what happened? When you left out you were fine, but all of a sudden you go missing for an hour?"

The good part is that I enjoy seeing this Noni. The outspoken one who's speaking her mind, the bad part is it's me she's standing up to.

I exhale then take a seat on the edge of the bed she just vacated. I didn't plan on the night taking this heavy a turn. I had planned to dick her down all fucking night, not argue and hash out our feelings.

"Is your mom right, am I just some passing phase for you?"

She goes completely still. She knew I saw the one message when her mother called her an ungrateful and useless bitch. I was livid about the text and had to force myself to calm down.

However, she didn't know I'd seen the one after where her mother told her she was obviously going through another phase. It's that message that made what Griff said feel like talons digging into my skin. It's plagued my mind all day.

"Of course not," her words are spoken softly.

"I'm supposed to believe that when just yesterday you gave your ring back to the man you've been with for six years?"

"Off and on," she clarifies like that's supposed to matter.

"Six years," I reiterate. "And now you're here ready to move on?"

"We talked about this last night. I told you I'm ready." She takes a step toward me. "Why are you acting like this?"

"Because in Vegas you ran out of my room so fucking fast the next morning, I thought you were going to hurt yourself. You wouldn't even let me walk you back to your suite. I'm guessing you didn't want to be seen with your bad decision. I'm fine with that, but now you want me to believe you're here because you want to be with me."

"Yes. And last night we were on the same page."

I shake my head. I'm done with the fucking lies, I had no problem being a chick's bad idea for a night, but I'm not going to play bullshit games. I won't risk my relationship with Ace, not even for Noni.

"Why are you here, Noni?"

She tilts her head back slightly and frowns. "You know why I'm here."

"Oh, that's right," I say, pushing my hair off my forehead and standing. "You're just here to get fucked."

I prowl toward her, my sights set on her. She slinks back from me. Not paying attention to where she's going, she backs herself right into the closed bathroom door. I take advantage of her situation, placing my hand by her head and caging her in.

"You want me to have that tight little pussy purring for days, just like I did in Vegas. Want me to have you coming so many times you'll beg me to stop again."

I drop my right hand to her shoulder and make a trail down the front of her shirt with my finger to graze her small, hardened nipple. She closes her eyes, and her bottom lip gets sucked in between her teeth.

With my finger, I find her bare thighs, right where the hem of my shirt hits. I push the fabric up her legs, feeling the trail of goose bumps as I go. The heat coming from her bare pussy damn near singes my fingers.

My dick is at full mast. I could knock a hole in the side of a ship with this damn thing. And it pisses me off further.

She doesn't get to use me. She doesn't get to treat me like I'm nothing more than a passing trend. Like I'm trash to throw away when she gets good and damn tired of it.

I fist the thick, soft curls in her hair and tilt her head back with more force than I should.

"Deacon," she purrs my name.

"This is what you want, right?" I snarl while taking a step closer, bringing our bodies to the point they're nearly touching.

With my knee, I knock at her legs, separating them, allowing my fingers to find the sticky residue on her thighs. I falter just a second. Having physical proof of how fucking bad she wants me—and this time she's sober—makes me reconsider.

The thought of fucking her into a coma and kicking her ass out doesn't seem like the best idea at the moment. She moans and calls my name. I remember again that she's using me.

I plunge my fingers forward, finding her opening. She gasps when I slip inside. I want to fucking explode from the death grip she has on me.

Noni releases a breath again as I use my fingers to fuck her while my thumb strums against her little pearl. She grinds her hips to the rhythm of my pace. I meant to only mess with her, prove to her I'm not some fucking toy to play with, but damn.

Having her right here, her head yanked back by the fist in her hair, her eyes shut tight, mouth wide open, panting and moaning. Her chest rises and falls rapidly as one hand wraps around the wrist between her legs and the other on my chest. It's the most beautiful sight I've ever seen, and just knowing that adds fuel to my fire. I tug her hair a little harder, exposing the neck I've wanted to mark up since that day I saw her in the diner.

"Deacon, wait," she cries out and I can feel the beginning spasms of her orgasm.

"You're almost there, Noni. I can feel it. Isn't this what you want? Just this, right? Nothing else. I'm no other fucking use to you."

This sobers her and the hand on my chest that was once fisting my shirt, now pushes me away.

"Not like this, please."

The sound of her whimpered plea makes me pull out of her so fast I stumble back, away from her. I turn my back to her tears. I feel like rocks have landed in my gut as my fingers open and close to calm me. I can't look at her. The only noise in the room is the sound of her sniffling and that only adds to the remorse I'm feeling.

"It's late," I start, looking over my left shoulder but not at her. "Stay the night, I'll sleep in the living room."

"Butterflies," she says the word so soft I have to turn to face her just to hear it. She's sitting down on the floor, her face in her hands and her legs crossed like a kindergartner.

"What?"

"From the moment I saw you at that club, that's what I felt." She drops her hands from her face but doesn't look up from her lap. "Porsha talked about them all the time when she met Marcus. I thought she was lying.

"I'd never felt them before. Not even when I first met Jason. At first, I explained it away as the alcohol playing tricks on me."

She lifts her shoulder briefly. "Only the feeling never left. Even when I was sober those butterflies never stopped."

She goes silent again, but I don't speak. I don't invade this moment. I allow her to get her thoughts together.

"When I rushed out of your room that morning it wasn't because I was ashamed of you, it was because I wanted to keep the butterflies."

"You're not making any sense," I say, shaking my head.

"In Vegas I was a different person. I laughed, flirted, and tried things I've never done before. That's the girl you asked to dance. The one you invited back to your room and made feel as if she could breathe for once in her life."

She wipes at her face, interrupting the track of tears on her cheeks. "If I'd stayed any longer, you were going to realize it wasn't the real me. The real Noni never lives. She overthinks, tries too hard, doesn't speak her mind and she suffocates herself every day just to please those around her."

The laugh that comes from her lacks humor. "If you would have met the real Noni, you would have taken away the butterflies. You would have looked at me the way everyone else does."

"Do you feel them now?"

At last, she looks up into my eyes. "Yes. Even more now."

I walk over to where she's seated and squat down in front of her. "For the last eight weeks, have I gotten to know the real you?"

"That's the thing, for so long, I don't think I was the real me. I felt trapped, caged even. I'm the most free when I'm with the girls, but I'm still not myself.

"It's like I'm squeezed inside a tight box, but then you came along and told me to tell you what I wanted. That's the most power I've been given in my entire life. When I'm with you, I feel like I can stretch out and be free."

"The woman that I met when I walked in this room, the one that was ready to hand me my ass, that's the Noni I want. The other one was the fake one."

She laughs and this time it's real.

"I won't lie like I have this figured out. I'm out of my comfort zone, but I'm here because I want to be, and it isn't because of this baby." She cups her hand to her belly. "This isn't a phase for me and I'm sorry my mom made you think it is."

I plop down on my ass across from her and pull at her leg to make her stretch out her feet toward me. I place one foot in my lap and start to slowly knead her arch.

"It wasn't just your mom. I already had some doubts."

"And let me guess, that phone call didn't help?" She observes me silently, not needing an answer to verify what she knows.

I shrug. "Yeah, it might have caused some doubts."

She rolls her eyes. "You're not the only one with doubts."

"What? What doubts do you have?"

She scoffs. "Like what happens when you get tired of this life? When the mundane kicks in and you'd rather be free and wild than stuck at home with me and a baby?"

The playfulness she starts off with disappears. Her brow creases and she takes in a deep breath before continuing. "What's to keep you from walking out that door when you realize we aren't enough for you?"

It's at this moment, I realize this has to do with her issue with her father. Just looking in her eyes tells me she's terrified of this scenario.

"Look at me," I demand when she cuts her eyes away from me.

I release her foot and slide closer to her, placing her legs on top of mine as we sit face-to-face. "Just like you, I can't promise you forever. All this is new to me, but here's what I can guarantee you. Never will I walk away from this child."

I place my hand, palm down, on top of her small belly. She runs her fingers through the front of my hair, pushing it off my forehead.

"I want this, Noni."

Her gaze connects with mine. "I want it too."

"Then from here on out, we keep the other shit out. All right?"

"All right."

"Come here." I tug her up and pull her down to straddle my lap. I cup her rounded ass in my hands as I pull her snug to me. "I'm sorry about earlier." I place a kiss at the base of her neck. "Do you forgive me?"

"Yes," her reply is nearly a whimper as I continue to lavish kisses all over her throat.

I swirl my tongue along the vein at the side of her neck before dropping a soft kiss there. My name slips off her lips and her hands find their way under my shirt. Her blunt little nails rake over my abs.

Finding the hem of her shirt, I pull it up and over her head, tossing the fabric across the room. I stop to take in her body. Her small breasts are tipped with blackberry-sized nipples.

That gorgeous fucking skin is on display, but the sexiest thing has to be staring at her small belly. I lean up, swallowing the little space between us as I take her lips. Parting hers with my tongue to taste her flavor.

I plunder her mouth, allowing my tongue to twirl and brush against hers. I dominate the kiss, claiming her warm cavern as mine. When I pull away, she's panting.

I lift my shirt over my head and toss it to the floor. I want to feel her skin against mine. I find her lips again, this time cupping one breast in my hand and flicking the puckered tip with my tongue.

She grinds down on my lap. The front of my pants gets soaking wet. Her head is tossed back, and her eyes are closed. I grip her ass, squeezing the plentiful flesh before I find the seam down the middle.

I slide my fingers further down, the slippery wetness leading me to my desired location. Her pussy lips are fat and spread open. I slip my digits through them before her heat engulfs me in her tight, hot box.

She purrs when I thrust inside. Her hips swirl around my digits.

"Fuck, baby, your shit's so wet," I say around her nipple.

She's soaking me like a fucking ocean. I release her breast from my mouth and kiss her chin. "Take me out."

She didn't have much work to do, my cock has damn near ripped a hole through these jeans. Noni raises up just a little to undo my pants. I slip my fingers out of her tight little cunt to rub over her engorged clit from behind.

I place my hand at the back of her neck and pull her mouth down to mine. She finishes undressing me with her eyes closed as I devour her lips. Once she has my pants undone, she gently pulls me out. The precum smears against my stomach right above my navel. I release her ass to hold my cock up for her to sit down on.

"Deacon, you know I can't do that. We tried, it's too big, remember?"

Yeah, I remember that shit, but tonight I'm making this pussy mine. That means I need to stretch it to be custom made for my cock.

"Yes, you can. Take your time, make that shit fit for me."

Her lip rolls between her teeth and her brow furrows. She places her hands on my shoulders as she slowly lowers to the head of my shaft. The heat nearly makes me burst all over her.

Slowly, I split her lips wide as she lowers down. She whimpers at the tight fit but like a soldier, she continues her descent. I grit my teeth and strain against how good this feels. Like a hot velvet glove sliding down my length.

"Oh gosh. Oh gosh," she cries out as she continues to lower. "That's it. Keep going."

As soon as she seats herself, I'm ready to bathe her walls in my seed, but I'm trying to do my best to hang in there.

In Vegas we used condoms. Even despite the broken condom incident, I didn't get to fully enjoy being inside her without a barrier. This is like heaven.

"Baby, you're killing me. You got to move up there."

She rolls her hips tentatively. I growl at the pleasure that rips up my spine.

"Did I hurt you? Do I need to move faster?"

"Hey," I say, capturing her face between my hands. "You're in control tonight. I want you to go as fast or slow as you want."

She smiles down at me, spreading those plush bow-shaped lips. She rolls her hips forward so agonizingly slow; I have to fist my hands at her hips to keep from slamming her down. I mean, what I said. I want her to take control tonight.

She sets the pace, riding my dick like she's trying to tame a rodeo bull.

"Baby, this pussy is amazing."

She has no idea. The fucking promised land is buried inside this pussy. When she starts to twirl her hips like she's hula dancing, I drop my forehead forward and it lands on her chest.

Our bodies are sweaty, our breaths are labored, but we're in no rush. She continues her slow grind. Her cries and whimpers grow louder.

As bad as I want to thrust up, flip her over and fuck her into this carpet, I don't. I let her keep her slow pace, but the slow grind and this superb pussy have me clenching my teeth and fisting my hands. She does something with her hips that makes me punch the floor beneath us.

The sound is loud, breaking into our moans and pants. I know when she starts repeating the word, please, she's near her release. I need her to come. I've been holding off from the moment my fingers were in her earlier.

"That's it, take from me all you need. Come for daddy."

I don't know why that comes out. When the fuck did I start wanting someone to call me daddy? I have no clue, but it feels right in the moment.

Her blunt nails dig into my shoulder. She bucks her hips on my cock and drops her head back, letting out a scream as she shatters all around me. And it couldn't have happened at a better time, because I just lost my fucking battle. My nut shoots out of me like water out of a damn hosepipe.

We both end up panting, sweaty and exhausted. I lift from the floor, standing her up with me. I fall from her tight fit. Walking her over to my bed, I pull the covers back and help her in.

"But we're all sweaty. I don't want to mess up your sheets."

"It's all good, besides no need for us to shower. I'll be right back inside you in about an hour, so rest up."

She laughs, but she doesn't complain. I fully undress, climb in behind her, and cover our bodies. Placing a kiss on her shoulder, I pull her into my chest and then rest my hand on my son. I fall asleep feeling like a motherfucking king.

CHAPTER TWENTY-ONE

Call to Service

Deacon

I laugh out loud at the inappropriate joke Mav just made.

"What the hell do you know about Black girl pussy?"

He shrugs. "All I know is, since she came along you've been a lot less of an asshole."

"I don't usually do this," Pat says, stopping in front of me with an armful of paper towel rolls. "But Mav has a point. You have been in a better mood."

"It's that Black girl magic. That shit is serious," Money Mike says. "Before long you'll be talking about oiling her scalp and asking me if I brought some shea butter to work. That Lubriderm y'all be using ain't shit compared to some shea butter."

I let out another laugh. I actually know everything he's talking about. Noni hasn't asked me to oil her scalp yet, but I have been with her on wash days, and I've seen her oiling her scalp and shea butter is the shit.

"Shut up, Mike. I've used shea butter before. It's not just an African American thing," Chloe says, rolling her eyes at Mike over her customer's back.

"I bet you used it wrong. Probably put it in some dry ass potato salad or something."

"You love my potato salad," She teases before shooting him the bird. I laugh again.

"Look, nothing has changed with me. I'm the same man."

Incredulous expressions stare back at me. I don't blame them. My head has been in the clouds lately. For four weeks, Noni and I have been going steady.

We've been taking turns at each other's place. One week we're at her condo and the next we're at my cabin. It's crazy how in the past that shit would have sent me running for the hills, but not with Noni.

We spend our days laughing, watching stupid shit on TV, talking about everything from the weather pattern to our future. And at night, I rock her body to sleep. Not once has she suffered with insomnia.

And the best part, her sex drive rivals mine. I'm happier than I've ever been and more terrified too. This is new territory for me and I'm more than positive this won't last. It never does for me.

My phone goes off in my pocket and I slide it out to look down at the screen. It's another call from Griff. I send it to voicemail before placing it back in my pocket.

I haven't been back to help him since that phone conversation. Part of me knows I'm being selfish, leaving him out to dry, but another part of me says fuck it. What I got right now, it means too much and I'm not trying to lose it. Not for anything.

"Speaking of your better half," Karly says, getting my attention. "Isn't that her outside? Does she know those guys?"

I walk toward the door before she can finish that last sentence. The scene before me makes me fume. Noni is standing at the trunk of her car with two bags in her hands, Chris is in front of her, and the pup is leaning against her car with one hand propped up caging her in.

I push the doors to the shop open, causing the bell to chime as I march over to them.

"I'm here to see my boyfriend," I hear Noni explaining. She tries to move away when the pup reaches out to stop her.

"Can I touch your belly?"

His hand is on her stomach before she can answer. I snarl as I walk up on him and snatch his hand away from her and shove him so hard he falls in Chris's arms. I glance at a startled Noni before facing the other two.

"Noni, go inside."

"Is everything okay?" I don't turn, not even for the concern in her voice.

"Oh, everything is fine, gorgeous. We're just catching up with our old colleague."

I'm going to kill this damn kid.

"Noni, inside."

The command comes out harsher than I want it to, but I'm too fucking pissed to be gentle. I don't see her, but I hear her retreat into the shop. Both Chris and the pup's gaze follow her.

"Yo, Titus, man, that bitch is fine."

My fist flies into his face, followed by the sound of bone crunching. The kid crumbles to the ground with a cry. As many times as I've had this kid on his ass, he should know to keep his mouth shut around me.

"Fuck, Titus. I think you broke my damn nose."

"You have to be the dumbest motherfucker alive," I snarl down at him. I catch Chris out of the corner of my eyes. It's always these dumbasses.

"We didn't mean no harm," Chris pleas.

He looks like he wants to help his friend, but he has enough sense to know I'm in a mood to fuck someone up right now. Pup is still on the ground rolling around. I kick him in the ass, causing him to cry out again.

"You approached my girl, you meant something."

"She was just here when we pulled up. Mad Dog remembered her from that day at the diner and wanted to say, hey. I swear man, we didn't come to start any problems."

Leashing my anger, I put my attention on Chris.

"Get the fuck out of here and don't come back."

I turn to head back inside. I know I'm going to have some explaining to do. I prayed my past would never come across Noni.

I hadn't even wanted her to meet Griff as soon as she did. I want to keep all that stuff away from her. I don't want her or Ace to ever know Titus or the shit he has done.

"Wait," Chris says, grabbing my attention. I turn back and Pup is off the ground. His hand covers his nose, but blood is pouring from underneath.

"I know you and Griff are beefing, but he needs you. He's not doing well."

"He's a grown man."

"His drinking has gotten out of hand," Chris explains.

"Out of hand is an understatement. He's never fucking sober anymore," the pup says, sounding like his nose is stopped up.

For a split second concern clouds my thoughts. Griff has been known for his drunken bets, hell, it's because of that we're in this fucked-up situation. However, his ass can keep it together long enough to run his business.

I shake my head. They were pulling me back into it and I wasn't ready to go back just yet.

"Not my problem." I cross my hands over my chest.

"What the fuck?" the pup says in disbelief. "I thought that was your dad. What kind of shit is that? I'm a fuckup, but I'd never do my old man like that. Especially not for some—"

"Come on, Dog," Chris says, interrupting his friend from saying something that will get him killed.

I watch them crawl into their truck and drive away. I don't turn back for the building until I know they're gone. My entire staff and one client scatter from the door like roaches when the lights come on.

I head back into the shop. Everyone pretends they're busy when I enter. I eye them all with a grin on my face.

The moment I enter the office, I spot Noni. She's sitting on the couch, one knee tucked under her. She twists her hands in her lap and her brows are pinched in concentration.

When she notices me at the door, she turns to look at me, but doesn't get up off the couch. I close the door behind me and lock it.

"You make a habit of letting strange men touch my son?"

I'm hoping that little comment will wipe that glimmer of anger off her face.

"I don't always expect to be stopped by baby gangsters."

Damn, I'd laugh at that if she wasn't mad at me.

"Well, for future purposes, I don't like people touching my girl or my Ace." I make my way over to my desk. I take a seat in my chair, keeping my eyes on her the entire time. "What brings you all the way over here? I thought I was coming to you tonight?"

She lifts one of those arched brows she spends thirty minutes in the morning shading in.

"Are we going to talk about what happened?"

"No."

"Deacon," she hisses through clenched teeth.

"Noni, I didn't mean to yell at you. I was pissed off that fucker thought it was okay to touch you."

"I'm not talking about that."

Shit, I was hoping that's what she's pissed at. That I can explain away and fix.

"Why did he call you a colleague?"

"He called me an old colleague," I joke.

She doesn't find it amusing. Her lips dip on the corners into a frown as she shakes her head. I exhale and drop my shoulders.

"I used to hang with a rough crowd. I wasn't always an upstanding citizen, Noni. But that shit is behind me. I've been out of that lifestyle for years. Those guys are old news."

This isn't the first time I lied to her. I wasn't exactly truthful with her with my plan to give up my rights. However, this one feels different. This is me blatantly lying to her.

"You promise?"

Her drawn eyebrows and pursed lips give way to her concern. She's not built for that life. If she knew the shit I was still tied to, she would run for the hills. Thankfully, I know how to keep that part of me separate. I pray like hell I don't regret this lie to Noni.

"I promise, baby. It's all in my past." Her sigh of relief makes the lie that much worse. "Now answer my question, what brings you to the shop today?"

She stands and picks up a bag on the floor. Her smile is blinding. I already know this has something to do with Ace.

"I was just in the mall to grab some more shoes and I walked by this store that had baby onesies."

She places the bag on my desk and stands between my legs. I've gotten in the habit of touching her belly every chance I get. Like right now, while she's talking to me, I place a hand over her six months pregnant belly.

She pulls a tiny onesie out of her bag and holds it up. My mouth drops open and I take the tiny shirt out of her hand.

"It's a baby onesie with tattoo sleeves," she says chipperly. "Since Ace will be biracial, I went with the tan color for the arms. But I have a few of them in all sizes. And look at this one," she's still talking, but I can't take my eyes off of the little shirt in my hand.

It's cute, with the colorful fake designs on the sleeve, but it isn't just the style that has me speechless. It's the first thing we've bought for Ace. She and I both wanted to wait until after the baby shower.

I know he's coming. I have felt him kick a thousand times. I've watched her stomach grow with him inside her.

I've even seen him in the picture I have tucked in my wallet. However, there is something different about holding this tiny little piece of fabric in my hands. Not only are all those reasons why this is such a big deal, but the first thing she buys our kid is a representation of me.

"Do you like it?"

I look up at the sound of her voice, taking my gaze off the little shirt. She's holding up another one, made similar to the one in my hand, but this time *tatted like my dad* is written on the front. I place the shirt down on the desk and stand.

"You don't like it?" she asks when I snatch the shirt out of her hands without replying.

I grab her by the neck and pull her into me for a feverish kiss. She whimpers into my mouth and digs her fingers into the hair at the back of my head. I turn her toward my desk, pushing everything to the side.

Pulling away from her kiss, I tell her, "Climb on."

Her eyes widen and she looks to the door. "We can't."

"Don't make me tell you twice."

For only a second, doubt and defiance flickers across her features. Then it disappears before she hikes up her sundress and takes a seat on the edge of my desk. I stand between her legs, cupping her face with my hand.

She has on one of her wigs today. The straight strands fall to her mid back. She's sexy in everything, but I love it when her natural curls are out. She's so fucking beautiful, it's hard to believe she's mine.

I seal my mouth to hers again as I taste her, enjoying the play of our tongues. Her soft lips feel like pillows against mine. My kiss works to distract her as I push her legs further apart. I take my seat back in my chair, coming eye level with my favorite meal.

"Deacon," she purrs my name as I move her dress even further up, exposing her little panties.

I slide the tiny hindrances down. She lifts slightly, allowing me to work them below her ass and down her thighs. She drops back on the desk when I lift her legs up and slide the fabric completely off, quickly placing them in my pocket for safekeeping.

Gently, I bring her legs back down, allowing them to hang off the table. A smile comes to my lips as I see her little botched shaving job. She's complained it's getting harder to shave since she can no longer see the coarse hair between her legs.

I run my thumb over her labia, splitting them apart, coating my finger with her essence. She hisses and tries to close her knees, but my head keeps her from blocking me out. My mouth waters at her sweet aroma. Dipping my thumb into her hot sex, I elicit a moan.

"Shh, you make a sound, they'll know," I taunt.

I don't give a shit who knows what I'm doing to my girl. As long as none of them can see her, I can't care less what they hear. I watch my finger disappear inside of her hungry pussy.

That creamy sound tells me she's well lubricated for me and has my dick hard as fuck. I squeeze her clit between my two fingers and continue to fuck her with my thumb. She moans, but quickly places both hands over her mouth.

I can't wait any longer. I suck her clit into my mouth. Her body arches off the desk. In response, I place one hand over her belly to keep her still.

This feeling, it's like I'm a damn king between her legs with how responsive she is. I roll over her little pearl with my tongue. Removing my thumb out of her pussy, I then seamlessly replace it with my two longest fingers, curving them up like I'm beckoning her to me. She creams all over my digits.

I take turns between sucking her clit and flicking it with my tongue, all the while my fingers do what my dick is begging to do. Her muffled cries grow louder. Her knees squeeze around my head, but I don't relent because I want her coming into my mouth so bad, I can already taste it.

I remove my fingers from her pussy to dip my tongue into her little cavern, she locks her legs around my head and lifts her ass off the desk as she comes all in my mouth. I drink every drop, sipping until she cries out for me to stop. Then, I slip my fingers back inside of her, moving in and out to extend her orgasm.

I shoot up so fast my chair hits the wall behind me. Not once do I take my eyes off her beautiful pussy as my fingers continue to make her spasm. With one hand, I undo my belt, unbutton my pants, and remove my cock out of my boxers. I spread the precum from the tip to the base.

"Don't make a sound," I demand as I hike her leg up and dip my hips to line up with her opening. I push forward, shoving my entire length into her at once.

She screams and I smile.

"You're going to pay for that."

I move my hips like I'm fucking to save my life. Like a demon has taken over my body and is now powering my cock. I'm egged on by her moans and fueled by the way her hands claw at the desk and press against my stomach.

I lift her legs straight up, her ankles by my ears as I slam into her and hiss as she finds another release. Her pussy clenches around me, her creamy cum leaking onto my balls. I lift her hips off the desk to get a better angle.

"Deacon, Daddy, please," she cries out when I pound her into another orgasm.

That name. Hearing it come off her lips does something to me. As I release her legs and grab her throat, lifting her off the desk, I bring her mouth to mine and let her taste herself as she sucks my tongue into her mouth.

I groan against her lips and apply a little more pressure to her throat. Hiking one leg over my forearm, I plow into her. She tries to pull away and cry out, but the grip I have on her neck keeps her locked in place.

"This is my pussy, Noni." My harsh words are said pressed against her kiss-swollen lips. "Who the fuck does this little cunt belong to?"

"It's yours, Daddy, all yours."

And just like that my fate is sealed. I come hard and fucking long. For a moment, I think I might actually die by ejaculation. A sound reminiscent of a tiger's roar leaves my lips as I look up at the ceiling.

Everyone in the shop definitely knows we are fucking. Our heavy pants serenade the room as we come down from our highs. I rest my forehead against hers, taking in the scent of our spent bodies.

"So," she pants in between her words. "I'm guessing you liked the shirts."

I lift my head and look down into her exhausted eyes and start to laugh. Damn, I'm falling for this woman. I've never thought those words would come to mind.

For thirty-six years, never have I even come close to this feeling. I'm not even sure how I feel about it.

I place a kiss on her forehead and pull out of her. Holding out my hand, I help her down off the desk. Fixing her dress first before I put my dick away.

She touches my arm, drawing my attention back to her face. The look in her eyes humbles me. Shining back at me is the proof I'm not having these feelings alone.

She's falling too, but I also see the same wariness I have. I imagine her trepidation doesn't come from the same place mine does. I draw her in for another kiss for two reasons.

Number one, I can't seem to get enough of her soft lips. And number two, I'm not ready to have that conversation with her. The one her eyes tell me she's ready to have.

I don't want to jinx this. Right now, we're good. I want to keep it that way because I've lived long enough to know the world isn't kind to people like me. I'm going to fuck this up soon.

CHAPTER TWENTY-TWO

Back in the Game

Deacon

"Are you sure you're okay with coming tonight?" Noni's sultry voice says through the other end of my speakerphone. "It's late and you were working all day. I don't want you getting sleepy while on your bike."

I chuckle. "Baby, relax. I'm good. I'm wrapping up here now. I'll be at your door…" I look down at my watch, calculating the time and distance. "By eleven thirty."

I power off my laptop and close it. Standing, I grab my jacket off the back of my chair before stretching my aching muscles. I went over the books most of the day today and ordered inventory.

"Look, tomorrow is your seven-month checkup and we've already rescheduled twice due to my schedule. Nothing is keeping me from that appointment in the morning."

She sighs. "Okay, just be safe. Oh, and I have a surprise when you get here."

223

"What is it?" I ask, turning off all the lights in the building.

"It's a surprise."

"You know I don't do surprises. Unless it has to do with that sweet little pussy."

Her laughter sounds like bells chiming. "You're so vulgar."

"You love my vulgar ass," I say before I realize what I've just said.

In total, I've only known Noni for about five months. It's too soon to talk about the L word.

"Yes," her voice is barely above a whisper, but I hear it. I stand dumbstruck with my phone in my hand.

We stay that way for what feels like an eternity. The pressure of her reply weighs on me. The dumb as fuck urge to tell her I feel the same beats at my thoughts wanting to come out.

"Your surprised," she says, clearing her throat.

I realize a moment passed between us and I just fucked it up. Not able to go back to it now. I hit my forehead with the palm of my hand, feeling like an idiot.

"The crib came today. The box is outside in the garage."

With this, I stop thinking about the lost moment and lift my head. "I thought we were still undecided?"

She and I have been going back and forth over a damn crib for weeks. Noni is into the French provincial style cribs with upholstered headboards that look way too fancy for my taste. I want simple, modern, or maybe farm style.

It's only because I'm dating an interior decorator that I know what any of this shit is. I'm just happy she's including me in the decision-making. I will accept whatever she got.

For the first few months, Ace will be staying solely at her place. Then as he gets a little older and stronger, he will get to come spend time at my place. We'll pick out another crib for that. No matter where he's staying, I'll be there with him.

"What did you go with?"

"I compromised. You got your farmhouse style crib, but I get a matching upholstered changing table and chair with an ottoman, thanks to the generosity of Daddy."

I laugh at her compromise. I already told her I would foot the bill for all baby furniture. With all the lights out, I head for the front door of the shop.

"Sounds like a plan. And Noni, don't even think about touching that crib. I'll bring the stuff in when I get there."

"Yes, Daddy," she purrs through the phone.

"Now you're playing a dangerous game. It will be a bad look for you to go to the doctor full of my cum tomorrow for your checkup."

Her laughter is drowned out by the appearance of the man leaning against the black Mustang beside my bike.

"Hey, baby. I have to go. Don't wait up for me," I say before we both say goodbye.

I slide my phone back in my pocket. Giving Griff my back, I lock the door to the shop. When I turn back to him, he's still in the same spot.

"How you doing, Titus?"

I cross my arms over my chest and take him in. His clear blue eyes don't look the least bit drunk.

"I'm good. How about you?"

He shrugs, pushes up from the car and walks toward me. "Been better, but I can't complain."

Awkward silence fills the space between us, something that has never been an issue before.

"I know you're not talking to me," Griff starts. I don't correct him. "What I said the other night... Well, I was trying to look out for you."

He runs a hand down his face, his discomfort with this situation obvious. Yet, I still don't relieve his frustration.

"I know you're not my real son, Titus. I tend to forget that sometimes and I overstep."

I hold up my hand and he stops. Neither one of us are good at this apologizing shit, however, we both need to do it.

"You're my pop's, Griff," I say, lifting my shoulders to my ears then dropping them. "That shit won't change. But family falls out sometimes. The stuff you said wasn't cool and I wasn't in the right mindset to hear it, but it had merit."

He shakes his head, cutting off my words. "Does this girl make you happy?"

"Very," I reply with no thought.

"Then that's what matters. Just know if shit goes south, I'm still your old man and I got your back."

He holds his hand out for me to shake. I clutch his in mine and squeeze before pulling him forward for a one-armed hug and a pat on the back. As always, Griff and I squash our shit.

This isn't the first time we've fallen out. I did stupid shit all the time when I was a kid that caused me and him not to talk for days. I release him and we both take a step away from each other.

"I don't blame you for pulling out of this bullshit. It's getting crazy, but the boys and I are faring well."

I lift a brow and take my earlier stance. Arms folded over my chest and legs shoulder width apart.

"That's not what I hear."

He turns to look at me, taking another step back. "Seems to me like you've been talking to the wrong people."

I nod, he may have a point there.

"What brings you to my shop at this time of night? I know you. You would have much rather squashed our shit over lunch."

Silence greets my question. He turns away, looking up at the sky as if the stars hold some kind of secret.

"I fucked up again," he says. I know right away the next thing that comes out of his mouth is going to be a problem. Blue eyes lock back on mine. "I needed to warn you about the Russians. They've started to make threats."

"What kind of threats?"

"Threats about the crew and at one point you were part of the crew. I want you to be careful."

"What kind of threats, Griff?" This time my question isn't as gently asked as the first time.

He looks away once more before back at me. "Threats to our loved ones."

I curse, turning away from him, running my hands through my hair.

"Let's not panic right now. So far I've been able to keep them happy…"

"Do they know about her?"

He lifts his hands as if he wants me to calm down. "Titus, just—"

"Answer my fucking question," I fume, taking a step toward him.

He sighs and drops his shoulders. "Yeah, they know about her and the baby."

"Damn it, Griff. What the fuck, man?"

"That's why I'm here. I'm trying to prevent anything from happening."

I ignore him and pull my phone out of my pocket. I have no idea what I will tell her. Just five weeks ago, I'd promised her I was out of this life.

Now I'm not only going to have to tell her the truth, but simultaneously explain I just put her and my son in danger. I go to hit her saved number on my phone, but the sound of a car pulling up and bright headlights cause me to turn to the sight of a dark SUV pulling up in front of us.

"You expecting company?" Griff asks as he comes to stand beside me.

"No," I reply.

All the doors open, and five men step out. They vary in size and shape, but the glares on their faces tell me they're here to cause trouble.

"You Griff?" The big one with the flat nose says in a thick accent. It's clear English isn't his first language.

"Who the fuck's asking?"

Flat Nose turns and smiles at the big guy with the scar on his cheek before turning back to us.

"You owe a debt. And we're here to make sure you pay up."

"And who are we?" I ask, widening my stance. "You and the rest of these pussies you brought with you?" I snort. "You need to climb back in your little minivan and get the fuck out of here."

Griff places a hand on my shoulder to calm me down. "Gentlemen, you don't want this trouble. Tell your boss I'll get his cars. It doesn't have to come to this."

The entire time Flat Nose is eyeing me down like he's itching for my foot up his ass.

"You got a fucking problem?" I ask him.

He grins, showing off a row of cracked yellow teeth. "You call us pussy?" he asks in his fucked-up English. "But I hear you got new pussy. Maybe, after we done here, we go show your new pussy what real men can do."

"Ah shit," Griff mutters at the same time I cut the motherfucker's words off with a punch to the face.

I round on his ass and only stop when Scar Cheek lands a thundering blow to my jaw that makes that bitch click. I can taste blood in my mouth. My lip is split.

I turn toward him. He runs at me. I kick his ass in the chest, sending him stumbling back.

Someone tackles me from the back, almost knocking me down. I toss my elbow back, connecting to my attacker. The crunch and squirt of blood lets me know I connected with his nose.

His howl of pain tells me he's down for a moment. I turn around just in time to see Scar Face coming at me again. My fist lands square on his jaw. Out of the corner of my eye, I see Griff laying out the other two motherfuckers.

One of the selling points of this property was that it is in a good district. Lots of shops surround us and it gets a ton of foot traffic. The downfall of that is they don't tolerate bullshit in this area.

A bunch of grown-ass men fighting in the parking lot is likely to draw attention and have the cops storming in. Which is why I'm not completely shocked when we are suddenly surrounded by police cruisers. Before I know it, I'm face fucking first on the concrete.

And no matter how many times I explain to them I own the shop, it doesn't matter, because I'm a big ass tattooed asshole, fighting in public. However, even though I know I'll have to spend the night in the tank, nothing compares to the disappointment I feel knowing my girl is at home waiting for me, and for the first time, I will miss Ace's appointment.

CHAPTER TWENTY-THREE

Disappointment

Noni

I've looked down at my phone so many times I've lost track. I'm beyond pissed. Last night I was worried, when twelve thirty a.m. hit I started to panic.

By two a.m. and after all my calls went unanswered, I thought of every scenario I could think of. Even visualizing him lying in the arms of another woman. By the time my eight a.m. appointment was over, I assumed he was dead and even drove over to his job and called the hospitals.

By the time I got home from work, I was livid. My doorbell rings and I jump up from the couch ready to give Deacon a piece of my mind.

"You have a lot of explaining to…" The rest is cut off when it isn't Deacon at my door but Jason.

"Hello, Noni. Can I come in?" his question is asked right as he walks into my house.

230

"Apparently, yes," I reply, shutting my door.

Jason looks around my condo as if it's the first time he's seen it.

"Your mom asked me to stop by and check on you. She's worried about you. Says you're not taking her phone calls, not going by the house after work."

He turns to look at me. His eyes land on my rounded belly. I watch as what seems to be regret fills his eyes and softens his features.

"Are you okay, Noni?"

"I'm fine," I huff. Screw his regret.

He tilts his head and takes a step toward me. "It's me, baby girl. You don't have to act tough for me. I can see it in your eyes."

"See what?"

"Your regret."

At this, I laugh. He completely missed the mark with that. If he can see anything in my eyes, it's the happiness of letting his ass go.

"There is no regret." I head to my door to see Jason out. I don't need his company. I'm too pissed to deal with him.

"Who did you think was at the door?"

I stop and turn to face him. I don't answer him because not only is it not his business, I don't want him to know I'm having issues with Deacon. That's all he needed to run back and tell my mama.

I shake my head at my plight. Things were going so well until that stupid admittance. All I had to do was keep my mouth shut, but I told a man I've only known for five months that I love him.

Is that even real? Do people get that emotionally attached in such a short time? Maybe it's just the hormones from the pregnancy. I can blame a lot of things on that.

Either way, I revealed my feelings to Deacon too soon and now he's ignoring me or worse. Lord, I hope it isn't worse. I place my hands on my hips and glare at Jason.

"Let me guess, your baby daddy?" He chuckles as if he just said something funny. "You know, it's a shame. I did all I could to give you a name, to keep you from people like that and you still found your way to that dirtbag."

He shrugs. "I guess it's my fault. Well, me and your mother's. We've babied you. Tried to keep you from the ugly truth of the world and we spoiled you."

"Spoiled me?" I mock. "Are you serious?"

"Oh, come on, Noni. I placed you on a pedestal and you were too unappreciative to stay there."

"Oh my gosh." I clutch my chest at his gall. "You really believe the bullshit that's coming out of your mouth. You didn't coddle me, you caged me. You treated me like a pet or an accessory you could take out and adorn yourself with whenever you felt the need to. You didn't give a shit about me or how I felt."

"Oh, and your little thug boy does?" He laughs tauntingly. "You're so naïve. You think you're the first girl to toss away her good man for a bad guy?"

He lets out another one of his annoying laughs. "Please, you're nothing new. And I bet if you ask those other women, they will tell you cautionary tales. Probably warn you to stay away.

"Here's a lesson I'm going to teach you, Noni. My final one, bad boys are fun until the novelty wears off. And trust me," he says, stepping close to me, closing the little gap between us.

"He will get bored with you. And when he does, he will toss your ass along with that baby back to the street, and the good guys like myself, don't take in the trash."

"Get the fuck out of my house." I open the door and stand there, waiting for him to leave.

"I'm only trying to help. For old times' sake."

"Get out."

Jason only smiles, then walks up to me. He stops in front of me, standing at the door. I don't realize what he's doing until it's too late. He plants a kiss on my cheek.

"You lost, cowboy?"

His voice makes me jump nearly out of my skin. We both turn to find a busted lip, bloody and torn shirt Deacon standing in front of us. He looks at me and I can see the accusation and anger in his eyes.

I hated that he walked up to see me like that. However, he doesn't get the right to be angry with me.

"Are you sure you want me to leave, Noni?" Jason asks, taking a step in front of me as if he's attempting to protect me from Deacon.

"She's sure," Deacon replies for me.

"You know, if you're trying to be a father, showing up looking like you got your ass handed to you isn't a good look."

Deacon takes a step toward Jason. I move to stand between them.

"You might want to reassess this situation. I didn't get shit handed to me and I promise you I have time to fuck up a pretty boy like you."

"All right, calm down," I say, placing my hands on Deacon's chest. "Come inside."

Deacon looks over at me, anger still obvious in his glare. He then walks into the condo without a backward glance. I watch him disappear into my kitchen.

"I bet that bad boy shit doesn't look as appealing right now, does it?"

Jason smirks before walking off. I watch him climb into his Jaguar and drive off before I close the door and go back inside. I find Deacon in my kitchen, standing in front of the fridge with a bottled water to his lips.

I wait for him to finish drinking before I say anything. I cross my arms over my belly and wait. He drinks the entire contents of the bottle before tossing the empty container into the trash and shutting the door. He turns and leans his back on the fridge.

"I had a long night, Noni. All I want to do is shower and get some rest."

"You have to be out of your mind if you think that's all you're going to give me. I waited up all night long for you, not to mention you missed Ace's appointment."

He looks up at me and remorse is painted across his features like an artist's brush strokes.

"Where were you?" Despite the pain in his eyes, I have to ask the question.

"In jail."

Okay, I wasn't expecting that answer. I honestly expected him to be lying in a ditch somewhere before I expected him to be in jail.

"Why were you in jail?"

He shakes his head before he grips the back of his neck. "Got into a fight."

The air whooshes out of my lungs and my mouth hangs open. My mind battles with asking him is he okay or wanting to fight him myself. The latter wins.

"Fighting?" I ask the question in disbelief. "You're thirty-six years old, Deacon, you don't know how to solve problems without using your fists? What the hell were you thinking?"

He turns to me, the forest green in his hazel eyes encroaches the brown as they flare with anger.

"You think if I had a choice not to fight, I would have made the fucking decision to do it?"

"Who were you fighting?"

He narrows his eyes at me. "You have a lot of damn questions." He pushes off of the fridge and takes a step toward me. "How about you answer a question for me. Why the hell was he here, huh? I miss one appointment and already you go running back to your lawyer fiancé."

With each step he takes toward me, I take one back until I hit the kitchen table.

"He just showed up out of the blue, I wasn't taking him back."

"Hard to tell when you had him kissing all over you."

"Kissing all over me?" I push away from the table and take a step toward him. "He wasn't kissing on me and... you know what?" I stop myself from explaining something I shouldn't have to.

"Don't change the subject. This is about you coming home looking like you went a round with Mike Tyson. Is this how you're going to show up for Ace? Are you going to tell him that Daddy can't control his temper and allows others to dictate how he behaves?"

"Enough, Noni, damn it, enough," he roars at me so loud the vein in his neck throbs. He turns his back to me and runs a hand through his hair. I focus on the tattoos on his fingers as he grips the strands and yanks them.

"It isn't just you anymore..." My voice is such a contrast to his tone it sounds as if we're having two different conversations. Deacon turns to look at me. "A lot has changed for me. This baby."

I touch the swell of my belly. "Means everything to me and I refuse to allow people in his life who will only hurt him in the end."

Silence surrounds us. Only the sound of the ice maker in my refrigerator makes a sound.

"What are you saying?" his question is spoken calmly, but the tension in his jaw tells me he is far from it.

"I'm saying you need to decide if Ace is as important to you as winning a fight."

His nostrils flare before his gaze drops away from me. "I'm sorry I can't be your perfect fucking man."

He storms past me toward the door. I didn't intend to make him feel as if he had to be perfect. Like how my mother made me feel as if I couldn't make a mistake.

I follow him, calling his name, but he refuses to turn. When I finally catch up to him, I grab his arm. He snatches it away, turning back to me with a glare.

"Call your ex up. I'm obviously not the man for you."

He storms out of my house, slamming my front door closed. I press my forehead to the cold surface, trying to calm my beating heart. A sharp pain hits my lower belly, and I gasp and clutch the area.

When the pain subsides, the tears come. I turn my back to my door and slide down. It would probably take me a while to get back up, but I don't care at the moment because I feel as if I've lost something I'll never get back.

CHAPTER TWENTY-FOUR

Too Soon

Noni

Five days have passed, and I haven't heard a word from Deacon. I've called his phone many times, but it continues to go to voicemail and my messages have gone unanswered. The one thing I won't do is show up at his house.

My pride refuses to let me fall that low. To distract me from the craziness my life has been, I decide to put the crib together. Now I'm sitting on the floor with a water bottle, three pages of instructions, and what looks like enough parts to put together two cribs.

I pick up the instruction manual one more time.

"Insert L bracket to long leg D."

I look around at all the parts again, continuing to rub my achy belly with my free hand. I've been having these little tightening pains in my lower belly since the day Deacon stormed out.

They aren't anything to fear. They aren't consistent and the books say as long as I don't see blood, I'm fine. At thirty-two weeks, aches and pains are pretty common.

"Ace, I don't know if mama will be able to do this."

The knock at my front door pulls my attention toward the sound. For a second, exhilaration coats my veins. My hope that Deacon is at the door brings me to my feet, but I immediately regret it when that cramping pain hits again.

This time a little harder. I grab for my belly and gasp. Taking a few deep breaths, I feel well enough to make it to the door. The pain has me a little scared, but all the books say it's nothing to be afraid of.

"It's not time for you to come yet, is it, Ace?" I rub my belly again as I get to my door and peep out.

A long sigh escapes my lips, and my shoulders drop. Now isn't the right time for this visitor. I open the door and plaster the best fake smile I can on my face.

"Hello, Mother."

She peers over my head, trying to see behind me. She has yet to look at me. "Are you going to let me come in?"

I step back and hold out my hand for her to enter. She walks in eyeing my townhome like the walls are painted in shit. I close the door behind her, preparing myself for what I know is about to be a stressful argument.

"I'm shocked you let me in. You've been too busy shacking up to check on your own mother." She drops her gaze to the scattered parts of the crib on my floor before she turns to me.

"Is that man here?"

"No."

I don't go into any more detail than that. My mother is the last person I want to tell that Deacon and I broke up. Is that what we did?

It feels like much stronger words than broke up are needed. The feeling of being caged has come back and those butterflies that once fluttered in my stomach every time he was near or if I even thought of him now feel like rocks in my stomach.

Even my sleep knows something is wrong. The entire time Deacon was sleeping beside me, not once had I had a problem falling asleep. Now, for the life of me, I can't get a full night's rest. So no, it doesn't feel like the words broke up are sufficient.

"Why are you putting that crib together? That's what a husband does. Something you would have if you'd stop playing these silly games."

I pinch the bridge of my nose. I can almost feel a stress headache coming on. "Did you have a reason for coming over?" I take a seat on my couch, keeping my mother in front of me.

"Oh, now I have to have a reason to come see my daughter?"

I don't give the question a reply. I just lift a brow at her. I can count on one hand the number of times she's come to my house. But why would she, I always went to hers.

She relaxes her stance and takes a seat on the love seat next to me. "Noni, I heard about the incident that happened here Monday night."

I open my mouth to defend Deacon, but she stops me. "Now I'm not going to tell you how I found out." Like there is any confusion about who told her. "But I wanted to come by and check on you and talk some sense into you. I'm worried about my grandbaby."

I snort and roll my eyes. "That's a first."

"What's that supposed to mean?"

Words fill my head. Words like, *you haven't asked about this baby since I told you I was pregnant, and it wasn't Jason's.* Or the words, *you don't give a damn about me or anything affiliated with me.*

Instead of saying anything like that, the word nothing comes out.

"Like I was saying," she continues. That sharp pain comes back just as bad as the last one.

"Are you listening to me, Noni? I think now is the time you call Jason back and apologize for behaving foolishly these last few months. Clearly this boy..."

She waves her hands dismissively around the room, as if she's trying to flick Deacon out of my life. "He's bad news. I mean, to show up at your house all beat up with black eyes, scratches all over his body, a broken nose, and a busted lip. I mean, come on Noni."

"He didn't look that bad. His lip had a cut in it, and he had a bruise on his cheek."

"Don't defend him. He's out here starting fights, probably over other women."

Damn, Jason told her more than I know. All I know is that he didn't start the fight. I never even asked what it was about.

"He didn't start the fight," I say, but she cuts my words off without even registering their meaning.

"Bringing that mess to your doorstep. What if his hooligan friends would have followed him here? What would have happened?"

She's jumping to all kinds of conclusions, making things much worse than they are. *Just like you did*, the nagging voice reminds me effortlessly. This time guilt washes over me, causing the heavy feeling in my stomach to increase along with that sharp pain again.

"The more and more I try to turn you into a daughter I can be proud of, the more and more you turn into your father. He did the same thing you did. He left a good woman for some young hussy. I can understand Jason's pain."

Her voice softens, as if she's reliving her situation. "You don't deserve him, but he's willing to take you back."

"I don't want him back," I say through clenched teeth.

My mother sucks her teeth and looks at me as if I'm insane. "Look at you, hair all over your head." My hair is, in fact, not all over my head. I actually have it in two neat braids.

"Where is your wig? You know you have that nappy hair like your father and with your dark color you need to make sure you keep a wig on, and your face done up. I mean, why would Jason want to come back to you looking like this and your nose has already started to spread, you're not even that far along."

This time the cramping hits so hard I cry out and double over in pain.

"Noni, what's wrong? What is it?"

I don't answer as I stand, stumbling into the bedroom, hand clutched to the pain in my lower belly. I can still hear my mother's voice through the house. My heart is beating fast and all I can think is that it's too soon.

All the books say his organs are still way too underdeveloped at seven months. I manage to grab my phone off the nightstand where it's charging. There's only one person I want to call. I only hope he answers for me.

CHAPTER TWENTY-FIVE

Mine Again

Deacon

"I'm just saying, it's been a long time since we… talked," Candy, an old flame from my past says, as she brushes against me.

She showed up at the shop today to get a tattoo filled in. She followed me into my office to talk afterward. Candy is half black and half white, with big gray eyes and a smile that deserves to be on television. She can also suck my balls out through my dick. She's the perfect mix of nasty and sweet.

A month ago, I'd have had her back at my place, riding my fucking face. However, at the moment, I glance at my desk, remembering being balls deep in the best pussy I've ever had.

I fucking miss that woman. My brain reminds for the millionth time since I stormed out of her house, but I can't make myself go back to her.

I have pride, and that motherfucker is a bitch sometimes. The way she looked at me like I was trash, the way she accused me of not caring about Ace. That shit cut deep.

Doesn't matter, she was kind of right. I was doing stupid shit. Just last night, I aided in the theft of damn near fifteen cars.

I jacked more earlier in the week. I'm not a saint, but I didn't start that fight on purpose. And I would never intentionally hurt my kid.

What do you think is going to happen if you get grabbed for these cars? Noni is right, you would hurt Ace.

I hate the fucking voice in my head. He's been eating away at my ass.

"What do you say, Deacon? You could come by on your break." Candy stands between my legs, her knee bumping into my flaccid cock. It seems old boy has made the decision for me.

"You know I want to."

"Want to what?" I look to my door and standing there with his signature cocky grin is Pit.

Of all the assholes, Pit and I have a lot in common. We both have shitty and abusive parents. His came by way of his supposed father, and me my mother.

I get up, making Candy take a step back.

"What the fuck are you doing here?" I ask, with a genuine smile on my face.

He shrugs. "Had a feeling in my gut I needed to check in on you." He cuts his eyes to Candy and then back to me.

Although the gang has never met Noni, Pit knows damn well Candy isn't my baby mama.

"Hi, nice to meet you, I'm Candy," she purrs at him. This chick was never loyal. She'd fuck Pit right in my face if he allowed it, but I know my boy.

"Not in the least fucking interested," Pit says, walking into my office, brushing past her to take a seat on my couch. Completely unbothered by the *asshole* she tosses at him.

"You can leave now," I tell her.

"Deacon, what about lunch?" She flashes one of her Colgate smiles and I try to think of how I ever found her cheap flirty tricks attractive.

"Get the fuck out of my office." She stumps her heeled foot and storms out.

"Now, Deacon, is that anyway to treat your pussy?"

"Fuck you, Pit. You wouldn't know the first thing about how to treat pussy if it wasn't for Skittles taming your ass."

He flips me off and we laugh as I take a seat at my desk.

"What the fuck are you doing over here, anyway? Don't you have a business to run?"

"I do, but it seems I have to leave my job to handle some bullshit."

I lean back in my chair, watching Pit cautiously. The crew and I tell each other mostly everything. Even the shit that's embarrassing to some. But I couldn't tell them this stuff about Griff.

They would either try to talk me out of it or attempt to help. And though we all have our shit on the side, I'm not trying to risk my guys going to jail.

"What bullshit?"

He shrugs, placing one arm on the back of the couch and the other hand rests on his knee.

"Laurence came into the bar the other night."

I know what this is about. Fuck. Laurence is a cop and was probably down at the police station when I got booked the other night.

Now I know exactly what bullshit Pit is talking about. Yet, I don't let on to it. I'm going to wait and see exactly how much he knows. With Pit's connections, it might be a lot more than I want him to.

"He told me some shit I just couldn't believe. One of my boys got pinched Sunday night." He scoffs and shakes his head. "I called him a fucking liar. First, none of my crew would go to jail without letting at least one of us know. So, I know damn well that didn't happen."

"Pit." He holds up a hand to stop my words.

"Secondly," he continues, placing his elbows on his knees. "Did it not come out of your mouth how important this kid is to you?" He doesn't even give me time to nod before he continues on. "What the fuck are you doing running cars in my city again? And for a Russian mob boss at that."

As I figured, Pit knows everything. "It isn't what you think."

"Oh, I don't think anything, because I still don't believe you thought you could keep this shit from me."

I run a hand through my hair, pushing it off my forehead. "It's not a big deal."

"The next words out of your mouth better be a fucking answer or I'm calling the crew and you're going to catch another ass whooping."

As serious as he is—because he would definitely call the other assholes to knock some sense into me, we've had to do that shit a few times with Tak—I still crack a smile.

"Are you back in the game?" Just like Pit to get tired of the back and forth and ask his question.

"Not really."

"Enough with the riddles. Look, we made a pact to call each other out on our bullshit. Well, I'm calling you out. You have a lot to fucking lose."

"You don't think I know that? I remind myself of that every damn day."

"Then why put yourself back in this shit?"

I sigh long and hard, drooping my shoulders. "Griff."

"Your old man?"

"Yeah, he got mixed up with the Russian. Got cocky and took an order too big for his plate. I'm only trying to help him out."

Pit stands dusting his hands down the front of his jeans.

"I know how much Griff means to you, so I won't tell you to turn your back on him, but the night you sat in my bar with the crew, you said you wanted to do anything you could to keep this kid in your life. This shit."

He points to the ground, but I know exactly the shit he's indicating. "This ain't it."

I get up, coming around to the front of my desk. I lean against it, my arms and legs crossed.

"It doesn't even matter anymore. She and I broke up."

Pit's head tips back and his eyes narrow. "Broke up? What is this, high school? I thought she was engaged?"

"She was, but her and Little Dick split, we were giving it a try."

"And?"

"And she's not ready for me. And I don't even know if I'm ready to be locked down."

"Bullshit. You sound like a pussy right now. Are you into this girl?"

"Yes," I say, standing up straight.

"Do you want her?" he asks.

"Hell yeah."

"Well, see, I belong to this club of assholes. Assholes take what belongs to them. They don't sit around bitching about shit. You want her and your son, you go for it. And stop sitting around here getting jerked off by fucking slut bags."

I crack a smile. He's right. I am acting like a pussy.

I got in my head and let my insecurities get the best of me. I saw Little Dick at her house, and I started to panic. There I was, showing up late from jail and he was already there.

I allowed the demons of my childhood to chase me from the one person I want more than anything. The one person who makes me feel like I'm worth something, like I'm not just one bad choice.

Of course, I don't tell Pit this. I glare at him.

"You an expert on relationships now because Skittles made your ass put a ring on it?"

"Fuck you, she didn't make me do shit."

"Let me call her and ask." I pretend to reach for my phone, and he punches me in the arm, halting my movements.

Just what I fucking thought. Skittles has his ass on a leash.

"And so, you know, the next time you get into some trouble and I have to find out my way, I'm coming over here and knocking all this silvery shit over. I mean, damn, you couldn't find none of this shit in wood?"

I crack up laughing.

"What the fuck ever. Your grumpy ass want to grab some lunch? I'm about to go on break."

He shrugs. "Yeah, that sounds good, but I promise you I'm not doing whatever shit she was about to do."

Before I can respond to his dumb ass comment, my phone rings. I grab it off the desk. Glancing at the number, a smile comes to my face. She's been calling me since that day, but I've been avoiding her.

"Hey, baby. We need to—"

My words are cut off by her tearful, "Deacon."

"Noni, baby, what's wrong?"

Never have I felt the fear I have at this moment. And I even outraced a fucking train. But nothing will ever hold a candle to this moment. Pit's brow is pinched as he stares at me, waiting to get more information.

"I'm heading to the hospital. Deacon, I'm scared. It's too soon."

"Noni, don't worry. I'm on my way, baby, I'm on my way."

I don't even have to explain my quick departure to Pit. He just nods as I rush out of my office toward my bike in the parking lot. I make the trip to the hospital in record time.

CHAPTER TWENTY-SIX

Rules

Noni

"Are you eating right?" My mother, who I begged not to come to the hospital with me, asks as she watches me from her spot in the chair. "You have to make sure you're eating well."

I ignore her. My eyes are trained on the white tile on the ceiling. I count the small holes in my head.

The sound of my heart monitor is drowned out by the fast thumping of Ace's heartbeat. It's his little heart that's keeping me sane.

The first person I thought to call was Deacon. For a minute I was scared he wouldn't answer again, but I don't want to do this without him.

When he did answer, I was a little thrown off by his cheerful greeting. We had just gone a few days without speaking. He sounded like he missed me when I called.

"You need to take better care of yourself. I left Jason a message and told him how poor of a job you're doing with this baby."

The beeping on my machine increases, almost drowning out Ace's heartbeat.

"I'm looking for room 453. Noni Scott." Just the sound of his voice makes my heart rate skip a beat and the flutters in my belly come back with a vengeance.

"Deacon," I call out his name.

"You called him?" my mother asks the question like it's the most disgusting thing she can think of.

I ignore her as Deacon rushes into the room. He stops at the door when he sees me, then rushes to my side.

"Are you okay? What happened?"

"I started getting cramps. The book said they were common, so I didn't stress about it, but they started to get worse. I should have called my doctor sooner."

I'd been holding back the tears pretty well until this moment. The doc still hasn't come to give me the verdict yet. I don't know if I'm going into early labor or if it's just false labor.

"Shh, don't worry. It's okay. Ace will be just fine. I know it." He pulls me into his chest, holding me tight as I bury my face in his shirt.

"You're the lowlife who ruined my daughter?"

Deacon's body tenses. I don't blame him. I almost forgot my mother was here, but her condescending tone quickly alerts me of her presence.

"Mother," I try to warn, but Deacon has already released me and turned to face her.

"Lowlife?" Everything about his stance from the way his fingers flex at his side to his feet planted shoulder-width apart, lets me know the question isn't an actual question but a threat.

And just like my mother, never knowing when to throw in a towel or to back off, she powers forward.

"That's right. Lowlife," she says the word slowly, sounding out every syllable. "You can just march yourself back out of this room. I've already called my son-in-law."

"Mother, I told you not to call him," I say, sitting up higher in my bed. The odd cramping has started back.

Neither she nor Deacon acknowledges my comment. "I don't give a fuck if you called Jesse Jackson and the entire NAACP, I'm not leaving my family."

For only a second, I allow his words to fill me with so much exhilaration. He called us a family. The one thing I've always wanted. However, I don't get to dwell on the word because again my mother doesn't stop.

"Family?" She snorts. "This is not your family. You stole this family while my daughter was drunk in Vegas. You seduced her," she says the last part as if she just realized it. Like it's a new discovery that justifies my situation.

"You're fucking right I seduced her. I seduced her all night and half the damn morning." Well, he ain't lying.

Mother scoffs and turns her face up as if something reeks. "Disgusting," she spits the word out at him before turning her gaze to me. "And this is the type of trash you let Jason go for? God, Noni, you are so much like your father."

She tosses her hands up after sending those barbed words tumbling toward me. The cramping starts back and this time, I have to place a hand over my pelvis.

"Don't talk to her," Deacon says, taking a step over to block mother's sight from me. "Your issue is with me, don't address her."

This takes my mother by surprise because for once she doesn't have a quick comeback. I imagine having a guy stand up for me is a new concept for her.

"Who do you think you're talking to like that? When my son-in-law gets here he is going to put you in your place."

"He will get his ass kicked if he shows up in this room."

"Why you—"

I cry out as the cramping increases. Both stop arguing. Deacon spins around toward me, and his face pales.

"Okay, I'm going to have to ask everyone to calm down," Dr. Shay says, stepping into the room.

She walks right over to me, a warm smile on her face. "How're you doing, Noni?"

"Having a little pain now."

She nods. "After checking a few things out it seems this little baby is doing fine, and not trying to make an appearance today, but baby does need his mom to relax."

She looks down at her tablet, sliding her finger over it a few times. "Your blood pressure is high. And I'm thinking it's due to stress. With this information, I'm going to have to ask that you limit some of your company," Dr. Shay says, turning to the others in my room.

"I'm not going anywhere. That's my daughter," Mother argues as if Dr. Shay pointed her out directly.

"If it means making sure Noni and Ace are okay, I'll leave," Deacon says, his color is back. He leans down to give me a kiss on the forehead.

That comment probably just made my heart rate spike again. "No, I don't want you to leave."

"Let him go, Noni. Jason will come and take my place," my mother says proudly.

Even though I see it on Deacon's face—the urge to tell my mother where she can go—he fights it.

"No," I say toward her. "You need to leave and while you're at it, make sure you tell Jason he isn't needed here."

For a long moment, my mother stands and gapes down at me in pure shock, but I'm not changing my mind. I didn't care about her being my mother. When it came to Ace, I will put my foot down, and her presence is stressing me the fuck out.

My mother turns from me, grabs her purse off the couch, and storms out of the room without a backward glance in my direction. The heavy energy in the atmosphere leaves with her, and the room seems to expand, making it easier to breathe.

"Now, Noni," Dr. Shay says, getting my attention. "If you don't want to be back in the hospital before your due date, you have to get rest and eliminate the stress in your life. It's not healthy for you or the baby. You also," she says, frowning at me. "Don't need to pick up heavy objects. That crib could have waited."

"You moved the crib?" His hazel eyes are lit with a fire as he looks down at me.

"You wouldn't take my calls."

Silence floats around us. Yes, I probably shouldn't have moved the crib, but it wasn't like he was around to do it for me. Dr. Shay clears her throat.

"We're going to keep you overnight to keep an eye on you. And if we can get your blood pressure to stay down, you can go back home tomorrow. But," she says, holding up a finger. "I'm putting you on a two-week bedrest. You need to rest, Noni."

"Don't worry, Doc, she will."

Dr. Shay smiles at me and places a hand on my knee on top of the covers. "I'll come back to check on you later." She nods at Deacon and then turns and leaves.

The moment the door closes, we both turn to each other and say sorry at the same time. I chuckle, and he shakes his head.

"I'll start," he says. "You were right."

The words are simple but powerful. In my entire six-year relationship with Jason, he had never muttered those words to me, even when I was blatantly right about something. He would always find some way to spin it so he was right.

Deacon takes a seat beside me on the bed. His hip brushes against mine as he looks down at me.

"I didn't start the fight, but I damn sure could have done more to walk away from it. Especially when you and Ace need me."

"Yes, we need you," I say, placing a hand on his knee. "But we don't need you to be perfect. And I'm sorry I made you feel that way." I flop back onto my pillow, looking up at the ceiling. "I don't want to ruin this kid's life."

"Hey, look at me." He pinches my chin with his fingers, tilting my head down so I can look him in the eyes. "We won't. Between the two of us, we can keep this parenting thing on the road. As long as we have each other."

"You promise?" I ask, with a teasing pout.

He leans forward and places a kiss on my lips before standing.

"How about we make some rules? Rules to follow to make sure we do all we can to make this relationship last."

I mockingly gasp, then touch my belly. "Do you hear that, Ace? Your daddy is following rules now."

He smirks at me and then winks. "Only this once and only for you. Rule number one," he starts. I pull myself further up in my hospital bed. "We listen to each other. Even if we're angry, we take the time to hear each other's side."

I rub my belly, finding comfort in the feel of it. "Okay, that's a good one. I have one. We never go to bed with unresolved issues. Even if we aren't in the same house."

He rubs his chin as if he's thinking it over. "Good," he says. "I got another one. We come to each other first with any problems. Doesn't matter how small. I want to be the first person you call if you have a splinter."

I laugh at the outrageousness of that one.

"Also," he continues. "Sex should be a daily part of life." I laugh so hard I snort.

"You wish, Mr. Clarke."

"Damn, can't blame me for trying," he says, coming to sit by me on the bed.

"All right, I have one," I reply, getting serious again. "We never lie to each other even when it feels like a lie would be better. We always tell the truth."

This time when he pauses there's no funny joke, wink, or teasing smile. He watches me with an unreadable expression in his eyes. The only sound between us is the rapid sound of Ace's heart monitor.

When it feels as if he may not approve of the rule, he takes my hand and holds it to his chest. The thud is a soothing rhythm under my palm.

He replies, "Deal."

I smile and lean forward to kiss him. The moment I place my lips to his, Ace kicks, and because of the bands wrapped around my stomach, it makes a loud thumping sound.

Deacon startles, rearing back and looking down at my belly. "What was that?"

I chuckle. "That was your son agreeing with our rules."

He places one of his large hands on my belly and smiles down at me. "We can do this," he says assuredly.

"Of course, we can," I agree emphatically.

CHAPTER TWENTY-SEVEN

Mundane

Deacon

"No, they should go with house three," Noni says loudly at the screen as I massage her aching feet.

"House three doesn't have the backyard for Steve's cookouts."

"But it's the better location."

If someone would have told me five months ago, I would be at home on my couch on a Friday night, rubbing some chick's feet and watching *House Hunters* like it's a damn competitive sport. I would've laughed in their fucking face. However, here I am in the only place I want to be.

Four days ago, Noni was taken off of bedrest and she is now in her eighth month. She was so tired of staying at home that after we got the all clear from the doctor; we came to my house to stay.

The entire time she was on bedrest I stayed with her. I put the crib and the changing table together and also helped her order the bassinet. On the outside, we're all ready for Ace's arrival, but on the inside, I'm a fucked-up mess.

It doesn't have anything to do with Noni or Ace, it's this shit with Griff. I felt like crap when I had to basically lie to Noni's face about her rule. I have no intention of her ever finding out, but even if she asks, I won't tell her the truth.

It doesn't make it any better that not long after the train shit our thefts have been all over the news. They have no suspects, thank God, but we are getting attention. Attention means the shit I'm doing is starting to get even riskier.

I may not know shit else, but I know I'm going to do everything in my power to make sure I keep my family.

"Ugh," she groans, rubbing her belly.

"Is he on your bladder again?"

She tries to sit up, and I quickly stand to help her.

"I swear he thinks my bladder is a soccer ball. Can you do that thing again?"

I've had a bunch of accomplishments in my life. I've won a shit ton of fights. I've stolen cars in less time than it takes you to tie your shoe. I even opened up and successfully run three businesses. Yet, nothing is more rewarding than her asking me to calm my son down because apparently only I can.

"Absolutely."

I squat down in front of her, leaning close into her belly. With one hand on each side of her rounded stomach, I press my lips to her navel and make car sounds. That's it, that's my magic trick. I rub the sides of her stomach at the same time, and underneath my hand I can feel Ace moving around.

Noni sighs above me, and I know my job is done. I place a kiss on her now protruding navel. She moans at the contact. My dick gets rock hard. Not that it's anything new. I'm always semihard around her.

She's already sexy as hell, but this pregnancy has made it harder to keep my cock in my pants. I pull away from her, standing to put distance between us.

"You want another banana?"

A heavy breath leaves her mouth. "No, I don't want anything else to eat."

She sinks back into the couch, her arms folded over her chest. She thinks I haven't noticed all the shit she's been doing, trying to get me to fuck her. Last night she slept without panties.

I almost went for it when she cocked her leg up over my thigh and smeared her wetness all over me. My dick tented the sheets like a pop-up tent.

"I can't give you what you want."

"Why? Dr. Shay said that everything is fine, and I could go back to my regular schedule."

"She meant work and standing on your feet. She didn't mean having my eleven-inch cock ramming against your cervix."

She moans. I shake my head. She fucking moans at just the mention of my dick. I would laugh if the situation wasn't so serious.

I don't blame her. I shook my dick after pissing today and nearly came. That's how in need of her pussy I am.

"I called and asked her if it was okay to start back having sex. She said it was fine. Unless that isn't the problem?"

Her words trail off at the end and they should. I can't believe she has the audacity to say that shit to me. I step between her legs, grab her hand, and place it on my hardened member.

"Does this feel like a dick that doesn't want you?" I groan at the feel of her hand cupping me.

Her mouth is slightly parted, and her nipples are like small nuggets underneath her tank top. Her breasts are nearly spilling out of the too-tight tank, heaving with each breath she takes.

She wraps her hand around my pole, over my shorts, and starts to stroke me.

My fucking eyes cross at how good it feels. I fist my hands at my side. I should stop this.

I know the doctor said it's okay, but she wasn't taking into account how big my dick is and how hard I like to fuck. When

Noni's wet heat wraps around me like a fucking small T-shirt on a fat man, I lose my shit and all rational thought. I start beating her walls down like I'm afraid someone is going to snatch the shit away from me.

"Babe, I don't want to hurt Ace." My fight sounds weak as shit. I don't even stop her hand from jerking me off as I make the bullshit argument.

"Please, Deacon, just let me taste you."

Fuck, she isn't playing fair. How the hell am I supposed to turn down head? She tugs my baller shorts down my hips, freeing my erection. I nearly poke her fucking eye out.

She licks the palms of her hands and grips my cock with both, still leaving a good four inches for her mouth. She starts to work me up and down, twirling her fists as she goes. I drop my head back and my eyes cross.

When I feel her warm breath at the head of my cock, I hiss. When that vacuum seal of a mouth locks down on my length, my damn knees nearly buckle. Noni has come a long way from Vegas when she had no idea how to suck dick.

Now her full lips wrap around my cock like she's had years of experience. She sucks me like she's starving for it. Slobber drips down her hands onto my balls, making it easier for her to jack me off.

She goes down too far and gags. Shit, that sound is fucking sexy. I place my hand in her hair, the thick puff feels like cotton in my hands.

I tilt her head back so I can see her eyes as I rock my hips back and forth.

She lets my dick go, dropping her hands at her sides, giving me permission to fuck her face. It's at this moment the three little words that've been running through my head for a while, like silent ninjas pop up again. This time loud and with authority.

I love this fucking girl.

I never thought the day would come when those words would mean anything to me. However, standing here now, with the most beautiful, loving, and caring woman's lips wrapped around my cock, looking up at me with so much trust, I want to shout those motherfucking words out loud.

Instead, I continue to look down at her, those big brown eyes glazed over with desire stare at me. My thick rod slides between those succulent lips, drool drips out of the corners of her mouth as I feed her this dick.

"Fuck, Noni, I'm going to bust down your throat. Can I, baby?" Only at the last minute do I think to ask her.

She moans around me and nods her head. I never take my eyes off her as I piston my hips, thrusting into her mouth. She hollows out her cheeks, tightening the grip she has on me.

When I pull out, nearly to the tip, she swirls her tongue around the head. I shove back in, her teeth scraping against me slightly. Turning my head up to the ceiling, I roar as thick jets coat her tongue. She swallows around me, trying to get all of me down, but even still, my cum oozes out of the side of her mouth.

I pull out of her, feeling weak and spent, like I've drunk an entire bottle of Blanton's. My legs feel like I just left the gym on leg day. I look over to Noni and she has a cocky smile on her face as she wipes the remnants of my nut off her lips. The little that dripped to her tank top she leaves.

"I guess I've gotten better," she says with a wink.

I don't care if I was about to keel over. There is no way I'm letting her get away without showing her who the king is in the bedroom.

"On your knees," I bark out the command.

She bites into her bottom lip but doesn't argue. She quickly gets up and shimmies out of the tiny shorts she's been wearing all day that nearly drove me crazy. When she's free of them and her underwear, she climbs onto the couch, facing away from me.

She pokes out her butt and I get a beautiful view of her pink center. My cock jumps, letting me know he's about ready for round two. I step out of my shorts and boxers, tugging at my length to wake him up.

I kneel behind Noni, placing kisses on her round globes down to her thighs. The smell of her center beckons me, making my mouth water. I insert two fingers into her tight little hole. She bucks, leaning away from me. I smirk as I tug her ass right where I want her.

I continue to trail tiny little kisses all around the area she wants me in most. I'm paying her back for her little taunting. She whimpers at the slow pace of my fingers moving inside her and my warm breath blowing over her wet lips.

"Deacon, please," she pleads, and it brings a smile to my face.

My cock is already hard again and pressing into the couch cushion. For a moment, I watch my fingers enter and exit her little slit. Enjoying the way it sucks my fingers in even when I try to pull them out.

I love the sight and the creamy sound it makes. I get hypnotized by the view until I can't take it anymore. I press forward and suck her swollen clit into my mouth as I pump my fingers into her.

She bucks against my face. I pop her ass cheek. Another one of her sexy whimpers leaves her lips.

She calls out my name like she's reciting a prayer. I swirl my tongue over her pearl, and she creams even more around my fingers. When she reaches her hand back and burrows her fingers in my hair to keep me right where I am, I know she's close to her release.

I smile as I yank my fingers out of her slippery cunt and slip my tongue in. I want her to come around my tongue so I can drink her essence from the source. I pinch her clit as my tongue buries inside her.

She screams, nearly collapsing on the couch, but I shoot my hand out to her hip, holding her in place as I lap up all her cream. When I have drunk every drop of her, I stand, run my tongue around my lips, and touch the tip of my nose.

"God, your tongue is the bomb," she pants.

I place one hand at her hip, using my other to line my head up to her pussy lips. "Yeah, but this dick is much better."

I push into her. She claws her nails into the cushions on the couch.

If there was ever a feeling of walking into heaven, it has to be the first slip into Noni's wet sheath. It's fucking perfection.

She moans and cries out when I rock into her and swivel my hips. My body moves as if it has a mind of its own. I have to remind myself to be gentle.

"Come here," I say, tugging on her hair.

She pushes up from the back of the couch, leaning back on her knees. I spread my legs a little more to keep me snug inside her. Stilling my hips, I tug her head back to my shoulder where I turn to take her mouth.

I allow her to taste herself on my tongue and my lips. I try to feed her my emotions through this kiss. I want her to feel how much I want her, how much I crave her tight pussy, but not only that, how much I crave her.

Just being near her, even to watch a dumb ass show on TV is the best feeling ever. I love this woman. I'm not ready to say it with my words, but I'm going to kiss and fuck the knowledge into her.

I release her lips, pull my cock out to the tip, and slam back into her. She cries out, placing her hand on my thigh.

"Don't cry now, baby, you asked for this dick," I growl in her ear.

Damn, her ass feels amazing bouncing off my pelvis. I continue to work her over, her cries and moans fueling my cock. Our bodies are covered in sweat. I run my tongue over her neck, licking up the droplets.

She lifts her arm as she comes around me, her nails digging in my hair. She pulls me down to her lips and again, I feed her my feelings through the connection. I drift my hand down to the hot center between her legs.

With my digits, I rub across her slippery nub. She spasms into an orgasm. Her mouth opens in a loud cry.

Nothing is sexier than the look of her coming for me. I power straight through her damn orgasm. When she starts to come down, I release her little nub, cupping her belly.

The place where she's holding my son. I lose my shit. Closing my eyes, I come so fucking hard I go deaf for a second. I think I lose all my senses—sight, sound, and taste.

After I have bathed her walls with what seems like everything inside me, I pull out and completely crumple to the floor. She gets down beside me. I pull her into me and we both laugh as we lie on the floor facing each other like we are in a bed.

When the laughter dies down, she gazes into my hazel eyes with her dark brown ones. Her kiss-swollen lips are parted.

"I think I love you," she says with a frown, as if she has no idea where that came from.

I reach for her face, rubbing my thumb over her bottom lip. "I think I'm in love with you too."

I don't tell her the truth. I'm past thinking and directly in the realm of fucking knowing. I also don't point out I'm one-hundred-percent sure she too is in that realm. Her eyes tell me everything.

"Come on," I say, smacking her ass. I get up off the ground and stand and then help lift her off the floor. "I'm going to run you a bath."

The smile that lights up her face makes me proud. She's always happy about the smallest things.

We enter the bathroom. I start the water, checking it to make sure it's warm enough. She hands me the huge bath bomb from that Sugah Bae place she likes. I place the bomb into the water and watch it fizzle.

Once the tub fills up enough, she places her hand in mine and I help her step over the high tub edge. Once she's settled, I pull off my shirt and climb in behind her. This is probably our favorite thing to do. We soak in the water, spend time together and talk.

"Did you get fitted for the tux?"

I groan. "Yeah, baby. Only for you will I put on a fucking penguin suit."

She chuckles as she gets comfortable. I lay my hands over her protruding belly, like always. As soon as we get in here Ace starts moving around.

"I think Ace is going to be a swimmer," I joke as I cup water in my hands and pour it over her belly.

She laughs. "Speaking of Ace, I think it's time we start talking about baby names."

"Easy, he's going to be a junior."

"Oh, excuse me for thinking I had an input in this," she mocks.

"You don't. My son will be named Deacon Titus Clarke Junior. I'll allow you to call him DJ for short."

She snorts and laughs. I place a kiss on her neck. "Whatever," she says while rolling her eyes at me over her shoulder. "I have no problem with naming him Junior. But what if he's a she?"

"Not going to happen."

"But what if it does?" she replies.

I grunt. "I don't even want to think about that. To even consider I would have to bring my baby girl up in this world with little boys swarming around her makes me want to lock her away. I swear, Noni, if someone makes her cry, I'm going back to jail."

She laughs, but I'm serious. I know the type of shit I pulled as a kid and a teen, hell a few months ago. To think of some punk pulling that shit with my little girl would cause me to lose my mind.

"Either way, if we have a girl, I'm thinking Charlotte for her name."

"Oh, hell no. I knew a Charlotte once. I will not name my daughter after her."

She laughs out. "If we're not naming after girls you know, she will never have a name."

"You got jokes," I say as I nibble her neck, causing her to laugh.

My phone goes off on the counter and Noni's shoulders drop, making me feel like shit. In order to stay on track to finish with these cars, I have to be out lifting four times a week. So it won't look suspicious, I have Griff call my phone.

I pretend it's Pit, needing me to help him at the bar. One day, I made it Tak who needed my help at a club. I feel like shit doing it, but we are right at two hundred and fifty cars away from ending this and I only have a month left.

That's all I can think of, ending this, so I can put this behind me and not have to worry about it anymore. Every night I'm out with this bullshit is a night I risk getting arrested. And I hate like hell I have to lie to her.

When the phone stops ringing, she sighs. "I guess you're needed tonight." She tries for playful, but it misses the mark completely.

"I'm sorry, baby. It's only for a little while longer."

"Don't apologize. You're helping a friend. I'm being ridiculous."

She leans up in the tub and then stands. Soapsuds cascade down her body. She reaches for the towel behind her and wraps it around her body.

I get up too, just in time to help her step out of the tub. She goes to the shower and turns it on, waiting for it to warm up. I follow behind her.

When I approach her, her back is to me. I turn her around and feel like a complete ass when I see she's crying.

"I'm just emotional. You know my hormones, I don't have a problem with you helping Pit," she tries to explain while wiping her eyes.

I pull her into me. She comes, wrapping her arms around my neck. She's not lying, her hormones do make her emotional.

Hell, last night she cried because she finished her bowl of ice cream. I know she's not upset with me for helping a friend, she just hates when we're apart. I don't blame her. I hate it too.

"I swear, when this baby comes, I won't be this clingy and whiny," she whispers into my chest.

"Yes, you will."

I laugh. She looks up at me with watery eyes and her mouth wide before bursting into laughter herself.

"Shut up, you were supposed to agree with me." She smacks my chest.

I place my hand on her rounded belly and drop a kiss on her pouty lips. "I don't want you to stop being clingy. I want you to want me with you all the time."

I get another smile from her. "Now get in the shower, I want to see if I can put that ass to sleep tonight before I go."

She slips her bottom lip into her mouth before she drops her towel and climbs in the shower. I spend the next twenty minutes with her hands pressed against the shower wall and her ass poked out as I give her enough dick to put her in a coma.

CHAPTER TWENTY-EIGHT

Ferrari

Deacon

I look down at my watch. This 1963 Ferrari 250 GTO is the last car of the night. All I can think about is getting it done and getting back home.

Noni texted about an hour ago that she was up and waiting for me to get back. She can never sleep through the night if I'm not beside her.

Another unbridled thought comes to my mind. I've been getting a lot of these since I met her. This thought screams at me. *I don't want to ever not be with her at night.*

Does that even make sense? Can one girl make me change my entire belief on love and marriage? I don't just want her to be my girlfriend or the mother of my child. I want her to be mine in the most official way ever.

"What the hell, Titus?" Chris says, bringing my thoughts away from the subject. "Can you not get that door open? We need to go."

The Ferrari belongs to some rich lawyer here in the city. He keeps it parked in a storage facility along with a Catamaran and a souped-up RV.

"I know what the fuck I'm doing. Just shut up." I use the dummy key to unlock the door.

I climb into the driver's side and start the engine. It purrs to life. I have to give it to the lawyer.

He kept this baby in mint condition. I pull out of the storage unit and Chris closes it back. Making sure to cover all evidence of us being here.

I had to choose between him, or the pup, and I took him. He's usually the less annoying of the two. I stop and wait for him to join me.

This night is almost over, and I can go home. Maybe I'll stop and grab some kiwi and bananas for Noni. My thoughts are so focused on making sure he shuts everything down and getting back to my girl, I don't see the cop car pull up in front of me.

I turn around just in time to see him walking over to the window. There is no fucking way I can outrun him. My heart drops to my feet and I feel like my entire world exploded.

No more Noni, no more Ace, no more plans for making this shit permanent. I'm about to ruin not only my life, but hers and Ace's too, and it's no one's fault but mine. The cop taps on the window and I roll it down without turning to face him.

"Deacon, is that you?" I turn to the window and almost fucking scream in relief when I see Laurence.

"Officer Laurence." I give him my most friendly smile. "How you doing?"

He scratches at the hair on his chin. "I'm good."

He steps back and looks at the car. My stomach tightens. I know Laurence.

I've had a few beers with him at Fuck Off and I've done eight of his ten tattoos. I know him, but he's still a cop. He whistles and then smiles.

"Damn, Deacon, I didn't know you were rolling like this. This is nice," he says, running a hand over the top of the car.

I have to think fast to get out of this one. "Hell no, this isn't mine. A friend of mine is loaning it to me for the night."

He smirks down at me. "Trying to impress the ladies?"

Motherfucker, I'm a six-three, two-hundred-fifteen pound tattooed man with an eleven-inch cock, I don't need a fucking car to pull pussy. However, I don't tell him that because tonight, I'd be whatever gets me out of this situation.

"You know how it is," I say with a smile and a shrug.

He chuckles. "Well, make sure you lock it up and keep an eye on it. There's been a shit ton of car thefts in the area."

He looks around then leans down as if he's about to tell me something top secret. "Between me and you, we're about to crack down on the fuckers. We've set up bait cars all over the city and we're patrolling the streets. We'll catch the assholes in no time."

"That's good to know."

Laurence stands up straight. "Hey, I have this tattoo idea, it's a unicorn sitting on a mushroom—"

"Sounds great Laurence, but I got to get going. You can set something up with Karly about the tattoo."

"Oh yeah, well you be safe."

He taps the roof of the car again, then walks off to his patrol car. He waves one more time before he drives off. I exhale so hard my entire body relaxes.

When there's another tap on my window, I startle, until I realize it's Chris. I unlock the door and he climbs in.

"Oh shit, I thought you were done for. I called Griff, he's sending the guys back over. What the hell?" It's clear Chris is shaken too, because he won't slow down. "My damn heart is still racing."

"Try living that shit." I put the car in reverse and take it back to the storage facility.

"Wait, what are you doing? We have to take the car to the drop-off."

"Are you fucking kidding?" I ask, slamming on the brakes, nearly sending his ass through the windshield. "If we take this car now, it will lead the cops directly to me. We have to ditch the car and wait to get another one from a different location."

"Fuck, we're already a month behind schedule."

I don't give a shit. I'm not risking my livelihood any more tonight.

"Yeah, well tough. Now get the fuck out and open that gate."

Chris climbs out of the car and slams the door. He opens the gate and I back the car back in its spot on the other side of the boat.

I wipe it down and cover it back up before leaving it behind. Steel meets us back on the other side of the storage facility where we slipped in and he takes us back to the shop.

***

"You made the right call," Griff says to me as we stand outside of the chop shop.

"I know," I reply, gathering my helmet and bike preparing to head out.

"He will move the car again. I'll keep Steel on the movement of it."

I nod to him but continue to pack up. "Hey, is everything all right?" he asks, grabbing my arm and halting my quest to get away.

I run my hand through my hair, pushing it off my forehead. "I'm just ready for this to be over. I'm ready to go back to normal and spend my time with my family."

"I know," he says. "I want the same thing. Just bear with me for a little longer. We're almost done."

I nod because I know this. We're almost down to the last few cars. If I keep up the pace, I'll be done with this shit before Ace gets here.

"Go home to your girlfriend," Griff says, releasing me.

"You mean my fiancée," I say before I catch myself.

Griff's eyes go wide. "When did this happen?"

I shrug. "I haven't asked her yet, but it's going to happen. I guess it's only right you're the first to know."

He doesn't speak, instead, he observes me, his mouth wide open.

"You going to say congratulations?" I say, laughing.

Griff shakes his head and blinks. "Congratulations, man. I get a daughter and a grandson all in the same year. I don't know what to say."

"Just keep your ass alive long enough to be around for the shit. I'll need a best man."

Griff looks down, trying to hide his eyes, but I see the tears before he can cover them.

"I'd be honored, son," he says with a raspy, tear-filled voice. I give him a quick hug before stepping back.

"I won't be available next weekend. I have that thing with her, remember?" I say, getting on my bike.

"I gotcha."

I nod to Griff before I start my bike and head home.

At first, asking Noni to marry me was a passing thought. Yet the more I think it over, the more it feels real. I want her as mine, and I want my son to know I love his mother. Maybe Pit, Luke, and Tak are on to something. When you find the right person, this marriage shit doesn't seem as crazy.

As I pull into my driveway, the excitement of knowing my little family is inside has me feeling anxious. It's ten after two in the morning, but it doesn't stop me from making a phone call.

"Hello?" Skittles groggy voice comes through the line.

"Who the fuck is calling you at this time of night? It better not be Kelex," Pit growls in the background.

"Will you shut up, it's Deacon."

"Deacon? Is he all right?"

"I don't know, Will, you won't shut the fuck up so I can find out," she argues like only she can.

"Hey, May, I need a favor."

"And it couldn't wait until morning?"

"What did he say?" Pit asks in the background.

"Oh my god, will you shut the hell up?"

I can't help but laugh. "Are you busy tomorrow? I need your help to pick out an engagement ring."

The line goes silent. I don't have to question if she hung up, I know she hasn't.

"What time tomorrow?"

"Around three, does that work?"

"Yeah, I can make it. I'll meet you at the shop."

The phone goes dead. I don't have to worry about telling Pit, because I know she will. I climb off the bike and head into the house. My phone goes off and it's a text from Pit.

Pitman: About fucking time. And if you ever call my wife at 2 in the morning again, I'll whip your ass.

Me: Fuck off, and thanks.

I put the phone away with a smile. I place Noni's fruit in the fridge and head to the bedroom. Stripping down to my boxer briefs, I climb in bed behind her and pull her body close to me. She's asleep as I place my hand over her belly. My son kicks, letting me know he stayed up waiting for me.

This is all that matters. I don't care about anything else.

CHAPTER TWENTY-NINE

Busted

Noni

"I look like a whale."

"Do you remember what happened last time you said that?" Deacon whispers in my ear.

A warm blush comes over me as I think back to earlier today as I was trying on the yellow empire waist dress with the gold accent cap sleeves. I made the comment about my thirty-five weeks belly making me look like the sun. Deacon immediately undressed me, set me on the bathroom counter, and proceeded to make love to me until I screamed to the ceiling that *I am beautiful.*

"Maybe you can give me another lesson tonight," I purr back at him.

He winks at me before tucking my hand inside his elbow and escorting me inside the building. I didn't want to come to this event. Especially since it's sponsored by my ex's aunt and uncle.

However, when I tried to cancel, Patricia Peterson wouldn't hear of it. She said she didn't care about what happened between me and Jason, she just wanted me here. So here I am, catching the eye of everyone who I walk past.

The old me would have felt out of place and even shied away, but not now. I'm on the arm of a sexy, intelligent, and strong man who treats me like a queen. I'm at an event where I'm being nominated for an award for a business I started. I belong here.

"You all right?" he leans and whispers as he brushes his lips over my temple.

"Yes," I say with a smile. "I am."

"Noni, darling, you are glowing," Patricia says as she approaches.

She has a timeless beauty, like an old Hollywood actress. Still trim at the age of seventy. Her salt and pepper hair is in loose curls at her shoulders and her light makeup is better applied than mine.

I let go of Deacon's arm just long enough to give her a hug and a kiss on each cheek.

"Sweetheart, pregnancy absolutely suits you," she says, taking a step back to glance at my stomach.

"Funny, I was just telling her the same thing," Deacon mutters, pulling me back into his side and planting a kiss on my temple.

I look up into his eyes and smile. I haven't officially said I love you yet. I told him I was falling for him, but I have yet to make the declaration that I'm wholeheartedly crazy in love with him.

"It's nice to meet you. I'm Patricia Peterson," she says in greeting, holding out her hand for Deacon.

I feel awful, I didn't even think to introduce them. Deacon takes her hand and brings it to his lips with a charming smile.

"Mrs. Peterson, this is my boyfriend, Deacon Clarke."

"It's nice to meet you, ma'am. And might I say, you look radiant tonight." He lets her hand go with a wink and even I blush.

Patricia clutches her chest and giggles like a schoolgirl.

"Thank you. You're too kind."

"I know that smile, who's flirting with my wife?" Mr. Peterson says as he steps up and places a kiss on my cheek before wrapping an arm around his wife. "Noni, you look amazing."

"Thank you," I reply kindly. "Mr. Peterson, this is Deacon Clarke, my boyfriend."

"He's more than that, I understand," he says with a wink at me.

A knot forms in my stomach. What did Jason tell these people? Deacon takes a step closer to me, and I can feel his body tense up.

He looks like a sexy beast in his dark gray tailored suit. But even all cleaned up, Deacon can't hide the rough around the edges tattoo artist that he is. Mr. Peterson laughs before placing a hand on my shoulder.

"Relax. Jason told many tales of the breakup, none of which I believe. That was even before Patricia told me the truth."

My shoulders visibly relax and I clutch Deacon's hand, giving it a calming squeeze.

"We know our nephew, Noni," Mrs. Peterson says. "Why do you think my husband hasn't made him partner yet?"

They both laugh. I knew that Mr. and Mrs. Peterson weren't fans of Jason. In fact, they liked me more than they ever did him, but I had no idea they felt this strongly about him.

"Thanks again for inviting me and nominating me for the award."

"You deserve it. The things you've accomplished in just five years are remarkable," Mrs. Peterson says with a warm smile.

"And you, young man," Mr. Peterson says to Deacon. "Don't be like my nephew. Hold on to this woman."

"I absolutely plan to," he replies, gazing down at me. I reach up on my tiptoes and he plants a kiss on my lips that makes my legs weak.

We part ways with the Peterson's and find our seats. Deacon seats me and then goes to find me some food. I'm completely content sitting alone until I hear his voice.

"Well, if it isn't my ex."

I turn around to find Jason looking as debonair as he always does. Holding tight to his arm is the same woman I found on her knees in his office. I offer them both a genuine smile.

The funny thing about being over someone, they no longer affect you. Seeing him with another woman feels no different from seeing Mr. and Mrs. Peterson hugged up. I wish Jason the best, and if this woman makes him feel the same way Deacon makes me feel, then I hope they find happiness.

"Hello, Jason. And I'm sorry, I never got your name," I say, holding out a hand toward the woman.

"Crystal," she says with a smug smile. She glances at my hand but doesn't shake it. I shrug and drop my hand back in my lap.

"Noni," Jason starts, glancing down at me. "I must say you look lovely to be so pregnant."

I take the comment as the insult he wants it to be. I don't get to reply, because a plate of fresh fruit is placed down in front of me.

"She looks stunning, you dumb shit. And if you ever insult her again, I promise it will be your last."

"Are you threatening me, thug?" Jason says, raising his voice over the crowd, drawing attention to us.

Deacon takes a step toward him, but I stand and step between them. I grab Deacon's hand and place it over my moving belly.

"Ace wants to dance," I say to distract him.

Deacon smiles as he looks down at his son.

"All right, little man, Daddy will dance with you." He takes my hand in his and heads to the dance floor, before getting too far away he turns back to Jason. "Oh, Little Dick, it was a promise, not a threat."

Jason's light brown skin reddens and so does his date's. I can't help but laugh. Deacon takes me to the dance floor and starts to sway me to the music.

"You are so bad." I laugh.

His smile grows. "Hey, he better be glad that's all I said. I wanted to make him eat his damn teeth after what he said to you."

I lift a shoulder briefly. "Who cares what he says. I look damn good."

His smile widens and a loud laugh leaves his lips. "You're damn right you look good."

What seems like apprehension pinches his brow again. He's been making this face a lot in the last week. He gets this serious face as if he's thinking over something and then eventually, he shakes his head and lets it go.

It takes me by surprise when he doesn't shake his head, but instead opens his mouth.

"Noni, I need to ask you something."

"Ladies and gentlemen if you would kindly take your seats, we want to announce the winners," the MC says. Everyone starts to migrate to their designated seats.

"What were you going to ask?"

He smiles, but it doesn't reach his eyes. "Nothing. I'll ask it later." Taking my hand, he walks me back over to our seats.

At our table are Mr. and Mrs. Peterson. Their son Parker and his wife Renee, and of course Jason and Crystal. I sit sideways in my seat with my back to Deacon, listening to the MC talk about the purpose of the banquet and its contributors.

I can feel Deacon behind me. He pulls me into his chest, allowing me to lean on him as he wraps an arm around me to rub my belly. Ace kicks for him and we both laugh.

I don't even have to look over. I feel Jason's glare on the side of my face like a light is shining on it. I look over to catch his eyes; I was wrong. It isn't a glare I'm seeing.

Remorse is written all over him. From the downturned mouth to the way his shoulders curl over his chest, and the way his eyebrows gather in.

For a second, I feel bad for him. He had me right where he wanted me, yet he was never content with that. He gambled with my feelings and lost the bet. And I'll never look back.

"And now for the reason most of you are here," the MC says to the crowd and a few of them chuckle. "The small up-and-coming business award is awarded to a business who has been in business five or fewer years." The MC goes on to list all the requirements for the award.

"Are you nervous?" Deacon whispers in my ear.

I turn my head to look over my shoulder at him. "No. I don't need an award to tell me I'm doing good. I'm proud of my business, and I have everything I need to be happy."

I lift my hand to cup the back of his head and bring his lips to mine. The kiss is short, but significant. I want him to know he's one of the reasons I'm happy.

"And the winner of the SUB award is..." She pauses for dramatic effect before saying. "Jeremy Watson of Watson's bakery and creamery."

I clap proudly for Jeremy. Their homemade milkshakes are delicious.

"Sorry, Noni," Patricia says. "I just knew you were going to win."

I wave her off. "No problem, it's an honor to even be nominated."

"Famous last words of losers," Jason says over the rim of his glass.

Patricia turns to him and glares.

"You would know, wouldn't you?" Deacon replies, his hand still rubbing circles over my belly.

"You think you won?" Jason gives a dry laugh. "I dodged a bullet." He reaches over and tugs Crystal into his side but from the frown on her face, I don't think she's happy about the way he's sulking. "You can keep the woman and the brat."

"Jason," Mr. Peterson says in a warning tone.

"It's all right, Mr. Peterson," Deacon says holding up a hand. "Jason's just a little bitter. You see, it took me one night to do what he couldn't in six years."

"And what's that?" Parker asks with a playful gleam in his eyes.

"Make me come," I say.

Renee chokes on her wine, Parker, and Deacon burst out laughing followed by Mr. Peterson. Mrs. Peterson hides her laughter behind her hands, but nothing is more satisfying than the open-mouthed shock on Jason's face.

Was what I said, rude, inappropriate and immature? Yes. Would I take it back? Hell no.

Jason has been trying to get a rise out of me since he saw me. He's mistaken me for the old Noni. The one who was silent and miserable on her quest to be perfect. The new Noni knows perfection is an illusion and I'm perfect just the way I am.

"Now, if you all will excuse me, my *brat* is dancing on my bladder."

Deacon jumps up first and then helps me up. We walk away from the table hand in hand.

Deacon

No one, and I mean no one, was expecting that reply from Noni, but damn, it was perfect. I love the strong woman she's starting to accept herself as. I already knew she had it in her. I'm just glad she's claiming it.

"Your mouth has gotten reckless, young lady. Where did you learn to talk like that?" I joke.

She looks up at me with a sexy little smirk. "An asshole taught me."

I toss my head back and laugh. We stop in front of the restroom and I watch her go in. The ring box in my pocket is feeling heavy.

Tonight, while we were dancing, wasn't the first time I've wanted to ask her. When I saw Little Dick and his date approach Noni, for a second, I thought I would see regret, or at least jealousy. However, I watched her face the entire time.

All I saw cross her gorgeous features was mild interest. She was entirely unbothered. There were no feelings left there for him.

That meant only one thing. She isn't just ready to move on, but she is truly in love with me. I know in the length of time we've known each other; it doesn't seem realistic, but I don't give a fuck about timelines. I've always done things at my own pace.

My phone goes off in my pocket and I dig it out. When I see whose calling, I step away from the bathroom, finding a quiet spot.

"Hell no, I told you I couldn't tonight," I say the moment I answer the phone.

"Calm down," Griff replies. "I know you're out with the family. I just need your help for a minute."

"What the hell aren't you understanding? I'm not leaving her tonight."

"You won't have to. That Ferrari from the storage facility is at your location. Mad Dog is already there, I just need you to go and supervise."

I hiss out a breath as I run my fingers through my hair. "Can this shit not wait for another time?"

"This car is rarely moved. If we don't take it now, it goes back in that storage facility and we can't get it from there."

"Find another one."

"I've tried, Titus." I can hear the weariness and frustration in his tone. "The only other car that fits this description is in London. And we don't have time for that shit. It's now or never and I want this job done before my grandson comes."

I let out a deep breath before dropping my head and closing my eyes. Griff is right. This shit needs to be over in the next five weeks.

That's hoping Noni goes the full forty weeks. We still have two hundred and twenty-five cars left to get.

"Fuck," I roar into the phone. "I'll go help. But I swear, if that kid fucks up my night."

"He won't. He's in the parking garage. Head there now."

I end the phone call with Griff and make my way back over to the restroom. I catch a woman on her way in and stop her.

"Excuse me."

Her eyes light up when she looks at me. She scans me up and down before looking back at me with a flirty smile. Damn, all I said was excuse me.

"My fiancée is in there. She's wearing a yellow dress, she's the pregnant one. Can you tell her I had to step out to make a phone call and I'll meet her back at the table?"

The way her face falls when I mention Noni would be comical if this situation wasn't so shitty.

"Yeah, sure," she says, tossing her hair over her shoulder and walking into the bathroom.

I quickly turn and head out of the building to the parking garage. The faster I do this, the quicker I can get back to my girl and maybe give her this ring I've been holding on to. I find the pup waiting by the parking garage door as soon as I step out.

"Don't you look like the proper gentlemen," he jokes. I cut my eyes over to him and he has the good sense to shut the fuck up.

We find the car parked in a reserved spot.

"Hurry up," I tell the pup as I turn my back to the car to keep watch.

The kid goes to the driver's side with the dummy key. The parking garage is completely vacant, which is exactly what we need.

"You know," the pup starts as he fumbles with getting the door open. "Griff was right, you're a complete asshole, but you know your shit."

"This isn't a Hallmark Original. I'm not here to bond with you, get the damn door open already."

He chuckles. "It's too bad you're going to go back to just tattooing after all this. With that kid on the way, you'll need the extra money."

"What part of my demeanor are you not fucking understanding?" I ask over my shoulder. "I don't want to talk. Do your job."

I turn back forward to keep a lookout. The fumbling with the door stops completely.

"Is Black girl pussy different from white girls'?"

Done. I turn from my watch to storm over to the kid. He backs away with his hands raised. But I'm not going to kill him. I don't want to go back into the building with blood on my suit.

I use the dummy key still in the door to unlock it. You have to push the key halfway in and lift the handle before turning. The exact moment I get the door open, I hear it. That breathy way she says my name.

"Deacon?"

I close my eyes and my world crumbles at my feet. I just fucked up. I look up to find Noni standing on the other side of the car. Her brows are pinched as she surveys the scene before her.

I don't speak. I don't want to say anything that will implicate me.

"What are you doing with Mr. Peterson's car?"

Shit, this is worse than I thought. I can't even lie like I know the owner of the car.

"Baby, I can explain." I can't. However, that doesn't keep me from stepping toward her.

"Titus, I have to go. Thanks," the pup says, jumping in the car.

Now his dumb ass starts moving faster. As he backs out of the parking spot, I watch as the pinched brow on her face turns from confusion to realization. When she looks up at me again, there's only pain and anger in her eyes.

"Old colleagues, huh?" Her nostrils flare with each word.

"Noni."

I take a step toward her. She backs away, holding up her hand to stop me from coming close.

"You promised me this was behind you, you said we wouldn't lie to each other."

"I know, and this was behind me, but my pops got into some hot water, I had to help him."

It fucking kills me when her eyes fill with tears that slide down her face.

"All those nights you were working at Pit's bar, you were out stealing cars?"

Silence greets us. There is no reason to lie. She caught me red-handed, yet I couldn't bring myself to say it out loud. My silence is answer enough. She clutches a hand to her belly.

"Are you okay, is Ace all right?"

"Don't touch me," she yells, and I feel helpless to do anything.

I take a step back because I don't want her to get worked up. Last time she got stressed, she ended up in the hospital. She goes for her phone and my heart drops. She's calling the police.

"Please don't do this." I'm not above begging. "If you call the cops, I can get real time for this shit."

I have no right to ask her this. In fact, I feel like shit for doing it, but I can't go to jail for this. I'll miss my son growing up.

"In a few weeks, this will be over with. My pops' debt will be paid, and I can put this behind me." I try once again, but she continues making her phone call. "They were going to kill him, Noni."

"Hello," she says on the phone.

I drop my head in defeat. This is it. I won't run or fight anymore. I'll face up to my mistakes.

"Hey, Mira, I need you to pick me up."

As soon as she finishes speaking, she starts balling. I fist my hands with the need to console her. A bit of hopefulness fills me. She didn't call the cops, that means she still fucking cares.

"Please, just come get me, I'll explain." She hangs up, and when she looks up at me, she shakes her head. "I love you."

Daggers, that's what it feels like slicing through my chest.

"I love you too." She holds up her hands to cut me off.

"Let me finish. I love you, and you're the father of my child, that's the only reason I'm not putting your ass in jail. But I don't want to see you again. I'll get my things from your house. Amira will notify you when Ace is born. I need time before I allow you to see him."

"Please, Noni. God, please don't do that."

She shakes her head. "Goodbye, Deacon." She turns and walks away.

"Noni," I call out to her back, but she doesn't turn back to see me.

The thing I prayed wouldn't happen, the one thing I've been fighting so hard against, just fucking happened.

CHAPTER THIRTY

Broken Hearts

Noni

I glance down at the phone again. The message from Deacon making these damn flutters in my stomach feel like I'm on a rollercoaster and I've just dropped from the top of the big hill.

Deacon: I love you. And when this shit is over, I'm coming for my family. Tell my son I love him.

"You're only going to drive yourself crazy if you keep looking at that text."

I set the phone back down on the table in front of me at the sound of Amira's voice. Today is my baby shower.

Since I opted to wait to find out what I'm having, the girls and I decided to have a diaper party. Basically, everyone brings me a box of diapers or a gift card.

Deacon didn't want anyone to buy anything. He wanted to purchase everything together, but he's no longer in our lives anymore.

I rub at my belly, trying to calm a restless Ace. Lately he just can't seem to get comfortable, it's like he knows his daddy isn't here.

"Are you ever going to tell us what happened between you two?"

"Nothing," I reply with a lift of my shoulders.

"She still telling that lie?" Porsha says, walking into the kitchen with a cake box.

She puts the cake down on the table and takes the top off. The cake is done in the shape of a pregnant belly with tiny feet sticking out. I grab my phone to take a picture and for a brief second, I think about sending it to Deacon, but quickly put the phone down.

"I don't know why you won't just tell us what happened so we can tell you it's nothing and you two can get back together," Porsha says playfully.

"Why do you just assume I want to get back with him?"

They both cock their brows at me like the answer was obvious.

"Reason number one," Porsha starts. "You won't tell us what he did, which means you don't want us to hate him."

"And you never did that with Jason. We knew every time that weasel pulled his shit."

Porsha nods her head in agreement with Amira.

"Also," Amira continues. "He keeps texting you and you haven't blocked him or deleted the texts."

"Admit it, you want this man back," Porsha sings.

I huff a breath before dropping into a seat at my kitchen table. "How can you want someone you know you shouldn't? God, I miss him so much, but I can't."

"Why can't you?"

I look to Porsha. I love my girls, but I can't tell them what Deacon did. I can't risk them finding out and reporting him.

I know he broke the law, and I should report him. Mr. Peterson was devastated to find his car missing. Thankfully, he had insurance, but still it was his property stolen. Yet, I can't for the life of me call in what I know. Does that make me a bad person?

"He's bad news."

"How bad?" Porsha asks with a pinched brow.

"The type of bad that could get him in trouble with the law."

Both girls are silent for a moment. I guess coming to their own conclusions on what I could mean.

"I have to trust your judgment," Porsha says. "But I will say this, everything isn't always what it seems. Sometimes it requires a conversation." She sighs before taking a seat in the chair next to mine. "When Marcus was younger, he went to jail."

"What?" Both Amira and I say at the same time.

Porsha nods. "Yeah, he was the oldest of four kids. His mother was struggling, and his father was long gone. He started selling drugs to feed his family.

"He served a year in jail for simple possession. When he came out, he vowed he never wanted to go back. He started taking school seriously and even worked a full-time bag boy job to take care of his siblings."

I had no idea about any of this. Not that it would have made a difference in how I saw him. Marcus is an amazing, kind, educated, and respectful man.

"I'm telling you that to say, when I found out, I broke up with him. I felt as if he had lied to me by not telling me he had been in jail, but we talked and I realized I was wrong for jumping to conclusions. Maybe you're doing the same thing with Deacon."

I shake my head. "Marcus was a kid. Deacon is a grown man making these decisions. I can't just think of me. I have to consider Ace. No child should have to see his father in a prison cell."

Both women nod quietly. They now see how much of a big deal this is. If it were just me, I don't even know that I could walk away from Deacon. However, any day now, I will have someone else who will depend on me to make smart decisions.

That's enough for me to walk away. I have to be strong. Maybe one day my heart will catch up to my head.

"Knock knock," someone says as they enter the house.

Porsha, Mira, and I both groan once we recognize the voice. Walking out of the kitchen into the living room, I spot my aunts and my mother. With them are my four female cousins.

"I'll take your gifts," Amira says politely, reaching for the bags in their hands.

I give my cousins and aunts hugs and thank them for coming before they take seats. I stand before my mother like a child who has a bad report from the teacher.

"I won't ask if he's here," my mother says with her nose turned up. "Jason told me he saw you leaving the banquet with Amira."

She shakes her head and steps around me. I don't take the bait. Instead, I shut the door and tell everyone the food is in the kitchen.

We all crowd in, my family, my best friends, and a few colleagues. It's a small gathering, but it fits me.

The decorations are all done in gold, gray, white, and yellow. Amira and I worked all night on a heart-shaped balloon arch that frames the table. On the wall above the table is a framed letter C.

The tablecloths are white with yellow runners and gold bows. Japanese lanterns hang over the gift table and little elephants are used as cardholders to direct you from the food to the gifts. I love the color scheme and how it turned out.

"I love this color," Maria, my secretary says parroting my thoughts.

The thank you never makes it out of my mouth. My mother's voice cuts me off first.

"I don't. Yellow is such an ugly color."

I catch Porsha's eye before she says anything. I shake my head.

"Are we going to have something other than these little finger foods?" Aunt Mildred asks, picking up one of the ham pinwheels and looking at it as if it's made out of paper towels. "When is the real food going to get here?"

"Mom, the invitation said the menu would be finger foods," my cousin Coco says. "That's why I ate before I came."

She ate before she came, yet still she has seven sandwiches in one plate, a half a pound of shrimp on another and now she's loading up the chocolate-covered strawberries in a small bowl.

"You know Noni tries to be fancy," Aunt Judy adds. "This isn't like when Kim had her baby shower." She smiles at her daughter. "I cooked a full dinner. We even had glazed ham."

It must have been glazed with sawdust. That ham was so dry, it broke apart in your mouth like overcooked turkey meat.

"The Popeye's down the street is still open," Porsha says.

Amira shoves at her arm to keep her from saying anything else. It grows quiet again as everyone continues to fill their plates.

"I thought you were going with the black and gold color scheme?" my mother's voice brings my attention back to her. She has yet to grab a plate. She's still looking around at the decorations like I painted shit on the walls.

"I never told you I was going with black and gold."

"I could have sworn we talked about black and gold," Mother replies.

We don't even talk, how the hell would we discuss a color scheme?

"Isn't black and gold Jason's fraternity colors?" Mira asks. We both have the same confused look on our faces.

"Maybe that's who I was talking to. He would be the only one to include me in plans anyway."

I try my hardest not to fall for my mother's attempt to bait me. She knows what she's doing. Had she ever taken the time to ask me what colors I was going with or even anything about the baby shower, I would have told her. But she's never been concerned.

"Well, maybe you should have let him plan it," Aunt Mildred says, picking up another melted ham and cheese slider. "Maybe if he did, we would have real food."

"You know, with all these complaints, it's odd how none of you returned our calls when we tried to plan this gathering."

Porsha's words don't shock me. I would have been more shocked if my family had offered to help. My cousins have been fed the same narrative my aunts have.

My mom loves to toss my accomplishments in my aunts' and cousins' faces. She uses me like a weapon against them but treats me like a disease. I have never been close to my family.

"If you wanted real food that was the time to voice your concerns, not here on her special day," Amira, usually the nicer one of my two friends, says.

"Well, you would've had help if you included Jason," Mother argues.

"Will you please stop talking about that fuck boy," Porsha snaps.

You can almost hear the tension creep in the room. My mother looks over to me.

"Well, there you have it," she says, throwing her hands out. "I tried to warn you about your friends. Now look at you, lonely and pathetic just like them."

"Who are you calling pathetic?" Porsha takes a step toward my mother. I grab her arm to stop her.

"Girl, you need to check your mama."

Mumbles of how shameful Porsha is acting circulate around my family.

"It's interesting you use the word pathetic," I say to my mother. "You of all people should know what it looks like. Lord knows, you've been pathetic for years."

"My word," Aunt Judy gasps.

"Now wait a minute," Aunt Mildred says, stepping forward.

My mother stops her sister with a raised hand. "Let her finish. I want you all to hear how unappreciative and disrespectful she is."

She's playing the victim. She wants me to be the bad guy, like she's been telling herself and others all my life. I chuckle and shake my head.

"You have no idea how hard I tried to please you."

"Please me?" she shouts. "You ran off to Vegas with those two hoes," she says, pointing at Porsha and Amira. "Just to come back pregnant with some lowlife's baby."

"And I would do it again in a heartbeat," I declare with absolute honesty. "I was drowning in my own pathetic life. That man did what no one else in my entire life could do."

"Oh, spare us your whore story. Jason told me about your comment the other night at the banquet."

"And I'm glad he did. Yes, Deacon made love to me in ways Jason never could have. And it wasn't just his giant dick and impeccable knowledge on how to use it that changed my life, it's the respect he gave me. Something Jason has lacked since the day I met him. I was suffocating in that relationship. And your issues didn't make it any better."

"What issues? I have no issues. All I've ever done is try to be the best mother I could to the ungrateful brat that ruined my life."

Her words are like a slap in the face. I'm officially done playing this game with her. Today, she will learn the truth, the truth she thought I didn't know.

"You've told yourself that lie so long you have started to believe it." I stand up straighter, squaring my shoulders. "When he walked out that door, he told you he never wanted to be a father."

"I know," she shouts.

"Nor did he want to be your man." The room gets quiet, and Mother stands stock still.

"He didn't mean that. He was saying that because he didn't want you around crying for him all the time. You wouldn't let the man breathe. Soon as he came home you were running up to him for attention."

"I was a child, that's what I was supposed to do. I just didn't know I was born to two of the most selfish and self-absorbed people in the world."

She gasps, clutching her imaginary pearls. "We were happy before you came."

"How many times are you going to tell that lie?" I scoff. "He was already leaving you when you got pregnant with me. You trapped him."

She takes a staggering step back, her hand moving up to cover her wide-open mouth. "Who told you that?"

I lied to Deacon when I told him I met my father, and he didn't speak to me. He did, he had a lot to say.

He still wanted nothing to do with me, but he admitted he had broken up with my mother. Yet, she wouldn't let him go. He was actively seeing other women but kept making the mistake of falling back in my mother's bed.

Then she told him she was pregnant. He had no doubt she did it on purpose. He stuck around, trying to be a father to his child, but soon realized he didn't want either of us. He hated her, and I made him feel stuck. He decided to abandon us both.

"I ran into Norman not long before I went to college and he had a lot to tell me. You see, all these years you've been lying to yourself and everyone else."

"What is she talking about, Shondra?" Aunt Mildred asks. "You told us Norman begged you to get back with him and that's how you ended up pregnant."

My mother never takes her eyes off me. She stares at me and for once the mask is off. The real Shondra looks back at me. The woman who hates her daughter because she wasn't enough to keep a man who never wanted to be kept.

"You'll need me before I'll ever need you." She spits out the words with so much vehemence. If I cared about how she feels about me, I'm sure they would have hurt me.

Instead, I shrug. "Until that time comes, get the hell out of my house."

Her mouth opens, but nothing comes out. She turns on her heels and snatches her purse off the table before she storms out of my house, slamming the door.

"And to anyone else who has a problem with my food, my color scheme, or my baby daddy, you can get out too."

I wait for my aunts and cousins to place their food down and walk out, but none of them speak. I catch my Aunt Mildred's eye, and for once, there isn't a hateful glare or a smirk. She regards me with a proud smile.

She then turns back to the table and starts to load her plate up. Everyone else follows suit. I stand there for a moment feeling confident.

That conversation needed to be had a long time ago. I fault myself for never owning up to it and speaking my mind. I let it go on for entirely too long.

Then someone came along and taught me perfection wasn't obtainable. They told me I needed to claim my space in the world. I miss him, but I'm not ready to allow him back.

"All right, ladies," Amira says, getting everyone's attention. "I'm going to pass this paper around, and I want you to write down if you think baby Clarke will be a boy or a girl and how much you think they will weigh."

Raised voices go up. It seems most agree I'm having a very big boy.

CHAPTER THIRTY-ONE

The Truth

Deacon

"Hey, Deacon, can I talk to you?"

I look up from the pile of paperwork on my desk to find Maverick standing there.

I lean back in my chair, running a hand down my tired eyes. I've been running myself crazy. All day I run the shops and at night I bring in cars like a crazy person.

In the two weeks since Noni and I have been broken up, I've brought our two hundred and twenty-five car total down to one hundred and fifty. I've powered through that fucking list like my life depends on it.

In truth, it does, because this shit—waking up every day away from the woman that I love, not touching my son and soothing him when he gets rowdy—this isn't living. I had no fucking clue how much I wasn't living until I got to sample the real thing.

"Yeah, come in."

Maverick enters the office and takes a seat on my couch. Mav is a good kid. In his mid-twenties, he lives a pretty quiet life compared to the shit I did when I was his age.

At almost seven feet, he's big as fuck. I thought it was strange he wanted to be a tattoo artist but has no tats of his own. When Pit brought him to me, I didn't think he and I would vibe. However, we've become close. I trust him, and I don't do that with a lot of people.

"You must have an early client?" I ask him, looking down at my watch. It's six in the morning.

"No, I actually came early to talk to you."

I sit up straighter in my chair. Not knowing what this could be about. "What's up?"

He sighs. "I don't mean to get in your business, but Mir has been asking me about you."

"Mir, as in Amira? Noni's best friend?"

He grins and those dimples Karly swoons over show up. "Yeah, we got to know each other. We're just friends," he assures me quickly.

"What about Amira?"

"Well, she keeps asking about what happened to you and Noni. She's worried about her friend."

"Tell her I'm working on it. I can't go back to Noni until I have this shit cleared up."

He rubs the back of his neck. "About that," he starts and trails off. "Look, you and Pit, you guys are like family to me. Probably more than my real family."

I don't know much about Mav, only that his real name isn't Maverick, his father is dead, and he doesn't talk to his family at all. He won't even mention them.

"I wanted to help you out of this mess you were in," he continues. "I wasn't trying to overstep but I have some connections, and I was going to reach out and use them."

"You don't have to do that. I don't want you involved. These men Griff owes, they're dangerous."

"That's the thing, Deacon. He doesn't owe anyone."

I'm tired. I can admit that. I've only had seven hours of sleep this entire week.

I'm stressed the fuck out worrying about Noni and Ace. I know I couldn't have heard or understood him correctly.

"What do you mean he doesn't owe anyone? He's working for a Russian. I met the guy's henchmen. They approached me at the shop."

Maverick shakes his head. "That's where I checked first," he says. "Turns out they're just some meatheads that had no problem roughing up a young punk."

"No way. What the fuck are you trying to say?" I ask, shooting to my feet.

"You need to listen to him." I turn to my door to find Pit. His arms are folded across his chest.

"After I found out about the meatheads, I took the info to Pit. I wanted him to double-check. I knew I couldn't come to you without being sure."

"I checked all my sources and turns out he was right. Those guys were hired by Griff. After I found that out, I went to Igor, the Russian Griff supposedly owes. Come to find out, your old man went to him with the job. Igor says all he was doing was shipping the cars off. There is no debt owed."

My head spins and for a moment I feel like I'm about to pass out. Everything I did, I did for him because I believed he was in danger. I fucked over my family, my happiness, everything for him, and this is what he does?

Why? What purpose does he have that he would pull me back in the game like this?

I'm damn sure not going to get answers by standing around. I snatch my keys off the table and storm toward the door.

"Deacon, wait." Pit says behind me, but I keep going. I'm going to make my first stopover Griff's to whoop his ass, and the next stop will be to Noni to tell her I'm done for good and then I'll plead with her to take me back.

"Deacon, wait a fucking minute." Pit catches up to me and grabs my arm. I spin around and snatch it away from him.

"What?" I shout.

"I'm trying to explain. He may know I was checking into him. One of my sources was found dead today. I think he got a little too close while digging up info. Griff knows I know. He may be ready for you."

In this moment, his words freeze me like an ice block. Every time Griff has pulled me back in or kept me going, he used the same two people.

Let's get this done before my grandson comes... They know about your family.

Every time he has used Noni and the baby and every time, I do everything he says.

"Fuck," the word is shouted as I storm out of the shop. I'm glad I chose my bike today, because I needed to get to my family fast.

Noni

The pounding at my door startles me. It's six in the morning on a Sunday. No one should be at my door.

"Coming," I call out to the person on the other side.

I look out of my peephole to find James, Deacon's father, at the door. For a second, trepidation hits me. Even Ace feels it because he does a somersault in my belly that causes me to grab my lower back.

"Noni," James calls out from the other side of the door. "I hate to bother you, but it's about Deacon," he says, the magic words to make me open the door for him. I swing the door open.

"Is he okay? Is Deacon all right?" Both sentences come out without me taking a breath.

Right away I know that I've made the wrong decision. James stands at my door and in his hand is a gun. Before I can push the door closed, a huge bald guy pushes into my house and grabs me.

I want to scream, but I don't get a chance to before he wraps a hand around my freshly done braids, pulling my head back and covering my mouth with his sweaty palm. James walks into the house and following behind him are the two men who cornered me at Deacon's shop.

"Have a seat. You should rest your feet," James says, as if he's concerned. The big bald guy guides me to my couch and shoves me down.

"What do you want?" My plan is to find out what they want so I can explain I didn't have it and they can leave.

"I just want your cooperation. Soon, my son will be here, and I need you to convince him to do his job."

"The job of stealing cars?"

James looks at me with a grin. He sits on the arm of my chair. The dark-skinned guy with the dreads is posted up at my front door while the skinny white guy stands at my window. The bald one continues to stand over me like I can move fast enough to leave.

"Did he tell you that that's how I found him?" James goes on to say, as if we're having a friendly conversation. "He was trying to steal my car."

He laughs to himself. "I'd watched him from my window the entire time. It took him a minute and twenty seconds to pop the lock with an old screwdriver. I could have been mad at him, but I was damn proud. The world looked at him and saw a delinquent little kid, but I saw dollar signs."

He shrugs. "The car industry is very lucrative, little lady."

"Fuck yeah, it is," the skinny, sick looking one says.

"It's also very competitive. It's about moving product fast, and there was no one faster than my little Titus. He was smart too, a lot smarter than others in this industry. He was my moneymaker.

"He was a natural at this shit. And then, well, he wanted out, so I let him go."

"Why did you let him go if he was that valuable?" I ask.

I don't actually care. This man is crazy, and he doesn't deserve the love Deacon has for him. But I need to keep him talking because if he's distracted, maybe I can find a way out of this.

"I got cocky." He shrugs. "I figured I didn't need him, and honestly, I thought he would come back. He wanted to be a tattoo artist," he scoffs at the comment like a car thief is better. "I had no fucking idea he would be successful at it."

The group of men all laugh like something is funny.

"Why bring him back now?"

James looks at me with a glare. "I'm a selfish man, Noni. I lost most of my money to gambling debts and bad investments. You see, Deacon was okay with being normal, working a normal job and being an upstanding citizen, but I couldn't stomach that shit.

"I missed the adrenaline, I missed the power, and the money. I wanted my lifestyle back, and I knew the only way I could get it was to drag Deacon with me. I thought that if I forced his hand back into the lifestyle, he would miss it too, but then you came into the picture."

This time all the playful banter is gone. He's not a fan of me, obviously.

"You see, I could have dealt with the kid. I could have simply shared him with the rug rat, but you can't pull a man away from pussy."

"Not good pussy anyway," this time the black guy speaks.

"With you in the picture, he would've never come back. Which is why I sent Mad dog there to steal the Ferrari at the banquet and I made Deacon go help."

"I'm guessing the text telling me to come to the parking garage wasn't from Deacon's phone?"

James laughs as if I just told a joke. "Steel doesn't look like much, but he's handy as hell with a laptop."

This time, they all laugh. Just then, the distinctive sound of a motorcycle rumbles into my driveway.

"Showtime," the skinny one he called Mad dog says.

All three men pull out guns to match the one James has.

"Now, Noni. If you follow my directions perfectly, I won't have to put a bullet in your head. And trust me, I have no problem doing that."

I can hear Deacon's footsteps coming up my front steps.

"Noni," he calls out my name before he knocks on the door. "Noni, answer the door."

"Tell him to come in," James whispers to me.

"Co… come in." My voice breaks, but I can't help it. The cold press of a gun is at my temple.

"Try again, this time a little more convincing," James directs.

I take a deep breath. "Come in." Instead of twisting the knob like we all assume he would. He doesn't enter.

"I know you're in there, Griffin. Let her go."

"Deacon," I cry out, trying to warn him, but the big guy named Steel yanks me by my braids, pulling my head back. A quiet yelp comes out of my mouth before he touches my forehead with the tip of the gun.

"I'm sorry, baby." Deacon's voice sounds broken. I want to tell him it's okay, but it isn't okay.

"You might as well come on in, Titus. We're all waiting for you," James says cheerfully.

The door opens and Deacon walks in. His eyes land on me and widen before he takes a thunderous step toward me. The clicking of guns causes him to pull up short.

"I'm here now," Deacon says with his hands up. "Let her go. I'll do whatever you want."

"Oh, now you're going to cooperate?" James laughs. "I know you, son. Remember, I raised you. The moment I let the little lady go, you'll find some kind of way to back out of this. No, I think I'll keep her."

I cry out when Steel yanks my head back further.

"What the fuck? I swear, I'm going to put a fucking bullet in your head if you touch her again." Deacon takes another step toward me, and this time he doesn't stop until Steel moves the gun from my temple to point it at my belly. That move brings Deacon to a stop and causes me to gasp.

"Here's the new deal," James says. "You have until tomorrow morning to get the other cars to the drop-off. When you deliver the cars, I'll drop the little lady and the kid back off right here. Completely unharmed."

"Hell no, no deal. Leave her out of this."

"You're not in the position to negotiate. You get me the cars, the girl will be fine. Unfortunately, I won't be able to offer you my help though."

Again, James laughs. "Get her up." He directs his statement to Steel, who grabs me and hauls me up too fast.

"Ow," I cry out as I clutch my heavy belly.

Deacon takes a step toward me. "Noni, are you okay? Is it Ace?"

He tries to come closer, but this time Steel blocks him, and the other two step up behind him. He clocks Steel in the face so hard the giant man goes down, but then he immediately takes a punch to the face that's so hard it should have knocked him out cold. However, Deacon comes back up swinging.

I scream his name and try to reach him, but James drags me out of the house while I watch the other three men take turns stomping him on the ground. I ignore the backache that has become a little more persistent. James pushes me into a car as I cry out for Deacon.

My hopes are dashed when James points the gun at my belly and tells me to shut up. After that, my fight is over. I cry silently as I'm driven away from my home and the man I love.

CHAPTER THIRTY-TWO

Last Chance

Deacon

My ribs ache, my lip is busted, and I may have a few sprain fingers from pounding on those fucker's hard skulls. But nothing hurts as bad as the back of my head. It's a possibility I have a damn concussion from where someone struck me with the butt of a gun.

The moment I woke up on the floor, I called Pit and told him what was going on. With just twenty-four hours to steal a hundred and fifty cars, I need to get moving. I'm good, but I'm not that damn good.

I pop another handful of Tylenols and finish them with what's left of the water in my bottle before going back to my map. I had the list of cars and their locations marked on a map. Thankfully, the rest of the cars were close by.

Some were harder to get than others, because they would come with trackers, but I already knew which ones had them. I have a damn good plan, but I still have no idea how I'm going to be able to pull that shit off by six in the morning.

It doesn't fucking matter how. You're going to get that shit done. I scold myself for even taking the time to think that bullshit. I let my girl and my son down. I'm not going to let that shit fly.

My doorbell rings, getting my attention. I have no idea who could be on the other side of the door. I limp over, holding a hand to my ribs. I definitely need to get those checked soon.

I don't even peek out to see who it is, at this point, it doesn't even matter. I swing the door open and have to take a step back.

"About fucking time you opened the door," Pit says, walking in the house with the gang right behind him. Leo, Pit's little brother, follows.

"Sup, Deacon. Got anything to eat?"

"In the kitchen." I direct him and turn back to the door. Skittles walks in and immediately punches me in the stomach.

"Next time, call us first, asshole."

"Love you too, Skittles."

She walks past me and Tak steps up and on his heels is his beautiful pregnant fiancée, Jazz.

"I tried to make her stay at home," Tak delivers in that deadpan way if his.

"Fuck off," Jazz says, giving me a gentle hug. "You know stealing cars is my shit."

"You're not driving a damn car," Tak says.

"You know how to make me stay home." Jazz calls over her shoulder as she wobbles into the living room.

"Fucking lunatic fan," Tak mumbles under his breath as he follows her.

Kelex is next. He claps my hand, giving me a one-arm hug. "You look like shit," he proclaims with a wink.

"Thank you," I reply sarcastically.

Reynolds is next and he has Syd with him. I stop him on the way in. "You sure about this shit?"

He and Tak are public figures, if they get pinched for this, they will never live it down. I'm not too worried about Tak because his ass has nine fucking lives. We would all go down before that lucky bastard.

Reynolds grabs my shoulder and squeezes. "Assholes for life. You need me, I'm here. Just don't make this bullshit a habit." He walks in hand in hand with his wife.

Jeff follows behind them, one hand in his pants pocket and the other holding a cell phone where his attention is glued. "I'm only here for moral support and someone mentioned whiskey." He never even looks up from his phone as he walks past me into the house.

Roman and Ox come through the door next. We nod to each other. I've come to know both of these men through Pit. The next faces stop me. Maverick, Q, and Shark are here.

"If I would have known," Q starts. "I would have warned you about Griff. We all jumped ship after you left. It was never the same, and he had lost his mind." I grab my old friend and give him a quick hug.

"Bring your ass, Deacon," Pit calls from inside the house. "We don't have all fucking night."

I shake my head, but shut my door and walk back into the kitchen. I don't have to tell them all what this means to me. They already know.

They also know that for any of these assholes in this room, I would have done the same. I go to the group around the table.

"All right, tell us what the fuck we're supposed to be doing." Reynolds says, looking down at the map and all the pushpin markings.

Q and I quickly give them a rundown on the system. We tell them the things to look for and what to do in what situation. When we're done, everyone has a car and a partner.

We're going to hit as many cars at once to make a wave. We have to cover a lot of ground in a short time.

"What about the Tesla?" Shark asks. "You know there isn't a jammer around to break that system. You would have to break into the motherboard on that thing and it would still take you thirty minutes to an hour."

"I know," I reply.

"Well, what's the plan for it?"

"I'll get that one."

"Titus, you're not listening," Q says, holding up a hand. "If you don't dismantle the tracker, you will have every damn cop in Vander City and Bridge Lake on your ass."

"I know."

Pit picks up on our conversation. He and Maverick walk over to us. "You're going to have to give us more information than that. We're not risking our lives to get you out of this shit just so you can go to jail anyway."

I run a hand down my face. "Look, we all know that someone has to go down for this. I just want my family safe. You get them out and I'll take the fall. No different from what you did that night of the race," I say, directing the comment to Pit.

"That's the dumbest fucking plan I've ever heard," Skittles says with her hands on her hips.

"Which is why I didn't tell you, because I didn't want anyone to talk me out of it. It's the only way."

"The only way that will send your ass to prison for ten to twenty years," Tak noted.

"It's the only way I can assure my girl and my son survive this. That's all that matters."

"What if we scrap that bullshit plan and plan a better one? One where no one goes to jail or gets killed."

"There is no other plan, Kelex," I growl in response.

"I might have one." We all turn to face Maverick. "But I'm going to need a fast driver."

Both Pit and Skittles step up. Kelex, Reynolds, Tak, and I all roll our eyes. This shit again.

"Are you fuckin' kidding me?" Skittles says to her husband.

"Not up for discussion, Mayven."

"I can dust your ass in a race."

"Yeah, so you say."

Before she opens her mouth to take this argument further down the rabbit hole I know it would go down. I cut in.

"Will you two shut the fuck up so we can hear his plan?"

They both shoot me the bird at the same time but do at least let it go.

"Here's the deal," Mav starts. "We're going to use the Tesla to bring down Griff. Q says that from the place we are taking the Tesla to the chop shop is about a fifteen-minute drive. If we can cut that time down to ten we can plant that car right at Griff's front door and along with it, every cop in Vander City.

"One car in his driveway isn't going to do shit. With the right lawyer, he won't get any jail time," Pit points out.

"He would have to be driving the car for him to go down," Roman advises.

"One car on his property might not do shit, but a shipment container full would definitely fuck him over," I speak the thought out loud as it plays through my head.

"I like where this is going," Mav says.

"Q, can you and Roman hack into Steel's laptop?" I ask both men.

Roman nods his head. Never one for many words.

"Yeah," Q says. "That shouldn't be hard, but what are we looking for?"

I smile. "You're not looking for anything. You're planting something. Griff is smart enough to know not to keep any of his dirty business records or files on computers.

"He's old school and doesn't trust the internet. However, I had a gut feeling and started keeping records of every car that was taken and every shipping order, number, time, and which shipping crate the cars were on. I need you to plant that information on every fucking computer system Griff owns. Including Steel's."

"About time your ass proved your worth," Reynolds says, smacking me on the back.

"We still need to get the cars to the shipyard tonight," Mav says.

"Not all of them, just enough to give the feds something to go on."

I scratch at my chin. This changes the game plan a little. I look back down at the list of cars. We need the big-ticket cars tonight.

"How do we keep Griff's guy from figuring out what we are doing? They are going to have eyes on our movement all night," Pit points out another good point.

"Leave that to me," Roman says with a bit of finality that lets us know he has it covered.

"Something else is starting to stand out," Pit says, leaning over Q's open laptop. "Didn't you tell me once that the carjacking business is lucrative but expensive?"

I nod, squinting my eyes at Pit, trying to see where he's going with this line of questioning.

"Looking at Griff's bank accounts, his ass can't afford toilet paper to wipe his own ass, let alone the amount of money that it would take to pull this off," Q says, looking up from his computer.

I lock eyes with Pit, undoubtedly thinking the same thing. Someone is bankrolling this for Griff. I'm pretty sure if we checked our sources, it would be the same one funding all the shitstorms coming for us lately.

I know eventually, we were going to have to figure out who this behind-the-scenes puppet master is. However, I can't focus on that right now. With our new plan in motion, we go over the car list again. We get one shot at this and we can't fuck it up. My family's lives are at stake.

***

"All right, everyone, game time," Q's voice comes over the headsets we're all wearing. Q has definitely upped his software and equipment since the last time we did this.

We are all in different locations around the city. The plan is to strike hard and fast.

"Once I say go, you turn on the jammers and wait until the light turns green. That light has to be green, or the tracker isn't disabled."

I make sure I repeat that little tidbit. "As soon as you have the okay, signal your tail and get in the car. When the driver is in the car, the tail needs to get out of dodge and get their ass to the drop-off. We're on a tight schedule tonight, let's make sure this shit runs smoothly."

"Damn, how many times are we going to run over this plan?" Kelex's voice comes through my earpiece.

"He's trying to make sure your ass doesn't go to jail," Pit says, coming to my defense over the headset.

"Thanks, Pit."

"You're welcome. Now shut the fuck up and let's do this."

"My god, y'all are like toddlers," Skittles' soft voice grumbles.

"Focus," I say, getting them back on track. "Are you guys ready?"

A bunch of readies come through my earpiece.

"All right, crew, let's steal some cars," Q sings. "Now."

I hit the switch on my jammer and hold it up to my first car of the night. Maverick is my tail for most of tonight.

The Plymouth Hemi Cuda is a classic and I doubt this beauty will have GPS tracking on it, but a lot of private owners put trackers inside the cars. The jammer will work to scramble those as well.

The tracking isn't the hardest part about this heist, it's the location of the car that will be a beast. I have to drive it off of a fairground. The fair is long gone, but every six months the Shriners host their car show on these grounds.

The cops are notorious for hanging out around here for the exact reason we're here. This is a breeding ground for car thieves. If they were going to set up bait cars, it would definitely be one of these.

"Team one is out," Pit says, coming over the headset. Leo is his tail.

"Team three is ghost," Reynolds' voice comes through loud and clear. He's the driver and Syd is his tail.

"Team four is done." It's Tak this time. He's the driver and Ox is his tail.

I'm waiting to hear from the other two teams before I climb in my car and get the hell out of dodge. I don't want any of these guys to get in trouble because of me.

"Team two is on its way," Skittles says, and I'm pretty sure me and Pit both take a collective sigh at that.

"What's the hold up, Kelex?" I ask, he has yet to call his all clear.

"This key isn't working," he rants.

"Kelex, make sure you're lifting the handle at the same time you turn the key." Q's calm voice comes through. That's the most important job for your tech, he has to stay calm when you're in a pinch. Q is a hundred times better at making dummy keys than Steel is.

I pop the lock to my Cuda and climb in before giving Maverick the sign to go.

"Kelex, all clear?" I'm not leaving until he is.

"Deacon, you got heat heading your way about a half a block out."

We knew patrols would be scanning the fairgrounds.

"Kelex," I call out.

"Got it," he finally says. "Team five is out."

I sigh in relief before starting the car. "Team six is all clear. Get to the shipyard. Roman, get ready to work your magic."

I peel away from the fairgrounds, feeling great about the first job. However, we still have a long night ahead of us.

Noni

The pain in my back is getting worse. It's probably because they've had me sitting on this hard chair since early this morning. It's nearly eleven thirty at night. I shift in my seat for the hundredth time, trying to get comfortable. It's not working.

I put a hand to my lower back and rub, trying to ease the ache. It only goes away for a short while before coming right back.

"They've cleared nearly fifty cars," the big one named Steel says across the room. He's sitting behind double computer screens at a makeshift desk. James stands behind him, looking over his shoulder. "There's no way they will get them all before midnight."

The reminder of James's threat has my heart hammering.

"I know my boy, he'll do it."

I hated the way he spoke of Deacon. He doesn't deserve to call him his boy. He isn't a father figure, he's a predator.

He preyed on the vulnerability of a young boy. He took Deacon's trust and toyed with it. Used his desire for a family like a weapon.

I hate this man.

"Hey, little lady, how you holding up?" James turns and asks me like he gives a shit.

I roll my eyes and look away from him. He laughs like he always does.

"You don't like me too much, do you?" He walks over to me, then takes a seat on the edge of the table in front of me.

"Gee, I wonder why?" I reply curtly.

He chuckles as he looks into the bag of fast-food burgers they brought me for dinner. Someone took a bite out of my burger and half of my fries were gone.

"Not hungry?" He quirks a brow. "You need to eat. My grandson needs sustenance."

"Don't call my baby your grandchild. You are not his grandfather. I'd rather have the absentee ass who left Deacon's mother take the role than you."

He grits his teeth. Tossing the half-eaten burger back in the bag, he jumps up, grabbing my chin in a painful grip.

"You should watch your fucking mouth when you talk to me."

"Or what?"

It's hard to believe I waited until I'm thirty-two to grow a backbone and speak my mind. It's even harder to believe I can no longer turn it off, even when I'm staring danger in the face.

"Hey, Griff," Steel calls him back over to the computer. "Something's wrong. The cars haven't been to the drop in a while."

"What?" James looks over his shoulder but has yet to let go of my chin.

"Shit," Steel's outburst is followed by his frantic movements, he's rapidly clicking keys on his keyboard.

"What's going on?" James lets me go and stands up straight.

"It's all here," he says. "All the car information, the logs of the shipments, someone hacked into the system and linked every damn car we took to you and me."

"What the fuck are you talking about?"

"I'm talking about my computer is now a fucking smoking gun," Steel shouts.

James goes to the device and starts smacking at the screen. I'm no tech person, but even I know that isn't going to help.

"Turn this shit off," he bellows to a panicked Steel.

"That's not going to help." Steel continues to work on the laptop, but I can tell by the way he's squinting and clicking rapidly on the keys he isn't going to be able to fix it.

"Call Deacon, get him on the phone now," James barks the orders at the other two who walked in when Steel started yelling.

A painful ache hits my back and moves to my lower belly. I close my eyes and breathe the way I learned in my classes. Oh my god, I think I'm in labor.

Really, Ace, you couldn't wait until tomorrow?

The rumble of a car pulling up over the gravel outside grabs everyone's attention.

"Get up," James shouts at me, but I'm in the middle of another contraction. He drags me out of my seat, and I cry out.

"What the hell is wrong with you?"

"I think she's in labor," the black guy who I discovered is named Chris says. He's watching me like a horror movie.

"Get up," James screams at me again. I barely stand without clenching my tightening belly.

"Griffin," Deacon calls out. "We got some business to discuss."

James drags me by the arm like I'm a child who just showed out in Walmart. We head outside of the warehouse. There's a large concrete deck that wraps around the front and side of the building. The thing is at least six feet high off the ground.

The only way to the gravel parking lot is by a concrete ramp on the side. With his hand still gripping my arm, James stands us on the ramp. In front of a black Charger is the only man I want to see. Maverick is also with him.

Deacon's gaze quickly turns to me, he scans my body from head to toe.

"It's done, Griff," he says, focusing back on James.

"No, it's not. There are still a hundred cars that need to be collected."

"No," Deacon replies quickly. "At this very moment, the feds have raided the storage facility. All the cars were seized."

James's hand around my arm tightens. "We were just watching the storage facility live. No fucking way the feds are there."

Deacon shakes his head. "You were watching footage of the facility that Roman fed you. The last footage you saw before it all went out, was a few hours ago. If you don't believe me, tell Steel to pull it up again."

James doesn't speak, but nods to Steel. Another contraction rocks me, and I clutch my belly and whimper.

"Baby, what's wrong?"

I don't answer as I breathe through the contraction.

"It seems our baby boy is making an appearance tonight," James says with a smirk.

"Noni, baby, look at me." Deacon tries to sound calm, but I can hear the panic loud and clear in his voice.

I have to wait until the contraction passes before I can look up at him. When I do, my heart breaks. Fear and concern crease his brow, and I have to fight the urge to run to him.

The parking lot of the warehouse is like a salvage yard. Cars, car parts, and towers of stacked-up tires litter the area. Getting from this ramp to Deacon won't be easy, but I want to be in his arms so badly I can feel it.

"Fuck, Griff, he isn't lying. Look at this." Steel breaks through my thoughts. He comes out with a laptop to show James what's on the screen.

With his distraction, I look back to Deacon. He smiles at me, then deliberately looks to my arm loosely held in James's. I get the feeling he wants me to run. I use Steel's distraction and push away from James, who lets me go.

However, I lose my footing and fall from the cement ramp. I go to scream, but it catches in my throat when a man with brown hair and green eyes grabs me and pulls me into his chest. Even standing up on the platform, we didn't see him tucked behind the stacks of tires beneath us.

"You got her, Pit?" Deacon calls out.

"Got her," the tall handsome man holding me says.

He pulls me back away from the platform, tucking me behind a large barrel and stacks of tires. Getting away from James brings a sigh of relief right before another contraction hits. I close my eyes and breathe through it until it passes.

"While you were distracted watching that video feed all night, I was busy mounting evidence against you," Deacon yells. I watch him through the break in the tires. Despite being in the middle of labor pains, I have to point out how fine my man is in his black Henley and dark jeans. Yes, I got it bad.

He continues to speak to James. "I know all the details, all the shipping numbers and routing numbers on the accounts. And with the help of friends, I was able to get that information to the right people."

"Why take the cars tonight?" James asks. He's stalling, I know it, and I think Deacon knows too.

"Because the records were fine, but nothing seals a case like hard evidence. And a storage facility with fifty-three cars looks a lot like hard evidence."

James does that crazy laughing thing I don't trust. "All that's good and fine, but none of that leads them here. And since it's just us here, I guess I need to clean up the loose ends and skip town." The guns come out and I yell just as Deacon drops to the ground.

I try to get to him, but the man holding me doesn't let me go. Maverick shoots back as he ducks behind the passenger door of the car.

"Get back," Pit growls low.

The roaring sound of a car racing down the street grabs my attention. Rocks fly up as the car pulls into the gravel driveway like a bat out of hell.

It comes to a screeching stop along with the shooting. The door opens and a beautiful black girl steps out. She quickly locates Pit and rushes over to us. That's when the guns go off again. The pinging sounds loud to my ears.

"Roman, move in from the back. We need to keep them here until the police come," Pit says. I have no idea who he's talking to. I don't get time to ask because I get hit with another contraction. This time it's followed by a gush of fluid.

"Fuck, did she just piss herself?" Pit looks at me like he actually thinks I did.

"Oh no, her water broke," the beautiful girl says. "Deacon we have a serious problem."

She doesn't say it loud enough for him to hear it over the noise. I haven't seen Deacon since he went down after the first shot rang out.

"She's in active labor. Her water just broke," she says, again clearly talking to someone.

Another contraction hits, and I scream. This one is so bad my knees give out. Pit wraps an arm around me, holding me up, but far away from him like I'm contaminated.

"Deacon told me to tell you to remember to breathe," the beauty says to me sympathetically.

"You tell him to remember to fucking breathe," I argue as the sound of bullets starts to get further away. I'm assuming James and the gang are retreating.

She and Pit look to each other and then to me before smiling.

"Where the hell are the cops, I thought they were supposed to trace the car?" Pit says, helping me lean against a stack of tires.

"Don't get mad at me because my driving skills are the shit. Q said I had ten minutes to get here, I made that bitch in seven."

"I could have made it in six," Pit argues without looking at the woman.

"No, you couldn't."

I scream again when this contraction comes with pressure. "He's coming."

The sound of sirens in the distance springs us all into action. Pit pushes away from our hiding spot and looks over the stack of tires. He then helps me stand upright as the beauty takes off.

I spot Deacon waving us toward his car. The moment I get to him, he cups my face and plants a kiss on my lips that nearly takes my mind off the pain.

"I thought you were dead," I cry.

He smiles. "Bulletproof vest." He taps at his chest before growing serious again. "Marry me?"

It's not the most romantic proposal, but it doesn't matter, my answer would be the same either way.

"Yes."

He grabs me and helps me into the back of the car.

"Pit is in the driver seat and Maverick in the passenger and the beauty and Deacon are in the back with me. We speed away from the wreckage shop they were holding me.

"Can you make it to the hospital?" Deacon asks when I get past another contraction.

"How far?" I ask.

"Twenty-eight minutes," Maverick says, looking at the directions on his phone.

"I don't think I can make it. He's coming," I start to panic.

"Pit, drive this fucking car," Deacon shouts.

"Hey, focus," the beauty says, snapping her fingers in Deacon's face. "You need to be prepared to deliver this baby."

"I'm not a fucking doctor, Skittles," Deacon argues.

"Relax," a voice says, coming through the speakers. It's a female.

"Syd?" Deacon asks.

"Yes, Q patched me through to the car's Bluetooth. Now I need you to calm down. I'm going to walk you through this.

"I need you to check to see if the baby is crowning. Just look between her legs and see if you can see the head."

With half of my upper body in the lap of the woman he called Skittles, I open my knees for Deacon to check. He pushes my dress up to my waist and slides my panties down.

"Oh fuck, I see his head." Deacon turns away like he's going to pass out.

"All right, no need to panic. What's your girlfriend's name?" the lady on the speaker says.

"Noni, and she's my fiancée."

"About fucking time," a male voice comes through the speaker from the background.

"Shut the fuck up, Reynolds," Deacon scolds halfheartedly.

"Okay, Noni," the female named Syd says calmly. "With this next contraction, I want you to push."

"Okay," I whimper.

I feel the contraction building up and prepare myself for it. As soon as it hits, I push down. It feels like fire between my legs, but I keep pushing.

"The head is out, Noni. Baby, look at his head," Deacon shouts happily. I can't yet participate in his enthusiasm cause this shit hurts.

"You're doing good, mama," Skittles says as she rubs my shoulder. Poor girl didn't sign up for this tonight.

When the contraction eases, I sink back and catch my breath.

"You're doing good, baby, the head is out." Lord, I wish this was over already. No one said it was going to be this draining.

"Deacon," the voice over the speakers comes again. "Is the baby facing up or down."

"Up, well up and to the right."

"That's good. You're going to have to help this next go round. I need you to support the baby's head when she pushes. Don't pull, just support."

"It's coming," I warn.

Deacon leans forward. I can feel his hands brush against my thighs as he supports our son's head. When the contraction hits, I push. I push with all my might. I can feel every inch of this baby moving through my body.

"That's it, Noni. He's almost here. Ace is almost here."

I give one final push and I can feel the moment my baby slips out of my body and into the world.

"Oh shit," Deacon swears as he quickly grabs our child before it slips out of his hands. Ace lets out a loud whine before quieting down.

"Did you seriously almost drop your baby?"

"Shut up, Skittles," Deacon grumbles.

Deacon places our baby in my arms.

"Hey, give me your jacket," he says to Maverick.

Maverick quickly slips out of his coat and hands it back to Deacon who quickly lays it over the baby.

"Well, what is it?" Syd asks.

I lift the jacket and peek down between the baby's legs and burst out laughing.

"It's a girl," I call out.

Skittles cheers over my head, but I can hear collective grumbles from the men.

"We didn't even pick out a name for a girl," Deacon reminds me.

I look down into the sweet little face of my baby girl and a name pops up in my mind.

"Asa," I say, thinking of the nickname dubbed by her father. "Asa Kaye Clarke."

Deacon repeats the name. "Yeah, I like that. Welcome to the world, my little Asa."

EPILOGUE

Happiness

Deacon

"Baby, I told you to get some rest," I say over the phone. Glancing into the carrier beside me, I smile as my baby girl looks back at me. She's two months today, and her eyes have yet to figure out what color they're going to be.

"Do you have enough milk? What about diapers? Is she covered up, and Deacon, I swear, if you let another woman touch my baby."

I laugh out loud at that last one. She knows damn well I wouldn't let another woman touch my daughter. Hell, I barely want anyone to touch her.

"Asa and I are good. I have everything she needs. Now, will you please get some rest? The whole reason I took her out is so you can rest."

She yawns and then laughs. "No, you're trying to get on my good side because I'm cleared for sex now."

318

She's not lying. My lady has been getting me right while she's been waiting for the all clear. Noni loves giving me head.

She thinks it's an accomplishment to make me come. I'm not going to argue with her. However, despite how good her head game is, I miss my pussy.

"Yeah, well, that's why your ass needs to get some rest because tonight, I'm taking back what belongs to me."

Her high pitch laughter dies out on another yawn.

"Go to sleep, I love you, Mrs. Clarke."

"I love you too, Mr. Clarke."

Noni and I got married two weeks after bringing our daughter home from the hospital. I called Pit and asked him to be my best man and stand with me at the courthouse. I should have known they weren't going to let it be that simple.

We had a small, close-knit wedding right in my yard. Noni's friends and Skittles decorated the yard, and Pit arranged for the priest to be there. All the guys showed up, even Jeff's ornery ass.

I turn my phone off and place it on the table. Asa and I have big plans for today. We're starting off at this coffee shop, because Daddy needs a little pick-me-up.

Then we're going to the shop to see the crew and then I'm taking her to Aunt Skittles so Daddy can go pick up a special surprise for Mama. It's a brand-new motorcycle that matches mine. We're going to have his and hers.

"The fuck, Frank. I don't need a new fucking assistant."

The familiar voice causes me to look up toward the door of *Smooth Roast*. Jeff walks in, oblivious to everyone around him. He's talking loudly on his phone. Not surprising.

"I can function without you for three months. Is that kid walking yet?" he says, stopping to glance at the line.

I smile. No way is his privileged ass going to stand in this line. As I assumed, he goes right around the line and straight to the front of the counter.

Asa coos and I turn back to her. She makes that face, the one that lets me know I'm about to be elbows deep in breastfed baby poop.

"I think you do this on purpose," I sing to her. She smiles, and my heart fucking melts.

"Oh, hell no," someone shouts.

I look back at the line to see what's going on.

"Did you just skip the line?" a lady wearing a business suit asks, her arms folded over her chest.

I chuckle to myself. I'd never let my boy get in any real trouble, if I thought these people were going to beat his ass, I'd jump in. Eventually.

When I tune back into the conversation, Jeff is arguing with the beauty with the ill-fitting suit on.

"What's your name?" Jeff asks.

Oh shit, I think he wants her. Please God, let her curse him out. I need this laugh today.

"None of your damn business. Get in the line."

Yes, hell yeah, I like this chick. I should buy her a better work suit. Jeff tries again to shoot his shot, even offers to get her order for her. I should record this shit and send it to the crew.

"You're a disrespectful, rude man." Damn, maybe she does know Jeff.

He laughs because he knows that shit's true. "Honey, you have no idea how accurate you are."

"I will not say it again, get to the back of the line."

Damn, she makes it clear she wants shit to do with him. I pick up my phone and send Pit a text.

Deacon: Rich bitch is at the coffee shop getting his balls handed to him. I guess his money can't buy all pussy.

Pit: That's what his dumb ass gets.

Deacon: Wait, he just paid for her food. He's trying really hard.

I watch Jeff take the bag to the girl, but I don't hear their argument. Not long after, he turns and dumps the bag in the trash. Oh fuck, that was cold.

He says something else to her and then leaves the building. I shake my head at him. His ass is going to get all the payback he deserves one day.

The tiny beauty storms out of the coffee shop not long after he leaves. I can only hope their paths cross again. I grab my shitty daughter's car seat up off the seat beside me.

"Time to get you cleaned up and start our day."

This may not be something everyone would enjoy but being here with her while the love of my life is back home waiting for me, that shit makes me the happiest man alive.

ACKNOWLEDGMENTS

To the readers that love my work, I thank you for keeping me going. To my writing sisters, this one is definitely for you. You guys pushed me on those late-night sprints.

To my husband, I won't say you were my motivation for this one, LOL. Last but never least, to my babies. All I do, I do for you.

ABOUT THE AUTHOR

Tiya Rayne is an avid reader and writer. She has an unhealthy relationship with coffee and is known to hide numerous bags of jellybeans around the house.

When she is not reading or writing—which is rare—she's trying to master this thing called parenting. She is married to her high school sweetheart and they live in Arkansas with their three—subjectively wonderful—children. Tiya also writes Young Adult Paranormal under the pen name KC Connor.

Wait, there is more! You can stay updated with my latest releases, learn more about me, the author, and get a free book as soon as you sign up and confirm to my newsletter at
www.TiyaRayne.com
If you enjoyed *Deacon*, I'd love to hear
your thoughts and please feel free to leave a
review. And when you do, please let me
know by emailing me at TiyaRayne@gmail.com
or leave a comment on Facebook https://www.facebook.com/AuthorTiyaRayne/
or Instagram @AuthorTiyaRayne

There is more to come from Tiya Rayne in 2021.
Want to keep up with Perceptive Illusions Publishing authors
and releases? Sign up to the newsletter for updates.
Go to PerceptiveIllusionsPublishing.com

BLUE SAFFIRE

TIFFANY PATTERSON

IVY HARPER

Continuing July 2022

A**hole Club

ARE YOU READY FOR THEM?

TIYA RAYNE

BLUE SAFFIRE

BLUE SAFFIRE